BORN IN THE SECOND WIND

BORN IN THE SECOND WIND

AJIT SHERAWAT

Srishti
PUBLISHERS & DISTRIBUTORS

Srishti Publishers & Distributors
N-16, C. R. Park
New Delhi 110 019
editorial@srishtipublishers.com

First published by
Srishti Publishers & Distributors in 2015

10 9 8 7 6 5 4 3 2 1

Printed and bound in India

Prologue

"I stand before you Mom, a lesser son, defeated and ashamed," Jeet's voice broke, muffled, struggling to come out, as an unseen force tightened its grip on his throat. He turned his head to look at his mother with his blurred vision. Numbed by the pain, he pinched himself, the nerves however refused to carry the sensation to the brain.

"There is no reason to feel defeated or ashamed son," Kamlesh looked at her son, "for you have been sincere in your efforts and results however are never in one's hands. And a son isn't less or more. A son is a son. He is the prism through which the white light of his parents' struggles pass through to get scattered into the radiant and vibrant colours of hope." Jeet felt reassured. As always, his mother's words had ignited hope. One more time, he felt the comforting touch. "Nothing can go wrong," his belief in him was back. As always, his mother's words had felt like soothing balm on his lacerated wounds.

"The inconsistencies of this harsh world have forced me to give up on my dream. It is an unfair world, Mom. I feel weak and let down." He looked at his mother, in hope of further encouragement from her.

"Don't try to bury your face in my lap, son," Kamlesh intuitively read her son's thoughts. "This world is your playground and though victory isn't in your hands, playing is. If you feel weak, then bide your time, go hide in the deepest of caves but only to strike back at the most opportune moment, with all your accumulated venom. Come from the hiding when you are once again strong and well-equipped. But remember, while fighting the world, do not become like the rest of them. For fight you will, but for your victory, and victory alone – and not for the destruction of the other. Remember, you are *my* son, and forgiveness, not revenge should be your forte."

"I cannot think of forgiveness for now; that is the jewel that adorns the strong. But right now, I promise you one thing," the determination and resolve had returned, "that whatever the circumstances, I will get the house freed from the clutches of Ram Sharan."

Jeet awoke abruptly, opening his eyes wide, surprised that even the hazy picture of his mother had disappeared. He looked around to find no one, not even the doppelganger. He felt choked and when breathing became impossible, he lifted his head from the soft pillow. He sat up on his bed and stared at his pillow which had absorbed all the stickiness of sweat and tears.

"Was it all a dream then?" he pondered, "but even if it was a dream, Mom's advice couldn't have been more profound." Jeet's resolve had grown strong. He missed the doppelganger though. Jeet hadn't met him for a long time now. Not even in a dream.

The Cycle Race: 1967

With the last three of the thirty laps remaining, the cycle race got more intriguing by the second. With Kanta and Anita ahead of her, Kamlesh – the focus of all – was in the third place. While for all the other thirteen competitors, it was a race against time, for Kamlesh it was against ill health as well. Despite the lack of strength, she pedalled hard. "Don't blame me if something happens," the family doctor had cautioned her against taking part in the strenuous and demanding exercise, as she was yet to recuperate from the stubborn fever that had gripped her for full seven days. Concerned as they were, her mother and elder brother were also not too happy about her decision to participate against the advice of the doctor.

"Maa, you have always allowed her to have her say," Rajender, Kamlesh's brother, had complained.

"You know how good she is at convincing, don't you? When she speaks, there is only one opinion that seems reasonable – her own. I hope she finishes the race without harming her health any further."

"Don't forget she has never lost a race."

"Yes, but this time, her ill health is a hindrance," their mother Rajkali had replied.

However, the thread of hope that her daughter would win it for her was still hinged in some corner of her heart.

For Kamlesh, taking the bull by the horns came easier than running away from a challenge. "If I should, let me lose inside the race track rather than outside of it." With that, she had sealed the debate with her mother for good.

The news of her fever had travelled far and wide. Not many outside of her family had believed she could take part. Kamlesh, however, had left the crowd not merely wondering but incredulous when she took her position at the starting point of the race-track that morning.

The status quo at the race track continued. Kamlesh was still at third place. She gritted her teeth as a drop of sweat slipped from the dishevelled brow, made inroads through her dusky cheeks and rested on her dry lips.

"Salty and sticky!" the taste buds cried.

"Defeat would taste worse," Kamlesh countered. The dreaded thought of insipid defeat sent shivers down her spine. With a grimace, she collected the almost non-existent ounce of extra energy and thrust it into the paddle, pushing it harder.

As the odds conspired against her, she was inadvertently united with her friend, philosopher and guide: her mind.

"One step at a time," she said, "let me focus on Anita first."

"You are on the right track," her mind reflected back. "Focus hard, for this is what stands between the winners and losers."

"I am the tortoise," she carried on the conversation, "and the hare too. I am required to be steady and quick at the same time. Time is of the essence."

"It sure is," said the mind. "Hang in there. With a little patience, you would be there soon."

Baoli was a huge village in the Meerut district of Uttar Pradesh and boasted of a population of over twelve thousand. It was, by far, the most densely populated amongst all its neighbouring villages. It stood for all the good and bad things that any other village in western U.P. represented. Patience and tolerance were hardly the traits that the notorious and infamous village was known for. Even a small dispute between the villagers had the potential to snowball into something very serious and gory. Keeping in line with other villages, the main occupation of the people was agriculture. Possession of land was sacrosanct. The more land a farmer possessed, the more clout he was likely to enjoy. It was from this big, hugely populated and notorious village that Kamlesh came. Rajkali, Kamlesh's mother was the village *sarpanch*.

Kamlesh had lost her father early. It was her mother and her brother Rajinder who comprised her world. With a stock of around one thousand acres of land, theirs was one of the wealthiest families in the village. Rajkali, like her late husband, was consulted in all matters of the village. The air of authority that ran in the family had rubbed onto Kamlesh too. Inheriting the best from both worlds, she got her height from her father and her looks from her beautiful mother. At 5'6", her dusky features only complemented her voluptuous figure. She was fiercely competitive and winning came naturally to her. She topped in studies, was second to none in extra-curricular activities. As much as she liked winning, she hated any short cuts that would give her victory. She preferred the hard grinding path, which according to her was the most appropriate definition of a win.

Kanta, her closest competitor in the cycle race, was the daughter of Shyam Singh. Her family too owned large tracts of land and like Kamlesh's family, had a huge following in the village.

The enmity between Kamlesh's late father Baldev Singh, and Shyam Singh went back three or four decades. The rift in the relations of the next door neighbours only worsened when Baldev

Singh defeated Shyam Singh by a narrow margin of nine votes in the elections for the post of sarpanch. Further, it didn't help the relationship in any way, when Baldev's son Rajender knocked down a Shyam Singh's son Pradyuman, who was heavier and taller, in a wrestling bout. The entire village was witness to the gory fight in which all rules of wrestling were broken. It hadn't stopped despite bleeding noses, and cries from the referee and the village elders to call it off. The egos of the fathers had mattered more than the lives of the sons. It took a clean and near-fatal blow from Rajender on Pradyuman's temple to at last end the fight. As Pradyuman lay unconscious on the ground, a delighted Baldev lifted Rajender onto his shoulders and danced a victory jig. But the joy didn't last long as a drunken Baldev couldn't wake up the next morning. For Rajkali and her kids, ecstasy had transmuted into gloom in the span of one night. Pradyuman's life, on the other hand, was saved by a timely surgery conducted by the team of doctors from AIIMS Delhi. A few hours' delay in taking him to Delhi could have resulted in fatality, the doctors had said after the operation. For Shyam Singh, it was a feeling of relief more than anything else.

For Rajkali, it was like starting from scratch once again. But rather than getting intimidated by the sudden bolt from the blue, she rose to the situation with courage and fortitude. Contrary to the assumptions of the villagers, she took the place of her husband not only in domestic affairs, but in village politics too. She defeated Shyam Singh in the village polls by a margin of 215 votes. Even booth capturing and other less than fair practices employed by Shyam Singh couldn't come to his rescue. It was a massive insult to his already injured pride.

Despite the bitterness between the families, Kamlesh and Kanta had managed to strike a bond of friendship. Studying in the same section of XII with science subjects, they would not only do their home work together but would play together too. Their friendship had been golden, until the appearance of a rift that arose with the advent of the cycle race.

There was extra excitement in Kamlesh's voice when she had returned home from college on an otherwise normal Friday evening. The date for the annual cycle race had been announced. With brightly lit eyes, she shared the news of the competition with her mother and brother. The exuberance of his sister made Rajender travel to Delhi the next morning to buy the latest model of a Japanese bicycle for the upcoming race. Dear as both Rajkali and Kamlesh were to him, it was his younger sister who occupied his thoughts. He had promised to himself to give his sister the very best. He couldn't allow her to lose just because her equipment wasn't up to the mark. Kamlesh hugged her brother several times after she had removed the wrapper of the fully-loaded, geared bicycle.

Her pride, however, was her peers' envy. Her classmates had started talking in hushed tones about how she would already be at an advantage as she had the best bicycle for the race. It was in this context that a careless comment by Kanta tied the first knot in their hitherto flawless thread of friendship.

"It's Kamlesh's bicycle that would win her the race." Kanta was speaking to her classmates, "I dare her to compete on a level playing field." Kamlesh overheard each word. The fact that Kanta had said it behind her back had caused more hurt than the comment itself. The injury hadn't lessened in any way even when she had reached home.

The night was more difficult. It was two o'clock. Sleepless, Kamlesh sat thinking on her bed. She was caught in a dilemma: whether to race with the new cycle or compete with the old one. Though she wanted to take up the challenge head on by relinquishing her advantage, she didn't want to cause disappointment to her brother. Indecisive and struck by insomnia, she decided to take her mind away from the issue. When she had drifted into deep sleep, her subconscious conjured up memories of stories she had read.

The Kauravas and the Pandavas stood facing each other with the armies stationed by their respective sides. The war of the Mahabharata was about to begin. Arjun was in conversation with Lord Krishan. "Help me, Keshav. My mind is troubled by this confusion," he addressed the Almighty.

"Go ahead Parth. Today, let me make you free from all your quandaries," the Lord said.

"You are aware, oh Lord, that I am blessed with divya astras gifted to me by Lord Indra."

The Lord smiled.

"And you are also aware, Keshav, that I can finish this war in just one single stroke by using any one of those astras."

"Without doubt, Parth," the Lord smiled again, knowing exactly what was coming.

"But Keshav, I do not want to use the divya astras. I want to defeat my enemy fair and square. Tell me Keshav, am I right in thinking that?"

The Lord nodded His head in affirmation. Arjun's mind was calm. He had got his answer.

The next Moment saw Kamlesh wide awake. The ambiguity in her mind had vanished. She too had got her answer. Her tentativeness gone, peace had at last found her.

The cycle race went on at its own pace. Far from being a mere tussle between the girls, the race in fact, was a tug of war between Shyam Singh and Rajkali. The supporters of both groups who had come in huge numbers, cheered incessantly.

It was the turn of Rajkali's supporters to roar in unison as Kamlesh overtook Anita just before the start of the final lap. The gloves were off: it was between Kamlesh and Kanta now. Rajkali and Shyam Singh fidgeted in their respective seats.

The beginning of the last lap brought about mixed feelings in Kamlesh. Whereas on the one hand it brought relief and hope for tired and overworked limbs, on the other, it meant she had very little time left to clinch victory almost from the jaws of defeat.

"Coming second is no good," her mind pepped her up. "Just one more lap to go."

If physical capacities were the parameters for victory, then Kanta was the clear favourite. She had trained well and was in the pink of her health. Kamlesh, however, outscored in the power of mind. Deep inside in her subconscious mind, there inadvertently dwelt a positive belief that she could not be defeated, irrespective of the circumstances. Kanta, however, carried an excess baggage of doubt in the form of a negative thought that Kamlesh would somehow win the race. It was this disparity in thought which made Kamlesh- despite her physical frailty- inch closer to Kanta with each thrust of the paddle. It was her potency of the mind and sheer will-power that had brought her this far. However, the question that mattered was: Whether the strength in mind was enough to help her get to the winning line first?

It was a mere one hundred yards between Kanta and the finishing line. Kamlesh was still behind, with five crucial yards separating her from Kanta. Despite her best efforts, Kamlesh wasn't able to overtake her.

With the winning tape just thirty yards away, victory appeared to be Kanta's, or so it seemed.

"Would I lose it then?" Kamlesh asked her mind again. "Opportunities would present themselves," the mind, brimming with optimism as ever, replied.

And opportunity did present itself. It was ten yards from the finishing line that Kanta made her first and the last mistake. It resulted from a lack of Kanta's belief in herself and an inadvertent, albeit strange move on the part of Kamlesh. In an ongoing effort to overtake Kanta, Kamlesh had run the entire race on the left side of her competitor. Getting no substantial results from the tactic, Kamlesh thought of trying something different. She positioned herself right behind Kanta. To start with, it saved Kamlesh a fair amount of energy as she had to deal with less air-pressure than before. Several times during the race, Kanta looked back over her shoulder to reassure herself about Kamlesh's exact position.

For Kanta, now almost within hand-shaking distance from the winning line, it was impossible to believe her luck.

"Am I really going to win?" she asked herself with a hint of disbelief. "Hmm... well..." The seed of self-doubt didn't allow the inner voice to answer with conviction. Then in an effort to find assurance outside, she looked back again, over her left shoulder to ascertain Kamlesh's position. She was most perplexed to not find Kamlesh there. Confused and caught unawares, her reflexes made her turn her head to the right with a massive jerk in anticipation of finding Kamlesh on the other side. As a result, her body, which was not ready for the sudden twist, lost balance and her cycle wobbled. In an effort to stop it from toppling over, Kanta applied the brakes and lost precious seconds. The realisation was immediate. She had faltered. She tried in desperation to regain the lost ground, but it was too late. Not the one to miss out on a God sent opportunity of such kind, Kamlesh whizzed past to overtake her. The next moment she crossed the finishing line.

In the audience, Rajkali and her acolytes thundered the roar of victory. Shyam Singh's camp witnessed dreadful silence. *Once again we managed to snatch defeat from the jaws of victory; why does it have to happen to me?* thought Shyam Singh, his head resting in his hands.

The Marriage Proposal

It was dinner time at Rajkali's house. Kamlesh preferred to have dinner in her room, while Rajender preferred to have it in the kitchen, sitting next to his mother as she cooked. It was also the time for the mother-son duo to talk of family matters and other issues. More often than not, the discussions would later continue in the drawing room, where Rajender would read the newspaper after he was done with his dinner. His mornings were reserved for *pranayam* and exercises in the village *akhara*.

"Maa, give me more dal."

"Is it nice?"

"It's delicious. Nobody can cook better than my Maa," he continued, hungrily wolfing down the food. Rajkali smiled and served him more of it. Words of praise from her children! There was little else in the world that made her this happy after Baldev's demise.

"Kamlesh liked it too. By the way, she did wonders yesterday, didn't she?" Rajkali wanted to relive the moments of the previous day.

"Of course she did. And why wouldn't she? After all she is *my* sister!"

"Shyam Singh really sulked," Rajkali chirped.

"Maa, we shouldn't see everything in the context of rivalry."

Having finished his meal, Rajender put his thaali aside and headed towards the washroom.

"Rajender," Rajkali called from the kitchen, "we should start thinking about Kamlesh now."

"What is there to think Maa? She is the brightest of all kids. She has everything that a brother wishes to see in his sister," Rajender said, wiping his hands with a towel.

After setting aside two small chapattis for herself, Rajkali doused the fire to join Rajender in the drawing room. She preferred to eat only after her kids had finished with their meals.

"Kamlesh is almost seventeen now. We must start looking for an ideal match for her," said Rajkali as she sat facing Rajender on the comfortable sofa. Rajender was engrossed in his newspaper.

"Ideal match! But she is very young for all that, Maa," surprised, he looked out of the newspaper to stare at Rajkali.

"I was sixteen when you were born to me," she smiled.

"Those were old times Maa. And she hasn't even completed her studies as yet!"

The strong and stoutly built twenty-five-year-old was sensitive when it came to his sister. He considered it paramount to look after her well being, especially after the death of his father. The thought of her leaving for some other family someday made him anxious.

"But you know our tradition very well," Rajkali stressed the point further. "Once the girl is past a certain age, it becomes tough to look for an ideal match. I don't want her to settle for compromises."

Rajender was aware that Rajkali's argument was well-founded.

"Maa, there is a good proposal from Ghata village. One of my friends talked about the boy to me, but considering Kamlesh's age and the fact that she is still pursuing her studies, I had rejected the proposal outright. But what you're saying is not completely wrong. In fact, it has dawned on me today that my little sister isn't that 'little' anymore. So we can take matters further with that boy. But you have to promise that we would let Kamlesh complete her studies before you decide to send her off."

Rajkali laughed, she wasn't blind to Rajender's love for his younger sister. "That can be decided taking the groom into confidence, once the match is settled. Tell me, what does the boy do?"

"He is a doctor, Krishan told me."

"Krishan who?"

"Krishan, my wrestling buddy. The news of Kamlesh's laurels has spread far and wide. It was the boy's mother who had approached Krishan knowing that he is my friend. There are more than a few proposals but I think this one suits us better than any other."

"What about his family?" Rajkali enquired.

"It's a small family Maa, just like ours. Two siblings. The sister is older to the boy and is already married. Unfortunately, the boy's father is no more. So it's just the mother and son."

"What about land. How much do they possess?"

"Come on Maa, the boy is a doctor. Why is land important here?"

"Doctor or no doctor, I am not marrying my daughter into a family which has no land."

"Five hundred acres Maa."

"What?"

"Yes, five hundred acres. That's how much they possess."

"Then why did you not tell me earlier?"

"To be honest, land isn't important to me. All that matters is the boy."

"Anyway, let's take the matter forward without further delay."

Rajender nodded.

"You know, you would laugh when you hear this," said Rajkali. "I too have received a proposal for Kamlesh. It's amusing how people can even approach with such lowly matches!"

"From where Maa?"

"From Gurgaon in Haryana. The name of the village is the same as that of the city it falls in. It is called Gurgaon Village. The boy's mausi came to talk to me. It's a huge family and the boy isn't even employed!"

"How many members in the family?"

"I don't know exactly, Beta."

"Even otherwise, I don't think it's even worth considering. But Maa, in whatever we decide to do, let's take Kamlesh's opinion too." Rajender reiterated.

"Of course we would. But I do not see any reason why she would have any objections to the doctor's proposal."

"Still Maa, we should involve her in discussions before we decide to move ahead."

"That you leave to me and now do not cause any delay in taking the matters forward."

"Sure Maa, whatever brings good to my little sister will be done in a jiffy. But what did you say to that lady?"

"I have politely refused her."

"Hmm..." Rajender heaved a sigh of relief, "Maa," he said thoughtfully, "this doctor boy looks really promising."

"For sure he does. After Kamlesh gets married, I would bring a suitable bride for you," she patted him on his cheek. Rajender blushed and said nothing.

Had the mother-son duo possessed the ability to look into the immediate future, they would have seen that Kamlesh would get married before finishing her studies and that her groom wouldn't be a doctor.

Two days later, Rajender sat engrossed with a paper and a pencil. Rajkali was out for a meeting of the panchayat and Kamlesh was studying in her room. The chart that Rajender was making on the paper compared and contrasted the two proposals for Kamlesh on five varied parameters. The doctor was the winner on all five counts by a considerable margin. *Have I missed something? Is there a sixth criterion?* Rajender thought.

Comparison Chart			
S.No.	**Assets**	**Doctor**	**Kanwar Bhan**
1	Land	Hundreds of acres	None
2	Bank balance	Huge	Depleted
3	Family	Small	Big
4	Future	Secure	Volatile
5	Profession	Excellent	Unemployed
6	?		

The series of thoughts were intruded by the knock on the door. Rajender placed the chart under the sofa cushion before getting up to see who it was. The middle-aged man was dressed in a white dhoti kurta and a white turban. The dust had settled not only on the face of the stranger but on his clothes too. Clearly, the man had endured a long and tiresome journey. There was, however, something strange about his eyes.

"If I am not wrong you are Rajkali ji's son?" he enquired.

"Yes, you are right."

"Can I come in Beta?"

"Of course," Rajender moved aside to let the man in.

"Might have come to ask Maa some favour," Rajender guessed.

The stranger was fascinated by the spaciousness of the drawing room. The fresh air carried the gentle chill from the nearby fields and brought it floating inside. Winter had given way to spring and summer was yet to fully set in. The man took off his turban from his head and wiped his face. The salt-pepper hair endorsed his middle age. The servant entered, carrying glasses of water and sharbat.

"Thanks Beta, the sharbat is really nice," the stranger gulped it down at one go.

"Please take some more, uncle."

The man refused with a signal of his hand. The servant picked up the empty glasses and left.

"I'm sorry, but my memory fails me in recognizing you," Rajender was polite to begin with.

"There's nothing wrong with your memory, son. It's just that you are meeting me for the first time. Actually I am from Jhanjho's village, the lady who had visited you a few days back regarding the proposal for your sister." The man stopped, anticipating a query from Rajender, but seeing his straight face, the man continued, "Actually Beta, I have come to extend a favour to you." It was at this juncture that Rajender saw the man's eyes. They were peculiar to say the least. He had seen them somewhere, but couldn't remember where. His gut feeling, however, cautioned him against the not yet manifested inconsistencies of the man.

"And what would that *favour* be?" Rajender measured each word.

"Can I meet your mother?" the stranger suggested.

"I'm sorry but she is out for some work. But please feel free to explain to me the real purpose of your visit." Rajender was curious.

"Beta, my name is Ram Sharan, and as I said, I belong to the same village as Jhanjho. In fact I am her neighbour."

"That's alright, but what brings you here?"

"Did you accept the proposal Beta?"

"Did Jhanjho not tell you?" Rajender was surprised. As far as he knew, his mother had categorically said a firm "no" to Jhanjho.

"Jhanjho hasn't sent me here. In fact, I would request you to keep this visit of mine a secret. It's for your own good that I'm here."

"Ok, please come up with what you have in mind, since you have come for my own good...?"

"Bhaiya, it's time for the fodder for the animals," Kamlesh barged in.

"You go, I am coming," Rajender didn't welcome her intrusion.

"Can you come here for once Bhaiya?" She stood there, ostensibly not taking the hint from Rajender.

"Arrey you go and ask Deepu to feed the cattle."

"Bhaiya, I want to talk to you."

A clearly irritated Rajender finally gave in.

"What is this Kammo? Why do you act so childish at times? Can't you see I am sitting with someone? Tell me what is it?"

"Sorry Bhaiya, but tell me who is he?"

"Who?"

"The man who is seated in the drawing room right now?"

"How does it concern you? And why is it that you have to know everything?"

"Bhaiya, I am just asking," she said with a hint of a smile.

"I am just telling you," Rajender responded in the same tone.

"No, but you aren't telling me anything!"

"That's what I am telling you that you need not poke your nose here. Mind your own business. Concentrate on your studies, and do not come near the drawing room. Ok?"

"Ok Bhaiya," Kamlesh responded with a sullen face, "but there is someone standing outside our house. He might be a friend of the person sitting with you."

"It's ok. I'll look into it."

Kamlesh went inside while Rajender came back to attend the guest.

"I am sorry to have kept you waiting. Is there someone else with you?" Rajender asked.

"Oh! Ghusadd! Yes Bete, I thought it's always best to travel with a companion".

"Why don't you call him inside?"

"No Bete, it's ok. As it is I wouldn't take much of your time. But tell me the girl who just came, is she the one? I mean is she your younger sister?"

"So, where were we?" Rajender ducked the question.

"We were talking about Jhanjho's proposal." Ram Sharan took the hint.

"We have not decided yet, Ram Sharan ji." Rajender thought it prudent not to divulge anything till he got a clear measure of the man sitting in front of him.

"That makes my coming to you all the more relevant and timely," Ram Sharan bent closer to Rajender, as if to unfold a grave secret. "See Beta, to be honest, the family from where you received the proposal is no match for your family and it would be an injustice to your sister if you were to accept it."

"Why so?" Rajender was terse.

"Well, for a number of reasons. I don't know where to start."

"I will make it easy for you. Start from the very beginning."

"The family has no land and whatever little they had, has been acquired by the government without any compensation as yet. God knows whether they would even get the compensation or not. Second, the boy is not even employed. The only source of income is his father's monthly pension, and that too is meagre if you consider that there are ten mouths to feed on that morsel of an income."

"Ten mouths?"

"Why! Did Jhanjho not tell you? I knew she wouldn't!" Ram Sharan's eyeballs circled along the borders of his eyes, making him look more cunning and dangerous.

"I mean she would have told Maa. As it is I never got to interact with her."

"See Beta, the boy that we are talking about – Kanwar Bhan – is the oldest of nine siblings, five brothers and four sisters. Mamchand, the boy's father, is a blind man and his wife, that is Kanwar Bhan's mother, died recently. If your sister is married into that house, the responsibility of bringing up all the siblings, and all other responsibilities besides, would fall on her."

For Rajender it was news. Not that he was interested in the match, still the impediments and the impossible situations that the family was in were challenging to say the least. He felt sorry for Kanwar Bhan. Sensing Rajender's concern, the wily fox continued with a renewed vigour.

"Your heart would further sink Beta if you knew the ages of the siblings. Anil, the youngest is four years old, and Mahendra is six. Therefore son, any girl who is married into that family has her task cut out. She would have ten kids plus her own with no income to boast of. Tell me then, is it prudent that you accept such a proposal?"

Rajender pondered over the issue for a while. He had now fully recognized the species to which Ram Sharan belonged. There was no dearth of them in his village as well. He belonged to the kind of people who found pleasure in the pain of others. Ram Sharan was a cheap, cunning fellow who knew that the proposal, if accepted, could benefit the situation of Kanwar's family immensely and therefore took the pains of travelling a long distance in order to stop any good that might happen to his neighbour.

"Ram Sharan ji..."

"Yes son?"

"I can understand the impossible situation that family is in, as of now. And taking your word to be true, I also agree that no brother worth his salt would let his sister marry into that household. But how does it affect you? Why are you so interested in my sister's marriage? After all, we hardly know each other. I mean, why this generosity towards us?"

Ram Sharan had not anticipated this cross fire from the young man. He was in such a flutter that he could hardly think of an appropriate reply.

"To be honest I don't want your sister to ruin her life by marrying into such a household. There is nothing more to it. Ok Beta, now I should leave. I have done my duty of telling you everything. Now it's for you to decide." Rajender returned to the drawing room after seeing Ram Sharan off.

Rajender's hands rummaged under the sofa cushion. He couldn't find the chart he had placed there a few minutes back. His surprise turned to astonishment when he lifted the cushion out of its place, and still couldn't find it. Lost in thought, he sank into the sofa. Then remembering something he quickly got up, enlightened.

He had at last recognized Ram Sharan's eyes. He had seen them in the recently concluded annual village fair. The eyes were bereft of eyelashes. They were the eyes of the serpent!

Kamlesh's Marriage

The villagers had exclaimed at the disparity of the match as joy came with nimble steps to knock at the doors of blind old Mamchand's heart. He was surprised by the advent of it. For some time, he was struck with disbelief. After all, it had been alien to him for a long time. But slowly, the almost jammed doors of his heart answered the knock and welcomed it. With the bride came good fortune too. Kanwar Bhan received his appointment letter from the state government on the second day after the wedding.

It was the third day of his son Kanwar Bhan's marriage with Kamlesh. The small house was flooded with guests and was abuzz with the post-wedding activities. Some relatives were preparing to leave, while others chose to stay back for another day. The ladies sang folk songs. Men danced to the beat of the *dholak*. Not a big house as it was, privacy was a luxury. The rooms were too small to allow even the free movement of limbs. Rajender, Kamlesh's brother, sat quietly in the corner of a crowded room. Despite the cacophony, he felt lonely. The high decibels of outside sound were no match for the storm that emanated from within.

As per tradition, the bride was required to visit her mother's house within a couple of days after the wedding. Rajinder had come to take his sister home.

"Have I made a mistake?" he felt his heart gripped. He could see Kamlesh surrounded by Kanwar Bhan's brothers and sisters. They wouldn't let her go, it seemed. Everyone wanted a share of their Bhabhi. The relationship between Kamlesh and her in-laws looked more than three days old. Whereas the grown-ups tried to go out of their way to secure her comfort, Santosh and Draupadi, Kamlesh's sisters-in-law aged four and eight were fighting to have their lion's share of time with their Bhabhi. Both fought with each other to sit on her lap. Kamlesh struggled to keep them both happy.

Is it fair? He thought, *After all, it's just her third day into married life. My sister surely deserves better.*

"Bhaiya, I m sorry but I won't be able to go with you today," Kamlesh's voice broke into his thoughts.

"But why? After all, it's the tradition, isn't it?" he almost cried.

"Yes Bhaiya, but these are special circumstances."

"What special circumstances?" Rajender struggled to control the pitch of his voice.

"Actually I have to accompany Anil and Mahendra for their admission to school tomorrow and there are more things to be done. Please try and understand. I really can't go."

"Really can't go? What does it mean Kamlesh? Have these strangers become more important to you in a matter of three days?"

"No, it's not that Bhaiya," Kamlesh warmly put her hand in her brother's hand and sat silently beside him. For several minutes, no one spoke.

"How would you survive here Kamlesh? These people don't even have proper beddings so that guests can get some peaceful sleep. How would you survive here? And it's not a single-day affair. It's your life, your entire life!"

Kamlesh didn't answer.

"You know," Rajender temporarily ended the uncomfortable silence, "the other match was really good. The doctor guy I mean."

"You mean I should have married the doctor?" she asked.

"Yes, in fact, there can't be two views about that. Maa and I simply bowed down to your wishes, as always. I now believe that at least this time we shouldn't have agreed with your stupid decision. Both of us should have forced you into getting married to the doctor."

"And be what Bhaiya? A decorated doll all through my life with no set targets to achieve? Look around Bhaiya, can't you see I have my hands full? With my hard work, I can change the track of ten lives. And if you look carefully into those ten pairs of eyes, you would witness the seeding of a new hope. With their silence they cheer, 'Thank you Bhabhi for choosing to come here.' Bhaiya, everyone is perplexed ever since you arrived. They are scared that if I go with you, I might take a long time to come back, or that I may not come back at all. This is the level of their belief that they have in themselves today. Their continued struggle has somehow instilled this doubt in their minds that nothing good can ever happen to them. And now, they can hardly believe their luck. I have to change all this Bhaiya. Yes, the house is small and life wouldn't be easy. But you should look at the bigger picture. Consider the amount of love and respect I would get here. Can I get it anywhere else? Tell me Bhaiya?"

Kamlesh could see his eyes welling up, and knew he wouldn't be able to hold back his tears. Rajender blinked quickly and tried to look away.

"I wish there were more like you Kamlesh. As always, go for the impossible. I can't be more proud of you. Thank you. Thank you very much for being what you are. But you know what Kammo, once again you have refused to ride the racing cycle that your Bhaiya had chosen for you." The tears flowed incessantly. Everyone looked at them, overwhelmed, as the brother-sister duo hugged and cried.

"Bhaiya," Kamlesh whispered as she opened a knot at the end of her sari with one hand and wiped her tears with the other, "Your chart that day was incomplete." She took out a white, worn out slip and gave it to Rajender, who quickly unfolded it. It was the same chart that he had made, but with one difference. The sixth column was filled too.

Comparison Chart			
S.No	**Assets**	**Doctor**	**Kanwar Bhan**
1	Land	Hundreds of acres	None
2	Bank balance	Huge	Depleted
3	Family	Small	Big
4	Future	Secure	Volatile
5	Spouse's Profession	Excellent	Unemployed
6	*Love*	*A leap in the dark*	*Abundant*

"I have filled the last column that was left incomplete by you. The asset in that last column outweighs all the other parameters." Her tears flowed while the lips smiled. Rajender's lips quivered, and then quivered again. The flood in his eyes had blocked the passage for words. He hugged his sister one last time and quickly moved out of the house, never once looking back. He sat in his car and drove. He was still within the periphery of the village when someone signalled him to stop. Rajender came out. It was Ram Sharan, the same man who had come to warn him before Kamlesh's marriage. Ghussad, his aide, stood by his side.

"How are you Son?"

"I'm fine," Rajender looked away.

"How was your first experience coming to your sister's house?" The sarcasm was obvious. Perceiving that Rajender was not inclined to reply, he continued, "Would you answer one question, Son?" he asked

Rajender nodded.

"Why is it that you chose to get Kamlesh married here? After all, she was in a position to get any groom of her choice."

"So, you want to know the reason."

"Sure, I mean if you have no objection."

"Though it's a private family matter and I am under no obligation whatsoever to make the communication public, still I would unfold the developments to you as you too in some direct or indirect way had played a significant role in this decision."

"Me! A significant role?"

"Yes Ram Sharan ji. You are the reason why my sister got married where she did."

"Me?" the day seemed engulfed by the night in broad daylight.

"Yes, I am sure it will be news to you if I say that before you had come to our house, we had already rejected the proposal."

"Then what made you change your decision?"

"It wasn't my decision. It was my sister's. She eavesdropped on you, overheard every word that you had said against Kanwar Bhan ji's family and decided..."

"Decided what?"

"That she would make it her life's purpose to change the fortune of each member of the family."

Ram Sharan's jaw dropped.

"And one more thing Ram Sharan ji, before I leave," Rajender hadn't finished, "Now this family is my sister's family. Any untoward comment from anyone, whosoever he may be, would be considered an intrusion on my self-esteem. And I don't need to tell you the name of the village I belong to. I am sure the notoriousness of our village precedes us wherever we, the people of Baoli go. Therefore, please be cautious where you tread."

"For sure Beta, I am of the opinion that we should forget all that has passed on either side," was all that Ram Sharan could manage.

"That would be better for you, Ram Sharan ji." Rajender entered his car and sped off, leaving behind a spellbound Ram Sharan. Rajender's bark had hurt him more than any bite. The inferiority in his character stopped him from answering Rajender with equal authority.

"That was an insult." said Ghussad.

"For sure it was." Ram Sharan stared at nothingness. Ghussad looked into Ram Sharan's motionless eyes. His pupils were still.

"When will he repay us then?" asked Ghussad

"No, he won't. Someone else will."

"Who?"

"His doting sister," Ram Sharan whispered

"When?"

"At the appropriate time."

The next day, Rajendar came back to purchase a big house just next to the one that belonged to Kamlesh's new family.

"To a lovely sister from a doting brother," Rajender said as he handed over the papers. This time, Kamlesh couldn't say no.

Jeet and Paddy

Kamlesh had little time to settle down in her new family. Confronted by more than a number of challenges, she chose to deal with them one at a time. She started with the most challenging of them all: lack of funds. With Kanwar's salary and Mamchand's pension being the only assets, there was wide disparity between income and expenses. She rented out the house that Rajender had gifted to her. But that wasn't enough. Despite the house being a huge one, it did not attract enough income to act as a panacea for lack of funds.

I must look for a job somewhere. The idea- however- was shrugged off immediately: it wasn't feasible for her, as she was required to manage household affairs on a daily basis.

She knew that there had to be a solution to her problem. She just needed to find it. She had the will... and then... she found the way.

One fine day, Kamlesh walked into the closest branch of the Gurgaon Gramin Bank and applied for a buffalo loan. After the necessary formalities and paper work, the loan was sanctioned. A penny saved is a penny gained. The purchase of three buffaloes helped the family in two ways: first, the expenses hitherto incurred on milk were saved and second, there was a considerable jump in household income. Milk from one buffalo was set aside for home consumption and the produce from the remaining two was sold to the milkman and within the neighbourhood. Owning buffaloes, however, didn't come easy. It required a considerable effort and a twenty four-hour vigil. Whereas in Baoli there were servants to look after the buffaloes, here Kamlesh had only herself to fall back on. Preparing fodder thrice a day to milking them in the mornings and evenings and maintaining an account of the milk sold, she managed everything. Whatever little time she was left with, was utilised in monitoring the studies of her siblings-in-law. Her day would start at four in the morning and end at eleven in the night. The effort was strenuous. There were times when she would feel dejected and demotivated. During such situations, she would go back to her books, the *Geeta*, the *Mahabharata* and others. Those books were her magnetic compasses to guide her in real life situations. She more than realized the value of treasures that the books held for her. "If there are a hundred problems, there are one hundred and one solutions for them," her books had told her during one of her regular conversations with them.

Kamlesh's hard work started to pay dividends and though she wasn't able to save an extraordinary amount of money, yet she could now meet educational, food and miscellaneous expenses of the family without much difficulty. The option to buy more buffaloes to increase the level of income further was always open. The wheel of fortune started to move forward. The villagers, being witness to the changes she was gradually bringing to the family, named her Lakshmi, after the Hindu Goddess of wealth.

It was after two years of marriage that Jeet was born. The family delighted in welcoming the newborn. Kamlesh promised herself that she would not let her child be pampered by her family. Rather, her efforts would be to let her son face all the trials that life presented him with, but only after she had done her duty as a mother in making him see the intricacies of the world to the extent possible. She knew that if she introduced the world to Jeet in the way it should be done, he would very quickly invent his own means of settling down well, without being a liability to anyone.

Jeet had turned four when Kamlesh gave birth to her second son Padam. The family nicknamed him Paddy, though the thought of giving a nickname to Jeet had never crossed the family's mind.

When the time came to choose a school for their elder son, Kamlesh and Kanwar were prudent enough to realize the imperativeness of the first school in shaping a child's future. Therefore, despite the village having its own primary school a stone's throw away, Kamlesh and Kanwar decided to get Jeet admitted to Our Lady of Fatima (OLF) Convent School, unarguably the best school in Gurgaon.

Admission formalities having been completed, Jeet was to join school the next day. Kamlesh was helping him get his bag ready when she heard the knock.

"My name is Munna," said the stranger after salutations. "I drop kids to the school in my rickshaw. I got to know you are looking for a rickshaw-wala for your son."

She looked at the rickshaw-wala closely. The man with thick moustaches and a missing tooth looked simple. He was wearing a striped shirt and a lungi, both of which had seen better days. But it was his toothless smile that stood out. All in all, the man had a hint of innocence in him, which Kamlesh was able to see through his less than the best appearance.

"Do you take kids to OLF too?" asked Kamlesh.

"Yes, I have kids from two schools only: OLF and St Michael's."

"And where do you pick them from?"

"Gurgaon village and from Bhimnagar."

"But as far as I know, there are hardly any kids who go to OLF from our village," Kamlesh said. "And by the way, who told you we need a rickshaw for our kid and that our kid would go to OLF?" Despite his outwardly honest appearance, Kamlesh was not the one to be taken in and wanted to cross-check things for herself.

"A kid's mother told me; her son goes to OLF too." His answer was straight and categorical.

She asked Munna to take her to a couple of parents, whose kids he ferried. He had no objection to it. On enquiry, she found out that Munna hailed from Meerut and was now settled in Gurgaon. He had no relatives and few friends. All in all, the rickshaw and the kids were his life now. No parent had anything adverse to say about Munna. Everyone praised him. Each family was of the opinion that Munna had a warm heart and poor that he was, would rather deny himself the necessities of life, than do anything wrong.

Satisfied that Jeet had nothing to fear from his association with Munna, the next morning she hugged the child and bade him farewell for his first day at school

It took Munna not more than fifteen minutes to cover the two-and-a-half kilometre stretch from Jeet's house to OLF. Having dropped the St. Michael's kids on his way to OLF, he helped the OLF kids get down from the rickshaw. Jeet was the last one to get off. Munna noticed the child eyeing the candy cart near the school gate, carried him over in his arms, and bought him some candy. Whereas Munna and Jeet hadn't realized it, the seeds for a long relationship were sown. Four-year-old Jeet was old enough to appreciate the sweetness of candy, but too young to be troubled by the weight of the debt of a poor man.

Those were not the only candies for which Munna was to pay from his own pocket.

Time flew and Jeet grew in size and years. The candies were transmuted to ice-creams. Each time Munna paid for them, his love for Jeet swelled further. There was no way Kamlesh could learn about their little ice-cream and candy story. For neither Jeet nor Munna talked about it to her. The relationship was symbiotic in love, but materially, one was the beneficiary and the other the benefactor. Only time would tell if an indebted Jeet would be able to repay Munna at some point in life.

The Siblings Settle Down

Time kept its pace and Kamlesh entered into the sixteenth year of her marriage. For all of sixteen years, she had lived along with her siblings-in-law under one roof. Considerable changes took place during this span. Mamchand had died sans worries, for he was convinced that the future of his children was secure in the hands of Kanwar and Kamlesh.

Both Kanwar and Kamlesh had now carried out almost all of their basic duties towards the younger brothers and sisters. Each of the sisters had been married off into decent households. The brothers were not only married but well settled too. Satya Bhan, the one younger to Kanwar was now a Bachelor-in-Law and now wanted to pursue a Master's degree in law in tandem with his professional practice. Anil- the next in line- had become a platoon commander with Central Police Organizations. Leelu had entered into a small business and Mohinder, the youngest had joined the department of education. Barring the higher studies of Satya Bhan, their responsibilities towards the siblings were complete.

Predominantly, her two kids were now the business of Kamlesh's life. For want of their privacy and future, the couple decided to move out of the ancestral house to live in the house gifted by Rajender that had earlier been put on rent. They, however, knew that their responsibilities towards the siblings wouldn't be counted as fulfilled till Satya Bhan had completed his higher education.

Jeet was now in class X and Paddy in class VI. As Jeet grew further in years and prudence, the debt of Munna's ice creams started nagging him. It occurred to him frequently that he should ask his parents to pay Munna for all the ice creams at one go. But Jeet brushed away these thoughts as he didn't want Munna to feel small. "But I can at least stop the debt from mounting further," he thought. He decided to walk to school. Munna was initially stumped by Jeet's decision, but later got a whiff of his mind. After all, Jeet was like his own son. The relationship, even after having come to an abrupt end materially, continued to grow in spirit and love.

Both Jeet and Paddy had developed a natural affinity towards cricket, so much so, that studies would take a backseat when it came to choosing one out of the two. Silently, Jeet nurtured a dream to play for India. Also, he was growing up to be a good son. He wasn't careless or extravagant like most kids his age. Kamlesh saw much promise in him.

Jeet's after school hours were spent in practice sessions with the village cricket team in the primary school playground. Sunday happened to be his favourite day for two reasons: first because it was his match day – every Sunday he played a match either representing his village or his school – and second, his dad was home.

Kamlesh was delighted when Jeet returned home after attending a month-long under-15 national level camp-held at Rohtak- during which he played several matches representing his state Haryana.

Kamlesh thought he looked a little subdued after his return, but he shrugged away any questions regarding the same. He only said, "It's nothing Mom." He was, however, eager to meet and narrate everything that had happened, to his best friend Dinesh.

"So, how did your matches go?" asked Dinesh. They were seated in their favourite Chinese restaurant and had ordered American chopsuey. In the fullness of his belief that Dinesh would come up with something worthwhile, he mentioned the circumstances that were troubling him.

Jeet was in class VIII when he had first heard of Dinesh. He was prudent enough to recognize his uncommon good fortune in having Dinesh as his friend, whom he could turn to in his hour of need. The friendship had grown to an extent where Jeet was certain there wouldn't be a time when Dinesh would no longer be important to him. He was convinced Dinesh possessed all the qualities that were needed to adorn a relationship as pious as friendship.

"A boy from our village spins the ball at least three feet," one of his village teammates had said during a cricket match two years ago.

"How old is he?"

"He is in college."

"Why is he not in our team then?" Jeet had asked.

"I have asked him to come for practice tomorrow."

Jeet's teammate wasn't wrong. Dinesh did spun the ball vociferously the next day. But it was his qualities other than cricket that had won Jeet's heart. Dinesh's simple demeanour and soft words were complemented by his heart of gold. It was not long before cricket debates were replaced by discussions on personal issues.

"Didn't go well at all," Jeet said with a hint of sadness

"Why, what happened?"

"I was asked to bat at number 11."

"Number 11?"

"Yes."

"You aren't a bowler for God's sake. You are an opening batsman. Why would they ask you to bat last?"

"I don't know."

"But only last year you were the opening batsman in the same tournament!"

"Yes I was."

"Then what happened this time?"

"Our team won the toss."

"Ok, and...?"

"The captain decided that we would bat first."

"Fine."

"And then the captain asked me to get padded up as an opener."

"But you just said you were called in at number eleven?"

"Listen baba."

"Ok, I am all ears."

"As I was about to step onto the cricket field, Topal appeared."

"Topal as in O.P. Topal, the selector from Gurgaon?"

"Yes, the one and only."

"And?"

"He asked me to untie the pads and asked Pankaj to get padded up instead."

"What the hell! He can't do that. One, because this is pure injustice and second, it isn't his business to interfere in the team decisions. It's the ballgame of the captain and the manager. Didn't you ask him why?"

"I did. During dinner at the hotel, after the day's play."

"What did he say?"

"That he wanted to teach me a lesson."

"Lesson! For what?"

"He said because he had seen me smoking a cigarette the day before, he decided to punish me."

"My God! I have never heard anything as bizarre as this. Did you not say you have never even touched a cigarette ever? And even if you did, it was your personal matter."

"I told him that I am willing to undergo any medical test regarding smoking."

"And?"

"He just ignored me, said nothing."

"This is a conspiracy."

"Sure it is. But can't say exactly who conspired."

"Of course Topal."

"But there has to be a reason why Topal did it. Was he staying in Rohtak, or did he come from Gurgaon that morning?"

"He came from Gurgaon."

"And the first thing that he did was to get your pads off."

"Yes, and I heard him saying to someone that he was glad to have reached before the openers could step into the field."

"Hmm, this is a clear case of conspiracy. Did he accompany someone from Gurgaon or did he come alone?"

"He came along with Ahlawat Uncle, in his car."

"Ahlawat who?"

"Ahlawat Uncle, Pankaj's father. He was the one who lifted my spirits when I was feeling down."

"And Pankaj was the one who replaced you as opener."

"Yes."

"It's two plus two four. Ahlawat is the culprit here!"

"I don't believe it. He was so kind to me, always is, but wait... !"

"What happened?"

"I think you have a point here... because once after the practice session, he offered me a lift in his car. He spoke about disinformation and the fact how much he liked it."

"Disinformation? What is that?"

"Casually, just to keep the conversation going, I had asked him whether he liked teaching History as he was a professor of that subject."

Jeet narrated the whole incident to him.

"You know Jeet, I like to study Chanakya in great detail," answered Ahlawat, his eyes fixed on the road as he drove.

"But that isn't a part of your subject, is it?"

"Of course it is."

"Tell me one thing that strikes you about Chanakya."

"There are lots of things. He was an institution in himself."

"Agreed Uncle, but tell me about one lesson that strikes you the most."

"Ok, let me think a bit." After thinking for a while, he spoke again, "See Jeet, there is this tremendous weapon he gave to the world. The beauty of this weapon is that it defeats the enemy even without a war. It strikes with utmost precision. In fact, I would go to the extent of saying that it hardly misses its target."

"And what would the name of such an incredible weapon be?"

"Disinformation."

"Disinformation? What is that Uncle?"

"It's a sure shot device to defeat your enemy or competitor by spreading rumours about him. It is done to create a rift between any two or more individuals, organizations or even nations in order to gain personal advantage. America did it to create a rift between Russia and its friendly nations, the British did it successfully for two hundred years and governed us. And it's so common with individuals. Several people do it all the time without even knowing it!"

"But how is it done Uncle?"

"As I already said: by spreading false information against your enemy."

"But how does it benefit the person who triggers it?"

"Your enemy's loss is your gain," Ahlawat had displayed a cunning smile.

"And he used this disinformation weapon against you," Dinesh looked at Jeet.

"Yes it appears that way now. More so, when the person who benefitted from my demotion was his own son. You are right. He was definitely the chief conspirator. It was he, who spread rumours that I smoked."

"Or maybe he said even more, which we don't know yet."

"Sure, and that is even more scary. So, are we dealing with a Chanakya here?"

"Yes, but Chanakya with a difference. Whereas, the original Chanakya helped a fifteen-year-old Chandragupta fight against the injustices and inconsistencies of the world, here is one who chooses to fight with hidden weapons against an unarmed fifteen-year-old, and that too in the garb of a friend. The modern Chanakya deserves kudos for explicit bravery."

There was silence for a considerable time.

"How much did his son score?" asked Dinesh.

"He scored a first ball duck. Zero."

"And how much did you score?"

"Just played a couple of balls and then ran out of partners, remained not out on two runs."

"So, despite all the cunning moves, the modern Chanakya still couldn't win!" Dinesh breathed, "What do you plan to do now?"

"Right now, I have no time for it. The boards are staring me right in the eye. But some day, Ahlawat will have to pay for it."

"Did you tell Uncle and Aunty?"

"No, they won't be able to tolerate it."

"But Topal can surely do it again."

"Of course he can. But don't worry, I'll try and find a solution by the next trials."

Dinesh had nothing more to say. Jeet felt lighter.

House Mortgaged

Like Robinson Crusoe's man Friday, Ghussad too had first met Ram Sharan on the same day of the week. Whereas Friday was sincere and loyal to his master, Ghussad was an out-and-out flatterer, a real sycophant. But like Friday, Ghussad too was the shadow of his master. Ram Sharan was one subject he had mastered himself in. He knew Ram Sharan's mind inside out. Be it preparing *hukka* or cocktail, he mixed them to the exact tee. He knew the exact words that would instigate his master and the ones that would please him. Ram Sharan too, felt inconvenienced if he did not have his chief flatterer by his side on any given day. It was the evenings that Ghussad looked forward to, when he waited like a jackal for Ram Sharan to dose off after a couple of pegs so as to feast himself on the remainder of the whiskey.

It was like any other morning when both of them were returning from Ram Sharan's fields.

"Huzoor, you were the talk of the entire village last night, hein hein, after all not everyone gets to be the chief guest of the village Ramlila," Ghussad took out his first card of the day.

"Stop it Ghussad, there is a limit to flattery. It's you who instigated me into accepting the offer of being chief guest. And I had to dole out five hundred and one rupees just for nothing. The one thing of interest in an otherwise boring affair was the dancer Shabnam. What a beauty!"

"But Huzoor! Shabnam was interested in you and none other. Didn't you notice how after every step she looked at you for approval?" Ghussad took out another card.

"Are you again trying to flatter me?"

"How dare I, *huzoor*! Did you not on your own notice her interest in you?"

"Yeah, it appeared a little that way!" Ram Sharan wanted to believe him.

"Of course huzoor, and five hundred rupees is small change for you. Why, it's even less than the amount that you squander for your daily drinks."

"My daily drinks! Your drinks Ghussad, your drinks! Till the time I have my two mini pegs, you gulp the entire bottle down your gut. Some gut, really I tell you! You are a tanker Ghussad, a big tanker. You don't even know how much you cost me!"

"I am all for you huzoor. Will live and die by your side. But there is one thing I didn't understand regarding the Ramlila."

"What is that?"

"Why did Ram ji hide behind the trees to hit Bali? I mean, for God to undertake such a cowardly act!"

"Arrey Ghussad! I had taken you to be a fool. I didn't know you had a mind too!"

"Hein hein huzoor, all because of you."

"Ram ji hid behind the tree because of the boon to Bali that whosoever would attack him in a battlefield will lose half of his strength to Bali. Had Ram ji fought an open war, he would have lost half of His strength to Bali. Then Bali, with all his strength and half the strength of Ram ji would be the stronger of the two and then it would be impossible for Ram ji to defeat him!"

"Is it possible in today's time, huzoor?"

"What?"

"That someone might get the other person's strength in a duel."

"How can it be possible, you fool? That was Satyug, anything was possible."

"But huzoor, there is one more thing that I didn't like."

"Now what?"

"The song sung by Kanwar Bhan's son Jeet. Did you not see how the crowd listened to him with rapt attention and later applauded for him? Have you forgotten our enmity with his family?"

"I couldn't sleep the whole night because the sound of applause resounded in my head and disturbed me. I am waiting for the right moment."

"Sixteen years have passed, huzoor, and you are still waiting. May be you have forgotten how Kamlesh's brother had insulted and threatened you."

"Believe me. When I say I am waiting for the right moment, that means I am waiting for the right moment."

"But slowly they are becoming powerful."

"You mean the brothers of Kanwar Bhan?"

"Yes."

"Hunh, they are not even worth considering. I am cautious of just two people."

"Kamlesh and Kanwar?"

"No. Kamlesh and Rajender."

"Talking of Kamlesh, huzoor, she had come to that Kallu Mahajan with her house papers."

"Why? For what?"

"Mahajan said she needed some money for Satya Bhan's law fee."

"When was it?"

"Last week, huzoor."

"And you are telling me now!" Before Ghussad knew it, Ram Sharan's fingers were etched on his left cheek. "Tell me what did Kallu Mahajan say? Was the house mortgaged?"

"No huzoor," Ghussad caressed his left cheek with his left palm. "Kallu said the money she asked for was too much."

"Ghussad," Ram Sharan spoke after thinking hard for a while.

"Huzoor."

"I was wrong."

"No huzoor you can't be wrong."

"Shut up and listen to me."

"Yes huzoor."

"Bali's story is still true. Even in Kalyug - the one who hides and attacks, wins."

"How huzoor?"

"I would hide and attack with precision. It would be a sure shot. If they don't see it, how can they defend themselves from it?"

"You mean Kanwar's family?"

"Yes," Ram Sharan's round eyes shone. "Ghussad!" he called again.

"Huzoor."

"I will gobble their house and for their entire lives, they would run helter-skelter to salvage their injured pride. That would be my revenge Ghussad. The time has come." His victim in sight, his serpent-eyes were still, venom ready to be exuded any moment.

Rajender had surprised Kamlesh by arriving unannounced.

"Surprise surprise Bhaiya!" Kamlesh smiled as she served water.

"Did you mortgage the house Kamlesh?"

"Yes Bhaiya!"

"For what?"

"Satya Bhan's fee for higher studies had to be paid Bhaiya."

"Kamlesh, you should have told me if you needed any money."

"Don't worry, we will get it back Bhaiya. We have eight years' time to return the money. The village Mahajan is not that bad a man."

"The house is mortgaged to Ram Sharan, not to the village Mahajan, Kamlesh!"

"No Bhaiya, the deal is with the village Mahajan."

"That is the conspiracy Kammo. Tell me, did the Mahajan not disagree to mortgage it initially?"

"Yes, he did."

"And then he came back again to do the deal?"

"Yes."

"It is Ram Sharan's game."

"We will prosecute him Bhaiya, if that is the case."

"We can't Kamlesh, he has done everything legitimately. I am told that the witnesses who have signed on the papers are his own too. The only solution now is that his money be returned. I have brought the money with me. We will get the papers back today itself."

"You know it can't happen. By getting me married you have fulfilled all your responsibilities. And you had gifted me this house too. So, you have already done much more than a brother is expected to. You want me to ask you to get it freed from the mortgage, so that I can mortgage it yet again at the first semblance of demanding circumstances. Let this cycle end here, Bhaiya. Now it's my destiny."

"But what about Jeet and Paddy?"

"What about them, Bhaiya?"

"Don't you think they need some security for the future, a safety net?"

"Ha ha," sarcasm spilled with her laughter, "Safety net Bhaiya! Coming from you, it surprises me. The ones with safety nets don't fly very far. And where was your safety net when you had jumped in that ring of death against a taller and stronger Pradyuman?"

Rajender didn't answer immediately.

"What is the period for the return of the money?"

"Eight years Bhaiya," Kamlesh answered, her voice dim.

"The period is substantial Kamlesh, and what are the conditions, in case the money is not paid within the stipulated time?"

"In that case, the house would belong to Ram Sharan. He might auction it, keep it for himself or do whatever he feels like."

"I know what he prefers doing with it."

"What Bhaiya?"

"Ram Sharan prefers to run a bulldozer over the house."

"How do you know Bhaiya?"

"He has been bragging about it in the entire village. Somehow, the news reached me as well."

Had a pin dropped, it would have made a profound sound.

"How will you get the house back now Kammo?"

"I don't know Bhaiya."

Rajender left, dragging his feet.

"I will get the house back Mom," Jeet whispered to himself in the adjacent room.

The Stone and the Destination

It was Sunday, the favourite day of the week for Jeet. His dad relaxed through the morning tea and the newspaper. Jeet and his younger brother Paddy were getting ready for the match. Kamesh continued with her morning chores. She was sorting out Jeet's school uniform.

"Jeet, what do you do with these shoes? Look at them," she threw the worn out shoe in his direction.

"Maybe the leg cricket sessions are taking longer," Kanwar suggested with a smile, looking out of the newspaper.

"Dad, leg cricket ball is a very soft ball made of sponge. It can't damage the shoe so much."

"Alright, then please enrich us by explaining how the shoe got damagèd so badly?" Kamlesh looked at him in mock anger.

"This happens when you kick a stone every day," he laughed in embarrassment, putting a hand over his mouth.

"You kick a stone, for God's sake! Do you mean a stone fixed on a wall?" Kamlesh looked astounded.

"No Mom," Jeet laughed heartily. "If I kick a wall people would stone me instead, thinking I am mad," all four laughed.

"What do you do then?" asked Kanwar

"I will tell you what he exactly does..." said Kamlesh, still laughing. "He chooses a stone and continues to kick it with his foot on his way to school. In a way, the stone heads towards the school with Jeet."

"Wow Mom, you are a genius," shouted Jeet as Kanwar and Paddy looked on.

"But why would you do that Jeet, don't you think it's weird?" asked Kamlesh.

"Mom, it may look weird, but it sort of makes it easy to talk to myself while I walk to school. I don't know how, but its helps me concentrate."

"And what is it that you concentrate upon?"

"Can be anything Mom."

"Give me one example."

"Like, in case I had played a stupid shot during a match, I concentrate on how to improve it."

"Do you take it right up to the school gate?" Kamlesh asked.

"Not always Mom, if sometimes it goes off the path then I don't get into the trouble of fetching it."

"Do you look for a new stone then?"

"Well, yes Mom," Jeet said thoughtfully, wondering how his Mom knew all that.

"Now listen to me."

"Yes Mom?"

"If you start kicking a stone on your way to school, then you should ensure you take the same stone always to the school gate, irrespective of where it goes."

"You mean even it goes way too far and even if fetching the same could make me late for school?"

"Yes, exactly," Kamlesh said calmly.

Jeet didn't exactly understand, but he nodded and went out with Paddy.

"And why should he do that? I mean it looks bizarre," Kanwar asked after Jeet and Paddy left.

"See," she replied, "he said he seems to concentrate better by doing it. When he walks to school he is alone and since there is no one with him, he is totally with himself. That's the time when his intellect would come into play and he himself said that he is able to concentrate and get answers or solutions to some of his problems."

"But why did you ask him to take the stone till the school gate?"

"To make him realize the importance of not leaving a task unfinished."

"And why did you ask him to not look for a new one and fetch the same one instead?"

"I did that in order to not let him get into the habit of running away from his ambition or relinquishing it on some pretext or the other, when he is faced with difficult situations."

"How?"

"See, assuming the stone has fallen off track, it would need an effort to fetch it, whereas the easier solution would be to look for a new stone. My idea in guiding him is to inculcate in him a habit of sticking to his ambitions even when his circumstances are difficult and not to look for easier options instead, in life that is."

"Hmm, I am impressed."

"I thought you were impressed already, for sixteen years," she replied playfully.

"But in his efforts to bring back the stone, what if he gets late for school?"

"Then he would realize that if he has to concentrate on the stone, he would have to start a bit early. It would in fact, further teach him one more thing – time management," responded Kamlesh.

"But how did you know about the stone incident even before he told you? I mean you were spot on, when you said what exactly he did with the stone!"

"Because I did it myself when I was a kid," she chirped.

"My God! So it's you who needs to be scolded then, for Jeet's bad habit!"

"For sure I should," Kamlesh replied with equal jest.

"On a serious note, tell me, did you take the stone to its destination?"

"Sometimes," she smiled.

"Why not always?"

"Because despite the best efforts, one cannot always win."

"But you didn't tell this to Jeet."

"Because some things he has to learn on his own. Time will be his teacher."

≈

Kanwar left by the 5 a.m. bus the next morning. Jeet and Paddy were ready for school. As usual Munna came to pick Paddy, while Jeet walked to school. He didn't have to wait long to find the right-sized stone. He kicked it gently and walked towards it to kick it again.

"Ram Sharan prefers to run a bulldozer over the house." His Mama's words disturbed him. Suddenly he felt grown up. Felt eager to the extent of gifting his Mom the house right then. But there were things to be done. Money had to be earned. He had eight years with him. He kicked the stone again. There was no doubt in his mind that his dream at that moment, was to gift the papers of the house back to his Mom. It was even bigger than his dream of playing for India. Would he have to now sacrifice one dream to fulfil the other, was the question that scared him. Can there be something common, so much so, that the fulfilment of one dream would automatically lead to the attainment of the other? He knew there wasn't enough money in domestic tournaments. He thought and thought hard, kicking the stone on his way to school.

It was just before he reached the gates of the school, that a conciliatory thought struck his mind. What if he played the Ranji Trophy for his state by the age of twenty and performed so exceptionally that the selectors would be forced to pick him for the Indian side the following year itself? And if that happened, certainly, he would have enough money within a year to snatch the papers of the house back from Ram Sharan. "Planning or dreaming is easy," his mother had taught him, "but it needed courage, hard work, and conviction to achieve anything big." He would have to pull his socks up and perform far better that he had been performing in the junior tournaments for a timely selection in the Ranji Trophy, and then take things further from there. He felt determined.

The Board Exams

"Shall I get you more coffee, sister?"

Raymond, Sister Fulgentia's aide had entered.

"No Raymond, thank you," she replied.

She had already had four cups of the brew, two more than usual. The headache, however, refused to subside. Raymond deftly cleared the table. Discomforting thoughts engulfed her once more.

"I will impound all your school buses," the words of the Deputy Commissioner returned to cause mental agony. The headache too, had worsened. Unable to bear the suffocation, the Principal of Our Lady of Fatima convent, came out of her office and strolled towards the beautifully manicured school lawn.

A graceful, double-chinned lady of fifty years, Sister Fulgentia was everything that a principal should be. Always in an impeccable white robe, she was polite yet firm. Just a stern look with a stiff upper lip could send shivers down the spine of the students. She was passionate about books. Whatever time she got for herself, was spent in their company. The no-nonsense persona wore a gentle calm. The well being and growth of the institution was the purpose of her life.

Her happiness, or the lack of it, depended on the health of the institution. Whereas, a victory at the inter-convent debate competition would make her evening cheerful, a runners-up position at a quiz contest was enough to spoil her day. Whenever she was confronted with challenging situations, her body clock would signal it to her through a headache in the left part of the skull. The tests and X-rays revealed no physical irregularity. The doctors had concluded that the reasons were psychological rather than otherwise. She was advised to take things lightly.

The cause of the recent headache lay in the occurrences of the previous day. She had politely turned down the recommendations of the deputy commissioner for an admission. The student was screened and was found to be way below the school standards. The deputy commissioner, however, wasn't amused.

After strolling for a few minutes, she returned to her office.

"Bring peace to me O' Lord," she offered a silent prayer. "Come what may, I would stick to my decision. The school's reputation is not to be played with." If there was any tentativeness regarding the decision, the same was now gone. Her gaze shifted to the ambience of her office. In front of her was the roll of honour board displaying the names of meritorious students, on her left were several cabinets that housed various trophies that the school had won. All of them adorned her office and gave her pride. Just behind her chair was a cabinet that displayed her collection of books. As her mind calmed a little, she turned to the routine administrative files placed on the left side of the table. She started clearing them one by one.

A gentle knock on the door made her look up. It was Sister Praseda, the vice-principal. She was the only one who, besides being part of the administration was a member of faculty too. She taught Physics to classes IX and X. Pleasantries were exchanged as sister Praseda occupied one of the guest chairs. Sister Fulgentia consulted her in all important matters, but when it came to decision-making, Sister Fulgentia's own mind, rather than anything else, was the decisive factor.

"Sister, has any decision been taken on the DC's issue?"

"What is to be decided in that, P?" Sister Fulgentia called her P. In fact, the whole school referred to her as Sister P.

"I mean, have you decided whether we should admit the child?"

"You were in the assessment board. In fact, it's your own note on file that the kid is not up to the school standards."

"Yes sister that's true, but I mean... it's the recommendation from the district administration."

"The recommendation was there even when you wrote the note in the file. So what has changed now?"

"Actually the DC's PA met me yesterday and told me the DC is genuinely interested in the case and requested whether it can be reconsidered."

"You know, P..." Sister Fulgentia had kept the file aside and started walking towards the only window of her office. "I too had a telephonic conversation with the DC and would say that he is not the politest of people around. But such threats or pressure tactics do not change one fact, that the reputation of this institution is paramount to us. Work is worship, and one should not be unjust or insincere during prayers."

"But sister, it's also true that the administration has immense powers, and all said and done, it's the question of just one kid."

"You are right, P!" the Principal laughed. "It's always the question of one kid and then the second and then the third and then we become redundant. Maybe mere puppets in the hands of someone powerful. And for once P, let's assume we admit this kid, would you then be doing justice to the hundreds of kids who were denied admission? At least most of them, if not all, were better than the child in question. You know how we all love children. In a way, they are no less than the reflections of the Lord Himself. But the same Lord is also looking at us all the time, expecting us to be fair and upright in fulfilling the tasks that He allocates to us."

There was an uneasy silence in the room. When the air of tension in the room made breathing impossible, Sister P bowed and left. The colour clearly drained out of her face. The thought that the DC's PA was waiting for her call only increased P's discomfort.

As the principal finished with the administrative files, her attention caught the pile of report cards kept on the right side of the table.

Must be the results of pre-boards, she thought. Invariably, she felt happy looking at the pre-board report cards. Browsing through, she signed them with an air of casualness. A gentle smile spread on her face as she picked up the next report card. Roll number 24, Jeet Singh. The name flashed an image before her eyes. An image of the class X boy with an athletic build. The smile, however, was short-lived. Tiny beads of perspiration appeared on her forehead as she scanned the marks in each subject. The headache had worsened. Her fingers reached for the buzzer and in came Raymond.

Hitesh Rustagi, Jeet Singh, Alok Maheshwari, Krishan Chutani, Chetan Gupta, Atul Jyoti and Neeraj Dogra formed the nucleus of the coterie of students of class X. They fought among themselves one moment and were buddies the next. Their bond of friendship had passed several tests.

It was recess time. Class X students were deeply engrossed in the leg cricket match. The under arm ball delivered by Chetan had met with the same fate as the other balls from the over. It was rocketed to the boundary by Jeet.

"How does he hit so hard with his foot? It's hardly a bat for God's sake," Chetan wondered. Sixteen runs in four balls. Just when Chetan's mind struggled to find a way out of the onslaught, the long bell signalled the end of recess.

"Recess is over." He kept the ball in the pocket of his trousers, taking back his tie and blazer from the umpire Atul. With everyone handing over his blazer to Atul, he was almost buried in the heap of blazers. Chetan's act, however, had not amused the batting side.

"But that's not the way. You can complete the remaining two balls," reacted Krishan, the non-striker. The other members of the batting side too joined in the protest. But Chetan was too assertive and too clever to let the clamour change his decision.

"You know it's Mrs Hans' class," he said with a flick of his head. No one had the wit to confront that masterstroke. Everyone knew that even a minute's delay could invite the wrath of the strict Maths teacher. Jeet was the one most disappointed. It was these thirty minutes that he looked forward to, in the entire eight hours of school time.

As always, Mrs Hans went about her task deftly. The students sat in rapt attention. Only Mrs Hans' voice was heard in the class, else it was pin drop silence.

After the period, Mrs Hans walked out and there were a few minutes before Mrs K. Yadav, the Hindi teacher stepped in. Sensing an opportunity, Neeraj Dogra scurried to Jeet's seat with a coin in his hand. He was the captain of one of the two cricket teams in the class. "Let's toss here itself for Sunday's match, skipper!"

"Here! You mean now? Have you gone mad Neeraj?"

The match had been a routine affair and had started in class VIII. Now, after two years of cricket madness, even the girls were divided on the team that they supported. All the team meetings, batting order, bowling schedule were the topics of debate for the entire week.

"What's the matter Jeet?" shouted a bespectacled Krishan, who was affectionately referred to as K.K. He was the wicket keeper in Jeet's team.

"Neeraj has gone mad. He says we toss today itself for Sunday's match."

"Come on Neeraj, what difference would it make? Irrespective of whether we bat first or second, we would thrash you all over the central ground like we did in the last match."

This was enough for Neeraj who possessed an unguarded temper.

"Oye Chashmoo!" he shouted back. "I challenge you to open the innings and face me with the new ball. The first ball would be a beamer aimed at your four eyes and that's a promise!"

"Hey, hey! Neeraj, try that with Jeet and you know where you would be fetching the ball from."

Neeraj picked up a notebook from his desk and threw it towards Krishan who, acting like a deft matador, took away his head just in time to duck the missile.

It was at this precise moment that their Hindi teacher entered.

The Hindi teacher was a person of strong likes and dislikes. She didn't appreciate students who came from a village background and had inferred on her own that Jeet was good-for-nothing. She seldom spared a chance of scolding him, or even caning him. Jeet's desk partner Shalini Sharma always teased him on his predicament while dealing with her. Though Mrs Yadav could communicate in Hindi, she chose to communicate in English, with all her grammatical errors and flawed diction intact. She peculiarly assumed that replacing the sound of 'j' with 'z' and 's' with 'sh' would give her a British accent.

The cacophony in the class turned to pin-drop silence the moment she entered.

"All are stand-up!" she ordered.

As everyone started to get up, sounds of controlled laughter at her faulty use of grammar emanated from all corners.

"Neeraz... why did you hit Krishan with the magajine?"

"Ma'am it was not a magazine," Neeraj stood up, uncontrollable laughter trying to escape him while he kept a straight face.

"Whatever it waj… "

"Madam, he was the one who was poking fun at me. Please ask Jeet… "

Before the Hindi teacher could respond, Jeet got up. Sensing danger, his desk partner Shalini laid a hand on him to stop him by pressing his hand, but the damage was already done. Jeet said, "Actually madam, it was just a casual discussion. No one is to be blamed." The moment the words were uttered, everyone in class, including Jeet himself, knew that he had presented Mrs Yadav with an opportunity that she would not easily let go of.

"All are shit down," the teacher ordered. 'Saved,' Jeet heaved a sigh of relief.

"Zeet, you come to me!"

Jeet sluggishly moved towards her, the class waited.

"Are you zzuzz?"

Jeet stared at her quizzically.

"Don't look at me like fools. Tell me, are you zzuzz?" she shouted at the loudest pitch of her voice.

Oh, she means judge! thought Jeet

"No madam!" he said loudly.

"Did I ask you to shpeak?"

"No madam," Jeet couldn't find a better answer.

Fachak!

Had the earth shaken? Was it a missile? Was it a thunderbolt? No. It was the sound of the fingers of Mrs Yadav's right hand slamming into Jeet's left cheek. The thundering sound echoed two more times. Her fingerprints stood out as glaring red bruises on Jeet's left cheek.

"Go back to your sheet!" she yelled.

The bell rang to end the class and along with it, Jeet's nightmare.

Jeet had just had the time to waive the encounter off when the physics teacher entered. She was getting ready to start her class when Raymond entered.

"Madam, Sister wants to see Jeet."

~~

It was not common to be summoned by the principal. Jeet entered the office and stood with hands folded behind his back. The principal's office had an air of discomfort. The vice principal too, was present. It was Sister Praseda who spoke first.

"Take a seat, Jeet."

"Thank you, Sister." Jeet sat on the seat adjacent to Sister P facing the principal. The pile of report cards kept on the principal's table had answered the question. Sister Praseda was holding Jeet's report card.

"Your scores in the pre-boards are miserable. I am afraid we can't allow you to appear for the boards," Sister Praseda's voice was devoid of emotions.

"But why, Sister?" Jeet was stumped.

"Why!!" She mocked Jeet. "Look at your marks," Sister Praseda almost flung his report card at him.

"But Sister, you know that I was away for my national camp and matches. In fact, the necessary permissions were obtained from the school beforehand," he responded, looking at the principal, hoping for her "divine" intervention.

"But then you had promised that the camps wouldn't have any effect on your academics and marks."

"I still maintain that, but these are the prelims marks and I hardly got any time to prepare for them."

"What makes you so sure you would perform miracles in your boards?"

"There are two months still to go for the boards, Sister, and in these two months, I would focus just on my studies and nothing else. In fact, I have informed the cricket association that I would not be playing any matches till I am done with the boards."

"Don't treat me like a novice, Jeet. Look at your science marks, in chemistry you have scored forty-two out of hundred. The rest is even worse. I am sure you are going to spoil our board results, if allowed to appear." She turned towards the Principal, "Sister, it's a hopeless case and I would not recommend it. As for the rest, it's up to you," she concluded, hurting Jeet's already dented pride.

The silence in the room was suffocating. The principal's body language did not convey anything. "Ok Jeet, you may leave. It's likely that we will call your parents tomorrow," it was P again.

Jeet rose with heavy feet. He was about to open the door when he heard the principal's voice.

"But tell me Jeet, what difference does it make? I mean let's say if you appear as a private student," the principal was looking at Jeet.

"I love my school, Sister. It's here that I have studied for twelve years. I would rather not appear for the boards at all, than appear as a private student."

♒

After school hours, the coterie of friends was engrossed deep in debate. Jeet's issue became a cause for concern. Chetan spoke first, "This is not how a school should treat its students."

"Chetan, the point here is not how a student should be treated, because it's a never ending debate. The school would have a point of view quite contrary to our line of thinking. The point is, how to find a solution to the present problem," Neeraj said.

Krishan took the discussions further, "So far as I can understand, it all depends on Sister P. If she doesn't cause any hindrance, the principal is not against sending the form."

"But the point is...who will convince Sister P?" Alok said to himself thoughtfully.

"Alok, you are her favourite student. She is a tough nut and you are our best bet," Neeraj urged Alok to think.

After a while he responded, "See friends, I know she has a soft corner for me but I believe it's limited to my performance in academics. I think we know her enough to anticipate her reaction."

Everyone knew what Alok had said was the bare truth.

"What if Ms Abha were to talk to Sister P?" Hitesh's proposal instilled life in a hitherto less-than-promising situation.

Ms Abha was the youngest member of the faculty. Standing slim and tall at 5'5", the twenty-four-year-old Army officer's daughter had charm written all over her. Her gait, combined with an occasional flick of her hair caused cascading ripples in her shoulder-length tresses. She had inner beauty too; an easy temper, combined with a resolve of steel. Though she appeared vulnerable and frail, she was rock solid from within. A girl with very strong convictions, she was unlikely to change her stance once she took it. She had chased one dream ever since she was a child, that of being a teacher. As luck would have it, she got an interview call from OLF just a couple of weeks after her B.Ed degree. Her spark and talent didn't go unnoticed in Sister Fulgentia's experienced eyes. Abha turned out to be a natural. She took to teaching, just like a fish takes to water. She seemed to have a sixth sense when it came to handling students; she seemed to know their psyche inside out.

Two years ago, Abha was made the class teacher of Jeet's class, that is, class VIII. She had found the batch extraordinary but it was the shy village boy who intrigued her. She decided to experiment with the introvert Jeet. She realized that he could do much better than the mere average marks he had scored in the first terminal exams. After carefully observing his behaviour and getting a feel of his psyche, she decided to go ahead. The plan was to help him examine his own feelings. This had to be done in a positive manner, or things could boomerang otherwise. She wanted to wait for the second term results. She knew she had to be very careful, for the minds of adolescents are impressionable and can bear permanent marks of any action, good or bad.

Abha entered the class with a pile of report cards in her hands. The sight made some students jubilant and some others nervous.

"Generally the results weren't surprising," she started to speak. "As expected, Alok and Manisha are the toppers and I congratulate them. I am sure they would continue to make their parents and teachers proud. For the rest of you, there is scope of improvement and I am sure you would realize that your board exams are just two years away. Please get the report cards signed by your parents by tomorrow. Neeraj will distribute the report cards."

She handed over the report cards to Neeraj and headed to the staff room. All of a sudden, as if on an impulse, she stopped, turned around and addressed the class again.

"And yes, if there is one thing that has surprised and disappointed me, it's Jeet's performance. I expected far better results from him."

A mere two lines. The message was subtle and sharp at the same time, aimed towards profound results. Ms Abha knew that in matters as delicate as these, less was more. The results, however, would only be known three months later when the answer sheets of the final term exams would be checked.

Jeet couldn't forget Ms Abha's remarks. He was hurt and astounded at the same time. He had almost the same marks as he had got in the first term. Then why the comment now? he thought. What is it that Ms Abha expects from me? Whether in the playground or at school or even at home, the two lines spoken by Abha confronted him at all times and at all places. He couldn't understand what to make of the whole situation. But he knew one thing: he had disappointed his teacher and it was this feeling of guilt that he wished to do away with. He had taken it on him that in some way, he had broken his teacher's faith. For an upright student, nothing could have caused greater injury than the feeling of breaking his teacher's trust, however involuntary it might have been. Probably, it would have been fine if Ms Abha had punished him. She could have turned him out of class, or asked him to stand in the sun, or even caned him. But she did nothing of the sort and merely chose to state it as a matter of fact. Her tone too, was devoid of any emotion.

Can the clock be turned back? Can I attempt the tests again and come up to her expectations? *he thought.*

It was time to act, not philosophize. He rescheduled his time table, set aside one hour for cricket in the evening, and earmarked all his hours, minutes and seconds for studies. Each subject had been allocated an exclusive time slot.

The note in Jeet's diary had surprised Kamlesh. Ms Abha had called her for a meeting the next day, despite the parent-teacher meet being merely seven days away.

She wanted to talk to Jeet, but then decided against it.

"Ms Abha is waiting for you in the staff room," she was informed at the reception.

"Sorry to have troubled you," Ms Abha's smile welcomed her.

"That's perfectly fine," Kamlesh too responded with a smile. "I hope all is well," the concern showed on her face.

"Yeah, yeah," Ms Abha grinned, "nothing to worry about."

Kamlesh felt re-assured.

"Actually I have a few questions regarding Jeet."

"What kind of questions?"

"Have you noticed any change in him in the last one month?"

"Change, as in?"

"I mean in his study pattern and in his overall behaviour?"

"Yes there is, indeed there is a very obvious and surprising change. So much so, that it has surprised me to an extent," Kamlesh was thoughtful. "Is there something that I am not aware of?" she asked.

"Of course I will discuss this in detail, but please elaborate the changes that you see in him," Abha brought her chair closer to Kamlesh, the curiosity growing in her voice all the time.

"His focus in studies for the last month or so has been remarkable. It has been as if he has to prove something to somebody. He has reduced the time he devoted to sports. Not only that, he attends additional tuitions for geography, as he finds it difficult. He seems to be studying all the time!"

Abha was happy. She told Kamlesh all about how she was trying to change Jeet's perception of life and how she was sure now that they would succeed. Kamlesh felt obliged. Abha now waited for the third term exams, when the success of her experiment would be known.

Focus and determination eventually won, when after three months, Jeet got the prize for the most-improved performance in the entire school. He showed a neat improvement of a hundred marks in the aggregate, when compared to the second term.

It was this out-of-the-box thinking that had prompted Hitesh to suggest Ms Abha as the teacher who could take Jeet out of troubled waters.

"It's a brilliant proposition but has riders attached to it," Atul responded.

"Riders like what?" asked Hitesh.

"Look, her positive point is that she would fight for Jeet, with all her might and without any prejudices. Leaving no stone unturned. But this straightforwardness can have a negative impact too," said Atul.

"How?" asked Hitesh.

"You know Sister P very well. She has her own mindset and it's very difficult to convince her against her will. If Ms Abha, with her no-nonsense attitude, says something that might injure her ego, then we would lose whatever little chance we have as of now," offered Atul.

"And what is the chance of that happening?" enquired Neeraj.

"Well, I don't know," accepted Atul.

"To be honest, I am not sure, so offence will be our best defence," said Hitesh.

"Yes, Hitesh is right. After all, the principal also needs someone to back Jeet to be able to rule in his favour. And there is none better than Ms Abha," Alok gave his approval too.

For the lack of any other idea, the decision was taken. The friends decided to meet Ms Abha at her residence in the evening. At the meeting, Alok briefed the teacher about the turn of events. Ms Abha listened intently and absorbed each word. When she didn't respond for some time, the friends looked at each other, unsure about what she had in mind. Neeraj gestured to everyone to be quiet and patient.

"So, what is it that you expect from me?" she asked.

"Ma'am, a meeting has been called tomorrow to decide on Jeet's case. We would like to request you to attend the meeting and represent him," Hitesh explained in a soft voice.

"But how can I attend the meeting when I am not invited for it?"

"Actually ma'am, we have requested the Principal to allow you to take part in it to represent Jeet."

"And she has allowed me?" Ms Abha said with raised eyebrows.

"Yes ma'am she did, as Jeet had requested her not to summon his parents," said Alok.

"But that's against the rules. Parents need to be informed in decisions such as these. After all, they are your guardians."

"Actually ma'am, we hope the Principal agrees to send his form. If she agrees to it, there would be no reason whatsoever to summon his parents," Krishan's sharp mind came up with a brilliant argument. Hitesh gestured a thumbs-up in his direction.

Ms Abha thought for a while before she spoke again.

"See kids, I have understood the matter and I can understand your concerns as well. But to be honest, I am not sure if anything can be done."

It was as if someone had mercilessly wrung their hearts. Hope seemed to be slipping away, like the granules of sand.

"You know it's not Jeet's fault. He had gone for the matches after taking permission. And these results didn't come as a surprise. In fact, these are only on expected lines. He had already planned to improve his marks in the boards. And he is leaving no stone unturned," Krishan pleaded.

"It's not that, Krishan. You know how strict the school rules are regarding pre-boards marks."

"Ma'am you have known Jeet. He is a hard working student," it was Hitesh's turn.

"That's not the issue Hitesh. It's unprecedented. No one in the history of the school with less than forty per cent marks in pre-boards has been allowed to represent the school in the boards."

Again, there was pin drop silence.

"And you talk about things following a certain plan, but did you include the school authorities in your plan? I agree Jeet had taken permission to take part in the national events, but was he also permitted to get sub-standard marks in the pre-boards, to be made up later in the boards?"

No one spoke

"Tell me! I am asking you something!"

All four shook their heads, gloom writ large on their faces.

"Ok, tell me who will be there at the meeting."

"Besides the principal, there would be Mr Daniel, Mrs Yadav... "

"Mrs Yadav, the Hindi teacher?"

"Yes ma'am"

"Hmm, who else?"

"Sister Praseda."

"Is that all?"

"Till now, that's what we know, and ma'am, we would also be present in the meeting."

"How can the students get permission to attend a meeting this important?"

"We requested the principal and she agreed," said Neeraj.

"Strange!"

"Yes ma'am, but she has allowed us on one condition," added Hitesh, "that we won't say anything."

"See kids, things do not look very bright. Jeet isn't exactly Mrs Yadav's favourite. In fact, she carries a fair amount of prejudice against him. Mr Daniel likes him but he wouldn't be able to say much, other than the fact that Jeet is a good sportsman. But the main opposition would come from Sister P. She has a lot of say in these matters and she is not going to make things easy."

"And what about the principal, ma'am?" asked Hitesh in a voice devoid of any life.

"Can't say for sure Hitesh," Abha said with a deep sigh. "It's unlikely that she would go beyond Sister P's opinion. All of you know her obsession regarding the reputation of the school and there has been a recent development that you might not be aware of, which in fact, is likely to work against Jeet."

"What is that ma'am?" they asked in unison.

"The Principal has denied admission to a kid who was recommended by the deputy commissioner. The DC was very adamant but she didn't budge. So what makes you think she would agree to play with the reputation of the school in Jeet's case?"

The faces of all the four boys went blank.

"Sorry kids, I wouldn't be able to help you. You know, considering the decision she took in the DC's case, it's more than obvious that for her, the reputation of the school comes first. There is no way she is going to recommend Jeet's form for the board exams."

Ms Abha and the students did not know that the astute mind of the brilliant young teacher had just misjudged the mind of the upright, yet ostensibly stern principal.

"Would you not come then, ma'am?"

Krishan somehow managed to ask a direct question. The coldness in Abha's eyes gave them the answer. The platform they had banked on so heavily on for their fight had just given way. They were alone in this fight, if at all there was any fight left, that is.

Ms Abha, the Saviour

It was exactly 8.30 a.m. when Chetan entered the principal's office followed by Alok, Hitesh, Krishan and Neeraj.

The principal was in conversation with the sports-in-charge, Mr Daniel. The three other guest chairs were unoccupied.

"Good morning Sister, good morning Sir," all of them said in unison.

They seated themselves on the corner sofa in the far end. Within minutes, Mrs Yadav and Sister Praseda came in and occupied their respective seats. Mrs Yadav looked every bit a bored middle-aged teacher in her green sari and a matching green blouse. Sister Praseda's white robe completely camouflaged her exceptional skills at teaching science.

The students were nervous. After Ms Abha's refusal to attend the meeting, the faint glimmer of hope had died. As a last resort, they had come up with a small plan for the meeting, though the chance for the success was less than dim. They had decided to inform the principal in as polite words as possible, that Ms Abha wouldn't be coming and instead, they themselves would represent Jeet's case. It was Krishan's idea and Hitesh had opposed it.

"This would not work," he had said like a seasoned lawyer. "It's like an accused arguing his own case in the court of law."

"Chetan," Neeraj whispered, "now they are waiting for Ms Abha. I think you should tell them right away that she won't be coming. The more you delay the matter, the more difficult it would get."

The others nodded.

"I am waiting for the right moment," Chetan whispered back.

"There is never a right moment. Tell them *now*," Neeraj was adamant.

"Ms Abha will be here any moment," all of them heard the principal announce. "Let's have some tea," she pressed the buzzer.

Minutes passed as Chetan deliberated the perfect moment.

"Does Ms Abha know when the meeting starts?"

The principal looked in the direction of the five students. The options, if any, had been exhausted.

"Excuse me ma'am..." Chetan stood up to speak. Before he could complete his sentence, the front door opened and Ms Abha entered the room, bringing considerable surprise and even greater relief to the students.

Ms Abha walked in with a pile of notebooks stacked by her side, as the bounce in her hair complemented the spring in her steps. With a black half-sleeved blouse contrasting her vibrant pink sari, she filled the room with unbounded effervescence. Courteously nodding and acknowledging everyone, she settled into the only unoccupied chair with great ease.

"Sorry Sister, got a little late," she apologised to the principal.

"Better late than never," Krishan whispered.

"Let's set the ball rolling without wasting another moment. This issue has been on my mind long enough." The principal was eager to put the matter to rest once and for all.

"In my opinion," K.Yadav seemed desperate to jump in, "there ij nothing to debate about. I am sure by allowing Jeet to appear for the eggjams, we would be rishking our board rejultsh."

"Well," Ms Abha smiled, "Sister, now that Mrs Yadav has come to a decision without the discussion even having started, I believe we should call off the meeting and hang the poor student."

"Don't take it pershnally Ms Abha. I hab neber shed anything of the short," retorted Mrs K. Yadav in a high-pitched voice. "Tell me, ij letting a shtudent appear aj a private student, equal to hanging? Whatever you may shay, shuch people sud not be encouraged."

"Such people!! What kind of people Mrs Yadav?" Abha responded with a hint of anger, "Do you mean people who come from a village background?"

"Calm down Ms Abha," the principal intervened. "Since this issue was raised by Sister Praseda, I believe it would only be appropriate if she starts with the discussions."

"Sister, first of all, I would like to make myself very clear to one and all. That I have nothing against Jeet and moreover he is a well-behaved boy and has never given us any reasons for concern till his attempts at the pre-board. Had it been any other class, we are sure this would have been a non-issue, as we know in due course, he would have caught up with his syllabus. But since it's just three months to the exams, I have my very valid doubts about whether he will be able to cover the entire syllabus, especially science. In view of all this, I believe the school's board performance is at risk."

"Do you have something to say, Mr Daniel?" the principal looked at the sports in-charge.

"Sister, being the sports in charge, all I can say is that the boy is my favourite. But since it's a matter related to the upcoming board results, I believe it's the teachers who should have more say in such matters," Daniel couldn't have been more categorical.

"Yes, Ms Abha, I am sure you would want to add something," the principal looked at her.

"Sister," she cleared her throat, "I totally respect Sister Praseda's thoughts and I also know that they emanate from only one concern:

the reputation of our institution. Having said that, I request you to consider the fact that it's we who had permitted Jeet to attend the sports camp and play matches. He hadn't gone on his own. Further, knowing Jeet as much as I do, I can safely suggest to the august gathering here that concerns about his performance in the board exams are unfounded."

She continued, "I would draw your attention to an incident when Jeet was in class VIII and I was his class teacher. I somehow felt he could do better than the average marks he had been getting. I pushed and challenged him to a certain extent, and in the following terminal exams he scored one hundred extra marks than what he had managed in the previous term. I mean, just in three months he showed enormous progress. I see no reasons why he cannot repeat the same feat now."

"Ms Abha," it was Mrs K. Yadav again, "I am syor you undershtand that there ij differensh between class VIII and class X."

"Sister, I believe we would like Sister Praseda's comments on it," Ms Abha ignored Mrs Yadav. "I would like to know if my arguments have created a feeling of re-assurance in her."

"As I said," Sister Praseda looked at Ms Abha, "I have nothing against the kid. And moreover, there must be something really good about him or why would you go to such great lengths to defend him? Still, I would like it if the principal takes a call, keeping in mind the decision we took in the case that involved a recommendation from the Deputy Commissioner. If merit is the criteria for not accepting his admission, then the in-house decisions too shouldn't be based on anything else but merit," her gaze turned to the principal.

"Yes, I think we have totally forgotten that part," Mrs Yadav remarked.

"The issue involving the DC has administrative repercussions," Abha looked at the principal and spoke. "Therefore, I believe, it's not a teacher's mandate to intrude on issues that are purely administrative. But as a teacher I would say that the principal couldn't have been more correct in denying that admission. Sister, you have upheld the parameters laid down by the school and clearly sent out a message that we will not get bogged down because of pressures and wouldn't compromise on merit just because somebody happens to be a kith or kin of someone in a position of power. Thereby, you have set an example for our students to emulate. But I would also go on to say that Jeet's case is totally different for a number of reasons. First, the boy doesn't lack merit. It's just that his merit has a different orientation, a different genre. Are sports not a part of education, Sister? After all, he is the only one in the school's history to have played a national level tournament. That too when the school doesn't even have a proper policy towards sports education. I think Jeet ought to be given some credit for that. Further, he is not an outsider; he has been with us for twelve long years. In case a student lags behind, can we as an institution wash our hands off responsibility for the same? Yes, it's easy to punish him, but in the process, shall we not as an institution punish ourselves too? After all, by providing twelve years of schooling to him, are we not responsible for whatever good or bad Jeet, or for that matter any other student, does? And let's not forget one thing: punishing Jeet would create fear in the minds of other students. It would send a message that in case going gets tough, this institution will turn its back on you, rather than stand by you in your hour of need." Ms Abha stopped to collect her breath and sip water from the glass lying in front of her.

No one tried to cut her short.

"By punishing Jeet, we would be crushing the very spirit of the system of schooling. We must allow enough latitude to our students and make them fearless, so much so, that the limitless sky becomes their vision rather than the shackles we tie them up with. Sister, just to let you have a sneak-peek inside Jeet's mind I would like to quote an incident. I had once asked the whole class to define the word 'respect'. I expected everyone to come up with the exact dictionary meaning as it's a fairly easy word for class VIII students, and most of them actually gave me the dictionary meaning. Do you remember what Jeet had said that day?" Ms Abha asked the five students.

While four of them shook their heads, Krishan spoke up, "Yes Ma'am, I remember. He said respect is divine. It is the greatest currency of mankind."

"Sister," Ms Abha addressed the principal again, "Today the future of this kid, whose upbringing has taught him that no currency can substitute respect, is in our hands and we have two options. Either to crush his future right here and now, or to let it flower so that we can be proud of him one day. I assure you sister, it's an extraordinary future. Let's nurture it, rather than nip it in the bud. I have nothing more to say."

For a considerable length of time, no one spoke.

"Would anyone want to make any further comment?" the principal asked in a calm voice. None spoke.

"Yadav," the principal looked at Mrs K. Yadav. "Do you want to add something?"

Mrs Yadav shook her head.

"And you P?"

"Just want to ask Ms Abha, does she really think Jeet would pass?"

"I feel it would be safe to predict a first division for him," Abha replied.

"That would be nothing short of a miracle I would say," P smiled. The smile, however, was more of a smirk.

"Right then," the principal took over, "I believe Jeet isn't at fault at all. The school had allowed him to take part in his games, and rightly so. And all of you will agree to the fact that the ultimate responsibility of the school rests with the principal. Therefore, I take a decision to allow the kid to appear for the exams as a student of this school. Irrespective of the marks he gets, I believe the kid is a winner already. Surely, I wouldn't want to face lack of sleep by clipping the wings of a student, more so when that student holds so much promise. I would like to quote Oscar Wilde here. He said, 'I never allowed school to interfere with my education'. So, Ms Abha is right when she says we should be the ones supporting a child rather than creating roadblocks for him. I would further go on to say that this institution is proud to have Ms Abha as a member of faculty. She has saved us from doing what would have been a terrible wrong. Thank you all for attending the meeting. Have a great day."

All five students hugged Ms Abha as they came out of the meeting. Hitesh uttered the first words, "I hate Mrs Yadav for what she turned out to be today."

"Hate whom?" Ms Abha's eyebrows were raised.

"Mrs Yadav."

"For what?"

"For disliking Jeet, when she herself comes from a village background."

"And who are you? Are you the Omniscient one, the Almighty God?" Ms Abha was angry.

"Ma'am... I... I...," Hitesh was taken aback.

"Do any of you know her circumstances, her situation?" her pitch was raised.

None of them spoke.

"And since all of you know next to nothing, let me shed a bit of light so that you can come out of the dark. She does not come from a village background. Yes, she has been married into a village family, and the rude treatment meted out to her is not even worth describing. Then her son was born and his behaviour too, wasn't respectful. She thinks it's the village atmosphere that has spoiled him too. And these collective experiences are the reasons for her prejudices. Yes, I know she is absolutely wrong in treating Jeet the way she does, but that wrong, Mr Hitesh Rustagi, does not change the fact that she is a teacher and you are her student. I am sure in future you would be within your ethical limits."

"I am sorry, ma'am," Hitesh's apology came straight from the heart.

Class X Results

"The results are out Jeet," Kamlesh called from the drawing room.

"So soon!" Jeet exclaimed from his room. "Only yesterday Neeraj had told me it would take at least one more week!"

"Yes, but they have been declared last night."

"How do you know Mom?"

"It's in the morning news."

Jeet said nothing and headed towards his room.

Kamlesh followed him.

"Nervous?" Kamlesh put her arm around him. Jeet didn't reply.

"I am not nervous Mom!" Jeet was visibly anxious. "How much do you expect Mom?"

"Whatever makes my kid happy!"

Through her calm exterior, she had hidden her anxiety successfully.

"Only sixty percent or above can satisfy Ms Abha. It's only if I get sixty percent that I would be able to look her in the eyes."

"In that case, Sister P would be happy as well."

"That hardly concerns me Mom."

"And why is that?"

"Mom, there was a story of a swan in my class VII text book."

"I am glad, today it's the kid who has a story rather than the Mom."

"This swan," Jeet smiled and continued, "was hit with an arrow by a prince called Devdutt."

"And then?" Kamlesh feigned ignorance. She knew the whole story.

"When the swan lay injured, battling for life, another prince Siddhartha picked it up, took it home and looked after the swan till the time it was cured."

"Hmm..."

"And when it got fully cured, Prince Devdutt staked his claim to the swan, that it belonged to him as he was the one who hunted it down."

"Hmm..."

"Siddhartha refused and the matter went to the king's court. The king let the swan decide for itself. He placed the swan in the centre, whereas Siddhartha and Devdutt stood at opposite ends. The swan remained still for a while, and then slowly walked towards Siddhartha and hopped into his lap."

"Amazing!"

"Everyone present in the king's court clapped and you know what the king said?"

"What?"

"That the saviour is always mightier than the predator."

"The story is a delight no doubt. But why did you narrate it to me now at this juncture and in what context?" asked Kamlesh.

"Just that Ms Abha is the saviour, Mom, and Sister P is the predator."

"A teacher is a teacher Jeet!"

"I don't know Mom. The fact is that Sister P had almost cut short my life as a student. I was saved because Ms Abha came to my rescue."

"But even if you get less than a so-called first division, it would still be an achievement, as the parameters for other students were different from that of yours. You couldn't even get three proper months to study."

"Still Mom, I don't want to be among those who score a second division as they are few and far between and would stick out on the school results sheet as a sore thumb. Let me go now, I can't take the stress any longer," Jeet rushed outside.

"And listen, come back soon."

"Don't worry Mom." Jeet shouted back.

Jeet was in front of the school gate. A crowd of students and parents were blocking the way to the notice board. With his heart in his mouth, after a considerable struggle, Jeet made it to the notice board. He searched through the rows on the printed sheet, and found his name with his marks written next to it. Instantly, he was overwhelmed with deep sorrow; the figure "59" stood starkly, against his name, causing him to lower his eyes in shame.

Am I the only one who got the second division? he thought, struggling out of the gathered crowd.

"Jeet, Jeet," someone called out to him. He looked back. It was Hitesh. He was circumspect, not wanting to face his peers. Indecisively, he waved at him with trepidation and the next moment, rushed out of the school premises. The journey back home was totally in contrast to the journey to school. The distance never seemed to end, or was it that he never wanted to reach home?

"Enjoy your breakfast," Kamlesh placed the tray of scrambled eggs and buttered toast in front of him. She was prudent enough to know that the situation didn't warrant any questions, not that curiosity wasn't killing her.

"Mom, will you not ask me about my marks?" the tears sat on the verge of his eyelids, threatening to spill over any moment.

"First have your breakfast son," she turned away to leave.

"No Mom, listen please," he ran after her and hugged her from behind. Gravity couldn't be defied any longer. The gloom of failure melted away by the warmth of motherly love, and he cried incessantly like a baby. Kamlesh wrapped him in her arms. The breakfast tray lay untouched.

"Mom, I failed," he said amidst sobs, "1 got fifty-nine percent. I believe I am the only who got less than sixty percent."

"But fifty-nine percent is almost sixty percent," Kamlesh said.

"Yes Mom, but *almost*. More than anything, it places me in a totally different category. Now it would be said that I was the one who spoiled the school result. Otherwise the school would have proudly claimed one hundred percent first division students. I have let everybody down Mom."

"Tell me one thing," she looked at him. "During these two exam months, did you ever watch TV?" She made him sit on the chair and sat on the floor in front of him.

"Mom but... "

"Tell me, did you ever watch TV?"

"No."

"Did you spend time with your friends, or even once touch your bat?"

"No."

"Then tell me, what all did you do these two months?"

"You know what I did, Mom!"

"Yes I know, but I want the answer from you. So tell me what did you do in these two months?"

"I studied."

"Which means you prepared for your exams."

"Yes Mom."

"And what does the *Geeta* tell us?"

"That we should do our duty."

"And not worry about the result."

"Yes."

"And now look at me, in my eyes. Do you see any shame here?"

"Tell me!" Kamlesh asked again.

"No Mom, I see no shame," said Jeet in a voice just loud enough to be heard.

"It means you didn't let us down, neither your parents, nor your teachers. Your job was to make the effort. I am sure your teachers would be proud of you too, including Abha and Sister Praseda. Sister P might be a little strict, but that does not change her identity as a teacher. Tell her you tried your best, and that you would continue to make her proud in the years to come."

The knock on the door broke the chain of discussion. It was Munna.

"The results are out I have heard," his voice carried urgency.

"Yes," Kamlesh narrated to him the entire sequence of events. Munna however wasn't convinced.

"I think we should go and check again, I don't know why, but I have a feeling that we should go and check again."

Munna's arguments didn't make any sense to either Jeet or Kamlesh. She asked Jeet to go with Munna to check his marks again.

"Congratulations!" Chetan had caught him before he could go to the notice board, "The principal wants to meet you!" he held Jeet's arm and pulled him towards the principal's office.

"Munna Bhaiya, you wait and I will be back in a moment."

"Is there someone else in the office too?" he asked Chetan.

"I can't say for sure," Chetan replied.

Jeet lifted his index finger to knock at the principal's door.

"Come in!" The Principal's voice increased his heart beats.

The scene inside the principal's office was contrary to what Jeet had imagined. The principal wasn't alone. Cups of tea and plates of sweets were randomly placed on the principal's table with at least twenty teachers surrounding her. Some were seated, while others stood for want of chairs. The little crowd was abuzz with joy. An air of hope hung all over the principal's room; the office smelled of victory, not defeat. Ms Abha hugged him and Jeet was overwhelmed by his teacher's affection. He wished that time would stand still and pinched himself to see if all this was really true.

Yes, it was all real. So what if no one brought up the subject of his marks?" he thought.

There were more surprises for Jeet. It was the turn of the principal to hug him. He wouldn't have traded these moments for anything in the world.

"Abha, it's all because of you." The principal was overwhelmed.

Whatever the marks, I must have done something good to deserve such love and adulation from my teachers who matter so much to me, he thought.

"Sister, I would go to Jeet's house to meet his Mom. After all, it's because of her efforts too," Ms Abha said.

"Sure, and congratulate her on my behalf as well."

"Sorry ma'am," Jeet said as he walked out of the principal's office with Ms Abha.

"Sorry for what?" she asked surprised.

"For not being able to fulfil my promise."

"What other promise did you make?" Ms Abha sounded doubly surprised.

"That I would get a first division."

"And how much do you think one needs to get, to be able to score a first division?"

"Why ma'am, it's sixty percent."

"And how much do you think you got?"

"Fifty-nine percent ma'am. You already know it!"

"Of course I do, but how do you know this?"

"I saw it myself!"

"Ok, we'll talk about this when we meet your Mom," there was mischief in Ms Abha's smile. Jeet was puzzled.

On the way home, Ms Abha asked Munna to stop and ordered a box of sweets.

"Congratulations," Ms Abha handed over the sweets to Kamlesh.

"Why did you take this trouble? Wait for a second!" Kamlesh went inside with brisk steps and brought the home made sweets for Abha.

"They are yummy, wonderful!"

"Did you like it, ma'am?" asked Kamlesh.

"Of course, it's just wonderful, but I am going to make you taste something that would taste sweeter than even your hand made sweets," Ms Abha chirped.

"Of course, the sweets that you brought must be very tasty," Kamlesh replied.

"No, I am not talking about these sweets. I was about to tell you that Jeet needs to grow up!"

Kamesh didn't know how to react. Jeet was speechless too.

"What I mean is, despite having passed class X, he still has to learn how to check the result sheet."

Their hearts missed several beats. Mother and son waited for more from Ms Abha, who held a mysterious silence. Kamlesh's mind was racing. *Had Jeet made a mistake in calculating his marks? Were his marks actually more than what he had made them out to be?*

"Ma'am please tell me my actual result," Jeet pleaded.

"You stupid, what you thought to be your percentage, were actually the marks you had scored in Hindi. The percentage is never mentioned in the result sheet itself. Only the marks earned in each subject are mentioned. And if you add all the marks earned in all the subjects, it adds to three hundred and fifty-five out of five hundred, making it a cool seventy-one percent, which puts you in the category of high-scoring students."

Jeet initially went numb hearing all this. Then it sank in that he was actually a first-class student. His reaction, however, was subdued. The feeling was more of satisfaction than overblown ecstasy. He bent down to touch Ms Abha's feet in gratitude and she hugged him again. The teacher then turned towards Kamlesh and hugged her. Jeet stared at Munna who was wiping away his tears through relieved smiles.

Why is this man happy? What is he to gain in this? I am not his son and materially he has nothing to gain from me. What is his relation with me? Whatever that relation is, does it have a name? Jeet wondered.

There were only questions and no answers. He looked at Munna again and saw something else too. For the first time in life, Munna seemed tired. Was it because he had pedalled hard? The greying hair around the temple said a different story. Munna was growing old.

> *How long will he be able to earn his living by pulling a rickshaw?* *In Jeet's mind, his marks had now taken a back seat. He thought, Maybe he will be able to work hard a few more years. What would happen to Munna after that?*

Jeet vividly remembered the long years of ice-cream treats from Munna, so much so that images of vanilla cups, orange sticks and cone-shaped softies danced before his eyes. *I stand indebted*, Jeet continued to think. *Something needs to be done so that Munna does not have to pull a rickshaw again.*

"Munna, please drop Abha Madam home," Kamlesh's voice intruded into his thoughts.

"Sure Bhabhi ji," Munna replied. The tears had dried. The eyes, however, were still swollen. Jeet saw him leave, but in his mind, Munna had stayed back. Jeet closed his eyes and thought hard. His task was definitively cut out:

1. Get the house back.
2. Pay back Munna's debt.
3. Represent the country in the sport he loved.

He knew that if he could fulfil his dream of playing for India, the other two dreams would automatically be taken care of. But for that, he needed to work at his game and uplift it to the required standards. And in order to do that, he needed an institution which could support him in his quest, even if it meant studies taking a back seat. A school where Cricket could be considered as important- if not more- as studies. Did such an institution exist? If it did, will he qualify for admission?

Tests at Rai

"MNSS Rai is your answer," said Dinesh.

"MNSS Rai! What's that?" Jeet asked.

The friends were seated in their favourite restaurant. Jeet had shared with Dinesh, his dilemma regarding the institution. "Where cricket could get preference over studies," Jeet had specified.

"Motilal Nehru School of Sports Rai. It's a school specially designed for students like you, who dream of achieving success through the prism of sports."

"Really! You mean there exists something of that sort for real? Where exactly is it situated?" Jeet was excited.

"It's exactly thirty-seven kilometres from Delhi."

"Tell me more!"

"It has huge lush green playgrounds and a budget that runs into multiple crores. To get enrolled in it is nothing short of a dream come true for any sportsman."

"Hmm, you said playgrounds! Do you mean it houses more than one sport?"

"Yes, besides cricket, it has athletics, hockey, gymnastics, swimming, boxing, volleyball, basket-ball, squash, tennis and a few others."

"Is the fee huge?"

"Not at all; the fee in fact is very nominal. The budget is taken care of by the Government of Haryana. The basic purpose of the school is to encourage sportsmen from the state. Moreover, employees from the state government have special preferences in terms of fee. But of course they do not have a head start when it comes to getting admission. There is no seat quota reserved for anyone. But there is one thing...," Dinesh paused and looked at Jeet. His eyes didn't blink.

"What?" asked Jeet.

"The entry levels for students are at classes IV and VII. Every year there are bulk admissions in these two classes and there are only a few seats in the other classes."

"You mean I stand no chance now...?" Jeet felt his heart gripped.

"Sure you do, but the seats might be less, in fact, they might not be any more than a couple."

"Two seats! That's all?"

"Hmm," Dinesh nodded.

"What about the number of applicants?"

"No idea. But since it's an open admission process, one can expect more than a fair turnout."

"But how do you know so much?"

"About the school?"

"Yeah, I mean there isn't one thing that you don't seem to be aware of."

"My elder brother's friend Manjit studied there. He got admission in class IV itself. I have visited the school a couple of times and whatever I know is from what I saw plus what Manjeet told me. If you want to meet him to know more, that can be arranged. But one thing I must tell you Jeet, MNSS Rai is what you need and MNSS Rai is what you should get. It is one of the very few sports schools in the entire country. The facilities for sports are incredible. How you secure admission is for you to figure out!" Dinesh concluded.

No sooner did Jeet tell Kanwar and Kamlesh about his interest, did they start their efforts towards fulfilling it. Kanwar took a couple of days' leave from office to visit the school and to get the admission form. The prospectus of the school endorsed everything that Dinesh had said. Further research suggested that Y.P. Bharadwaj, the principal and director of school, had a mind of his own. "Merit is what he seeks, and merit is what he gets," they were told. The vacancies in class XI were just four and more than a hundred forms were sold against the same.

"It's tough Kamlesh," said Kanwar.

"But Jeet is a sportsman, and a sportsman is what they should look for. After all, it's a sports school, isn't it?"

"That's right. But don't forget Jeet is seeking admission in class XI, so the marks obtained in class X would surely be given some weight. Jeet's marks are good no doubt, but there are just four vacancies against a hundred odd applicants. Every fraction of a percent will count."

"What will the criteria of selection exactly be?"

"The collated performances of class X boards, physical test, sports credentials and the interview will be the criteria for selection."

"And if Jeet doesn't make it to the list?"

"I don't know how to answer that question?"

"I mean is there a way out in such a scenario?"

"Not really," Kanwar paused, and then continued, "But yes, there is an outside chance in case that happens."

"What is that? Tell me!"

"They say the principal has the discretion to increase one more seat for a student if he sees some spark in him."

"Sees a spark in? What does that mean?"

"In case the principal finds a special capability in a student other than the ones who have made it to the merit list, he uses his discretionary powers to add one more seat and then that student is given admission against that additional seat. So no name gets cancelled. This way, as you would appreciate, it's a win-win situation for all."

"Hmm."

"But there are too many 'ifs' and 'buts' in this issue. We can't sit back and hope that the principal finds a spark or fire or whatever it is and the seat falls in our lap. Jeet has to work hard to be among the meritorious ones," said Kanwar.

Kamlesh too, was of the same opinion.

Jeet was leaving no stone unturned in his preparations. He had increased the intensity of his training, and was working on a set plan based upon the events mentioned in the form:

1. Hundred metre sprint
2. Eight hundred metre race
3. High jump
4. Long jump

In order to prepare for his interview, he read various magazines. All the material he read, suggested two things:

1. That it's possible the interviewee, rather than the interviewer, takes control and defines the terms of an ongoing interview.
2. That the interviewee should always think on his feet.

Go by your instincts, was the advice he got from his parents.

⁂

Kanwar and Jeet reached the school at around 6.30 a.m., half an hour before the stipulated time, on the day of the competition. With a sprawling area of three hundred and sixty-five acres, the school was self-sufficient in almost every aspect and looked more like a mini-world rather than a school. To read about it in the prospectus, and to actually see the institution directly, were two different things, Jeet realized.

At 7.00 a.m., all the candidates were directly escorted towards the stadium, the venue of their physical test. The sight of the administrative block, the auditorium and the school library on the way to the stadium was grand. "The school houses the best auditorium and the largest library, compared to all other schools in the entire country," they were told by a proud instructor.

The stadium was equipped to hold top international sports events. The scenario had become even more tempting. With enticement came desperation. *What if I don't make it?* Negative thoughts intruded, but they were quickly brushed aside. *I have to emerge a winner despite all odds.*

Mr Chikara, the swimming coach and in charge of the physical test had divided the candidates into groups, wherein each group consisted of seven to eight students.

The events started with the hundred metre sprint. Jeet came first in his group. In the eight hundred metre race, he was once again the first one to cross the finishing line. The other events, high jump and long jump, did not present him with an extraordinary challenge. As the competitions were held in short groups, there was no way that Jeet could gauge his performance in respect to all the other contestants. However, on an average, he wasn't dissatisfied with his efforts.

After the physical test came the interview. Based on whatever small conversations he had had with fellow candidates, it appeared to him that most of them preferred studies over sports.

What are they doing in a sports school? They could study in any school and get excellent teachers to guide them. But where else would a sportsman like me get such facilities? Certainly, my need exceeds theirs by some distance Jeet continued to grapple with his thoughts.

Though the performance in the physical test had added to Jeet's confidence, it had not stopped him from getting rid of his nerves altogether. Seated in the administrative block, he looked around towards his fellow aspirants. The well-dressed first batch of twenty-five was all set and raring to go. *To say that the competition is tough would be an understatement*. He cast a casual look at his attire. The impeccable white shirt went along well with the navy blue trousers.

Not bad at all!

Excelling at the physical test is fine but it's your performance in interview that will count the most, his dad had said after he had completed the physical tests.

Jeet was ninth in the order. As the candidates kept moving in and out, he was enticed to ask some of them how they thought they had fared in the interview and also about the questions that were put to them, but he decided against it.

It was Jeet's turn. He gently knocked the door, just as any well-informed interviewee would, and entered, careful not to cause an unnecessary disturbance.

"A very good morning to you all, sirs!"

There were five people in the board. His eyes were, however, fixed on the figure in the centre. He had seen the pictures in the prospectus and could make out that it was none other than the principal and director. The principal had big hands. His salt-and-pepper beard was thick and full, and rested on his chest to form an intimidating semi-circle. He looked neat and tidy in his white shirt. But that was not all. His eyes stood out as the most dominating factor. Whatever emanated from them, virtually pierced through Jeet.

Dad was spot on in analyzing his personality, he concluded.

"So, you are Jeet," the Principal spoke. The voice seemed to come from a well.

"Yes sir," Jeet tried to speak but could manage nothing more than a whisper.

You can do better than that, Jeet thought, trying to pull himself together. He rubbed his perspiring hands against each other.

"So, you are a cricketer," the principal continued.

"Yes sir," the voice was louder this time.

The topic was in line with his interest.

So far so good, he thought. My best chances are in being questioned by the principal as he is likely to talk about cricket, he guessed.

"So, what do you do in cricket?"

"Sir, I am an opening batsman."

"Opening batsman!" the principal's eyes lit up to exude a hint of excitement. The ice was broken. It was now a question of consolidating upon a job well begun. Jeet had inadvertently peeked into the heart of a fellow cricketer. A bond was struck between him and the principal. The thought that the interviewee was controlling the interview, kept him in good spirits. However, he needed to think on his feet now. Jeet was in his comfort zone with the principal and it felt like his own backyard where his faults, if any, would not be given undue weight. Under the given circumstances, the principal was his best bet.

"So, why was it that you chose to be an opener and not, let's say, a middle order batsman?" the principal continued.

"Sir it's ironical," Jeet was ensconced in his chair, as he now commanded the complete attention of the Principal, "and at the same time, a blessing in disguise."

"Sounds interesting, please tell me about it."

The other members of the board also looked interested in what Jeet was about to say.

"Actually sir, in my village I used to play with older friends. When I was in class VII, I used to play with people who were already in college. Most of them were uncomfortable with the new ball and as I was the youngest, I was often bullied into opening the innings," Jeet was smiling, and so was the interview board. "I had no option but to accede to their demands. As I played more matches, I developed a bond with the new ball. I sort of started to understand it fairly well and the new ball too, had a fair measure of my personality." Before Jeet had finished his sentence, the board members were laughing out loud.

"So tell me, who said cricket is a game of gentlemen?" it was the principal again.

Jeet paused – he knew the answer – but the science teacher decided to interrupt with his question, "How many marks did you get in science?"

In an effort to duck the question, Jeet pretended not to have heard it at all and looked in the direction of the Principal instead, "Sir, Don Bradman was the one who said that cricket is a game of gentlemen." The Principal nodded in satisfaction.

"Baweja, do you have any questions?" The principal looked at the vice-principal.

"Don't you think seventy-one percent marks in class X boards aren't enough for a competition as tough as this one?" the vice-principal threw a missile.

"Sir, most of the time during the academic year, I was out attending cricket camps and tournaments."

"And the information in the form says you are a national level player."

"Yes sir, that's right."

"This means you have represented your state in all-India tournaments."

"That's correct, sir. I have attached the necessary certificates in the file."

"Thank you Jeet. Have a great day!"

Jeet came out of the interview room realizing he hadn't breathed for some time.

His parents were happy with his performance, but also anxious about the interview results.

"The letters to the successful candidates would reach in approximately ten days," they were informed. It went without saying that the unsuccessful candidates wouldn't receive any communication.

As a farmer's eyes never leave the sky in anticipation of clouds, Kamlesh's eyes never left the door in anticipation of the postman. The minds of Kanwar and Jeet too, oscillated between hope and despair.

Fifteen days had passed since the interview. Jeet was at the practice sessions at Nehru stadium, Gurgaon. His mind, however, was elsewhere.

Only the selected candidates would be intimated, the thought troubled him.

"Pad up, Jeet," shouted Kishore, Jeet's coach. He noticed that Jeet was lost in a world of his own. Kishore shouted again, "Jeet, pad up!"

Awakened from his thoughts, Jeet headed towards his kit bag and first took out the left leg guard.

At around the same time when Jeet crouched to tie the left leg guard, a few learned academicians, seventy kilometres away were getting together to decide his fate.

Kulbhushan Kain was one of the youngest members of faculty at Rai. The thirty-two-year-old bachelor was very passionate about teaching history. There were instances where the students opted for history only because it was Kain's subject. History, however, wasn't the only interest that Kain had. He loved cricket equally, if not more. Like the principal, he too, as a student had represented Delhi University in cricket. The commonality, however, didn't end there. Both of them were teachers of history and both were splendid orators. A defeat of the school cricket team, even in a friendly match could cause agony to both.

In the absence of a cricket coach, it was Kain who looked after the school cricket team.

Kain looked forward to a relaxed Saturday evening with pleasure written all over it. He had planned a dinner with his friends at Murthal – a place five kilometres from Rai and famous for its exquisite *paranthas*. He was ready and about to step out of the house, when the phone rang.

"What's up Kain?" the voice seemed to come from a deep well.

"I am about to leave for Murthal for dinner, sir. How may I help you?" Kain answered.

"Lucky you – to have time to enjoy the Murthal *paranthas* and here we are, stuck in administrative matters."

"Why don't you come along, sir? Let work take a back seat, at least on a Saturday evening?"

"No Kain, but I request you to let Murthal wait for a little while. Pick me up from my residence for a small meeting at the administrative block. You can carry on with your evening after the meeting is done. I won't take much of your time."

"What is the meeting about, sir?"

"We are shortlisting the lateral entries."

"Are we recruiting any cricketers this time, sir?" Suddenly Kain was interested.

"You come over Kain. Let us discuss things in person."

"Sure sir. I am coming."

"So are we getting any cricketers this time?" Kain asked, as the principal got in the car beside him.

"Let's see Kain," the Principal replied. "You know that I do not interfere in the selection procedure. I have asked the committee to select eight boys, and then we will further shortlist it to the final four."

"We desperately need an opening batsman, sir," Kain continued. "We have lost several matches last year for the reason that the team didn't get to a decent start as much as one would have liked it to."

Each member of the selection committee stood up as Y.P. and Kain entered the conference hall in the administrative block for the meeting.

"So, let's see what my team has come up with?" Y.P. thundered.

"Sir, we are through. As per your instructions, we have shortlisted eight students," said Vashishtha, the second in command of the selection committee.

"Can we come up with the names please?"

"Sir, everything's there in your file, if you could just go through it..." Vashishtha managed.

"Cut the red tape Vashishtha. Forget the file, come out with the names. The country has enough bureaucratic hurdles already. Let's not add to them. Please be quick. I stand here guilty of having delayed Kain's dinner. I am sure none of you would want to further delay his meeting with the paranthas at Murthal."

Everyone laughed.

"Sure sir," continued Vashishtha. "Mr Salaria," he addressed the Maths teacher, "Could you read the names aloud please?"

"Right away, Mr Vashishtha." He opened the file: "1. Sanjeev Faujdar, 2. Neeraj Rohilla, 3. Sanjeev Tanwar, 4. Manish Arora, 5. Vikas Sharma, 6. Shashikant, 7. Amitabh Sharma, 8. Rupali Rathore."

"Is that all?" Y.P. asked

"Yes sir," replied the committee in unison.

"But the names don't sound familiar – I am sure I must have met all of them during the interview, but none of the names seems to ring a bell."

"Do you think something is missing sir?" asked Vashishtha, sensing something wrong.

"No, it's ok Vashishtha. Are the names in the order of merit?"

"Yes sir, they are."

"Then let's select the top four and finish with this. Get the letters sent to the selected candidates by tomorrow."

"Sure sir."

"And by the way Vashishtha," YP scribbled something on the slip pad placed on the conference table.

"Yes sir..."

"Add this name to the list of selected candidates. I am using my discretion to increase the vacancies to five." He tore off the piece of paper from the pad and handed it over to Vashishtha.

"No problem, sir."

"Job done. Let's go, Kain!"

"So, sir it's about having the 'spark' again I guess," he smiled as he took the driver's seat. Certainly he could ask the question now, far away as they were from the formal settings of the conference room.

"Yes Kain, sure it is. But he should have been on the list anyway. The selection committee is disappointing at times. The boy is really bright."

"And who's the lucky one, sir?"

"Jeet Singh."

"A cricketer, sir?"

Y.P smiled and nodded.

"An opening batsman, sir?"

Y.P. nodded again. Kain was delighted. His appetite had grown. Dinner would surely taste better.

As the letter for admission was dispatched, there were three people at Rai who waited eagerly for Jeet.

Kain waited so that Jeet could come and strengthen the school cricket team. Y.P. waited for the boy with the spark. But there was one person who waited for Jeet for a totally different reason. Roshni hadn't seen or known Jeet before; or had she?

The First Day at Rai

A fifty metre gallery separated the junior boys' hostel (classes VII and VIII) from the senior boys' (classes IX–XII). Both the hostels had the same setting. Both were four-storey structures with each floor accommodating one house. Surya on the ground floor, then Soma, Indra and Varuna on the first, second and third floor respectively. Each floor consisted of several rooms and one big hall. Whereas, the board classes, that is, classes X and XII, were housed in the rooms, classes IX and XI occupied the hall. There was the privilege of a separate room with bathroom facilities for the head-boy and the vice head-boy of the house. For others, there were common bathrooms in front of the hostel. Situated along the gallery was the mess, large enough to accommodate all the students, girls and boys of the school at any given point of time. The infirmary, headed by Dr Bansal, was situated across the road and on the opposite side of the senior boys' hostel. The girls' hostel was located three hundred yards away from the infirmary. Mrs Datta, the English teacher, was the matron and was responsible for overall supervision of the girls. Equidistant from the infirmary and the boys' hostel was the lavish two thousand square yards bungalow of the principal and director. The houses for the teachers and administrative staff were scattered around the infirmary and on the opposite side of the girls' hostel.

The road from the school gate led to the sports courts and fields. Further towards the highway was Kamla Nehru School, the junior wing of the school for classes IV to VII.

It was to be a hectic first day for Jeet. The predominant part of it was spent in completing all the documentary work in the company of the warden, Mr R.K. Gaur. It was past 6.30 p.m. when he had completed all formalities, and got his uniform and accessories issued. S-383 was his school number where S stood for Surya House.

The formalities over, a tired Jeet lay down on his bed and surrendered to sleep only to be woken up by his peers at dinner time.

On the dining table, he was introduced to the five students from his house: Rakesh the high jumper, Rajbeer the medium pacer, Rajesh the leg spinner, Sushil the volleyball player and Sudhir the long distant runner. All of them would be his pals for two years in school as they were his classmates and also housemates. After dinner, Jeet went back to sleep with dreams in his eyes and a defined work plan for the next two years that he was to spend at Rai.

Roshni, the tall and dusky volleyball player, was the most talked about girl in the boys' hostel. She presented a lively disposition which triggered delight in everyone around her. Despite the wish to befriend her- the boys couldn't muster enough courage to approach her. Hence, they tried to make up by watching her from a distance whenever she jumped high into the air to smash the ball in the face of opponent, or walked to and from the girls' hostel with springs in her steps. The mole in the centre of her forehead added further to her attractiveness. But it wasn't only volleyball that found favour with Roshni. She was equally partial towards literature. She wrote poetry, which she preferred keeping to herself.

"The skies from above will someday send my soul-mate to me," she would often tell her roommate and team member- Neelam; Roshni believed in destiny.

"But how would you know about his arrival?" Neelam would often tease her.

"The skies will bear the signs and I would know," Roshni's belief was unshakeable.

It was a long day for Roshni. An extra drill session during the morning games was followed by three back-to-back class tests during school. Though the afternoon siesta was routine, it was much needed that day and therefore, more satisfying than any other day.

Her roommate and fellow volley ball player, however, chose music over sleep. Although Neelam was careful to keep the volume low, Roshni could hear the melody subconsciously and relaxed deeply in sleep.

When she woke up, she felt energetic and bright. She also felt strangely happy. She had never felt this way before.

It had to be the song she remembered from her sleep.

"Neelam...," she called.

"Yeah," Neelam answered. "Rise and shine madam, it's just ten minutes to the games whistle," she was in her evening games track suit.

"Do you remember that song?"

"Which one?"

"The one that was playing on the radio while I was asleep."

"Yes of course I remember it. But how are you aware of it? I thought you were asleep!"

"Yeah, I was half-asleep. The song was *Rangeela re*, right?"

"Yes."

"The tune is still going round and round in my mind."

"In that case, you are Wordsworth's solitary reaper."

"Maybe, but with one difference."

"And what is that?"

"What the solitary reaper had experienced was something melancholic and sad, and here I am, almost dancing in excitement.

And if I may ask you, who was referred to, as *Rangeela* in the song?" Roshni asked.

"Her boyfriend, of course," Neelam answered.

"No, not her boyfriend."

"Honey, who else then, if not her boyfriend?" Neelam rolled her eyes.

"Her soulmate. She calls for her soulmate."

"Oh my my...!"

"Yes, you know it's a beautiful word the lyricist has used, *Rangeela*. I believe it can only be used for 'soulmate'."

"Boyfriend is also synonymous, at least for lesser mortals like us, my dear goddess of spirituality."

"Boyfriend, I would say, is a lesser word. Soulmate fits it perfectly. There is something unique about this song, something that cannot be bracketed in words. That something may be in the lyrics or the music, or both."

"Yes, it is a beautiful song and I like it too. But beyond that, I am not sure. I mean it's just a song, after all."

"Why then can I still feel it within me?"

"Only you can tell baby, or may be...," Neelam seemed to have remembered something. "Oh yes! Maybe it's a signal from the skies that your soulmate is on the way."

"No, the skies do not signal that way," Roshni got out of bed to get ready for the games session.

"Then how do they signal?"

"The signals from them are distinct, clear and without any ambiguity."

Neelam merely smiled. They headed to the volley ball courts.

For Jeet, the first few hours were enough to cement his belief that this was where he belonged. "I wish I had taken admission in this school in class IV or VII," he lamented.

It was the morning assembly time. Jeet walked with a sense of urgency along with his friends Rakesh and Devender. They were headed to the auditorium.

"Move around fast kids!" Jeet heard a thick accented voice, "Come on Surya house boys, don't walk like tortoises. Aren't you aware what you are destined for? How will you win all those trophies with this pace? Come on, come on!"

The pace became brisk.

"Rakesh, who is this new boy?"

"It's his first day in school, sir!"

"Ohh, the lateral entry?"

"Yes sir."

"Come here young man. The rest of you... run to the auditorium."

An overawed Jeet walked towards Kain with measured steps.

"What's your name?"

"Sir, Jeet."

"I never knew you have been knighted Jeet. Ok, we will all call you 'sir' now."

"Ha ha, no way, the sir was for you...sir." Jeet smiled.

"So you are the cricketer."

"Right, sir!" Jeet smiled again.

"Mr Bhardwaj thinks very highly of you. Are you as good he thinks you are?"

"Well sir," Jeet tried to think of something, "I try my best."

"Oh, so you try!"

"I believe so, sir!"

"Is it the same wittiness that got you through the interview son?"

"I absolutely have no idea sir."

"Fine, now hurry up or you would miss your first morning assembly."

Jeet rushed off to catch up with his friends.

"What does he teach?" Jeet asked Rakesh.

"Who?" Rakesh looked at him.

"The teacher I spoke to?"

"He is Kain, the history teacher. We call him 'Mr Carefully Careless'."

"What does that mean?"

"Didn't you notice his sense of dressing up and his hair?"

"Yeah, it seems sort of unique, different from others I guess." They kept scurrying towards the auditorium.

"One half of his shirt is always tucked in, and the other half is carefully left to dangle out."

"Hmm... and he has an amazing style of speaking, very different from the others."

"Yeah, he shows off a little bit."

"Whether he shows off or not, he really can leave others awestruck with his diction!" Jeet was impressed.

"Don't worry." Rakesh laughed. "He is also in-charge of cricket, as no coach has been appointed yet. You will interact a lot with him."

"Is he a cricket player?"

"He represented Delhi University in his college days."

"Don't tell me!"

Jeet found himself in the extraordinary ambience of a wonderful auditorium. The interiors were that of a luxury multiplex. It was a far cry from the open air morning assemblies he had attended at OLF in the heat of the scorching sun.

"The principal generally addresses the assembly," Rakesh informed Jeet, "but on Thursdays, the music teacher supervises it."

"It's Thursday today," said Jeet.

"Yes, and here comes Mrs Soni, the music teacher," Rakesh whispered.

"What will she do?"

"She will play some bhajans or songs and then we will head for our classes."

Everyone stood up to the sound of Lata Mangeshkar's recorded bhajan, '*Tum asha vishwas hamare, Rama*.' After the bhajan, everyone sat down in their seats. "If you want to sing a song, please volunteer," Mrs Soni announced.

Jeet wanted to raise his hand, but he got nervous and his courage faltered. The music teacher left and Rohit, the school captain, took charge of the assembly. Seeing more than a couple of lateral entries in the audience, he didn't want to let go of the opportunity of having fun at the expense of the newcomers.

"Let the lateral entries introduce themselves please. As it is your first day, we would be glad if any one of you can come to the stage and sing for us," he announced.

Seated in the first row, Jeet turned out to be the nearest target. He was forcibly pushed and nudged by the class XII students. Jeet, however, didn't like to be forced. He freed himself and walked towards the stage. *He could now either make a fool of himself or win their hearts with his singing,* he thought.

By the time he reached the stage, he knew what he wanted to sing. So far so good! But when he started to sing, the words refused to come out of his mouth! The unfriendly crowd certainly wasn't helping. Suddenly, a pleasant thought struck his mind. He recollected how confidently he had sung at the village Ramlila.

"Kishore Kumar please start," he heard a voice say from one section. "Did you forget the lyrics?" said another voice from the other section. The school crowd was getting restless. *The audience here is less than friendly*, Jeet thought. *But it certainly isn't as hostile as the Ramlila crowd!*

He started singing *Rangeela re*. The girls Neelam and Roshni looked at each other, perplexed.

"Isn't it the same song?" whispered Neelam to Roshni.

"Sure it is," Roshni whispered back.

"It is an amazing coincidence."

"It is more than a coincidence."

"More than a coincidence- What are you trying to say?"

"It's a signal from the skies."

Roshni started scribbling in her pocket diary.

"What are you doing?" whispered Neelam.

"Nothing."

"I know you are writing a poem."

It was Jeet's day. The applause didn't die down even after Jeet had finished singing and was seated. A clear blessing in disguise, the circumstances had taken care of themselves. He had made a name for himself on the very first day. He had achieved in a moment what under normal circumstances was difficult to achieve in years. Jeet stood outside the auditorium receiving accolades. Among those who wished him were the girls' school captain, the boys' school captain and other girls and boys from all the four houses. It was a dream first day.

"Hi!" Roshni smiled. She had waited for Jeet to be alone. Rakesh and Devinder, however, were still with him.

"Hi!" Jeet replied.

"Really well sung!"

She held out her hand and Jeet took it with all grace and chivalry.

"Do you know who she is?" Devender asked after Roshni had left. The compliment from the volleyball player had surprised Rakesh and Devender.

"How would I know?" Jeet shot back.

"She is Roshni, every boy's dream girl. I have never seen her complimenting anyone."

That Roshni had complimented Jeet was the topic of discussion in the Surya house hostel that evening. He was teased by one and all. Jeet, however, didn't seem to mind; he was lost in the reverie of the softness of Roshni's hand. It had felt good – the blood rushing through his adolescent veins. Life was good.

"This is just a beginning," Jeet reminded himself. "The developments of the day are a blessing. Now it is for me to capitalize on the excellent start."

Jeet now looked forward to play his first match for the school. Had he been blessed with clairvoyance, he would have known that he was going to strike gold in his first match.

≈

Roshni couldn't stop thinking about Jeet. At night, all by herself, she took out the piece of paper on which she had written the poem and worked on it some more. Then she addressed it to Jeet and read it to herself one last time.

Dearest Jeet,

I have waited forever,
Longed for this interference divine,
The blessings, however, couldn't have come
At a more opportune time,

As the song that perched on your lips
Was the one that occupied my mind.
You scurried through
But not before your eyes had met mine,
In your advent though, was the delight of sun shine
If not this, what else then would be a heavenly sign?

Roshni

As she read on, her facial expressions changed. Tension replaced the easy smile. In no time the frown lines deepened and were accompanied by tiny drops of sweat. A nightmarish storm had gripped her mind. An unseen force seemed to take control of her – and the poem she had written with her heart and soul was torn apart by the hands that had written it.

Neither this was the first time in life that Roshni had torn up her own poem, nor was this to be her last. The trigger lay in an incident that had occurred in her childhood; an event that she was too scared to recount even to her own self. But the more she tried to run away from the pain, the more it returned to haunt her.

For years together, she had been living with her past. Volley ball and literature were the only indulgences that brought her succour.

Sanawar Match

Jeet was happy with his practice sessions and as a result, his batting got better by the day. The team was a fairly strong unit with six main players forming the nucleus. Alok – the opener – was the most accomplished batsman. Ajay Yadav – left-handed and the number three batsman in the batting order – had been temporarily playing the role of an opener in the absence of a regular opener. With Jeet in the team, he was looking forward to get back to the number three slot. The new ball pair of tall and fearsome Ashok Bhatotia and Rajbeer Choudhary was extremely effective. Ashok was the captain of the team too. Rajesh Bhambha, the wily leg spinner, and Vinay Kaushik, a very agile wicket keeper-batsman, further strengthened the team. Two out of the six best players – Rajesh Bhambha and Rajbeer Chaudhary – came from Jeet's house, Surya.

The practice sessions gave Jeet a fair idea of what his role in the team was likely to be. Despite being a lateral entry, the team had accepted him with open arms. He was almost certain of his place as an opener. He now waited eagerly for the first match to experience the thrill of representing an institution he believed was always his and which he thought had awaited him for a long time.

The prestigious Lawrence School, Sanawar, was to be the first to lock horns with Rai at the start of the season. Carrying tremendous repute, Sanawar was expected to pose a stiff challenge. The importance of the match could be gauged by the fact that it was declared a no-class day. For the whole school it meant a day's respite from classes and morning drills. It was mandatory to watch the match till lunch time. After that, it was optional. A student could choose between watching the match and following his normal routine.

The Sanawar cricket team arrived two days before the match. Separate nets were arranged for them for practice and also to help them get acclimatized.

It was the match day. At 8.00 a.m., while their peers from other sports enjoyed a rare, extended sleeping session, the three Surya house cricketers, Jeet, Rajbeer Chaudhary and Rajesh Bhambha were getting ready to win the battle that lay ahead. As always, Rajbeer's off-whites looked impeccable.

"After all, Sofia would be there too," Rajesh winked at Jeet, a clear effort at poking fun at Rajbeer's extravagant efforts at looking good. Rajbeer couldn't restrain his quiet smile. That he had more than a soft corner towards Sofia, the brightest student in the medical stream, was hardly a secret. Rajbeer's friends never let go of an opportunity to tease him. The way Rajbeer blushed on such occasions cleared any doubts one might otherwise have had about how he felt about her. But whether Sofia too shared Rajbeer's sentiments, was the million dollar question.

"Rajbeer, today you are the closest that one could get to Mr Bhardwaj's definition of a gentleman," said Jeet. After his admission to Rai, the definition of good or mediocre, started and ended with

Y.P.'s perspective. The ghost of Y.P. was now omnipresent in him, so much so, that there were no other parameters other than how Y.P. would judge a certain thing.

"You are right I suppose," replied a proud Rajbeer, smiling from ear to ear. "According to him, a gentleman means someone who is spotless. And today I am spotless."

"You aren't spotless, dear Rajbeer," said Bhambha. "Your off-whites are spotless. I am sure Y.P. would kick you out of the team if he knew you wanted Bhatotia to lose the toss."

"Lose the toss!" exclaimed Jeet. "Why, for God's sake! I don't believe this!"

"I am sure you don't," said Rajesh with an intriguing smile.

Jeet looked at Rajbeer. Again his blushing, quiet smile gave it away.

"I got it," said Jeet.

"Let's see if you really have," said Bhambha.

"It's simple actually. Bhatotia would choose to bat in case he wins the toss."

"So far so good," Bhambha chuckled.

"But Rajbeer wants to bowl first."

"But why?"

"The crowd, as it is, is not likely to return after lunch. Rajbeer wants to perform in Sophia's presence and she too, he hopes, would want him to perform in her presence, and that can happen only if we bowl first."

"Bingo!" shouted Bhambha. "But there would be someone else in the crowd who would want us to bat rather than bowl first."

"I am sure the entire school, except Sophia, would want us to bat first."

"But I am talking about a special person with her special reasons," Bhambha winked at Rajbeer.

"Roshni!" Rajbeer shrieked as it was Jeet's turn to blush.

"Come on now! It's nothing," Jeet continued to blush.

"Tell this to the marines buddy, don't play ball with us. Don't we know that she is always looking for reasons to interact with you, say 'hi' to you, not that you seem to mind it yourself. Yes, both of you look very patient and the dish is on a low flame, but it is on the flame nevertheless."

"Yes, I can smell something cooking," Rajbir said.

Jeet lowered his gaze and didn't answer.

"So it's not as much between rival captains, as it is between Sophia and Roshni, the battle of the toss I mean," Bhambha shouted. "In which case, the two sides of the coin shouldn't portray heads and tails, but the picture of Jeet on one side and Rajbir on the other."

"Or maybe the picture of Roshni on one side and Sophia on the other," Rajbir offered.

All three had a hearty laugh.

The walk towards the ground was rather quiet. They concentrated and planned in their own way. Jeet started concentrating on, and planning his innings just like any good batsman would, before a match. He drew a virtual replica of the field and pitch with player positions. He had not yet decided which bat he was going to bat with. He knew that a good bat is more than a tool for a batsman. In a way, it's an extension of the batsman himself. A batsman's real personality is transmuted into the bat as he grips it. The reflexes are attained after hundreds and thousands of hours of practice, and are transferred into the bat from the player's soul. It is then that the batting becomes a poetic fusion of the bat and the player. Therefore, the choice of bat was very crucial. Jeet had had a few good ones till then, but none that could be termed as perfect. The school kit bag had two excellent pieces of willow that were balanced to his liking, and could deliver a fairly good punch. Both these bats were from the maker Sunridges or SS.

Someday I would lay my hands on a Symonds Super Tusker bat, Jeet thought to himself. Symonds bats, however, didn't come cheap.

Once I perform well, I would request Y.P. to get one for the team, he thought. Jeet didn't know that Mr Kain owned a wonderful piece of the very same brand.

Mr Kain too, was getting ready. He looked in the mirror. The image satisfied him. The uncombed hair, the new white-coloured Adidas track suit, with the carefully half-tucked T-shirt that could be seen through the upper, completed his "carefully careless" look. The unkempt bed and unorganized toiletries added up to his bachelor lifestyle. With the Symonds bat hanging on his shoulder, he headed straight to the cricket ground and was the first to reach.

"The kids would be coming anytime. Let me get warmed up."

Placing his prized possession on one of the chairs in the pavilion of the home team, he jogged towards the far end. He had hardly gone a hundred metres, when he heard the sound of a ball hitting a bat. As he turned to look, he saw Dinesh, the all-rounder of the team, practicing with the Symonds bat with another player Khapra bowling at him.

"Dinesh!" he shouted.

Dinesh looked in the direction of the voice. A huffing and puffing Mr Kain in a white track suit, headed towards him. "Do you know what my bat is to me?" he shouted angrily. Dinesh didn't know what to say. Mr Kain continued to shout, "I treat my bat with the same sanctity as I would treat my sweetheart. So don't ever dare touch it again. Can't you think of better things than to spoil your mood and mine on the morning of such an important match?"

Dinesh gently placed the bat on the chair, his head bowed down. Through the corner of his eyes, he could see Khapra making valiant efforts at concealing his laughter. Mr Kain resumed his jogging.

Dinesh and Khapra waited for him to get out of earshot, before they laughed their hearts out.

⁂

Both the teams had occupied their respective dressing rooms. The spectators too had started to fill the seats.

If Rai School was the universe, the cricket ground became the centre of it. With every colour present on the ground, it appeared to be a carnival of sorts with the weather playing its part to the 'T'. It was the beginning of September and the weather was best suited for a cricket match. A clear blue sky, without a speck of cloud presented a picturesque backdrop. The sun was mild and bright – as if it had left all the excess heat back home – and shone with radiance. A light breeze made the afternoon pleasant and welcomed the cricketers with open arms.

While the students sat on the ground around the boundary line, colourful tents were erected to accommodate teachers and coaches. Some of them preferred the comfort of the green grass and were seated along with the students. Two dressing rooms were erected for the two teams. Makeshift washrooms were also there. A separate tent had been erected to accommodate the principal and the vice principal. Two separate breakfast tables were set aside for the two teams. The buttered cucumber sandwiches and luscious vegetable cutlets were too good to resist.

Y.P. – partial towards cricket as he was – loved such events. Cricket wasn't merely a sport for him. It formed an integral part of his nervous system. It was in his DNA. The extravagant arrangements were a cricketer's delight.

The winning of the toss was acknowledged by a huge roar from the crowd.

"Roshni has won," Bhambha whispered to a smiling Jeet.

"We are batting first. Alok and Ajay Yadav will open. Vinay at number 3 and Jeet Singh at number 4," Bhatotia announced before occupying a vacant chair next to Mr Kain.

The first four batsmen started putting on their gears.

"Why isn't the new boy opening the innings?" asked Mr Kain.

"Sir, it's his first match. I didn't want to put him under pressure."

"Kid gloves; you are treating him with kid gloves! Throw him in the deep end skipper, for God's sake!"

"Sure sir, in the next match I will ask him to open the innings."

"What about the rest of the batting order?"

"You mean after Jeet?"

"Yes."

"Let it be horses for courses, sir. We will decide as the situation demands it," Bhatotia replied.

"Hmm... fine," Kain agreed.

Jeet put on his pads and headed towards the washroom.

"What are you doing here?" he was surprised to see a smiling Roshni. Jeet quickly looked around. The washroom was camouflaged between two tents. The chances, therefore, of someone seeing them together, were remote.

"I saw you heading here," she was calm.

"Have you gone mad?" Jeet sighed. "Please go," he gently pushed her.

"Don't worry, I am going. I know you are scared of Y.P.," she teased. "Just came to give you this," she pushed a slip of paper into his hands and walked away. Jeet's heart missed a beat as he unfolded it.

"I wish you all the best for the match. Your thoughts catch me unawares at odd places and at odd times. Tell me...what to do?"

The handwriting was as beautiful as the message itself. He looked around once more. There was no one. After coming back from the washroom, he surreptitiously slipped the piece of paper into the inner pocket of his kit bag. He took a couple of deep breaths. It was extremely important to focus on the job at hand now.

He moved towards the school kit bag to get the SS bat he was to play with. All of a sudden, his eyes shone. On one of the kit bags lay his dream Super Tusker. With disbelief, he lifted the bat.

Hope it's not a fake, he thought. But the genuine looking logo and perfectly parallel seven grains suggested otherwise. He requested Rajbeer to toss a ball at him, so that he could have a feel of it. As the ball hit the "sweet" part of the bat, a musical sound emanated and the ball travelled far, hit the sight screen wall, and ricocheted back to create a perfect symphony. Jeet looked at the bat in admiration.

"You know what," Dinesh looked at Khapra. He had a naughty smile on his face. "The morning scene is going to be repeated."

"How?" said Khapra, busy gulping cucumber sandwiches.

"Look at Jeet. He has Mr Kain's bat."

An oblivious Jeet continued to look at the bat in admiration. Satisfied with its balance and stroke, he moved towards his chair as Dinesh and Khapra giggled in their seats, anticipating the impossible.

"What about the new kid?" Mr Kain was in conversation with Bhatotia.

"I have already announced it. He bats at number four, sir."

"That I know. I mean you must have seen him. Is he good?"

"He looks alright in the nets, sir. Today is the real test."

"The principal has very high expectations of him."

"As I said sir, today is the real test."

It wasn't the best of starts for Rai School. Trying to cover drive a swinging new ball, Ajay could only manage an outside edge. The ball flew towards the first slip. The fielder did the rest. The score in the very first over read: 3 runs for 1 wicket. Mr Kain shifted worriedly in his chair.

"No worries, Alok is still there," he mumbled to himself.

"Did you say something sir?" Bhatotia asked as Vinay reached the crease to try and repair the early damage.

"No, nothing," responded Kain. "Is Vinay in proper touch?"

"Yes, sir."

"Hmm," Kain breathed. "Tell everyone to initially play with caution."

"Yes sir," Bhatotia looked in the direction of Jeet and saw the Super Tusker in his hands.

"Jeet Singh," Bhatotia called.

"What happened? Why are you shouting at him? Let him concentrate in peace. He is the next to go for God's sake," Mr Kain was clearly irritated.

"Sir, he has your bat in hand. Not his fault actually. He might have assumed it belongs to the school."

"Oh my God! But Bhatotia, you and the others should have told him. This is so frustrating. Ask him to change the bat immediately."

Jeet walked towards his captain, focussing on the field. Before he could reach Bhatotia, another wicket fell.

Alok had thought the ball from the fast bowler was either a harmless full toss or a juicy half volley. It was, in fact, a deadly yorker. The best batsman's stump lay uprooted on the ground.

Kain and Ashok found it difficult to breathe.

"Yes Ashok," Bhatotia and Kain looked at Jeet, and they realized why he had been called in. Kain pressed Bhatotia's hand before Ashok could utter a word, and spoke to Jeet himself.

"See Jeet, the team needs you. It's your first match. Give it all you have. And please do not rush things. All the best."

"Thank you sir. I would give my very best," replied Jeet and entered the ground, the Symonds proudly tucked under his right arm.

"What about the bat, sir?" whispered Bhatotia.

"No bat is greater than the team's cause. Only that he must justify this exceptional piece of bludgeon that he has so proudly and so authoritatively tucked under his arm," Kain replied. Bhatotia smiled.

Jeet took his guard. The fast bowler reached his mark. At the other end was Vinay. He too was surprised to see him carrying Kain's bat.

"There is no need to hurry, Jeet," Vinay said. "We need to reconstruct and then consolidate here a little bit. Let's see the new ball off and keep wickets intact. The onslaught can come later," Jeet nodded in agreement.

"Steady," Jeet told himself. The ball was pitched short. Jeet's reflexes took over and all care and caution was thrown to the winds. He rocked on to the backfoot and dispatched the ball to the boundary. Two thuds emanated within a fraction of a second. One was the sound of the bat meeting the ball and the other of the ball making a dent in the boundary wall. The roar from the crowd was deafening.

Jeet carried on with his innings and hit two more boundaries. On executing one of his shots, he heard a very distinct, heavily accented voice that pierced through the cacophony, "Good shot Jeet," Y.P. was on his feet.

"Thank you sir," Jeet's lips moved. The resolve to do well became stronger.

Mr Kain, however, was furious.

"Has he gone mad?" he looked at Bhatotia. "The best batsman has just got out. The score is a meagre 15 runs. And look at what our very own Viv Richards does? He jolly well plays to the gallery. After all, the girls are watching!"

Bhatotia gestured towards the batsmen. With fingers pointing upwards and palms facing the batsmen, in cricketing parlance it was a clear signal to be calm. Vinay and Jeet acknowledged.

There was no looking back for the two batsmen. Slowly and steadily, the situation of the team got better. By the end of the twentieth over, the score board read 91/ 2, with Jeet batting on forty-eight and Vinay on thirty-two. This showed considerable progress, when compared to the earlier score of 15/ 2.

It was with a massive swing of the bat that Jeet reached his half-century. The ball landed a couple of feet away from where Y.P. was seated.

"Why don't you come home tonight? Y.P. asked V.K. Verma, the Maths teacher seated close to him. V.K. and Kain were of the same age. In fact, both were buddies and shared secrets.

"Something special, sir?" V.K. asked.

"I have an eagerly waiting bottle of Chivas Regal at home."

"Waiting for what, sir?"

"Waiting to be consumed V.K. It begs to be caressed, to be felt V.K, whenever I open my cupboard."

"You are in a mood to celebrate, sir. But don't you think it's too early. I mean we haven't won the match yet."

"We have already won V.K. Just that you haven't realised it as yet. You know what?"

"What sir?"

"This boy reminds me of my playing days."

"Are you referring to Jeet?"

"Who else? I see so much of me in him. I want the Chivas Regal's wait to end tonight."

"I got it, sir."

V.K. knew the principal drank rarely. But whenever he did or looked forward to it, it was safe to presume that he was in an ecstatic state of mind.

"Let me go and sit with the principal." Kain got out of his seat.

"Sir, please keep sitting. We are playing well," requested Bhatotia.

"And what has our batting got to do with my getting seated with the principal? You mean if I change my seat, a wicket or two will fall? Come on Bhatotia grow up, get rid of your ancient thinking." Kain moved out.

"It's nice to see you having a great time, sir." Kain pulled a chair close to the principal.

"Kain, why are you roaming around like this? Don't you see we are playing so well?" Y.P. said in a loud voice. Kain hadn't completely occupied the chair as yet. He could see several pairs of eyes staring at him.

"S...sir," Kain stammered as he glanced towards Bhatotia who was looking in his direction with a 'didn't I tell you' smile. He left the chair and headed towards where he was earlier seated.

"Where exactly do you think you are going now, Kain?" It was Y.P. again. "You seem to be in some discomfort today."

"No, Sir... just that... because you said..."

"Now be seated with me and don't get up unless we have played out the entire innings."

"Sure sir." Kain sat down. Adding insult to injury was V.K. with his sheepish, suppressed smile. It was unusual for Kain to get rubbed the wrong way. But there was nothing much he could do about the situation.

"So, Kain," it was Y.P. again. "I did see the spark alright."

"There can't be a better judge of talent than you, sir! The boy surely isn't doing badly," acknowledged Kain.

Not able to suppress himself any longer, V.K. burst out laughing, causing even more discomfort to Kain.

"Is there something I should know V.K.?"

"Sir," V.K. managed to speak in between intervals of laughter, "Nothing much, just that Jeet is batting with Kain's favourite bat."

"Oh really!" exclaimed Y.P. "That shouldn't a big deal, or should it be, Kain?"

"No sir, it certainly isn't." Kain managed.

"In fact, I would suggest we should let the kid keep it, I mean, if he is really fond of it. We can always get you a new one," Y.P. looked at V.K. and winked.

"I am afraid that's not possible, sir," V.K. chirped. "Kain says he adores his bat as much as he would adore his sweetheart."

No sooner had V.K. finished speaking than Y.P. burst into laughter. Kain didn't know which way to look.

"In that case Kain," Y.P. said, "First thing the comparison is absurd..."

"I don't mean it, sir," Kain intruded. "Just that in cricketing parlance we kind of use this comparison; V.K. has misquoted me on purpose. What I have in fact always said is that I hold my bat in the same regard and sanctity as I would hold my sweetheart."

"I got it Kain, but you cannot correct a wrong by hiding behind the pretext of cricketing parlance, and moreover if cricketing parlance is what you understand then believe me, the boy is a real gentleman. He would return to you whatever is yours, unscathed. Be it a bat or..." All three laughed spontaneously.

Vinay and Jeet went about their tasks in a surgical manner. It was on his personal score of eighty-nine that Jeet made his first mistake. Unfortunately for him, it turned out to be his last as well. A hundred had seemed just around the corner. Trying to clear the long-on fence, Jeet mistimed the shot. The fielder at the long on came under the skewed-up ball and took a comfortable catch. The crowd, stunned initially, applauded his innings as he started to walk towards the pavilion. Although a bit disappointed on missing a hundred, he was satisfied for being able to stand up and deliver for the team. The dressing room, however, was surprisingly quiet. Jeet had anticipated sounds of 'well played'.

Doesn't make sense, he thought as he removed his pads. And then suddenly, it all fell into place.

"Well played Roshni," everyone shouted in unison.

"How could they know?" Jeet was embarrassed and stunned.

"You threw it away kid," Kain's face seemed to show concern but the next moment the smirking lips were stretched into a wide smile. "Well played Roshni," the dressing room exploded one more time.

Rai's innings ended at 12.30 p.m. After the allotted thirty-five overs, the score was 186 for the loss of five wickets. Jeet with his eighty-nine runs, had scored the highest.

As expected, not many turned up to watch Sanawar's innings. Both their openers were back in the pavilion before the third over. The visitors never recovered from the early blows. The entire innings unfolded in the thirty-first over with the score at a hundred and twenty six. MNSS won by a decent margin of sixty runs.

It was party time in the dressing room. The sounds of laughter emanated from all corners with empty bottles of energy drinks scattered all over.

> "Everyone's attention please," all eyes focused on Kain as he stood up for the pep talk. "Congratulations once again for a fine victory and a good start to the season. But we must also not forget that it's a long season ahead..." Kain stopped as he saw a familiar, intimidating figure walking in. Y.P. was dressed in an impeccable white Kurta and a black pair of jeans. The trademark spectacles, as usual, hung on his chest.

Y.P. looked glad. "Well done boys. Keep it up! I will be brief and leave the boring job of pep talk to Kain," he paused and then continued amidst subdued laughter. "All of you, along with the guest team are invited for dinner at my place at 8.00 p.m. tonight." He turned to go and then suddenly turned back, "And yes, before I forget," he was looking towards Jeet. His eyes almost drilled holes into him, "Well played Roshni," Y.P. smiled. The dressing room had erupted again. Jeet suddenly became oblivious to the surroundings. He could see the exaggerated hand movements of his team mates but the sounds of cacophony died down on the way before reaching his eardrums. The only thing that he could hear clearly was the principal's compliment. Hitherto, he hadn't known a feeling more ecstatic than the one that the present moment carried. That the dream run would end soon, he didn't know.

Jeet and Roshni

"My dear book-worm, how about a song?"

Roshni's sudden intrusion made Jeet fidget in his seat. He sat in the library engrossed in the book *The Art of Batting*. He had sought special permission to be in the library on a Saturday evening, when the rest of the school was watching a movie in the auditorium. Roshni had come in unannounced, without making a sound.

"Why are you disturbing me?"

He looked at her, feigning irritation. Within, he was happy she had come. He liked her and looked forward to everything associated with her. The teasing of his friends, her appearing from nowhere at odd hours, all delighted him. She was the good that had happened to him. With her, he always lost track of time.

"Disturbing you? May I ask what important task were you involved in?"

She walked towards one of the four chairs around the table where Jeet was seated and ensconced herself comfortably beside him. Jeet looked at her. He couldn't hear what she said; he could only see the quivering lips, the expressive eyes, her slender fingers pushing away the hair from her face. This moment came with no baggage.

It was for moments such as these that God must have decided to create life, he thought. *But then, why isn't our whole life made of such moments and such moments only? Maybe because in that case the real worth of such moments would go unrealised. So God chose to keep them few and far between.*

"Hey, where are you?" she snapped her fingers in front of his eyes and he was back in the real world.

"What happened?" he managed.

"Yes, what happened to you?"

"I am fine, I am reading."

"Reading yes, of course, what else do you think people do in a library? But reading what?" she took the book from him, "*The Art of Batting*?"

"Of course, I am learning more about my game."

Roshni burst into uncontrolled laughter.

"Why are you laughing so hysterically?"

"Oh my cute innocent cricketer," Roshni was still laughing, "The last time I heard, a game is learnt by practicing on the field, and not by reading about it from some book. Would you face a fast bowler coming at you, all guns blazing, with a book in your trouser pocket or with a bat in your hands? Will you ask the umpire to stop the game so that you may refer to your pocket-book, my Sunil Gavaskar?"

"I don't want to argue with you."

"That's because you have no ammunition to argue with."

"By reading, I get to know more about the nuances and subtleties of the game, else why would I miss a movie to read it?"

"Good point, but not so good actually. I know why you missed your movie." Roshni was in no mood to loosen her grip on the situation. She continued to tease him.

"You mean is there some other reason?"

"Of course."

"Do me a favour then by telling me about it!"

"The reason is the diction."

"Diction? As in?"

"The diction in Hollywood movies is like a bouncer that flies over your head and you cannot make out the heads or tails of English movies."

"You..." Jeet tried to grab her arm.

"Ok... ok... sorry," She folded her hands. "I was kidding. But on a serious note, what are the coaches for then, if you have to refer to the books for nuances and subtleties!"

"Coaches..."

"Oh I forgot! You don't have a regular coach but then there's Kain, does he not... " All of a sudden she burst into an incessant laughter.

"Don't laugh so loudly, this is a library."

"Talking of Kain," she continued, "it reminds me of the other day when you played with his bat... "

"I didn't know it was his bat," this time Jeet smiled too.

"You should have seen how Y.P. reacted when V.K. told him about the wife and bat comparison. Y.P. said, *Kain don't worry, the kid is a gentleman. He would return to you whatever belongs to you, unscathed.*"

"Y.P. said that?" his smile got wider.

"Yeah, and you know what my friends said?"

"You mean Neelam?"

"Yeah, and the others too!"

"What?"

"Roshni, forget Jeet, he is now Y.P.'s property."

"Y.P.'s property? As in?"

"Yeah, you have floored him with your batting. He says he sees a lot of him in you."

Both of them laughed in unison.

"I felt very bad when they said that," said Roshni, "despite the fact that they were merely teasing me. Now sing."

"Sing! Now where does this singing come from? You abruptly change topics. I was about to tell you... "

"Tell me...what?"

"I forgot...yeah...was telling you how my friends congratulated me."

"Congratulated, as in, after your innings?"

"Yeah."

"Yeah tell me... "

"They said *well played Roshni!* And Y.P. and Kain followed suit."

Roshni blushed and said abruptly, "Now sing please. The movie will soon get over."

"Sing here in the library? Have you gone mad? And by the way, who gave you permission to be here?"

"I, me and myself."

"You, and who are you by the way, Cleopatra?"

"Listen," she ignored Jeet's sarcasm, "please sing."

"Please behave. It's a library, for God's sake."

"Yes library my dear Gavaskar, but without readers. Tell me, who will I disturb here? These tables and chairs?"

Jeet felt like a fool. "But the attendant is here. He can complain to Y.P. and I won't get permission to sit here again."

"Oh my God! I don't know when you will free yourself from the ghost of Y.P. Wait... " she walked towards the reception.

"Where are you going now?" he admiringly watched her, as she walked away from him. *This girl could put any ramp model to shame,* he thought.

The next minute, she was back with the attendant in tow.

"Tell me Bhaiya," she looked at him. "It's Saturday evening so it's off for you, isn't it?"

Jeet looked down holding his head in his hands.

"Yeah normally it's an off," the attendant replied.

“So, Jeet has spoiled your off day, has he not?”

“No it is our job...so we have to do it.”

“Of course you have to do it, but not on off days.”

The attendant couldn’t find any words to respond. Jeet’s head was still in his hands.

“So, tell me,” there was no stopping Roshni, “What were your plans for Saturday evening? I mean, if Jeet had not fiddled with it.”

“I would have gone to Murthal with my wife.”

“For paranthas?”

“Yes.”

“So, is it not his responsibility to make up for your lost evening?”

The attendant looked up and down, not knowing what to say.

“Ok,” she looked at the attendant, “do you like songs?”

“Yes.”

“So, won’t you be happy if Jeet sang nice, melodious songs for you to compensate for your evening, because he can’t make paranthas for you, and for your wife?”

Enough was enough. Jeet couldn’t take any more. He took Roshni’s hand and headed towards the library gate, leaving behind a relieved attendant. Roshni smiled.

“Put the book back on the same rack,” he looked back towards the attendant. Both were now out of the library.

“Have you gone mad?”

Only the streetlights glowed in the dark.

“Yes, a little bit. But why are you dragging me? Just tell me where we are going... and... ”

“And?”

“And I would come with you to... wherever... ”

“Hmm... very funny, go to your hostel.”

“I can’t go to my hostel,” she teased. “Don’t forget, I am still in the auditorium... officially, I mean.”

“You mean you have bunked?”

"Come on Jeet, you don't bunk a movie, you bunk something like a class or a lecture, *for* a movie!"

"When you go against the school schedule, it's called bunking."

"Don't bore me with your lectures. Let's go and sit somewhere."

"Where?"

"Someplace I know; and you know as well."

"Stop talking in riddles, you have irritated me a lot already."

"Ok, to the cricket field."

"But why do you want to go to the cricket field, that too at this hour?"

"Because you are stupid. My hostel is closest to the cricket field. We can talk there for some time and then in no time I would be in the hostel before anyone could know about it. Don't forget, there is a roll call after dinner. If I miss that, I'm gone."

"You are a gone case anyway."

Roshni laughed, and both of them moved towards the cricket field. They sat beside the roller close to the cricket pitch. It was dark and they could hardly see each other.

"Sing for me now."

"No."

"Don't worry, Y.P. won't come. Don't be scared."

"Ok, let me go then. Why should I be sitting here, if I am scared of Y.P.?"

"Sorry baba," she pulled him back. "Achcha please sing, if we stay here for long, your worst fears might come true. Both of us may get rusticated."

"You are embarrassing me by asking again and again. I am not some Rafi or Kishore."

"You are my Mohammad Rafi and Kishore Kumar both rolled into one," she wrapped her arms around his shoulders. "So, I will name you my Kishore Mohammad."

"Then I will be a Muslim and then your parents won't allow... "

"Allow what...?"

"Allow..."

"Say it... allow what...?"

"Ok, which song?"

"You mean you can sing any song?"

"Yeah, at least I can try."

"Ok sing a song of your own choice first!"

Jeet sang two songs. Roshni was lost in the romance that the songs exuded. The stillness of the night added to the ambience.

"You should seriously pursue singing professionally, Jeet!"

Jeet didn't answer.

"Can you sing *Tere bina zindagi se koi shiqwa to nahin*'?"

"From the movie *Aandhi*?"

"Yes."

"Yeah, I can. This too is a Kishore song."

"Yeah, but more than Kishore, its Gulzar's song, I like it for its lyrics. You know...," her voice shook and her eyes became moist. She fell quiet. Her exuberance diffused. What remained was a vulnerable and emotional Roshni. In the darkness, Jeet couldn't look into her eyes, but he could hear her tears. Her sobs hurt him. It was after prolonged persistence that she started telling him her story.

"This is my Mom's favourite song. She cries each time she listens to it."

"But why?"

"Because Dad has left us."

"Dad left...as in?"

"No, no, not that way. I mean he is very much alive... may God bless him with a long life. For me, he is the greatest dad in the world."

"But what happened? You mean he doesn't love your Mom?"

"He does. In fact, he more than loves her. It may be his possessiveness that triggered all the trouble."

"How can you say that?"

"I say that because I can see no other reason. It started slowly. And then he wasn't the Dad I had known all along. He started getting drunk, started getting violent with mother at smallest of issues."

"And?"

"We didn't know what to do. And then one day... it was a bright and pleasant January day and we were on the terrace. My neighbours were on their respective terraces too. I sat with a pencil and paper trying to make a portrait of Mom and Dad, while Mom was busy in her household chores.

"I completed the portrait and just then, Papa came along. He was at his worst that day. I had never ever seen him so angry. He started shouting at Mom in full view of everyone around. Dad said something about my Mom's parents and Mom retaliated for the first time. She shouted back at Dad, with anger and disgust in her eyes.

"She called him a coward and asked him to immediately leave the house. And then Dad was quiet, as if a storm inside him had died down. He moved towards the stairs. But there was no stopping Mom that day. Just as he started stepping out, Mom threw a bucket, half-filled with water, at him. The blood that oozed out of his head, just didn't stop.

"I ran towards him with the portrait in my hand ...but stopped... as I saw papa struggling to stop the incessant flow of blood. I managed...somehow... to turn his attention towards the portrait ... in the hope that my first work of art will make him forget his anger and... his pain. He took the portrait in his hands and looked at it very carefully and then he looked at me and smiled. The blood still oozed out of the wound. I could look at Dad and see that his smile was fading. Till this day, I haven't forgotten that sad smile. He tore the portrait neatly into two, bisecting it perfectly, separating the two individuals who had promised themselves to be forever counted as one. And Dad hasn't returned since... "

Roshni was quiet. She didn't speak for a long time.

"But didn't you or aunty try to find the reasons for his sudden change in behaviour?"

"We did... we went to a doctor and he said it's a very common illness."

"You mean the doctor agreed that it is some kind of illness?"

"Yeah and there's a cure too!"

"What is the cure?"

"Counselling and some medicines."

"Doesn't sound tough. Why don't you go for it?"

"I asked Dad to start with the treatment, but he refused. He doesn't accept that he is sick. It's for this reason that I want to be a doctor, Jeet."

"Neelam told me," said Jeet, "that you write very good poems, but you don't allow anyone else to read them and then you tear them up."

"But how does she know they are good? I never showed them to her."

"She says she read a couple of them from under your pillow."

Roshni kept quiet.

"Is this tearing away of poems something to do with how your Dad behaved that day?"

Roshni nodded her head in affirmation.

"And when you write a poem, are you reminded of that incident?" asked Jeet.

"Yes," Roshni nodded, "and then a thought grips my mind, leaves it senseless, the thought that it's a useless piece of paper and will fail to draw any appreciation from the people who really matter. What use then, is such art? And then the sound of the tearing of paper reverberates in my mind and some force inside me asks me to tear the poem, and I tear it up, despite not wanting to do so."

Another long silence ensued.

"Can you sing that song for me, Jeet?"

"Sure, but I ask this just for curiosity's sake, why this particular song?"

"My mother can connect with the song. Her husband is the only complaint she has from life; but without him, life in fact is no life, and that's exactly what the song says."

"I have been singing this song for ages, never realizing the impact of the lyrics. I feel small Roshni, so small. Today you have given a totally different meaning to the song, and may be to life too."

Jeet started singing. Roshni experienced a dull throb in her heart, in her head, as the lyrics took her back to those days, but the pain transmuted into relief as the song progressed. By visiting her pain once again, she had in fact, found her way to peace.

"See me off to the hostel Jeet, the movie has ended it seems."

Fifty yards from the girls' hostel they stopped and hugged. Roshni watched as Jeet moved away from her.

I have been living two lives, Jeet. The life of the past now haunts me, troubles me to death. It's high time I made it disappear now. With you, I am more than assured I can do it.

Jeet had reached the infirmary. He just needed to cross the road that separated the hostel from the infirmary. It was then that he was blinded by the headlights of the approaching car. The persistent honking further irritated him. He was about to ignore it and enter his hostel, when he saw the shadow of a hand wave at him from the driver's seat. His eyes scanned the number plate. It was the principal's white Ambassador.

"You were supposed to be in the library," Y.P. almost shouted.

"Yes sir, I came back from there."

"But the library is on the other side if I know the locations right, and you are coming from the girls' hostel side."

"Yes sir... I... sir, went for a walk."

"A walk!"

"Yes... sir"

"Alone?"

"Yes sir."

"Hmm... Ok."

Y.P. put the car into gear. He was eager to reach home, desperate to grab the phone. Jeet stood numb, didn't move a muscle till Y.P.'s car had disappeared.

Why did I have to lie? Why couldn't I see Roshni off a moment earlier or a moment later? He wished for the earth to open up below him.

The library attendant had placed all the scattered books back in their respective shelves. He was satisfied. He wouldn't need to work that hard on Monday morning now. He had closed the gate and was locking it when he heard the ring of the telephone. He thought he should ignore it, but then rushed inside and picked up the receiver on its last ring.

"Good evening sir," he said to the principal at the other end. *Good that I came back*, the attendant thought.

"Yes sir, he had left early."

"Around one hour ago, sir."

"No sir, Roshni was with him."

"Yes sir, the one from class XI."

"They sat and talked for some time and then they left, sir."

"Towards the cricket field, sir."

"Yes sir. Good night, sir."

The attendant locked the library and went home.

In the drawing room of his palatial bungalow some five hundred yards away from the library, Y.P. walked around aimlessly in his drawing room thinking, "Was a lie really needed? Shouldn't he have told the truth?" The principal was angry. "But he's a kid after all. Might have got scared; what are we other than our fears?" He tried to justify Jeet's actions.

He somehow managed to forgive Jeet's first lie, but would the principal be magnanimous enough to forgive the second one?

Under-17 Trials

Their love continued to blossom. Despite strict schedules, they managed to steal their minutes, if not hours, of togetherness. With Jeet and his songs around her, Roshni inched steadily closer towards him and towards freedom from her past.

For Jeet, the immediate challenge wasn't love, but cricket. Going by his experience in the under-15 tournament, he was sure that Topal, the selector from Gurgaon, wasn't going to recommend him for selection. On the contrary, if the cigarette episode was any indicator, Topal was likely to leave no stone unturned to stonewall his selection.

Seeing no solution in sight, his mind turned towards two people who had invariably managed to tilt the winds of circumstances in his favour whenever the air of adversity threatened him.

"Topal isn't going to back me in the selection meetings," he wrote to his parents. "To act is better than doing nothing at all against the anticipated storm. I am coming home." He had written about the entire cigarette episode and the reasons for his fears of failing to make to the list of selected players despite deserving a place in the side.

It was 7 p.m. when he knocked at the front door. Kamlesh and Padam were delighted to see him. The paranthas tasted divine. He ate till he could eat no more. Then he sat in his room, discussing batting techniques with Paddy.

"So, how were the paranthas?" Kamlesh asked on entering the room.

"Divine! Not even Mr Joon can make better paranthas than my Mom."

"And who is Mr Joon, who stands to compete with your Mom?" Kamlesh's eyebrows went up.

"Our mess manager, who else Mom?"

"You mean the mess manager cooks paranthas at Rai?" she joked as all three broke into laughter.

"I am glad everything is to my son's liking," she wrapped her hand around Jeet's.

"By the way Mom, what time is Dad supposed to come?"

"He would be home anytime now. Why? Are you worried about the trials?" she asked with a smile.

"Yes Mom. Hope I am not doing anything that is to your dislike. I mean, the way I am trying to set things right with the selectors and looking for recommendations and stuff like that."

He wondered if his thoughts and actions were aligned to his Mom's.

"With your hard work and passion," she said, "I am more than convinced of your right to make it to the state team. Also, it wouldn't be a delightful feeling for a mother to learn that her kid wasn't given his rightful place for reasons other than merit. Moreover, when one's adversary is as cheap a person as Topal, everything is fair." Kamlesh's tone carried a hint of anger.

"Do not worry," Kamlesh continued. "Your dad has been on the task ever since we had the letter in our hands. In your language I would say, his eyes are on the ball. But Beta, why is Topal against us?"

"I cannot pin point the exact reason for that Mom. But you know, he treats the players like his servants. Whenever there are election rallies, he calls all the cricketers to be present to add to the crowd and please the politicians, so that he can ask for favours from them in return. That I could never make up my mind to accept any such invitation, might have added to his hatred towards me."

"Did other players succumb to such untoward demands?"

Kamlesh felt indignation stirring inside her.

"Most of them yes, because they were scared that if they don't, then he wouldn't help them get selected."

"But why is he so... important?"

"You mean Topal?"

"Yeah."

"He is important because he is the selector from Gurgaon. As per the board's policy, the selector from each district recommends his players for selections in the meetings for the state team. So, in case the selector from the district chooses to ignore a certain player, then it is likely that the player's name would not even come up for selection."

"And Topal takes advantage of this."

"Exactly."

Just then, the doorbell rang. It was Kanwar. The overflowing curiosity in his son's eyes along with the hint of desperation didn't go unnoticed. He freshened up and joined Kamlesh and Jeet at the dining table. Paddy lay sleeping in his room.

"So when is the trial?" Kanwar came straight to the point.

"It's on Sunday, Dad. Didn't I mention it in the letter?"

"Sure you did. I wanted to ensure there are no last-minute changes to the date. Does the venue remain unchanged too?"

"Yes Dad, Bhiwani it is."

"I met the Chairman of the selectors Mr Raj Kumar Gupta through a common friend. He said two things. First, that it if the trails are at Bhiwani, Raghubeer Singh, the president of the association, will be at the trials. In this case, the other selectors will be redundant. Second, Raghubeer Singh doesn't usually encourage recommendations of any kind, but if someone very close approaches him, then things can move but that too, if the recommended player is really good."

"Where does this situation leave us, Dad?"

"Raghubeer Singh has a friend named Vishwapal. He is a friend of mine too. I spoke to him and he said we need not worry, he would take care of the issue."

"Do you really believe he will be able to help us, Dad?"

"You can just go ahead with your preparations. Leave these things to me. I will ensure that Vishwapal has a word with Raghubeer Singh."

Jeet reached Bhim Singh Stadium, the trials venue sharp at 8.30 a.m. on the D-day. Kanwar had left for Karnal the previous day itself to meet Vishwapal and ensure everything was in place.

The stadium was crowded with cricketers from all over the state. Jeet met Pankaj and Mansoor, his fellow cricketers from Gurgaon, who had also come to attend the trials.

The trials were yet to start. Jeet saw someone bowling in the nets. The man was dark, in his mid-forties and definitely above six feet tall. Jeet could see fairly thick grey hair peeping through his centre parting. There was something unique about his persona. All the selectors stood around him, at times even fetching balls for him.

"Is he...?" Jeet's mind was at work.

"He is Raghubeer Singh." said Pankaj.

"Are you sure?" Jeet asked.

"Of course, don't forget my Mamaji stays in Bhiwani," he said with a cheeky smile.

"Raghubeer Singh has been a student of his Mamaji," elaborated Mansoor.

"Student! Do you mean Pankaj's Mamaji was a teacher?"

"He was the director of physical education in the same college where Raghubeer Singh studied," completed Pankaj.

Uncertainty gripped Jeet's heart again. He tried to weigh his own chances – was Vishwapal the right man? Had he conveyed to Raghubeer Singh? What if he forgot? What if Raghubeer Singh didn't pay heed to Vishwapal?

"Let me focus on my batting," Jeet pushed his intruding thoughts away.

The players started filling their forms. Everyone was nervous about the selection. Arun Singla was the only player assured of his place. The seventeen-year-old left arm spinner from Chandigarh had done well to earn himself a place in the Ranji Eleven the previous year. The remaining fourteen slots were wide open.

In the presence of Raghubeer Singh, the job of the selectors was restricted to the collection of forms and segregation of players into various categories like opening batsman, spin bowlers, and so on. Singla, being the senior most, was asked by the chairman of the selection committee, Mr Raj Kumar Gupta, to assist him to distribute the forms to the players and collect them. It turned out to be a bad call for Singla as Raghubeer Singh took this as an act of indiscipline, unaware that it was Raj Kumar Gupta who had asked Singla to assist him.

"Singla, come here!" Raghubeer Singh's voice reverberated.

"Yes... sir."

"Are you a player or a selector?"

"A player, sir."

"Do you think you are a big player or something?"

"No... sir," Singla struggled.

"Get out of the stadium, you won't be considered for the trials," a sheet of silence got spread all over.

Gupta mutely watched as Singla picked up his kit bag and, hoping against hope, looked one last time at Gupta. The eyes begged loudly for intervention. Gupta shifted his glance and looked the other way.

"Don't you think Gupta should have defended him?" Mansoor asked Pankaj after Singla had left the field.

Fearing the thin air would carry his words in the direction of Raghubeer Singh, Pankaj chose to ignore Mansoor's question.

The episode triggered a wave of fear amongst the players. From then on, everyone went about his task in a very cautious manner.

During the trials, each player was to be given a certain amount of time to display his talent. The amount of time depended on the selectors. It could be as short as two minutes or could even stretch to several minutes. The trials started. There were five nets in all, two of them turf wickets and the remaining three were cemented ones. It wasn't long before Jeet and Pankaj had put on their gears and awaited their turn at the trial nets. Raghubeer called the shots, while the rest of the selectors including Topal, Gupta and Sushil Kant stood and watched as mere spectators. Only Sarkar Singh, the selector from Faridabad seemed to hold his own. Raghubeer Singh was meticulous in his actions. He monitored all five nets in tandem.

All the openers including Jeet and Pankaj were asked to get ready and padded up. It was Pankaj's turn to go into the nets. In a mere two minutes, he was asked to come out. His performance at best could be termed as average. He was beaten a couple of times against both pace and spin. Jeet was the next.

"Leg stump," Jeet requested for the guard after walking into the cemented nets. There were five medium pacers ready to hurl the brand new red cherry at him. Majumdar, who was from Gurgaon as well, was the quickest among them. Having played a couple of matches against him, Jeet knew what to expect. As for spinners, there were three of them. As Majumdar stood at the top of his run-up to hurl his first missile at him, Jeet planned his strategy. He decided to use his feet against the spinners and play the quick bowlers on merit.

"Right arm over," declared Majumdar as he rushed in to bowl.

The ball had no real pace and pitched just right for Jeet to extend his front foot and drive it towards the mid-on. On meeting with the sweetest part of the bat, the ball whizzed through and travelled in the direction of Raghubeer Singh and missed him by a mere whisker. Reminding himself of the Singla incident, Jeet decided not to hit in the direction of Raghubeer. That hitting the first ball in the direction of Raghubeer Singh was the best stroke of luck he could have had, was something that Jeet was to realize only after the trials.

"Good shot," whispered the wicketkeeper from behind.

"What's your name?" the authoritative voice belonged to none other than Raghubeer Singh himself.

"Jeet...sir," said Jeet, careful with the tone. Raghubeer watched Jeet for a couple of minutes. Jeet played as if he could not go wrong. The extended practice sessions at Rai were bearing fruits.

"Stop!" Raghubeer Singh halted the bowlers in their run-ups. He ordered for new balls. The spinners were rested and five of the quickest bowlers from all the nets were called in to bowl. Jeet was now the centre of everyone's attention. He was asked to resume batting against the fresh bowlers.

"Play," Raghubeer gave the go-ahead.

"Right arm over," declared Rajesh showing Jeet the red cherry. Raghubeer Singh stood crouched at the vantage point, exactly where the umpire stands during a match. The moment the ball was released from Rajesh's hand, Jeet sensed that it was a long-hop. His right foot went back in quick reflex and the ball was sent racing.

"Power shot!" This time the wicket keeper almost let out a shout. Jeet continued in the same fashion comfortably. Raghubeer Singh watched his batting minutely, as if through the magnifying glass. He seemed to enjoy.

"Stop," the high bass voice reverberated again. "Jeet!"

"Yes sir."

"Get to the extreme right turf net."

"Yes sir."

"New balls please." Topal came running in with the new balls.

Jeet had walked into the turf nets.

Standing perpendicular to the nets, Pankaj and Mansoor were not the only ones surprised and envious with the developments.

"What's going on Pankaj? Jeet is getting extended sessions to bat."

"I am as much in dark as any other. I believe it's the first shot that pulled Raghubeer's attention towards Jeet. Moreover, you cannot close your eyes to the fact that Jeet is batting like a dream."

"Agreed, but what's the point in making him bat against every bowler and in every net? I am sure someone has recommended Jeet's name to him."

"Then you don't know Raghubeer Singh," Pankaj smiled. "Recommended players are the first ones to be scratched off his list."

"What about your Mamaji? Did he not recommend your name to him?"

"Mamaji knows this fact like the back of his hand. Therefore, he has very subtly informed Raghubeer that I am his nephew. He has never requested him to select me."

"So you attribute merit to be the cause of Raghubeer's current obsession with Jeet's batting."

"Absolutely."

In the nets, Jeet continued to bat in the same elegant and powerful way. Also, he continued to thank Vishwapal, his guardian angel for the moment.

The amount of respect I am getting from Raghubeer Singh is phenomenal. Other batsmen got around two or three minutes in the nets and here I am, batting for such a long duration. I'm enjoying the personal attention of the man himself! he thought. Raghubeer Singh at last shouted, "Thank you," signalling the end of Jeet's trials.

"Well played," said Pankaj as Jeet took out his gear and stood next to him.

"Raghubeer Singh was really impressed," Mansoor complimented Jeet, "and rightly so. I mean he tested you under all conditions that he possibly could and you came out a winner."

"Thank you, Mansoor." Jeet replied with a smile. *If only they knew that the real compliment should go to Vishwapal,* he thought.

As expected, Jeet's name was second on the list. Jeet was happy that he had been selected, but he was more pleased with the fact that he had shown his talent and resilience at the trials. Singla was elated and relieved at the same time to find his name in the list.

"Sir, I apologize once again," Singla addressed Raghubeer as Gupta stood alongside him, "and I thank you for selecting me while ignoring my faults." Raghubeer Singh nodded his head in affirmation. Gupta looked down towards his shoes and said nothing.

"Mom, I have been selected!" Jeet shouted with joy as he entered the house. Kanwar and Kamlesh came rushing outside, and

Jeet hugged his mother. After telling them all that had happened during the trial in great detail, Jeet waited for dinner to be served before he discussed Vishwapal Uncle.

"Dad I want to personally thank Vishwapal Uncle."

"Sure!"

"Dad you had to see it to believe it. The amount of respect I got because of him!"

"Yeah, I can see it in your eyes, son!"

"Dad, let's go and thank him as soon as possible."

"But why do you bother? I will do it on my own. I mean kids should keep themselves out of such things."

"I do understand your concern, Dad, but I still want to accompany you. Please Dad"

"Ok, whatever the champion says!"

"Dad, one more thing."

"Go ahead!"

"Gupta disappointed me both as a human being, as well as a cricketer."

"Why so?"

Jeet narrated the entire Singla episode in detail.

"It was Gupta who had assigned the form related task to Singla and not once did he come forward to claim that it wasn't Singla's fault."

"But that's how life is sometimes," it was Kamlesh. "Unfair... I mean."

"It was a scary situation to be in Mom! Thank God that Singla could come out of it. With friends and guardians like Gupta, there is hardly any need for enemies. Thank God I wasn't in Singla's place."

What Jeet did not know was that in a few days, he was to face a similar situation. He too was going to be unfairly accused of something he hadn't done. The question was how Jeet would come out of it.

The next day, Jeet and Kanwar went to Karnal, to Mr Vishwapal's government allotted residence to thank him.

"Sahib is coming in two minutes," said the domestic help as he served them coffee in the well-furnished drawing room. Jeet and Kanwar waited with the box of sweets they had purchased from Rewari sweets, Kanwar's favourite sweet shop in Gurgaon.

"Oye Kanwar, how are you yaar?" a voice reverberated as Jeet saw a bulky middle-aged man enter the drawing room.

"This is Jeet, my son," said Kanwar as he freed himself from Vishwapal's tight embrace.

"Uncle I... " Jeet started to say something.

"Yaar Kanwar, I want to apologize to you yaar," Jeet was interrupted.

"Apologize?"

"Yaar, I totally forgot one small thing that you had requested me."

"What are you talking about?"

"I mean I couldn't do what I had promised. Is he the one who was to face the trials?"

"Yes."

"Yaar, I just couldn't speak to Raghubeer Singh. It's only now, when I see you with your son, that I am reminded of my mistake."

Vishwapal approached a dumbstruck Jeet. "Beta, do not worry. Next year, we will surely get you selected."

Liar-Liar!

For the next couple of months, it was only cricket for Jeet. He attended camp as part of the under-17 team, and then there were the matches. Unfortunately, the Haryana team had lost in the very first knockout match and the tournament was over for them. Jeet scored forty-five runs in the match and his performance was far from the kind that could open the doors of the Ranji Trophy for him.

He had no option, but to pin his hopes on the under-19 tournament the following year. It was going to be a do or die situation for him: failure in that tournament would be tantamount to his dreams meeting with sudden death.

From Rohtak – where the tournament was held – Jeet headed straight to his school. It was past 2 a.m. when he entered the hostel premises. He was to play an important match in the school the next morning.

Jeet was just three hours into his well-deserved sleep when Bhatotia and Alok entered the hall. Rajbeer and Bhambha were already up. The rest of the students were out on routine morning drills. It was a match day, and the cricketers were exempted from drills.

"Hey, get up opener!" Bhatotia pulled his blanket, "Rise and shine!"

An irritated Jeet rubbed his eyes. It took him a good few minutes to realize he was in his tidy hostel room bed and not at the camp's stinking dormitory. But he needed more sleep and was reluctant to get up.

"Come on, skipper," he drawled and looked at Bhatotia through half-closed eyes. "What do you want? Don't you know I slept only after midnight?"

"My dear Sleeping Beauty, in case you have forgotten, the match with Rohtak starts at 9 a.m.," retorted Bhambha

"I know that, but it's just 5 a.m. for God's sake!"

"Don't worry; we just came for this mandatory form. You know, it's a school level official tournament so we have to get these forms filled up by every player. It has to be submitted before the match starts. Everyone has filled it, except you."

Jeet took the form, grabbed a pen from his almirah and filled it.

"Here you are," he handed it back to Bhatotia.

"Didn't I say it's a cake walk?" Bhatotia started to say, "Hey... but you didn't put your photograph."

"But I don't have a photograph."

"It's incomplete without the photograph. The other team will scrutinize our forms with magnifying glasses. They will look for every opening to get the team disqualified. Their prowess in hitting their opponents below the belt is well known. No photograph means you can't make it to the team and you know we can't afford that. It's after all, not a friendly match but the Indian School's Trophy Tournament."

"He can get a photograph clicked," Bhambha suggested

"The shops don't open before ten and the match starts at nine. But what's the big deal? We can tell them we don't have the photograph and in case they insist, we can get it clicked during lunch," Jeet said.

"Jeet, you are saying all this because you don't know about them," Bhatotia seemed eager. "I assure you they won't allow you to join the eleven if you don't have a photograph. Don't forget the adjudicators will be there too and that makes it even more complicated.

"Arrey Nilesh looks exactly like him," Alok intervened. "Let's fix his photo. After all, they will check it at random. We can replace it by Jeet's photo later."

Nilesh was Jeet's classmate from Indira house. There were similarities as far as looks were concerned, but not to the extent that one's photograph could be placed on the other's form. The absence of a quick fix solution and the desperate situation, in a way coerced Jeet to agree to the bizarre suggestion. The fact that the forms were then to be sent for Y.P.'s signatures had not dawned on Jeet. He could feel a knot in his stomach as he fixed Nilesh's picture in the space provided on the top right corner of the form.

The match was on. Bhatotia won the toss and decided to bat. Jeet was tying his right leg guard when he saw Ramanand, Y.P.'s peon rushing towards Bhatotia and then talking to him in hushed, hurried tones. There was gloom writ all over Bhatotia's face as he listened to what Ramanand was saying.

"Y.P. has called for you," Bhatotia came to Jeet, while Ramanand stood at a distance.

"At this time? What for?"

"It's the photograph thing. We made a blunder."

"What do you mean? How did Y.P. come in the picture?"

"Don't know much. Ramanand says Y.P. has called you."

"But I have to go and bat."

"You don't worry about that. We will send Vinay. You can bat at number three or four when you come back."

"Is it that urgent?" he asked Ramanand.

"Principal Sahab said that you should meet him immediately. He looks very angry," Ramanand replied.

"Where is he?"

"He is waiting for you in his office."

Jeet took out his pads.

"Jeet, one second," Bhatotia called him as he started to leave.

"What?" Jeet's heart was in his mouth.

"Please tell him it was by mistake. Don't tell him about our early morning meeting and that I knew about the problem regarding the photograph, and was party to the suggestion."

Jeet nodded.

"You liar," the sound of the slap echoed in the entire administrative block. "You scoundrel, how dare you paste someone else's photo under your name? And you have the guts to send it to me for my signatures?" Y.P. rushed outside the administrative block. Jeet stood there, not knowing what to do. Eyes from all over the administrative block cut him in half. The earth and sky, both turned out equally unkind to not have swallowed him up.

For Jeet, it was the longest day at Rai. After contemplating and negotiating with unprecedented mental agony, he decided to tell the complete story to the principal. He didn't care what Bhatotia or other people thought about it. He would tell the principal that he was ready to be punished, but punished for an act of stupidity and not for being a liar. To lie – that too to his God – was never an option.

"Yes, what is it?" the question from Y.P. was terse. Jeet had gone directly to his office after the morning assembly, the next day.

"Sir, I... I... wanted to say something."

"Regarding what?"

"Regarding yesterday's incident."

"What is there to tell? You pasted someone else's photo, did you not?"

"Yes sir, but it was an important match and I didn't have a photograph."

"So you would paste someone else's photo?"

"No sir, actually Bhatotia suggested this."

"Did Bhatotia also tell you to tell me you were alone in the library, when in fact you were with Roshni?"

"Sir?"

"Yes yes tell me, shall I refresh your memory about what you had exactly said?"

"Sir..."

"What sir... were you with Roshni or not?"

"Sir... I..." the words didn't come out of his mouth.

"Speak up, I am waiting... tell me I am wrong... for a change I am eager to learn that I am wrong. Let me tell you that there's nothing as insipid to me as a lie and that too, from a cricketer. So for God's sake, prove to me you were alone that day and you would do me a favour. Can you prove that?"

"No sir. I wasn't alone..."

"Please close the door while going out."

A week had passed since Jeet had sluggishly walked out of Y.P.'s room that day. It wasn't, however, the old Jeet anymore. The vibrant and effervescent Jeet was gone and in his place was someone embraced by gloom and deserted by hope.

The changes in Jeet did not go unnoticed by Roshni. She could sense his lack of interest in everything, even in his game. After several failed attempts at asking him to tell her what actually had gone wrong, she managed to get the facts out of Jeet one day. He told her about the photograph episode and the resulting ire of the principal. He, however, was cautious to not let her get the whiff of the incident involving her, regarding the evening when he had unfortunately and accidently bumped into Y.P. after he had seen her off at the hostel. Roshni wanted her old Jeet back, but how? She had no idea. The fact that Jeet revered Y.P. was hardly hidden. She knew if Y.P. forgave Jeet, her old Jeet would come back to her.

She grappled with similar thoughts as she headed out of the mess after lunch. It was the sixth continuous day that Jeet hadn't met her. When she reached the hostel, she saw the notice board outside and her eyes sparkled. She turned back.

"Where are you going?"

Neelam called her.

"Nowhere."

"But what would I tell Mrs Datta if she asks?"

"Tell her I have gone to the principal's house."

The Inter-House Music Competition

"Good evening madam!"

It was Ms Mondira Bhardwaj, Y.P.'s wife who answered the doorbell. Ms Mondira was music in-charge of the house that Jeet and Roshni belonged to: Surya House. She also taught English to the kids of classes VII and VIII.

"Good evening Roshni, come on inside. Good that you came, I was about to call you in any case."

"Anything specific ma'am?" She entered.

"Arrey, the inter-house music dates have been announced. The committee has finalized your name for anchoring the show."

"Yeah, it's for the same that I have come to you."

"But who told you about your name getting finalized? The meeting has just ended."

"No ma'am, I didn't know about my role as an anchor. Actually I..."

"Yeah tell me, why do you stammer?"

"I wanted to meet you regarding the representations from our house."

"I didn't get you."

"Actually... ma'am... can I have some water please?"

"Oh how stupid of me to have kept you standing. Of course! First you sit down." She held her by the hand and led her to the drawing room. Ramu, the domestic help, served them water.

"Madam, last year we couldn't win the inter-house trophy," Roshni kept the empty glass on the side table. Both of them sat facing each other on the sofa.

"Why only last year, we lost the year before that too, because we don't have a decent male singer in our house."

"This is the very reason why I came to see you. I came to know about the competition from the notice board outside the hostel."

"I don't believe there is a dearth of talent in our house, Roshni. All said and done, this time I do not want to lose this inter-house trophy. I am not worried about the solo and instrumental part. We are alright there. It's the duet that gives me the jitters. Even if we score well in the other sections of the competition, the duet can bring us down. Sangeeta as a female singer is just fine. What we lack is a boy who can match her."

"Actually ma'am, there is a singer."

"There is a singer...and you are telling this to me me now, after so long, when all the rehearsals are almost done!"

"Ma'am please listen to me."

"No, you listen to me Roshni. Tell me who is he?"

"Jeet Singh."

"Jeet Singh? The cricketer?"

"Yes ma'am!"

"Does he sing?"

"Yes ma'am. In fact, he sings very well."

"In that case, why didn't you tell me about it? And why was he not asked to participate?"

"Actually ma'am, he wants to concentrate on cricket, so he sort of avoids other things."

"He thinks taking part in a competition once in a year is going to affect his game...strange!"

"Ma'am, he avoids music competitions because of the rehearsals. He knows that if he takes part in the competition, then he has to take part in the rehearsals too."

"In that case, what makes you think he will be ready to take part in it now?"

Roshni hesitated at first, but then told her about the developments between Y.P. and Jeet and how much Jeet revered Y.P. She tried her best to make Jeet's good qualities known to Mondira.

"That issue has affected his game too."

"Yash hates lies like anything, and even more if it comes from a cricketer. But how is the music competition related to this issue of his?"

Mondira was curious as to why Roshni was going to such pains in helping the cricketer. *What does she stand to gain out of it? Maybe I will embarrass her by asking directly. Let things unfold on their own,* she decided.

"There is a faint hope that things will turn out better for him."

"But how?"

"Music is your soul ma'am, isn't it?"

"Sure it is."

"I don't know much, but I have heard if one is a liar, he or she cannot be gifted with music."

"Ha ha...well you have touched such a sensitive topic. Will you have coffee?"

"Sure ma'am, I mean if you so wish," she pushed herself back into the sofa, sat more comfortably and was more re-assured. *So far so good,* she thought.

Coffee was ordered.

"You know Roshni, I will answer your queries in one single sentence and that is, only the ones with souls can claim to be close to music. Cheap, cunning people cannot find themselves equal to it."

"Exactly ma'am," Roshni replied with a hint of excitement in her voice, "so when you practice with Jeet, you would be able to understand whether he is a liar or not. Maybe then you would want to have a word with sir and get the matter resolved. I mean, it is a humble request, ma'am!"

Coffee was served.

"Hmm, you are very bright, I must say," Mondira smiled broadly. "But what does Jeet say about whether he actually lied or not?"

"Ma'am he says he can be accused of being stupid, but he is not a liar."

"Sounds interesting," she smiled, "do you know what exactly the issue was?"

Roshni narrated the whole incident regarding the photograph for the form. Mondira listened to each word patiently. She thought hard before she allowed the first word to escape from her mouth.

"Roshni, you send him to me. I do not promise anything. Let me see how it goes."

"Sure ma'am, when can I send him in?

"Send him today evening at 5 p.m. sharp."

"Yes ma'am, I will inform him."

"And in this madness, don't forget to prepare for your part. You are our anchor, remember that?"

"Sure ma'am. I shall take your leave now."

Mondira accompanied her to the door.

It was two minutes to 5 p.m. when Roshni returned. Ms Mondira opened the door and saw Jeet almost hiding behind Roshni.

"Let's sit in the music room."

All three were seated on neat white sheets in the aesthetically done music room. The domestic help served them water. Mondira sat with her harmonium and asked Jeet to sit on the opposite side facing her.

"So Jeet, you joined us in class XI?"

"Yes ma'am!"

"Did you learn music in your previous school?"

"No ma'am, I did not."

"And do you attend Mrs Soni's music classes?"

"No ma'am, actually I didn't get a chance to."

"But you do know something about music, don't you?"

"Beg your pardon ma'am?"

"Roshni says you are a singer. So one could expect you to know a thing or two about music?"

Jeet wasn't ready for this question. He shifted uncomfortably and looked at Roshni.

"Ok, tell me, which is your favourite song?" Mondira had been a teacher long enough to recognize unease in a student.

"Ma'am, I usually like Kishore Kumar's songs."

"Ok sing for us."

"Any particular song ma'am?"

"Sing whatever you like."

"Hmm..."

Ms Mandira noticed that Jeet was constantly looking at the inner door. She pondered a little and smiled. *He thinks Yash is at home and is therefore unsure of himself.* Once she diagnosed his problem, she set to work upon the remedy.

"Ramu, what did sahab say before going?" she called to the domestic help.

"He said he would return by eight in the evening."

Now the ice was broken.

Jeet started to sing. Mondira instantly liked his voice. He sang a few more songs while she played the harmonium.

"The trophy is ours, Roshni, I believe we are far ahead of the competition," she concluded.

"Ma'am...I was saying...!"

Mondira understood that Roshni wanted to speak to her in private.

"Alright Jeet, you may leave for your cricket practice now. I will let you know about the rehearsal schedules."

"Right ma'am."

She looked at Roshni as Jeet rushed out.

"Ma'am I had requested for a favour!"

"Yes I will do it Roshni, but on one condition," she had a smile on her face.

"What's that ma'am?"

"He should win the trophy for me."

"Surely he will, ma'am... he will..."

"Ask Jeet to be regular with rehearsals, leave the rest to me. Both Sangeeta and he need to practice together. He shouldn't forget that it is a duet and it takes two to tango. It is the camaraderie between the two that will matter, rather than any individual."

It was the day of the competition. The auditorium was packed. The teachers occupied the front rows and the principal was seated right at the centre of the very first row. To his left was seated the short and stocky vice principal. There was a special vantage point earmarked for the judges. All four of them had come from different schools and colleges in Delhi. The participants were all in the respective green rooms adjacent to the stage on each side.

Roshni, the anchor looked stunning in the pink sari and impeccable white blouse. The contrast accentuated her already radiant skin. She looked taller than she was and her lithe frame with dusky and sharp features appeared sharper. Her movement to and from the stage carried the potential to stop heartbeats. She was the unanimous choice of the selection committee for the same reason.

"Ladies and gentlemen," she started to speak, "I welcome you all to this wonderful evening of melody..."

Ironically, thought Jeet as he watched Roshni, *the one with the most silvery voice isn't singing this evening.* He continued to watch Roshni in admiration. His eyes, however, weren't the only ones watching her.

The evening went on to be an evening of melody. Jeet and his partner Sangeeta sang the duet well. It was time for the results to be announced. Roshni was to get the marks from the judges.

"We just have marks from the three of us." She was told by one of the judges, as she went to them to collect the marks that they had given.

"What about the fourth one?" she was puzzled.

She learnt that the fourth judge had to leave for an emergency and though he had awarded the marks, by mistake, he had carried the sheet away with him. Roshni knew that under the circumstances, the marks awarded by only the three judges would count for the results. She quickly looked at the one result that interested her most. Surya house had won the trophy in the overall tally, but Jeet had lost. He was in the second place with only one mark separating him from the duet sung by Indira house.

"What time did the gentleman leave?" She hurriedly asked.

"He left just a moment ago," she was told. She rushed out of the nearest exit and ran towards the parking. For once, she couldn't believe her eyes. The fourth judge was only ten yards away from her, trying to get into his car.

"Sir, by mistake you are carrying the sheet of marks with you," she said in a hurried tone.

"Oh you are the anchor, aren't you?"

"Yes sir."

"You mean the sheet isn't there?"

"No sir."

"Oh how stupid of me, let me just check," he rummaged his hand bag and the next moment he handed the sheet to Roshni.

"Have the results been announced?"

"No sir, not yet," Roshni's voice carried eagerness.

"How stupid of me again! Why would you come running for the sheet had they been announced already?"

Despite the urgency in circumstances, a smile got perched on Roshni's lips. She had opened the sheet and was in the process of scanning it for the marks that mattered most. Her eyes lit up; she had found exactly what she was looking for.

"Where had you been, everyone was looking for you," Mondira scolded her.

"Ma'am the fourth judge had left, taking the sheet along. I mean, he hadn't submitted his sheet."

"Yes he had informed me that there was an emergency. But so what? We could have considered the marks given by three judges only."

"But he hadn't gone far... so I thought, why not try and access it too?"

"Ok, did you get the sheet then?"

"Yes ma'am."

"Tell me the results, fast. Have you tallied the marks?"

"Yes ma'am, we have won the trophy and Jeet has won too!"

"Great rush it then, go announce the results!"

"Ma'am I... was asking about Jeet. Now that he has won..."

"Arrey don't worry. I have done the homework. You just wait and see. I was kidding the other day when I laid down the condition of him winning. It was a non-matter. I was determined to resolve it otherwise too, but good that he has won. It will give him some added confidence."

Roshni smiled from ear to ear. She turned to go.

"Roshni..." Mondira called as if she remembered something that needed to be tallied.

"Yes, ma'am!"

"Did we win the trophy with the three judges too? I mean, in case we were not to count the marks by the fourth judge."

"Yes, ma'am."

"And was Jeet winning... with three judges I mean?"

"Ma'am actually I... it was..."

"Ok, ok don't answer," she had a teasing smile on her face. "Rush to the stage and announce the results."

The results were announced. The victory of the Surya house was received with much fanfare by the students. The trophy and the prizes were distributed by Y.P. Roshni requested him to speak a few words of encouragement.

"It was a wonderful evening," Y.P. started while Roshni stood by his side. "Far away from the monotony of everyday life. All I would like to say is that only a voice of truth can create the sound of music. I congratulate all the winners and all those who have taken part too. I have a special word of praise for Jeet. Despite the demands of his game, he not only participated, but won too! To be honest, I was surprised to see this fresh lease of talent in him. Thank you everyone. Good night!"

Roshni and Mondira looked at each other and smiled. While one smiled in accomplishment, the other smiled in gratitude. Jeet stood quiet, too numb to realize what was happening.

The Last Rendezvous Before School

The issues with Y.P. settled, Jeet moved ahead with renewed vigour. His target now was to perform in the under-19 tournament, which would open the doors to Ranji trophy for him. A good performance in Ranji trophy meant the honour to represent India, which was his ultimate ambition. *Once I get into the Indian side, paying Ram Sharan's money and getting the house back isn't going to be a big deal,* he constantly thought. The road, however, was tough and he knew it.

The two years had ended sooner than anticipated. Jeet had appeared for his class XII board exams and was to soon leave school.

After lunch, Jeet was headed towards the library to meet Roshni. *In our last meeting, we will chart the path for our future and I will also share a secret with you,* Roshni had said while scheduling the library as their last rendezvous. It was the penultimate day for Jeet. He was to leave the next morning.

"Here you are! Hidden from the world while I search for you all over!?" Jeet manifested mock anger as he took the seat opposite her. Dressed in her sports outfit, she looked at him teasingly with all the impish naughtiness that her eyes could gather.

"But why are we seated here? At this hidden place?" Jeet asked.

"In your question lies the answer," she kept the book on the table.

"What does this mean?"

"This means you are a tubelight," she chirped. "We sit here today because we are talking at length, about our future, about getting married and so on. As you are leaving the school for good, we must have a plan in place and there is something else, something really special that I need to tell you."

"A secret, that's what you said!"

"Yes a secret it is, till it is revealed to you!"

"Don't murder me with your suspense. Tell me what it is."

"It is a riddle actually. In a way, it will be a final confirmation, sort of a litmus test, that we indeed are soul mates. The clue for the riddle lies in today's evening movie."

"And what is the riddle?"

"The riddle is that I have written a note in a book in the library, the clue for which, as I said, is hidden in the evening's movie. But don't sleep during the movie today, else you would miss the clue."

"I have not clearly understood it."

"It is so simple my dear tubelight, that if you are able to see today's movie without falling asleep, and therefore are able to get the clue, it will be an endorsement that we are soul mates. So you have to win today. Please do not fail me and do not fail yourself. But that comes later in the evening. First let us deal with this," she rummaged a hand under the table to bring out a packet.

"What's this?" Jeet stared at the brown wrapper.

"For you."

"For me! But what is it?"

"Sandwiches."

"*Sandwiches*?" he almost shrieked and realized the next moment that he was in the library. "Sandwiches? But you know, we aren't supposed to eat in the library... ohhhhh... this is why you needed privacy?"

"Yes, my tubelight, but the main reason is that we would be talking in detail about you and me and..."

"And...?"

"And about me and you," she giggled as she opened the hot case and offered it to him. As always, the sound of her laughter touched a chord somewhere deep in Jeet's heart.

"Where did you get them from? Ohh, you made them yourself...!" Jeet munched on the first one.

"Yes, tubelight!" She laughed again and then all of a sudden turned quiet. Her eyes, however, were anything but silent. They expressed so much more than Jeet could figure out. The subtleties of the silent language, however, made Jeet a little uncomfortable. He shifted his gaze away from her.

"But tell me, why did you come so late?"

"Come on, you know I am not an expert at packing my stuff," he took another bite from the sandwich.

"Hmm," she smiled all naughty-naughty again. "You could have called me for help!"

"Called you for help? Sounds enticing, but a girl's presence in a boys' hostel, well, can't be further from reality. You would have got me rusticated."

"Come on, don't be silly! You have appeared for your board exams. You are leaving school in any case. You cannot be rusticated. This Y.P. effect isn't going to leave you, I know that. His commands are likely to be instrumental in driving your life forever." However, the comment was meant to lack seriousness, but Roshni wasn't aware that the truthfulness of the comment was to dawn on her in a few minutes' time.

Jeet sat with a blank face, not knowing how to respond to Roshni's wit.

"Oh, ok let it be," said Roshni. "Arrey what happened to the aquarium you were planning to gift to the school?"

"I never planned to gift anything ma'am!"

"By you, I mean the school leaving class, dear tubelight!"

"So, you haven't seen it as yet?" It was his turn to tease her a bit.

"Of course not."

"Then it's you who is the tubelight, not me!"

"Oh my, I didn't know the tubelight comment had hit you that badly. Ok, if it makes you happy, I agree to be the tubelight in this conversation. But then at least it's me who is exuding radiance here, making things glow in my own light, and not in a borrowed one."

"Borrowed? Who is the borrower here?"

"Who else but...you, borrowing light and radiance from me, just as moon borrows from the sun."

"You are the sun, you mean?"

"Of course!"

"Then why don't you locate the aquarium yourself? The sun, after all can see everywhere."

"No, I can't locate that."

"Why not?"

"Because it must be placed in shade. The sun can only locate outdoor objects."

"You and your stupid reasoning!" Jeet picked a magazine from the nearby section and rolled it to hit Roshni. They laughed loudly, the echo reverberating in the library. Several pairs of eyes stared at them.

"Tell me please, I really want to see it," Roshni pleaded.

"Well, it's placed at a distance of not more than twenty metres from you."

"Ohh! You mean you got it placed in the library itself?"

"Could you have suggested a better place?"

"I think not. Where is it exactly? Come on, don't play Sherlock Holmes with me!"

"Just look towards your right."

"Right, where?"

"Right means right, shall I now explain to you the directions too?"

Jeet held her face in his hands and tilted it towards the right.

"Ohh my! How did I miss it?"

Roshni moved towards the large aquarium. Red, blue, green, multicoloured – fish of almost all colours swam and glided in the crystal clear water.

"Oh myyyyy, it's beautiful!" she gently ran her hands against its glass walls. "Look at the fish Jeet! They are simply amazing."

"Yes they are beautiful!"

"Ok tell me, if I had been a fish, which one would I be?"

"I think this blue one."

"No, I would be this red one. This one is the most vibrant and..."

"And the one who can jump six feet into the air to smash the ball right in the opponents' face...?" Jeet jumped in.

"Ha ha, no... fish do not play volleyball stupid!"

"Then tell me, what is it that they play?"

"Look at the way she swerves around in the most carefree manner possible... as if..." she continued to admire the red fish.

"As if?"

"As if... she is dancing in love."

"Just like you?"

"Just like meeee!" She put her hand around Jeet's waist and performed a subtle twist.

"Library, ma'am, library. Control yourself!"

Jeet could see some students looking at them through the corners of their eyes. *But this is my last day in school,* he tried to brush aside all concerns.

"Ok, tell me," Jeet asked Roshni.

"What?" asked Roshni.

"There must be some 'he fish' too."

"Ha ha! Of course there are... my naïve love!"

"So if you are the red one, which one of these would be me?"

"Hmm," Roshni started to think, "good question."

"Maybe the black one?" Jeet suggested.

"No, not that one."

"Then... Maybe the grey one!"

"No, not even that."

"Then?"

"Actually you aren't any of these."

"Then who am I?"

"Not 'who am I', but, 'what am I' would be the correct question."

"Ohhk baba, what am I?"

"You are the water."

"Water!"

"Yes, water – the very substance that supplies life to the red fish, because of which the red fish is alive, which makes her dance without care, without which the red fish would die," suddenly her naughtiness had disappeared from her eyes once again, and what remained was unpolluted emotions of pure and simple love.

"Jeet!" someone called from behind.

It was Ramesh, the assistant librarian. "Yeah," Jeet looked in his direction. "The principal wishes to see you in his office," the assistant librarian said.

"The principal? Who told you?"

"The principal himself."

"Was he here?"

"Yes, he was doing the rounds."

"Did he see us?"

"Yes, he came to me and pointed his finger in your direction and asked me to tell you to meet him in his office."

"But how could he see us. The seat where we sat is hidden in a sense."

"I have no idea, he is the Principal after all, you know," he smiled.

"Yes, of course he is-What were we doing when he saw us?"

"How would I know?" Ramesh responded.

"Oh my God!" Jeet looked at Roshni

"Oh my God what?" Roshni jumped in. "Come on Jeet! You are no longer his student and he is no longer your principal."

"That's fine, but I can't ignore him."

"I am not asking you to ignore him. All I am saying is, stop getting so scared of him. Get his ghost out of your mind, for God's sake," she almost shouted in desperation.

"Ok, thanks I will go and see him," Jeet said to the assistant librarian in hinting to him to leave them alone. Then turning towards Roshni he said, "at least you should have waited till the time the librarian had left."

"Sorry," Roshni held her ears in an attempt to lighten the situation, "now go and come back soon. I have to tell you something important. Remember I told you... my little secret?"

"What is it? Tell me now."

"Don't be impatient. Come back soon, I am waiting for you."

Jeet rushed outside.

≈

"Sit down," Y.P. said without looking up, his face buried in a file.

Jeet sat down.

"So," Y.P. took off his spectacles.

"Sir," Jeet looked everywhere but in the principal's eyes. The deep reverence for Y.P. hadn't diluted one bit.

"Set for the challenges ahead?" he smiled.

"Sort of...sir!"

"You must be wondering why I have called you!"

"No sir, not really!"

"What are your plans, Jeet? Now that you will be out of school, you must have thought of something for yourself."

"There are certain dreams, sir, and certain responsibilities."

Jeet told him everything, about his dream of representing India and getting the house back. He talked about Munna too.

"You know Jeet," Y.P. stood up and started strolling around the room. He had attentively heard each and every word that Jeet had said. "When the young ones get out of the safety of their home for the first time, the guardian is worried because the young one is weak, frail, and most of all, knows nothing about the outside world. In case the young one has almost impossible dreams like you have, the guardian's worries are justified even more as there are chances that the little one might become the food of the hawks that venture in the world. Tomorrow, when you step out of the safe surroundings of this school, you will step out with all your frailties and gullibility. You know little about the cunningness of this world. As a principal, as a guardian, and most of all as a teacher, it becomes my duty to place before you not only a likely scenario that you may face outside, but also equip you with the relevant tools for the same. It might not be a panacea for ills of all kinds, but it could definitely be a formidable weapon to deal with the inconsistencies of this cruel world."

"Sure sir, that is really kind of you."

"Don't be in a hurry Jeet, let the feelings of gratitude wait a little bit. Who knows when this conversation is over, you might find me to be the first person making an unreasonable and unjustified demand.

"I am sure your stay here, though only for a short period of two years, has been anything but inconsequential. You have seen quite a few crests and troughs in this short span of time. You know, I have put in more than a little effort to know you, in a way to study you Jeet, especially after the photograph episode. And whatever I could gather after having visited even the tiniest nuances that your mind presented, and also adding to it what my wife Mondira had to say about you, I would say I was not wrong in my decision to admit you in this institute."

Y.P. stopped to breathe.

"Why do we study, Jeet?" He continued while Jeet listened in rapt attention. "Or let me put it this way, for you: what is the meaning of education? How will you define it?"

"To learn is education, sir."

"Learn about what?" asked Y.P. gesturing animatedly with his hands.

"Anything sir!"

"What is anything? Be specific Jeet! If by learning, you mean knowledge, then in my opinion, that can be gained by reading books and through other sources. Where then, does the school come into the picture?"

"Sir... I... sir..."

"I would say Jeet, we come to school to gain wisdom through our teachers. But then you may ask what exactly wisdom is. You know, the great author Bertrand Russell has put it very appropriately. Do you know what he said?"

"I am eager to know, sir."

"He said freedom from fear is the beginning of education. So, this is lesson number one for you Jeet. Your first and one of the most crucial of all tools. Learn to be free from fear."

"Yes sir. Can you give me one example of what you mean by fear... I mean, I don't get it."

"Hmm. Why don't you give me an example? An example of a fearless person, just try to name a person from history. Just try Jeet, it's not a test, so don't bother to get it exactly right."

"Hitler, sir?" Jeet uttered the first name came to his mind.

"Haha Hitler, well, you know what, when Hitler was about to be captured by his enemies, he committed suicide. If there ever was proof of an act of cowardice, it was this. So yes, Hitler was a tyrant for sure, but fearless? Never – because cruelty isn't lack of fear, it's lack of courage. It's the most glaring example of cowardice. If I say be fearless like Mahatma Gandhi, Jeet?"

"Mahatma Gandhi, sir?"

"Yes son, like Mahtma Gandhi. You must be thinking that the person who has always been criticized for being soft, for his policies like offering the other cheek; and here we are equating Gandhiji with words like courage, fortitude and fearlessness."

"Yes sir, it's something like that."

"Something like that! Ha ha! I love the way you respond Jeet. But coming back to the topic, I would say it's not your fault. Many people, irrespective of the generation they belong to, have misunderstood Gandhiji. For example, let me come to the 'offer the other cheek' part. Its meaning in real terms is that one is most welcome to hit the other cheek as well. It means Gandhi ji refused to succumb to the violent measures and hitting back was just not an option. In short, I can describe it like this. Gandhi ji said, 'You may hit me and you may hit me again, but I would continue to do what I want to, without hitting you back.' People mistake him for a coward. Do you know what his views about cowardice are?"

"What sir?"

"In his article 'The Doctrine of the Sword,' Gandhi ji wrote, 'I do believe that where there is only a choice between cowardice and violence, I would advise violence'."

"Did Gandhiji say that?"

"Yes, in exact words, and to bring my point home I would quote him from the same article in which he wrote, 'But I believe that non-violence is infinitely superior to violence, forgiveness is manlier than punishment.' Do you get it now Jeet?"

"Got it sir, got it loud and clear."

"So you learn two things. The first is to be fearless so that you do not shy away from taking even the toughest of steps towards achieving your goals. Second, you should be forgiving because in your path towards achieving your dreams, you will meet people who will be unjust and unkind to you. Do not waste your time thinking about punishing them, because that will take your focus away from your goal. But remember, a weak person cannot talk about forgiveness. So be strong and then forgive. The Mahatma said, 'Strength does not follow from physical capacity, it follows from indomitable will. Forgiveness adorns a soldier. But abstinence is forgiveness only when there is the power to punish. It is meaningless when it pretends to proceed from a helpless creature. A mouse hardly forgives a cat when it allows itself to be torn to pieces by her.' And now the third lesson, Jeet. Like the Mahatma, you should possess a strong-willed mind. Do you know what a strong-willed mind is?"

"The mind that can achieve goals sir, even the impossible ones."

"No, those are the results you are talking about. Will power is all about the processes which leads to great results. Let me explain again by one example. Assuming that you plan to run five kilometres every morning, and one day you see it's raining and therefore confine yourself to the comforts of your bedroom. That is an example of a weak will power. Now tell me Jeet, what exactly do you mean by a person with a strong-willed mind?"

"One who can follow the schedules despite hardships?"

"Exactly; now we come to our last lesson. Chances are that you wouldn't like the lesson as much. In fact, I wouldn't be surprised if you hate me after that."

"What's that, sir?"

"When you play cricket, Jeet, do you play in the shade or in the sun?"

"Of course in the sun."

"What do the sun rays do to you?"

"In winters they seem soothing, while in summers they are a bit of discomfort, and may tan my skin."

"But they don't burn your skin, do they?"

"No sir."

"That's because the rays are scattered. When you concentrate those rays through a magnifying glass on a small piece of paper, what do you see?"

"I see that the paper burns."

"That is 'FOCUS' for you, Jeet. It is the difference between the winner and the loser."

"Yes sir, my mother too has endorsed the importance of 'focus' on more than a few occasions. In fact, for a moment it was as if my mother who was speaking in your place."

"And I repeat that the impossible dream that you have dared to dream would require unhindered, unadulterated focus in case you are to come anywhere near achieving it. Nobody should stand between you and your goals, not even Roshni."

"Roshni! What does she have to do with this, sir?"

"Everything Jeet! Your love towards her would dilute your focus towards your real goals. Your mind, Jeet! If it keeps oscillating between your love and your real goals; it would never be able to burn the paper."

"Are you suggesting something, sir?"

"Nothing, I am not suggesting anything. I am just telling you the scene as it appears from here, from my point of view that is. How you take it is entirely up to you. Don't forget that from now on, it's you who would be taking decisions. This can, of course, be your first tough one, to choose between love and the purpose of life. As for me, mind you I am not against love. In fact, a teacher shouldn't be the one to preach against something that he himself practices. I had married Mondira because I had fallen in love with her.

"Do you read the *Geeta*, Jeet?"

"No sir, but my Mom reads it regularly and quotes several times from it."

"Do you know about the Jayadrath episode?"

"I don't know much about Jayadrath sir, other than the fact that he was married to Duryodhana's sister."

"Yes, you are right. But Jayadrath's importance in the *Mahabharata* is far beyond that. He was instrumental in the killing of Arjun's son Abhimanyu during the chakravyuh episode. Arjun had then taken a pledge to kill him before sunset. However, had Lord Krishna not come to his rescue, Arjun would have failed.

"Can you tell me Jeet why did Arjun falter? What made the finest archer seek help from the Almighty in killing one single person?

"You tell me, sir."

"Because his focus had shifted; only one of his eyes was on his target: Jayadrath."

"Where was his other eye then?"

"On the sun; Arjun was anxious about the sun getting set, but the more he looked at the sun, the more nervous he became. Lord Krishna cautioned him several times, saying, 'Arjun, the sun isn't your target, Jayadrath is. The sun will set at the scheduled time. You can't do anything about it. Both your eyes should focus on Jayadrath.'

"Just one more thing before you go, Jeet."

"Sure sir."

"You know what Lord Krishna's weapon was?"

"The Sudarshan Chakra sir."

"And do you know who gave it to him?"

"No sir."

"Lord Krishna was given that weapon by Lord Parshuram; and do you know what he said before handing over that weapon to him?"

"What sir?"

"He said, 'Krishna, you have played enough flute for the cows and for the maidens alike, played enough games with your peers, now it's time to move forward towards your real purpose in life.' So Jeet, it's the real purpose that counts. Love can wait. Please be mindful of the fact that I am not asking you to discard love, just advising you to forget it for the time being. So Jeet, enough of venturing around, enough of holding hands in the library, enough of passing slips, now concentrate and focus on the real job at hand. The meeting is over Jeet- I wish you all the best."

Y.P. had again succeeded in creating turbulence in an otherwise peaceful scenario, he thought. Once more, the principal had managed to pierce the stillness and calm of Jeet's heart with sharp, pointed reasoning. But his arguments were hardly out of context. In fact, they were valid and justified. Jeet told himself, "He is not wrong in endorsing the importance of focus in achieving tough goals in life. Given the situation, love surely will have to take a backseat. Shall I ask her to wait? But then what about Roshni's dreams of becoming a doctor? Will her desperation in awaiting my return not take her mind away from her studies? And then he took his decision. But will Roshni understand?"

Oblivious to the developments and overflowing with the spirit of love and hope, Roshni waited for Jeet. She now regarded Jeet as an example of everything that was good or even great. The fact that he had allowed her, and no one else, to possess, to own him, brought a deluge of emotions to her mind. She was so grateful to him. He symbolized everything that was respectful, gracious and confidence-building. He was now, by far, her dearest object of affection.

Come quickly Jeet. I am dying to tell you the secret: that I no longer tear my poems. There is a lot I have to tell you. I will tell you that you are the one who has cured me. It's you who made me realize that the path to freedom from pain lay through the pain and not beside it. But there is another fear that has replaced it, Jeet. The fear that you may leave me. I know it's bizarre to think that way, as I know you are mine forever. I believe my insecurities have given birth to such fears and in due course, I will be relieved of them all.

Then she opened her hand bag she had brought and took out the small Sanyo tape recorder.

You will have to record songs for me Jeet, songs of love and hope. The songs that I will replay again and again till you come back to replace these songs with your love and take me away to your own world forever. Then I won't need any recorded songs Jeet.

~

"What happened?" Roshni could sense something had gone wrong. The person who had returned from the meeting wasn't Jeet.

"Tell me for God's sake, what happened?"

Jeet explained everything, very slowly, without a trace of emotion on his face.

"So...what now?" she asked when he finished.

"I don't know," he looked away, meekly.

"I don't know? Is that all you have to say Jeet? Tell me what have you decided... or wait... wait... listen... don't tell me. Shall I not know? Don't I know you enough Jeet?"

"I don't know what to say. But... we.... will have to forget our love."

"Forget love? For good?"

"For good."

"I knew Y.P. will spoil it someday."

"It's not Y.P.'s fault Roshni, and he never tried to spoil anything. In fact, he is not against love. He has merely asked me to wait."

"Then why are you running away? Listen Jeet, I can wait. You can take your time. As it is, we are not getting married tomorrow. Why should we call it quits? And moreover, I find this idea of choosing one thing out of the two really laughable. Tell me Jeet, do people become averse to success after they get married? I mean there are loads and loads of people who are successful and married, both at the same time!"

"Yes sure, none can deny that. But I have dared to dream an almost impossible dream. If to dream to get into in a team of eleven players out of hundred crores isn't an impossible dream, then I would like to know what is. To achieve something of this magnitude requires undiluted, razor-sharp focus. Everything else, including love has to take a backseat."

Jeet told her about the dream of getting back the house.

"You mean getting the house back is the first thing in the list of priorities?" Roshni tried hard to look for an opening of any kind to save her love.

"Both are my dreams and are interconnected. I achieve one and automatically I achieve the other too."

"But getting the house back is your priority, right?"

"Right, the house is ahead in the list of priorities because it's very dear to my Mom."

"That means if the house is freed tomorrow, the liability on your shoulders would be lessened considerably?"

Jeet soaked her words in.

"I know where you are headed, Roshni."

"What do you mean?"

"I know what your next question would be."

Roshni stared at Jeet, but said nothing. The silence- like the sweat on his palms- was sticky.

"You would ask me how much money is required for the house to be freed from the moneylender."

"Absolutely Jeet, I mean efforts can be made- is there any harm in it?"

"No harm actually- what is it that you have in mind?"

"Jeet, we...I mean my family has enough land. My dad is one of the most flourishing landlords in the entire district. Sure he lives away from us but he is my father and he can't say no to his doting daughter and that too on financial matters."

"How much land does your Dad possess, Roshni?"

"Don't take me wrong Jeet. My efforts are simply to find a solution, and if no solution exists, then to invent a solution if possible."

"I have no doubts in the sanctity of your efforts, Roshni. Your eagerness to solve the riddle is honest. Still, let me know how much land does your family possess?"

"We have around fifty acres, give or take."

"My Mama, my mother's real brother has nine hundred acres. In legal terms, half of those nine hundred acres belongs to my mother if she claims her right to it. And to be honest, it's not land but a goldmine- situated next to a perennial canal, its fertility should be seen to be believed. Probably the costliest agricultural land in the country and nine hundred acres of it! My Mama can give away all his land just like this," Jeet snapped his fingers, "for the happiness of his sister. But my Mom, she wouldn't have an inch of it.

"My Mom, Roshni, brought up eight of my Dad's siblings, got them educated and later got them married into respectable families; all on predominantly one asset: my father's salary. She never took a penny from my Mama. She, in her heart of hearts, believes that it's her older son who is going to give the house back to her, though she has never said it in exact words. She hasn't asked me for that. She is too proud to ask for anything, Roshni, even from her son. I had eavesdropped once and got to know about it. Now you tell me Roshni, shall I go and tell her that she shouldn't bank upon such dreams, now that her son has fallen in love? Shall I tell her that she has put her stakes on the wrong horse? That what she thinks is her biggest asset- is actually a soldier who has surrendered before even going to war?"

Tears flowed from Roshni's eyes incessantly; while the red fish in the aquarium continued to swerve carefree.

"Now when I think in hindsight, I believe," Jeet continued, "love isn't made for me Roshni, and I am not made for it. I apologize to you for having come this far. Might be that your innocence conspired with your beauty and the two together succeeded in pulling the wool over my eyes and I couldn't see what was otherwise so glaringly visible."

Roshni sat down absolutely blank. Her eyes had dried. No more tears remained to be shed.

"Jeet," at last she spoke, "Forgive me for what I am going to say, but what if you aren't able to get the house back or let's say you aren't successful in representing India even after sacrificing love?"

"That might happen," said Jeet. "It's possible that I lose this war, Roshni. But if I am satisfied with my efforts, at least I would be able to look in my mother's eyes."

"Jeet!" Roshni looked in his eyes. "The question is: why can't we put love on hold, rather than kill it completely?"

"When one ventures out to achieve something, there are no sureties. Neither for its success, nor for the span of time required to achieve whatever one has set out to. Would it then, not be unfair to ask you to wait for something that exists only in my dreams? Moreover, our love is in its infancy. It's like a sapling."

"And because it's a mere sapling, it wouldn't be that difficult to uproot, right? That is what you want to say?"

"No."

"Then?"

"What I mean is that it's easier to replace a sapling rather than replace a full grown tree."

A grappling silence ensued. No one spoke for some time. For a considerable amount of time, Roshni scribbled something on a piece of paper.

"Can I ask you something?" she had finished scribbling.

"Sure."

"What is my identity, Jeet?"

"Identity- What do you mean?"

"My identity as in- who am I, Jeet?"

"You are Roshni."

"Just Roshni, nothing more?"

"Well, you are Roshni, the volleyball player."

"And?"

"And you are a student of Rai School."

"And?"

"And you are Mr Dalbeer Chaudhary's daughter."

"You know what I am asking Jeet. Don't beat about the bush."

"I don't know. What is it that you want to hear?"

"Go Jeet," she stood up decisively. "Where ever you are destined to!"

With heavy feet and bowed head, Jeet stood up, turned and started towards the exit.

"Listen Jeet." Jeet turned back. Roshni's voice carried calm. A deadly, silent calm, "You are a coward Jeet, like my father was. And you are as cruel, it's just that you don't shout that much." Jeet said nothing. He turned back and continued in the direction he intended to. When he didn't react, Roshni's calm transformed into anger. She took the tape-recorder in her hands. In a knee-jerk reaction, she pulled her hand back aiming it in the direction of Jeet. Love had suddenly changed its form. From being a thing of sacrifice and reverence, it became a vehicle of violence. It was crude, repugnant and hideous form of something otherwise divine, a form nevertheless it was. For a moment, Roshni had thought of causing injury to Jeet. But then, in an instant, love regained its originality.

A fraction of a second before the tape-recorder could leave her hand, Roshni realized the blunder she was about to make. But it was too late, as the grip on the tape-recorder wasn't strong enough to stop the missile altogether. The extra flick of the wrist, however, effected a change in direction. Instead of flying towards Jeet, the dreaded missile now flew in the direction of the aquarium. The glass of the aquarium was undoubtedly thick, but not thick enough to bear the jolt of several hundred grams of metal hurled with such great force. The sounds of splish-splash of water and the scattered pieces of glass resonated in the library. The red fish was thrown out on dry ground, as she fought for life and tried in desperation to reach a drop of spilled water. She could find none.

Jeet was already out of the library and out of her world. Roshni unfolded the slip and started reading what she had scribbled.

So near- So far

The velocity in the wind was absolute,
I struggled- with the waves,
Canoed my boat all the night through;
Cruel lightening struck at dawn,
In the morning was I to meet you.

Roshni

Next, she saw herself tearing up the poem. Not that she didn't try to stop herself from doing that, but a voice in her head didn't allow her to.

Meeting with Doppelganger

The night is likely to be the most troublesome one. I can see a multi-headed demon gripping my heart in his filthy grip? Have I done the right thing by discarding love? There seemed no end to the incessant questions that flooded his mind. It was pitch-dark. Besides him, every other soul lay asleep. *Why not lie down? Maybe I would be able to get some sleep that way.*

He slid himself under the blue bed cover. Disquiet had gripped his mind; as if ripples had being caused by a pebble in an otherwise still lake. He looked around. The shadow sat at the edge of his bed, towards his feet. Strangely, the shadow had a hint of illumination.

"Hey what's up?" the shadow smiled.

"Who are you?" An astounded Jeet sat upright, his legs still under the bed cover.

"Didn't your mother tell you about me?"

"How do you know my mother?"

"First answer me- did she not tell you about your soul?"

"Yes she did- so..?"

Jeet looked around. His friends lay asleep in their beds.

"So nothing. I am the one."

"You mean you are the one- my soul..?"

"Yes I am your angel, the true reflection of your soul." The smile still danced on the shadow's lips, "What exactly did your mother tell you?"

"That the soul speaks to us whenever we are at crossroads."

"So- aren't you standing indecisive at crossroads, Jeet?"

"Yes I am- but why do you look like me?"

"You know souls have no shape or size, but to make myself visible to you, I had to take some form. Why then not be your lookalike then Jeet?"

"Yeah..."

"Call me doppelganger."

"And your purpose is to guide between the right and wrong?"

"That's right. So tell me what's up?" doppelganger asked

"Nothing much," replied Jeet

"Why then are you not able to sleep?"

"If you are my soul, then you know it all. Why do you pretend ignorance? You very well know my soul is in dark here. I seem to have failed everybody."

"You can't be more wrong. I am your soul and you can see I am illuminated even in the dark."

Jeet didn't answer.

Doopleganger stood up, held Jeet's hand and made him sit down on the bed, close to him.

"Now tell me- whom have you failed?"

"A whole lot of people."

"But as of now, you are not worried about a whole lot of people. You are worried about Roshni, right?"

"Yeah, she doesn't understand me. She called me a coward."

"But are you one- in the real sense I mean?"

"I don't know."

"Then let's find out. To find that, first of all let's try to define who exactly is a coward, and then you will see that you don't fall in that category. So, go ahead, tell me who is a coward in your opinion?"

"A coward is...." Jeet said after pondering over it a little, "a person who is scared."

"Scared of what?"

"Scared of...anything."

"Everyone is scared of something or the other. But not everyone can be called a coward."

"Hmm." Jeet sat thinking, pondering.

"Some people fear heights," doppelganger continued, "some people fear congested places, some fear their enemies, and some even friends and...."

"Friends!" Jeet was astounded

"Of course," doppelganger replied. "There is no worse thing than a friend turned foe- but let's not deviate from the topic. And why just friends, some people fear their own selves. So the bottom line is that fear is a common thing and everyone has it."

"But Y.P. says we should not be fearful. So if everyone has fears... then is it possible to be fearless?"

"Good question. But what your principal might have meant is that we take actions despite the fears, which is as good as being fearless because your actions are not hindered because of fear. Would you agree with me if I were to suggest that a courageous person is someone who moves ahead despite the fear, and takes a decision, a stand, despite the odds being against him?" Doppelganger responded in just one breath.

"Yes, I believe one has to agree to that."

"And considering the present scenario, are the odds not against you? I mean you have to choose one out of the two things that are close to your heart. And under such less than favourable circumstances, you somehow managed to take a decision, a stand, that you would just focus on your goal and ignore all other things, including Roshni's love. And you have to believe me when I say that it needs courage for a boy your age to say no to a girl like Roshni."

"Hmm."

"Hence the point is proved," chirped the doppelganger. Jeet smiled too.

"I am really thankful to you. This discussion of ours is bringing some relief to me. But please tell me, is it the right thing I am doing by ignoring Roshni? She says both of us are soul mates. And this is what I am doing to her."

"If what she says is right, and if both of you are in fact soul mates, then destiny will work overtime to bring the two of you together."

"Do you think we are soul mates?" Jeet's eyes were lit with hope.

"That's for destiny to decide. I am not destiny itself but a mere servant of it; but you will know the answer at the right time"

"But you are my soul, aren't you?"

"For sure I am." Doppleganger smiled. He knew what was coming.

"Then are you in touch with Roshni's soul?"

Doppleganger didn't reply. He continued to smile.

The morning whistle woke Jeet up. He looked for the doppelganger but could see him nowhere.

"Where has he gone? Was it a dream?" he asked himself and then he saw the clear impressions, the silhouettes, on the bed sheet: someone was seated there for long. The entire conversation replayed in his mind in a micro-second. He felt light, confident. The excess baggage of the mind had been shed. The real Jeet was back.

The Under-19 Match

Jeet had taken admission in government college in Gurgaon. He got selected to play in the under-19 trophy. Once again, Topal couldn't obstruct his selection because of the presence of Raghubeer Singh.

The person who was appointed as manager of the team wasn't all that heartening news for Jeet. Subhash was after all the right hand man of Topal.

After attending a fairly lacklustre fifteen day camp at Bhiwani, the team assembled at Delhi to board the train to Jammu where the tournament was scheduled at. It was an overnight twelve hour journey from Delhi to Jammu.

Subhash hailed from Rohtak. Although he was an experienced manager and loved the game to a certain extent, everything wasn't hunky dory with his behaviour. On any given day, he could gulp one full bottle of whiskey down the throat without batting an eyelid. His bias towards the players from Rohtak in matters of selection made the players from other districts quite uncomfortable.

Exactly one hour had passed when the train had left from Delhi. With their bag and baggage in place, the players were properly ensconced in the compartment. Being in a jovial mood, some of them played *'teen patti'*, some were hooked to their walkman, and others sang songs. Subhash had settled on the lowest berth whereas Jeet's berth was the top one.

Subhash had taken out his Bonnie Scott and had covered it with a newspaper. He had surreptitiously started to make pegs for himself in the plastic cups. As he continued to gulp down, the Rohtak players quietly came and sat around him. It was the best time to get some match secrets revealed.

"Sir, is the final eleven decided?"

The voice was clearly Gobind's, the third opener in the team other than Pankaj and Jeet. The question had invited every player's attention. All ears ready to catch the most hushed syllable uttered by Subhash. Jeet took his eyes away from the book and looked down.

"Not yet Gobind, but I can confirm one thing," he said with mystery in his eyes.

"What sir?"

"You won't be in the playing eleven."

There was absolute silence, as if a bomb had exploded on Gobind's head.

"But sir, you had promised I would be playing the first match."

"Yes I told you Gobind, but I didn't know there is a back door entry amongst you."

"Who is that, sir?" all the Rohtak guys asked in unison.

"The one sitting right up," Subhash pointed his finger towards Jeet's berth, "The great Jeet Singh. There is a message right from the very top that he should be included in the first eleven."

"But why is there a message to drop me, sir?" asked a bewildered Gobind. The other players were no less surprised by the revelation.

"No, dear Gobind, the message isn't to drop you."

"But sir you said...."

"This is the problem with you guys. You don't listen properly. The message is to include Jeet in the team, nothing less nothing more. But a team just requires two openers. Pankaj, being captain, automatically selects himself. So, there was just one slot. Now with the diktat in favour of Jeet, the doors for you, my dear Gobind have automatically shut." Subhash's devious smile appeared draconian.

Subhash didn't stop. Partly because he was in spirits, and partly because he didn't care. Seated on the top berth, Jeet listened to each word.

"But I can assure you of one thing," Subhash whispered in Gobind's ear. He had to struggle to tolerate the stench of alcohol that entered his nostrils.

"What's that, sir?"

"You will surely be playing the second match."

"How sir?"

"Because the great batsman that Jeet is, he is going to score a big zero and then what I would do to him in the next match I need not tell," he made another peg for himself.

"Why, are you not happy?" he patted on Gobind's cheek and without waiting for his reaction, he continued spitting venomous words. "I literally hate the guy. I have never seen any other guy to match him in being a liability to the team. I have never seen such a *sifarishi*. You know he dropped three catches in under-15 against Delhi and batted at number 10."

"But sir, he had opened the innings in the under-17 tournament last year and had scored 40 odd runs. He didn't bat badly, sir." Singla, the left arm spinner spoke from the aisle berth.

"I know how nicely he batted Singla, don't try to teach cricket to me. Had it not been for his recommendations, he wouldn't be in this train right now."

Singla wished to reply but then decided against it.

"Come on Singla," Subhash wouldn't stop. "I am sure you want to add something."

"No sir, nothing," replied Singla.

"Very good, Singla. After all, you are actually not as stupid as I had considered you to be."

Jeet couldn't take it anymore. Subhash's words had pricked him hard. Not knowing how to react, he slowly came down from the berth and wandered directionless towards the washroom. As he reached near the window, sudden gusts of wind felt soothing. Jeet stood there for what appeared to be forever. When at last he returned to his berth, all lights were switched off. Jeet slowly lay down on his berth before sleep came quietly to take him far and away from the heartless world.

It was early morning when the team reached the hotel. The players were allowed rest till afternoon. After a small nap and a heavy lunch, the team was taken to the ground for practice. The ground, as expected, was lush green with picturesque mountains forming the background. It was a small session of around two hours. After that, the nets were handed over to the Jammu & Kashmir team.

Failure to perform today would mean curtains to my dreams, Jeet told himself on the morning of the match. He knew the importance of the day in his life.

As he sat in the team bus, his mind went back to the story of a sage that was narrated to him by his mother.

> *Once upon a time, a sage who had been living in the Himalayas came to live for a few days in a town situated on the banks of river Yamuna. He made his abode under a Peepal tree besides the river. The sage was believed to possess immense powers. Struck by his fame and aura, the people from the nearby town started visiting him to help them fulfil their wants. But he ignored all*

of them. Some people stopped coming to him, taking him to be rude and stubborn. Some continued coming for a few more days but seeing the sage not relenting, discontinued too after some time. But there was one determined old man. He would sit all day near the tree where the sage sat but never disturbed him in his prayers. Though the sage was busy in his prayers, yet, he wasn't oblivious to the elderly person's constant dedication.

One day he gestured him to come near him. The old man, hardly able to believe his luck, went towards him.

"What makes you come here?" the sage asked.

"You would agree that the cycle of life if full of pain. I want you to free me from the cycle of life. Give me moksha, O enlightened one."

"Come at dawn tomorrow."

The old man was very happy. Fearing that he might get late, he slept on the bank of Yamuna itself and went to the sage with the first rays of the sun. The old man greeted him. The sage asked him to walk along with him towards the river bank. Just as they reached the river bank, the sage caught hold of the man's neck and submerged it in water. The old man struggled with all the might to get himself released from the clutches of the yogic powerful sage, but the sage wouldn't let him go. When the old man thought his end was near, he held the sage by his neck and the sage was forced to release him out of his grip. The old man brought his neck out to breathe.

"Tell me, O great soul", he pleaded, "What wrong have I done to invite such wrath from you?"

"Tell me how you felt inside there?" the sage seemed to show zero interest in his plight.

"I almost saw my death."

"Tell me, what was the one thing you desired most when you were helpless, with your head inside the water," the sage asked.

"I wanted you to release me from your iron like grip."

"Yes, but why did you want me to release my grip?"

"So that I can bring my head above water."

"Above water, but for what?"

"To breathe."

"To breathe yes, but breathe WHAT?"

"Breathe air."

"Yes, means you wanted air. Now tell me, would you have traded your entire wealth in exchange of air?"

"Why only wealth, I could have traded anything for it."

"It means you were desperate, to get air, so desperate that you could have traded anything for it. Now if you show the same desperation for moksha, if you want it as much as you wanted air, there is nothing that can stop you from achieving it."

My desire to perform today is even more than the old man's desire for air, Jeet thought. So will I get what I want?

The bus continued on its journey towards the ground. He looked for doppelganger. Maybe he could clear the doubts.

"What if the first ball gets the better of me?" Negative thoughts tried to gain control.

"But even Sunil Gavaskar has lost his wicket on the first ball a couple of times," the mind replied rationally, the optimism had not died down. "That means that any batsman in the world can get out on any score, because not all depended on the batsman alone. There are other factors too, like the bowling attack and most importantly, your luck on that particular day." Jeet had suddenly started to find pieces to the puzzle. His mind was coming up with answers. "So what really is within the powers of a batsman?" this time the question was even more categorical, but the next moment the answer was presented too. "To avoid making mistakes and play to the best of one's abilities. For everything else, the decision rested with someone up there." The clouds of doubt had started to melt away. Jeet started to plan his innings. Since it was a three-day match, patience and the score that a batsman would put on the board was all that mattered. The longer the innings, the more the runs scored. He knew his forward defensive shot was his best bet. As it almost negated any chances of getting bowled or LBW, if used properly, it could help him play a long innings. Then came the wicket keeper and the slip cordon, as it was here that most of the openers usually got out. That point too did not worry him too much as he was more than aware of where his off stump was. So he wasn't going to chase deliveries that were way outside the off stump. Getting reassured on defence, he now needed to weed out risky strokes. Square cut was one of the shots he thought he didn't play too badly. But since it was a horizontal bat shot, it carried fair amount of chances of the ball being carried away towards the slips. Hence on better judgment, he decided to take that stroke out of his innings completely. Then he thought about the cover drive which carried minimum risk and was the best bet in these kind of matches. Jeet's strategy was made.

a. Have patience; try to stay at the wicket
b. Cut down on risky shots like the square cut
c. Play cover drive to score but with a not so high bat lift
d. Try to play session by session as it would not let the mind have windmills of any kind

The bus entered the stadium. The captain asked everybody to come down to the ground for light warming up exercises. Subhash had come in another vehicle. As the players started running on the periphery of the boundary, the sight of a familiar face brought Jeet's heart to his mouth. Subhash was standing in the centre of the ground with somebody. Pankaj who was running just next to Jeet spoke first, "Is that Jadeja?"

"He is none other than Jadeja."

The voice had come from behind and Jeet knew it was Mahesh Ahlawat, the left arm spinner. He knew his teammates were looking at him from the corners of their eyes. It was an open secret that the presence of Jadeja meant that the doors of the match were shut on Jeet. Since he was busy with his junior international matches, it was expected he wouldn't be joining the state under-19 team. But here he was, in flesh and blood.

Is it over for me then? Jeet felt something insipid had entered his mouth.

"But things are not in my hands," he tried to rationalize. There were no further thoughts. The mind had turned blank. As they approached their last round, the manager called Pankaj. As the three of them, i.e Jadeja, Subhash and Pankaj seemed to be in a discussion, the rest of the players slowly finished the last lap and started with the stretching exercises. The J&K team was doing the same at the far end. The umpires too had arrived. It was less than twenty minutes for the match. As the umpires signalled for the toss, Jeet saw Pankaj rushing towards him with a sense of urgency.

"Jeet, you are in the team. Jadeja wants to bat at number three," Pankaj whispered in his ear before announcing the eleven for the match.

Pankaj's words didn't sink in immediately. Jeet tried to be calm and not show his trepidation to the teammates. But deep inside him, the feeling was of having fallen from the crust to trough and then back to the crest again. He closed his eyes and tried to concentrate back to the plan of his innings. He tried to get his focus back in his efforts at getting mentally prepared to go out there in the middle.

Pankaj lost the toss and J&K chose to bat. After a small pep talk from the manager, the team entered the field with a lot of enthusiasm and chirpiness. The presence of Jadeja had lifted the spirit of the team.

The J&K batsmen didn't offer much resistance. The wickets fell at regular intervals. As their eighth wicket fell at just ten minutes to tea, Jeet knew he would be facing the J&K new ball bowlers at the difficult twilight hour. He wasn't wrong. It was two minutes to tea when J&K's last wicket fell. Singla had captured three wickets while Mahesh had two in his kitty. The rest were shared by the three medium pacers. Jeet and Pankaj padded up as openers. Jadeja had padded up too for the number three.

It was Pankaj who took the first strike. The wicket still had moisture. The first over was played without any runs and it was Jeet's turn to face the other bowler from the far end. The ball was seen just for a split second as it left the bowlers hand, Jeet's left foot went impulsively forward for a defensive stroke but the ball was of a more fuller length than was anticipated and, therefore, Jeet had to drag his foot back to the crease. Everything happened in a fraction of a second. The ball swerved from the off stump and was really quick. As it finished on leg stump, Jeet somehow managed to get his bat to the ball and it went racing away towards the long leg. *Four runs* thought he, but as his eyes followed the ball, he could see the fielder getting behind it. He had to settle for just a single.

Pankaj and Jeet played quietly for a while. Jeet's plan to play on the front foot worked fine, as the idea was to survive the difficult period and come back afresh the following morning. The first forty-five minutes witnessed nothing dramatic. The score read at twenty for no loss. It was the first ball after the drinks that dealt the first blow. As Panjak went forward to an incoming delivery, the ball swerved more towards inside after pitching and got Pankaj on the outstretched front pad. The ball popped towards short leg where the fielder grabbed it with ease. To Jeet, it appeared to be a harmless shout for a catch. As all eyes followed the umpire, the dreaded finger went up. Jeet looked at Pankaj for his reaction. He didn't look all that surprised and quietly headed towards the dressing room. The fall of wicket had rattled Jeet's concentration for a brief moment, but the advent of Jadeja at the crease instilled a feeling of re-assurance in him. Both of them continued to chat and play without much discomfort. Jadeja was more of an adventurous sort trying out ideas like who to face whom. He asked Jeet if he was uncomfortable with any particular bowler. What he meant was that he would save Jeet from any bowler that he found difficult to handle by taking most of the strikes against him. For Jeet, these were misadventures that were likely to take the focus away from the batsman.

"We should focus on seeing off the day without trying anything away from the normal," Jeet requested Jadeja.

"Exactly my thoughts," he had replied with the wink of his eye. The medium pacers had had their quota of spitting venom and it was now the turn of the spinners to get introduced. It was a Sikh guy Paljeet who came as the first replacement. He gave the ball more than normal flight and didn't look threatening enough to create problems. Jadeja continued with his chirpy self while Jeet tried to concentrate on each ball. Not for a moment did he deviate from the plan. He had to survive and survive at all costs. He did not play even a single square cut to the medium pacers and had no intention of using it against the spinners as well. His runs came slowly, mostly in singles, whereas Jadeja was the more aggressive and the more flamboyant. But even a friendly attack can sometimes prove hostile. That's exactly what happened as Jadeja in his carefree manner offered a forward defensive stroke to a Paljit delivery. But this one turned a fraction more than the rest and took the inner edge of Jadeja's bat, deflecting off the pad towards the waiting short leg fielder. Jadeja's wicket was a considerable setback to the whole team and it had made the otherwise chirpy dressing room go quiet. Next to come in was Sanjeev Arya, the team's wicket-keeper batsman. The rest of the twenty minutes didn't hold any more surprises and the day was over without any further damage.

At close of play, Haryana's score read 62 for 2 in reply to J&K's 232 all out. There was still a lot of work to be done. Jeet's personal score was 25. Twice he got the opportunity to execute cover drive and on both occasions he was rewarded with four runs. The batsman in him was thrilled with both those shots as both fetched runs and didn't look all that bad to the eyes.

It was a restless night for Jeet. Subhash's words were almost etched in his mind and the scars so formed hindered the path of sleep. A mere 25 runs were hardly a panacea for those scars. "It's tomorrow that matters," a determined Jeet said to himself. At last, the tired muscles got an upper hand over anxiety, and surreptitiously sleep found its way to sooth the tired body and mind.

The medium pacers started their attack the next day, but after a couple of overs it was once again the spinners' turn to attack. Jeet continued from where he had left the previous day. Following his plan, he continued to build upon his score. Only the balls that were perfect half volleys were driven. Otherwise the runs came in singles and twos. All was going well and Jeet counted each run that he scored. He could tell his score at any given time without asking the scorer.

The wakeup call came when his individual score read 37. The left arm spinner offered him a least expected full toss that lobbed around his waist. Having nothing planned for such a delivery, he played with an impulsively natural, knee jerk reaction. That was just swinging the bat at it to let it bounce outside the boundary, the treatment that it richly deserved. The occasion though demanded something different. The ball instead of going out of the boundary lobbed up in the air and he saw the fine leg fielder coming in. Jeet forgot to breathe.

"I have never seen such a *sifarishi*." Subhash's voice haunted him as the fielder came under the ball to catch it. The hop from the batting crease to the non-striker end appeared to be one of the longest. But it turned to be Jeet's moment and he continued to live to fight another day. The fielder dropped the easy catch. The manager of the J&K team was furious, and could be heard swearing at the fielder. The dropped catch instilled more confidence in Jeet and he became more cautious and more assured. Now that the first half century seemed within sight, he couldn't afford to let it go.

"First let me complete my half century, and then I would take it from there," he said to himself. He didn't have any target score as yet. The aim was still the same, to survive at all costs. The continued nudges and pushes got him to his half-century. He heaved a sigh of relief. The team's score read 120 for the loss of four wickets. Still, there was work to be done. Subhash too pestered Jeet to stay on for as long as possible.

Jeet thanked the almighty for his small achievement. It was his first 50 in any board's trophy. Certainly he would be able to make a call home now. He had now started seeing the ball better compared to when the innings had started the previous day. The bowlers too appeared far less hostile. However, there was still a lot of work to be done. A 50 against J&K certainly could not take him notches ahead of his competitors. But the innings was not over yet and it was not the time to get out. Jeet thought of starting all over again as if he had just come to bat. The theory to survive seemed to be working fine and there appeared to be no reasons to change that. It was the first time Jeet had a target in mind.

If I could continue for a little while more, this 50 can be converted into 70, he thought and went on to play without making any alterations to the plan. One hour after lunch, Jeet's score read 74 while the team stood at 162 for 7, still 50 runs away from the target set by J&K.

It was during the drinks interval that Subhash seemed desperate to talk to Jeet.

"Look Jeet, you don't need anybody to tell you the importance of this match. I mean for God's sake we have never lost to J&K and certainly not with somebody like Jadeja in the team. To be honest, I don't really know if he realizes this as you can see how carefree he appears to be." And as both of them looked towards him, they saw Jadeja chirping with teammates looking oblivious to everything. Subhash's face had turned red.

"That's his nature sir, he can't help it. But I don't think he is non-serious. I'm sure he realizes the intensity."

"I really don't care what he thinks Jeet, but I don't want to lose this match, not when I am the in-charge. And you know what, you are my best bet. See, you are the set man in and I want you to carry on, and do take the tail along with you."

Jeet gently pinched his thigh. The talk was for real.

"I would give my best sir," there was nothing but sincerity in Jeet's voice.

"I don't know what's your best, Jeet, but I want you to stay there. And keep playing as well as you have been. Please beta."

Jeet was even more determined after this small dialogue. Personal target was now replaced with the target of team's victory. "I will be at the crease till the team overtakes the score," he set up a fresh diktat to himself. The plan was now to overtake J&K's score, as the game in all probability was to be decided on the first innings lead itself. Fifty runs were still needed with just three wickets remaining. The last man Mahesh Ahlawat was not considered worthy of even a couple of runs by the team, hence in real terms there were just two wickets in hand. Rajesh was the new man in, as the seventh wicket had fallen at the stroke of tea.

"Rajesh, you have to block everything that comes your way. The runs would automatically come, but we need to stay at the crease."

"You don't worry about me Jeet. I assure you they can't get me out."

The calmness with which Rajesh spoke those words suddenly made Jeet take a crucial decision which was to prove decisive. Jeet had it in mind to save Rajesh from the bowling by taking single off the last ball of each over and avoiding the same on first to fifth ball, even if it meant the loss of a few runs. But Rajesh's words made him alter that decision and he felt no fear in getting Rajesh exposed to the bowling attack. Both of them continued taking singles and doubles. The tactic worked well and the scoreboard kept ticking along slowly yet surely. Rajesh was totally focused and showed a fair amount of resistance and grit. The partnership swelled. Slowly the bowlers became hapless and the match seemed in the team's pocket with just 5 runs needed. Jeet's score stood at 98, but the fact that he was just two runs away from a well-deserved century was the last thing on anyone's mind. Just then, against the run of play, Rajesh made the first and last mistake of his innings. He chased an outside ball from the medium pacer and the catch was plucked by the wicketkeeper out of thin air. Rajesh stood his ground for a considerable time. His eyes manifested the pain and disappointment of throwing all away after coming so close. Jeet came to him and patted him for his determined effort. He could see the salty droplets tickle down the cheeks when the moisture in the eyes became too heavy to be contained. Rajesh had to at last drag his heavy feet out of the ground.

Ajay, the left hander, was the next man in.

Ajay did exactly the opposite of what he was asked to do. The totally harmless first ball that he faced from the spinner had pitched outside the off stump and was going further away. All that Ajay was required to do was to leave it alone. Instead, he seemed to finish the match in just one shot by trying to sweep it out of the ground. The ball had gained more height than the distance and the man at square leg did the rest. If that wasn't enough, the ball also brought the egoist Mahesh Ahlawat to the crease. As the shot from Ajay was in air for quite some time, Jeet had had the time to cross over and therefore, it was he and not Mahesh who was to face the last ball of the over.

As Jeet got ready to face the next ball, he could see the whole team standing and signalling to him to remain calm. Even from a distance, he could see Subhash being the most tensed. He had a cigarette in his hand. The frequency of his puffs manifested the storm within. The moment he saw Jeet looking at him, he threw the half burnt cigarette and signalled frantically towards him. "Keep your calm," he seemed to plead. Jeet thought of talking to Mahesh before facing the last ball.

"Put a dead defence to the ball; it's just a matter of a couple of balls," Jeet told him

"Please mind your own business and play. I would do what I have to," Mahesh said with a straight face and turned his back. Jeet had considered him to be a rude person, but that he would stoop to this level was something that he could never expect from a sportsman... that too, when the team was standing on the crossroads of victory and defeat.

Considering Mahesh's attitude, Jeet had to decide and decide fast. There were five runs needed to take over the projected score. Whether Jeet should play his normal game and take ones and twos as the opportunity comes, or try to hit a six off the last ball and leave nothing whatsoever for Mahesh. The second decision was a difficult one because if the shot got miscued and he got out while trying to hit a six, the whole blame would fall on him. In that eventuality, even the exceptional innings he had played till now was sure to come to naught. He would be criticized for playing a rash shot and could suffer in further selections too. But, given the situation, the more difficult and the risky of the two options appeared to be the best bet for the team. There was no fielder on the fence and Jeet knew for sure that he would be able to clear mid off and mid on. The risk was if he missed the ball completely and as a result got stumped or bowled. As Paljit started his four yards bowling run up, Jeet had made up his mind. He was going to go all out and hit Paljit out of the ground. Certainly the joy of looking Mahesh in the eye and asking him to go to hell after the ball would have cleared the ground made the decision a little less difficult. Jeet issued a fresh diktat for himself – "Watch the ball till the last moment and try to time it with perfection without caring to hit it too hard."

As paljit's hand went up to deliver the ball, Jeet committed a blunder that was virtually fatal. His anxiety got the better of him and he jumped out of his crease a little too soon. He was stranded in the middle of the pitch with the ball still in Paljeet's hands. The off spinner realized this and dropped the ball short, flat and wide. Jeet found himself far away from the pitch of the ball. But it was too late to retract. With all his might, he heaved the bludgeon with his eyes getting closed, just like that of a pigeon when it's about to be pounced upon by the cat.

A complete life span existed in that one moment – Jeet's ears got ready to listen to the death knell of the bails being dislodged by the wicket keeper. Finally the sound did reach his ears. But it was hardly the death knell. Instead, it was the sound of music. The sound of rain drops falling on the tin roof to form a divine orchestra. The sweet sound of bat hitting the ball. As Jeet's eyes opened to the dazzling sunlight, he saw the ball souring high into the sky. He fell to the ground but not before he had seen the umpire's hands going upwards to signal a six. Among the cacophony of his teammates, there was a whisper that was distinct and clear. It was the sound of the doppelganger. He had been there all along.

"That was the real plan." Jeet heard doppelganger say in his ear.

Munna's Debt

Jeet scored tons of runs during the season. He was also selected for North zone under-19 team and he scored two centuries in zonal matches due to which he was also selected for the junior India camp. All in all his performance was better than any other junior player from the country.

The place in the Ranji Trophy team in the next season is now assured, he thought.

Not only did he score runs in the season, but also earned money in the form of his match fee. He was to attend a camp before the season officially ended. The season now over, he was headed home after playing the last match at Visakhapatnam. He was in a dilemma how to best utilise the money earned. Whether to save the money for the house or get something done for Munna?

For the house, we still have time and as it is, the amount of money that I have in hand cannot solve the mortgage issue altogether but If utilized for the benefit of Munna, it can go a long way in helping him.

He decided in favour of Munna. He decided to contact Dinesh - the person who he trusted the most, outside of his family.

"We can get a second hand taxi for Munna in the amount that you have in hand," Dinesh said.

"But he doesn't know how to drive a car."

"Ha ha."

"Why do you laugh?"

"You don't look like a Ranji Trophy player."

"Why so?"

"How many days does it take to learn driving?"

"Hmm. But Dinesh, will it really help him?"

"For sure it would. He can drive it easily till he gets ninety years old. And moreover, he can buy another taxi after earning some money and appoint a driver. He can get into real business with this."

"Yeah, that looks promising. And as you said- we can also help him get another taxi after some time."

"Yeah, correct."

"You know Dinesh, I will request Munna to make Mom and Dad his first passengers once he learns driving."

"That is some idea, I tell you. This would make your efforts even more worthy."

"It's decided then. I am sending the money to you. It will take me another week or so to come to Gurgaon."

The same day the money order was sent to Dinesh.

The two-year-old doctor driven Ambassador looked almost as good as new. Although it was a second hand car, it hadn't been driven around too much by its first owner. There was hardly any wear and tear. Dinesh had got it washed and serviced. Jeet had arrived and was pleased with Dinesh's choice.

"Good job! It must have taken some effort in finding this car out, provided the limited money that we had in hand." Jeet hugged Dinesh.

"The joy in your eyes has properly compensated for the effort." Dinesh smiled.

♒

It was Sunday- Jeet was to deliver the car to Munna. Paddy was out for his cricket match, while Kanwar relaxed with his morning tea and newspaper. Jeet was talking to Kamlesh.

"I have planned everything Mom."

"Yeah I can measure your efforts by merely looking at the car outside. Adorned with flowers- it is no less than a new bride."

"Finally Munna has a bride; so what if a little late in life!" Kanwar looked out of his newspaper, making the three of them laugh out loud.

"Mom," Jeet complained. "Papa is still in his kurta pyjama."

"Don't worry," Kanwar said before Kamlesh could reply. "I have got my favourite pair of trousers and shirt ready." He went back to his newspaper.

"But what is the exact programme?" Asked Kamlesh.

"First, I will present the car to Munna."

"Ok and..?"

"And feel rejoiced through the joy in his eyes."

"But have you got the address confirmed. What if he is not staying at his old place? After all, so much time has passed since we last saw him."

"I don't think so, Mom. He has been living in that place for a long time and there is no reason why he would have shifted to some other place. And even if he has, we will find him some way or the other."

"Yeah, there shouldn't be any cause for worry, I hope." She thought for a while and asked, "But how will you take the car to him? None of us know how to drive."

"We have hired a driver, Mom."

"Wow !" Kanwar again looked out of his newspaper. "I wish I were Munna today."

The wittiness triggered the laughter again.

"And then, Mom," continued Jeet through the bouts of laughter, "we will come home along with Munna and go for a drive, eat out and also go for a movie."

"But why go and watch a movie outside when the day's hero will be sitting next to us," Kanwar said. "I for one will take Munna's autograph and will consider my day made."

"Today, Dad is in full form, Mom. He will score a century today, it seems."

"No way," replied Kanwar, "I am not even playing today. There is only one batsman and one bowler today, and one man of the match and man of the series – Munna."

Jeet had been thoughtful to have hired the driver for tendays, so that he could also teach Munna how to drive. Jeet was looking forward to see Munna's reaction.

Today I will thank him for all his ice creams, éclairs and toffees and tell him that his love cannot be measured in any way. That this car is just a way of telling him that his Jeet has now grown up and he won't allow him to pull rickshaw anymore. Then probably he would laugh, or maybe cry in joy. And maybe he would hug me and try to pinch himself to check if the joy was for real. And he might also say, 'Jeet, I don't know how to drive a car son!' and then I will push the driver ahead and will tell him, 'Munna Bhaiya, Raju has been hired to teach you exactly that.' And then maybe he would ask a stupid question like, 'What will happen to my Rickshaw?' and I would then suggest it to be donated to someone.

When they were one street away from Munna's house, Jeet was surprised to see a swelling crowd. His surprise didn't end there. As he entered Munna's street, the presence of cops near his house astounded him even more. *Why so much police in a not-so-happening street?* He was to get his answer soon.

"Bhaiya, has something happened here? Why all the police?" he asked a bystander.

"I am a new tenant here, but they say it's the house of a rickshawala, not getting his name... Yeah...Chun mun."

"Chun...mun? Do you mean Munna?"

"Yeah, yeah Munna."

"What happened to him?" Jeet hoped his worst fears weren't true.

"He died last night. The police are waiting for someone to claim his body."

The Selectors' Conspiracy

In each and every measurable parameter, Munna's death was a major loss to Jeet. One of his three dreams had slipped out of his hands. As the cricket season was fast approaching, he couldn't afford to succumb to gloom. With considerable effort, he pulled himself together to get back on his feet again. His focus was now the Ranji trophy.

He- however- was oblivious to the fact that some ninety-five kilometres away, a conspiracy to injure his second dream was taking roots.

Like any other day, Gupta – the chairman of selectors – had returned home after his day at his office at the SBI branch. As usual, he had handed over the briefcase to his wife, loosened his tie and sat on the sofa in the drawing room.

"Has Hitin returned from practice?" he asked his wife.

"Yes, he is in the other room. Hitin!" she called out to her son.

"So, how was the practice?" asked senior Gupta as Hitin entered the room with a glass of orange juice. Both of them now sat facing each other in the comforts of their beautifully furnished drawing room.

"There was no practice today, dad. We played a match instead," he looked away missing the gaze of his father.

"And how much did you score?" asked an enthusiastic Rajkumar as he bowed down to untie the laces of his shoes

"Actually dad, the ball had kept low," the son replied in a whisper.

"That's not what I asked?" the chairman got irritated.

"But that's a fact dad, that I got out because the ball had kept low."

"And what was your score when the ball kept low and you got out?" The sarcasm was evident

"It was the very first ball."

"So, it's a zero."

Gupta's mood turned sullen. Nothing else mattered to him as much as his son's performance. While there was no joy that could equal the ecstasy of seeing his son score runs, there wasn't a greater pain than seeing him fail on a cricket pitch.

The incumbent chairman of selectors was an exceptional left arm spinner in his playing days. With more than seven hundred wickets in his kitty, he boasted of more wickets than any other bowler in Ranji Trophy. Though he richly deserved to represent India, it was by a mere whisker that he missed playing Test cricket. A fairly large section of the cricketing fraternity believed injustice had been done to the exceptional talent. His humble upbringing was considered one of the reasons for his non-selection. The more sophisticated ones moved ahead in the race for selection where competition was no less than cut throat. Once he had made it to the fifteen of the Indian cricket team, but was later dropped without being given a chance to perform. The father now wanted to fulfil his unrealised dreams through his son. But the two had little in common. The senior was a left arm spinner and the junior a left hand opening batsman. The son was not even a shadow of his talented dad. Reaching the Ranji

Trophy stage had been a cake walk for the junior- given the clout that the senior had in the matters of selections. But his constant poor performances in the Ranji games never allowed him even a sneak peek into the higher levels. The father was determined to see his son wearing India colours, even if it meant stepping over the careers of people with more talent and promise. As chairman of selectors, nothing else mattered to him but the selection of his son. The once tormented was now the tormentor.

"Dad..."

"Han?"

"What were you thinking dad?" the junior shadow practised as if he had a bat in his hand.

"I think you should shadow practice for the balls that keep low," Rajkumar tried a jig at Hitin.

"Common dad, get over it. It was a practice match after all."

Rajkumar didn't reply. "I want to discuss something important with you."

Rajkumar didn't pay any attention to his son's statement and simply stared at him. His anger clearly manifested in his eyes. Junior couldn't bear the gaze for long and looked away.

"Look at me!" Rajkumar stood up, held Hitin's face in his hands and forced him to meet his eye.

"What is it, Dad?" The son was visibly irritated and still looked away.

"When I say look at me, then just look at me!!"

Hitin obeyed.

"You know the kind of competition you face. Every single day, some newcomer performs and knocks at the doors of Ranji Trophy. I mean- except you- everybody is performing. Look at this new kid Jeet. He is doing wonders."

"I know," he replied pensively.

"Just knowing isn't going to help. Do something about it. Score some runs so that your place is secured and I don't have to eat a humble pie in order to keep you in the team."

"It's about Jeet that I want to discuss."

"Tell me what is it?" Rajkumar looked at him with a new-found interest.

"Either Jeet's luck seems to be favouring him all the time; or he is getting poor bowling attacks to face. He never seems to get out."

"You mean he gets to face poor bowling attacks?"

"Yes, or else how would he score those runs?"

"But the other players play against the same opposition, don't they?"

"Yes dad they do. I don't know. Maybe it's his luck then. In that innings against J&K, he was dropped at 37 and went on to score a hundred. It has to be his luck dad, nothing else."

"But your catches have been floored too. Why is it that you never seem to take advantage of those floored catches?"

"Dad, I believe the topic of conversation is Jeet, not me."

"What is there to talk, other than the fact he has been scoring in tons of late?"

"That's the trigger of worry dad. My sources tell me- Deepak has become fond of his batting and follows his performances keenly."

"Do you mean Deepak Sharma, the Ranji captain?"

"Yes."

"Hmm."

"We have to do something about it dad, or this Deepak will make me sit out of the playing eleven."

"But it's the captain's prerogative to choose the eleven of his choice. That's his right. What have I got to do with that?"

"Is this the chairman of selection committee speaking, who happens to be my dad as well?"

"What can anyone do anything about it? After all, it's Jeet's bat that does the talking. How can anyone silence that?"

"I am not talking about silencing the bat, Dad. I am talking about snatching it altogether."

The chairman of selectors didn't answer. The dad was silent too.

"Dad, all said and done, if you select him, I am going to have sleepless nights," the boy continued to spit venom.

"Maybe one day you would understand, that it's not the good performances of others but the lack of performances by you that are going to show you the door out of the Ranji team." There was frustration all over Rajkumar's face. "Till the time your dad is able to sacrifice the careers of others for your good, he will continue to do so," he murmured, almost to himself.

"I will score runs this time, Dad. I have practiced a lot this season. I assure you this time I am going to be the most prolific scorer all over India. Just this time Dad, don't let this Jeet stand in my way. Because if you do select him, I am sure that Deepak is going to play him in the eleven and I am surely to be kept out. There is only one way for me to prove myself, and that is to keep Jeet out of the squad."

"But with his performance, how can someone keep him out? The press will surely eat us up."

"We are not Delhi, we are Haryana. We hardly have any press presence. On the contrary, the press gives a hoot to what happens in Haryana cricket."

"You very well know it's not in my hands entirely. He is from Gurgaon and once Topal recommends his name in the selection meeting, by no means can I say no. How can one turn a blind eye to such massive performance? And suppose by hook or crook I am able to keep him out of the squad, and tomorrow Chaudhary sahab asks me about his non-selection, what will I say?"

"You mean Raghubeer Singh Chaudhary?"

"Yes."

"Dad, Jeet isn't exactly the apple of Topal's eyes, and moreover, I have the solution. If you act in accordance, Topal won't be a hurdle."

"Yeah, I am aware of that- but what if he recommends?"

"No he won't. But only if you listen to me carefully," Hitin was smiling.

Raj Kumar's eyes split wide in astonishment with each word as Hitin unfolded his plan. He didn't know whether to be proud of his son for having worked out an almost unbeatable plan or to despise him for trying to stab a fellow cricketer in the back. Raj Kumar kept thinking for a considerable time. Once again, the ambitious father emerged victorious against the chairman of selectors whose job was to do justice. Raj Kumar tried hard to figure out if something was missing, "There shouldn't be any loose ends."

O.P. Topal was the joint secretary of the Haryana Cricket Association and represented Gurgaon in the matters of selection. His interests were quite different from Gupta's. But like Gupta, he too was least bothered about selecting the best available team. He had one single agenda, to get rich through cricket. His modus operandi was simple:

1. Organise a Ranji trophy match in Gurgaon.
2. Hoodwink the District Cricket Association by collecting funds to be given to players as match fee.
3. The fact that the actual match fee was given by the BCCI was hidden from the members of the association.
4. If at all some ex-cricketer who was privy to this fact raised his voice, he was silenced by the clamour of a simple

point: That money will be returned to the association once it is reimbursed by the board. The fact that it was hardly ever returned was another matter altogether.

It was on this weakness that Hitin had planned to attack.

The chairman of selectors was sharp on time to meet the joint secretary. The trial was two days away. The moment couldn't have been more appropriate.

"So tell me Gupta sahab, how can I help you?" Topal came directly to the point. The chairman and he sat in the tastefully designed drawing room. The chairman was surprised to see the progress that the joint secretary had made in a span of a couple of years. The scooter parked in the lobby was now replaced by a luxury car. The house too had been recently re-furbished and the old furniture was now gone.

Organising matches isn't that bad a business, the chairman had thought as he had placed his finger at the doorbell. That Topal had no other means of income was an open secret.

"You know it's always about Hitin. He is the only worry I have."

"That shouldn't be the cause of worry Gupta sahab. By God's grace he is regularly playing Ranji trophy and now he has been appointed by the bank too. It can't get better I suppose."

"Maybe the grass looks greener from where you see it. The fact remains that I cannot get more worried. If things go like they have been going, I doubt whether he would be able to hold his place in the team."

"Yes, I believe he should be scoring more runs. That will make it easier for you in the selection committee."

"I understand that Topal sahab. This time I have changed his coach. I am sure this time he will perform better, but that's possible only if he finds a place in the eleven."

"What makes you think that he wouldn't be playing in the eleven?"

"See, Topal sahab, we will select him in the fifteen. No issues with that. But the point is, we hardly have any say when the eleven gets picked up. You know it's the captain's ball game once we give him the fifteen. After that who he chooses and who he does not, is completely up to him."

"But Deepak Sharma is a nice boy Gupta sahab. And he respects you a lot. I am sure he won't do anything to hurt you."

"Things are different this time."

"How?"

"I have heard he is mighty impressed by Jeet. And if he plays Jeet in the eleven, Hitin will have to sit out."

"I am afraid that cannot be ruled out Gupta sahab. So, what is it that you suggest? I mean where do I fall in the scheme of things?"

"The kid is from Gurgaon and it's you who should be recommending his name to the selection committee."

"True."

"And if you don't recommend him, the issue will be nipped in the bud. Deepak Sharma would then have no option but to play Hitin in the eleven."

"But Gupta sahab, you know how difficult that would be for me? I mean, the guy has scored runs in tons. What justification will I have if Chaudhary sahab asks about Jeet not getting selected in the team?"

"You very well know I am the last person to spoil anyone's future. You know how many careers I have made. Even this Jeet, it's I who had encouraged him and shown him the way; and here he is now, threatening the chances of my own son. What I mean to say is, we can include him in the team in the next season. After all, he is not even twenty yet."

"That I understand Gupta sahab, but my only concern is Chaudhary sahab."

"That issue I will handle; you don't have to worry about that. After all, I am the chairman of the selection committee. In case some justification is required, I will provide that justification to Chaudhary sahab. But you please do not recommend his name. I will be more than obliged."

"But Gupta sahab..."

"You don't worry about anything Topal sahab. And one more thing, we have decided to shift the Rohtak match to Gurgaon. All of us know how good an organiser you are," Gupta laughed sheepishly as Topal's eyes lit up.

"Means I will be getting two matches this season? You are too kind."

"But please don't forget my request."

Topal came out with to see him off. The driver opened the car's door for him.

"Is this your office car?"

"Yes, I made this trip as the official one."

"Ha ha," Topal laughed out heartily. "I salute you."

The conspiracy had taken the shape of a fully grown tree, with its roots penetrating deep into the soul of an innocent sportsman. The pain, however, was to emerge only later.

Rejection in Ranji Trophy

"Chaudhary sahab isn't coming to the trials" was certainly not the best piece of news that Jeet could have received on entering the Nahar Singh Stadium, Faridabad. *But I have scored enough runs. My performance will speak for me. I shouldn't be bothered. Topal can't play his games against me anymore. The press will eat them up if they don't select me.* He felt reassured.

It was just two balls that Jeet was allowed at the nets. "Thank you," Rajkumar Gupta had shouted just as the second ball that Jeet faced met with the sweet part of the bat.

"We have seen enough of you, Jeet, you don't need nets to showcase your talent," Rajender Gupta smiled as Jeet came out of the nets. After properly placing his gear in his kit bag, Jeet came back to stand at the back line along with his peers from Gurgaon.

"That seals your selection," said Pankaj standing next to him.

"Let's see," Jeet managed.

"What's there to see in this?" Pankaj said. "By scoring those many runs, you have hardly left them with any choice."

Jeet began saying something, but stopped midway. Someone tapped his shoulder from behind.

"Hey, how are you doing Bradman?" Jeet looked back to find Ashok Singh, his under-15 captain, with his trademark smile.

"Oh, hi Ashok, hope all's well," Jeet smiled back. Ashok, the all rounder had last year been included in the Ranji squad and had had a fairly good last season. He had hogged the headlines when in an Escorts sponsored tournament, Kapil Dev passed on his man of the match award, a Rajdoot motor cycle, to him. Far from the prize itself, it was Kapil's decision to choose Ashok amongst the galaxy of young and emerging players that had caused the buzz.

"Yeah, I am fine dear. But what happened to you? You created quite a stir last season, didn't you?" He smiled

"Hardly anything in comparison to what all you have been doing lately," Jeet returned the compliment.

"Actually, Deepak Sharma wants to meet you," Ashok whispered.

"You mean the captain!"

"Yes the man himself." Ashok replied.

"Now?"

"Right now."

They both went to where Deepak Sharma stood.

"Bhaiya, he is Jeet," Ashok introduced him to Deepak.

"Oh, well played man," Deepak shook Jeet's hand. The firmness of the handshake manifested mutual joy.

"Thank you, Bhaiya," Jeet was thrilled.

After the initial salutations, Deepak suddenly touched a sensitive topic.

"See Ajit, our Ranji Trophy team has been struggling for the last couple of seasons. And more than anything else, it's the opening partnership that has been letting us down."

"Yes, I am aware of it."

"I have been keenly following your performances this year and the brightest spark that I have seen in you is your patience. And it's this patience of yours that we would need in abundance. You will get all the support from me. Moreover, it would be your first season and you have to ensure that your entry happens with a bang."

"I will try my best, Bhaiya, but first let the team get announced." Jeet smiled

"What team?"

"The Ranji Trophy team, I mean after the trials"

"Does it mean you have a doubt on your selection?"

"Actually Bhaiya, I am not Topal's favourite player. And Chaudhary sahab is also not at the trials. To be honest, I am a bit tentative."

"Come on! Don't be a kid. I know these things matter, but not to the ones who are way ahead of the curve, Jeet. Concentrate on performing well in the forthcoming matches. And dispose these negative thoughts off."

A delighted Jeet took Deepak's leave.

≈

The names of the selected players were to be announced in the next day's newspaper.

"I won't be able to sleep the whole night," said Kamlesh at the dining table. Kanwar and she had been waiting eagerly for Jeet to give them the good news.

"The hawker will deliver the newspaper around seven. You mean, you would be awake till then?" countered Kanwar.

"Sleep peacefully Mom, there is no way I can be left out. Moreover, I will go to the main bus stand early in the morning to fetch the newspaper. I am sure I will be home with the newspaper by 5, with my name in it. But only if you promise to sleep peacefully."

"Alright," smiled Kamlesh.

Kanwar was not the one to be lagged behind in enthusiasm. He announced he will get a box of sweets in the morning when Jeet leaves to get the newspaper.

"Not possible Dad; I will be here by 5 a.m. and no shop opens that early."

Jeet's comment made the husband and wife smile at each other.

"What?" Jeet wondered, looking at Kamlesh and then at Kanwar.

"Shall I tell or..."

"You tell," said Kamlesh.

"Beta, when you were around four years old, you got this habit of asking for sweets as early as four in the morning."

"Me?"

"Yes, who else?" replied Kamlesh, smiling ear to ear.

"The first couple of days we ignored, but you never relented. So on the third day, I took you along and went to the Rewari wala shop cum residence. The poor man came out rubbing his eyes and opened his shop at 4 a.m. to give us sweets. Only after eating those sweets did you go back to sleep. Then this became a routine with you, and someone ended up waking the poor guy up at that unearthly hour for your sweets."

"I don't believe this, Dad. Plus, you could have bought and kept the sweets at home so that I could eat them at home at odd hours!"

"And you thought we didn't do that, dear intelligent son?" said Kamlesh. "You were adamant that you would get the sweets from the shop only and not the ones that were at home."

"It's incredible Mom. And for how long did it go on like this?"

"It lasted around one year and then your peculiar habit stopped as abruptly as it had begun. Tomorrow that practice will come to life again for a day, when your father will bang at the poor man's doors."

As planned, Jeet left for the bus stand at 3.30 a.m. Kanwar woke up a little later and left to get the sweets. It was 3.45 when Jeet reached the main bus stand. The place looked like a sea of newspapers. The hawkers were segregating and arranging the newspapers to be delivered.

"Bhaiya, please give me a copy of *Hindustan Times*," Jeet said to the vendor nearest to where he had parked his bike. Jeet gave the vendor the exact change and jumped to the sports page. There wasn't any brief.

Strange, he thought. *Maybe it's in some other newspaper.*

"Bhaiya, give me *The Indian Express* and *The Tribune* also."

"Haryana team announced," read one of the headlines in *The Tribune*. Whereas it took not more thirty seconds to go through the news brief, it was likely to take years to negotiate the jolt of the effects it was to have. He read the list again, and again, and again. Unfortunately, each time the names in the list remained the same.

No sooner had Kamlesh heard the vroom of the bike than she came rushing from the kitchen. There are times when words aren't required. Jeet's countenance gave it all away. Kamlesh felt weak. Just then, Kanwar entered home with the box full of sweets in his hands, struggling to keep it away from the street dogs that had been attracted by the aroma. Kanwar's smile faded as he looked at the blank faces of his wife and son. Sensing his mind getting distracted from the box of sweets, the dogs pounced at it. The sweets lay scattered on the floor as the two devils fought to get the lion's share. Topal and Gupta slept peacefully at their respective homes dreaming of their respective shares out of the deal while the two dogs continued to feast on the box of sweets.

The Prime Minister's Office 1

If I can do away with the gloom of not getting selected and if I can jettison my cricketing dream for good, I would be able me to plan and do something concrete about getting our house back. You win some, you lose some. Let me at least salvage whatever pride I can. Certainly not all was lost.

Jeet thought hard, tried to bring his injured parts together and regain his lost morale. A thought got triggered and he rushed to kick start his bike. He was headed towards Dinesh's house.

"I don't want to play cricket anymore," Jeet said with a face that lacked emotion.

"But why?" asked an astounded Dinesh.

" I don't have the under-19 with me any longer."

"Yes. So?"

"That means that the entire season, I will have to practice, with the hope that I get selected for the next year's Ranji Trophy."

"Yes."

"And if I don't get selected the next time too, then again the same thing will repeat next year."

"Well..."

"Do you agree this was my best chance when I had performed better than anybody else?"

"Even your biggest critic has to agree to that."

"So, what makes one believe that the cruel Topal will have a change of heart the next year or the next to the next? The only thing that my continued efforts would ensure is that I will be a a liability for my parents till I continue my struggle."

"But that will also mean a premature end to a really promising talent."

"Ha, talent!" Jeet laughed with sarcasm. "What results has this talent given, Dinesh? At the end of the day, it's the success that matters, isn't it? And my success as a cricketer is in the hands of one human being called Topal. If he pushes my name in the selection meetings, I get selected, else I fail. It's laughable. It's my life and my career, and the success of it does not depend on how many runs I score or how fit I am or how many hours each day I put in the nets. It depends on one thing and one thing only: whether or not Topal recommends me. I don't want the life of charity. I can't plead with him. I want a life where I am judged by the talents that I possess and not by the number of visits I make to Topal's house to satiate him." Jeet said in almost a single breath.

"See Jeet," Dinesh held his had, "I understand each word that you have said. Tell me what you have in mind. How do you want to go about your career?"

"I don't want to play cricket anymore."

"And do what?"

"I need your help."

"Tell me."

"Do you remember once you told me about your uncle?"

"Which one?"

"Your father's cousin; who is a manager in some bank."

"Yes, Mukesh uncle. He is the manager at Oriental Bank of Commerce; but what about him?"

"I want to enquire if I can get some loan, so that I can get back my house. I can no longer bank on my game. I have to look for other avenues." The words manifested Jeet's pain.

"When do you want to go to him?"

"How about now?"

~

"See beta, in banking terms what you are referring to is called personal loan. "

Mukesh, Dinesh's uncle, had spoken after giving a patient hearing to Jeet. He was in his mid-forties. Dressed in a light blue striped shirt and dark trousers, his countenance matched his job from all possible angles. His dyed hair, however, had failed in its efforts at making him look younger.

"Like any other bank manager," Dinesh had said categorically on their way to the bank, "my uncle is very particular about the documentation. Despite the proximity, he wouldn't compromise on that."

"Alright, so can we get it uncle?" Jeet crouched a little, shifting his weight to the table.

"The bank gives loan on two accounts: either against an immovable property which in your case is already mortgaged, or in case the concerned person is a government employee. I mean these are the policies of the bank; immovable property and a job with the government act as sureties for the bank that the money will be returned."

"But we will return each penny," Jeet pleaded.

"Sorry beta, I cannot go against the policies set by the bank."

Mukesh had put his foot down. His emotionless countenance had left no room for further negotiation. Jeet thanked him and moved out. Dinesh followed him.

"Why don't you try for a government job?" Dinesh said as he sat behind Jeet on his bike.

"Don't kid around Dinesh. I am not even a graduate."

"But you would be, this year. You are in the final year, and don't forget, you are a sportsman."

"Don't talk about sports to me now, please."

"Ok, but see," Dinesh continued as they headed towards Gurgaon, "You know there is a quota for sportsmen in all government jobs."

"You mean they appoint sportsmen?" Jeet saw a ray of hope peep through the dark clouds.

"Yeah, there is a five percent reservation."

"I am sure I have seen some vacancies in the sports section of the *Employment News*, Maybe in Railways. Wait here, I would rush and get the newspaper from my study room." They were at Dinesh's house. Within minutes Dinesh was back with the newspaper.

"Don't be over zealous." Jeet smiled, Dinesh's eagerness hadn't gone unnoticed as he flipped through the pages, "There can be so many disciplines covered under sports. We have to look only for the cricket vacancies."

"Oh! I hardly knew! By the way, thanks for telling me you don't play football," Dinesh mocked before coming out with the required page.

"I hope it's not football that gets mentioned here." Dinesh winked as Jeet almost snatched the weekly from him. It was cricket alright. Although the exact number of vacancies wasn't elaborated, yet the date for the trials and other requisites were mentioned without any ambiguity.

"It's just one week for the commencement of trials," he said, deeply engrossed in the advertisement.

"That's pretty quick," asserted Dinesh. "And the best part is that the interview would be held the very same day of the trials. That's jet speed man. Suits you Jeet; appears to be tailor-made for you." He was clearly excited.

"Can I keep this paper-cutting?"

"All yours, brother. Keep the whole newspaper instead. As it is, there are no engineering vacancies in there to interest me."

"Will take your leave now."

"So soon?"

"You know there is one thing I am fighting against, and that's time." Jeet smiled.

. "There is something I want to tell you." Dinesh looked serious,

"Sure, go ahead" Dinesh's tone had ignited his curiosity

"Maybe you won't like it"

"But still you have to tell it to me, now that you have brought it up"

"It's about Ram Sharan."

"What about him?"

"He keeps saying to the entire village..."

"Keeps saying what? Come on Dinesh! Don't move in circles, for God's sake!"

"He met Babuji the other day."

"Ok, and then?"

"He said that you people won't be able to get the house back."

"And what reasons did he give for that?" Jeet kept a straight face, hiding the trigger of the volcano somewhere deep inside.

"He said you people won't be able be able to get the money arranged till the specified date, and then he would keep the house for himself."

Something painful had gripped Jeet's heart. Despite the volcano inside, he didn't want his emotions get the better of him. But Dinesh was too close a friend to not know the storms that had got erupted.

"I knew it would hardly be pleasant for me to say and for you to listen to such things," Dinesh held Jeet's hand, "but I thought you should be made aware of what lies hidden in Ram Sharan's mind, as it should make your resolve only stronger."

"Don't worry, Dinesh," Jeet tightened his grip as they shook hands. "Let's wait for the right time, and we should let Ram Sharan wait for the right time too. I promise all his queries will be answered."

"You know, all the village cricketers miss you," Dinesh walked outside with Jeet to see him off. "We all miss your numerous innings that lifted our team out of trouble now and then. I know your hands are full. But let's arrange one match. It's not a big ask, or is it?"

"You know more than anybody else, that for me, there can be nothing better than a game of cricket. But these are hardly the ideal times Dinesh. I believe we should wait for the atmosphere to get a little more conducive, shouldn't we?"

"Sure we should, Jeet."

Jeet increased the intensity of his practice sessions. He wanted to utilize to the extent possible the seven days between the notification date and the date for trials. Everything happened quickly. As had been stipulated, the interview sessions were conducted the same day at Baroda House which was just a couple of minutes' drive from the Railway stadium where the trials were held.

Within one week, the report of shortlisted candidates was dispatched to the administrative section. One copy of the trial report was also handed over to the candidate concerned. "I find the candidate fit to be appointed under a suitable post in the Railways," the trial coach had categorically mentioned in Jeet's report. What wasn't received, however, was the document that mattered most, the appointment letter.

"In all likelihood you will receive your letter within one month," Jeet was told when he queried about the same at Baroda House. But when the appointment letter appeared nowhere in sight even after the month had long passed, Jeet thought of meeting with the trial coach.

"It's not in my hands now," the trial coach was straightforward. "My job was limited to holding the trials and submitting the reports in all fairness. I have not been a part of the rest of the process and can't help you. Why don't you approach the administrative bench? Amit Srivastava is your man."

Securing appointment with Amit Srivastava was anything but cake walk. More often than not the officer was on tour. After repeated attempts, Jeet at last managed to meet him.

"Please take a seat," the tobacco-chewing- fifty-something Srivastava had appeared to be polite initially. "Let me see what all we have here!" The officer perused the file meticulously, turning page after page. After a few seconds, Jeet noticed the impassive face of the officer turning into one with frowns.

"We will see what can be done. And by the way, you have no business in having this trial report with you; it's a confidential document." He looked from above his reading glasses- that were perched on the edge on his nose. He now sounded and looked like a wily old fox.

"But this is my trial report, how can it be a confidential document?" Jeet retorted. He could sense that he had ended up sounding rude, despite his efforts at being polite.

"Well, let's see." The officer clearly wasn't amused.

"When can I come next?" Jeet shot back

"Come next- for what?"

"For the letter of appointment."

"You don't have to come for that, we would be sending it in due course."

"But when?"

"Soon," Jeet saw hints of anger as Srivastava pressed his buzzer to summon somebody- a clear signal that the meeting was over.

Another month had passed but there were no signs of the letter. Even after continuous efforts, Jeet couldn't secure another appointment with Srivastava.

"Sahab is busy," was the routine reply he got from his secretary. Kamlesh could see the grind that her son was going through. The hard work didn't trouble her, for she knew that struggles and hard work are only going to make him tougher. It was the 'almost chronic' failure that accompanied the struggle that didn't find fancy with her. She would see Jeet start in the morning with the file of his testimonials in his hand and radiance in his eyes, but each time when he returned, the file would still be in his hands but the eyes had lost the radiance.

"Is it justified?" she would at times think. "Am I doing the right thing by allowing him to face the adversities of this world single-handedly? Is getting the house back really worth the pain my son is going through?"

Despite her concerns, she didn't want to act in haste. Having pondered over the issue for a considerable while, she thought it best to bring up the issue, but in not so serious a manner. By doing that she would be able to gauge the potency of tools that her son was fighting the battle with.

"Jeet," she called out to him just as he was about to sleep after another tiring day.

"Yes mom," he opened the door and came out to speak to her.

"Not that it's that much of an issue, but don't you think you have been to the Railways office quite a few times?"

"Yes mom, you are right. But are the circumstances anything even close to being normal?" the shakiness in his voice hadn't gone unnoticed.

"Do not give way to gloomy thoughts, son. Listen to me carefully: nothing is more important than the happiness of my son. Remember, your courage should always rise with every effort at intimidating you." Kamlesh hugged him. Jeet felt the stubborn, frozen lava move within him. By biting his lip hard, he tried to stop the flow, but to no avail. He could fight, and fight well with the ridicules of the world, the indirect taunts of Ram Sharan and even the tormenting cold shoulder of the Railways officials. But the warmth of a mother's bosom proved no match for his resilience. Tightening his embrace, he broke down. Tears that had been frozen for months flowed incessantly, and he cried like a baby. Kamlesh kept a stern upper lip. She was hardly surprised at Jeet's outburst. In a way she was happy that a free release of the lava could get the volcano to its calmer self once more. Minutes later, the tears had dried up, but the sobbing continued.

"Wait, let me get curd and sugar for you," Kamlesh tried to move out to diffuse the situation to some degree.

"Sorry I cried, Mom," Jeet called as she looked back smiling at Jeet's innocence.

As Jeet slowly ate the curd and sugar she brought, she knew now was the time to talk. She asked Jeet to tell her everything that had been happening at the Railway department and Jeet unfolded all. Kamlesh listened in rapt attention without interruptions of any kind. She allowed everything to sink in.

"When are you supposed to go there next?" she spoke after a prolonged silence.

"Tomorrow," Jeet replied

"Don't go," she said plainly.

"But mom..."

"Jeet," she cut her son short, "By whatever you have told me about Srivastava, I perceive in him no inclination of serving the much deserved appointment letter to you on a platter. In my opinion, pursuing things with him any further would be nothing more than a mere waste of time."

"But why do you think he is doing it?"

"His partiality seems to rest elsewhere. Maybe he wants to wear you down by constant humiliation, so that when you are tired and don't follow things anymore, he may grant the job to someone of his own choice."

"But he can do it right now also, Mom. After all, he has the power."

"He is finding it difficult to do it right now."

"I fail to understand why?"

"Your trial report clearly mentions that you have been considered fit for the appointment. He cannot ignore the report. Moreover, the trial coach has done you a huge favour by handing over the copy of the report. He is surely a righteous and an honest man."

"You seem to be right Mom, because when I showed Srivastava the copy of the trial report, he seemed to be slightly uncomfortable. He said that it was a confidential document and that I should not be having the copy of it."

"Then what did you say?"

Jeet told her what his reply was.

"You shouldn't have shown the copy to him, because he can try to harm the trial coach. But I believe since the coach was in the right by doing what he did, there is nothing much that Srivastava can do against him other than swearing at him, that too in his own mind."

"But what should I do now?"

"We will write to the highest authority."

"Do you mean the chairman?"

"No, still higher."

"Do you mean the minister of Railways then?"

"No, still higher."

"Then who?" Jeet's curiosity was sky high.

"The Prime Minister."

"What...are you kidding, Mom?"

"No son not at all. I mean every word."

"But with the degree of issues that our PM faces every day, why would he be bothered in the least about somebody by the name of Jeet not getting his due."

"Let the injustice be reported at the highest level, Jeet. Do as I say."

"For sure, I wouldn't do it any other way Mom, but...I mean... are you sure?"

"As sure as daylight."

"Whatever you say, Mom," the tone spelled tentativeness.

"Tell me what troubles you, son?" Kamlesh had noticed the hesitation.

"Nothing as such Mom, but..."

"But what?"

"What if people come to know that we have written to the highest authorities against them?"

"By people, do you mean Srivastava?"

Jeet nodded.

"And you fear that they may delay things on purpose?" Kamlesh continued.

"Something like that."

"But he is already against us, isn't he?"

"Yes he is. But..."

Kamlesh took a deep breath. She had assessed, quite accurately the reasons for Jeet's tentativeness. The house issue was getting to the boy. He wanted it back at any cost, and that's why he was being driven crazy for the job in question. She decided to tread carefully.

"Shall we do one thing?"

"What?" responded Jeet.

"Shall we take your dad's opinion on this before deciding upon anything?"

Jeet agreed to the proposal. Kanwar was to come home in two days. "But till something gets finalized, you will not go to meet Srivastava." Kamlesh strictly told him and he readily agreed.

Two days later, the matter was brought to Kanwar's notice. First the three of them had a heart to heart discussion and then Kamlesh made Jeet talk to his father in privacy so as to get his concerns- if there were any- addressed against her own opinion. Kanwar heard Jeet out patiently. Only after Jeet had poured his heart out, Kanwar began to speak.

"Beta," Kanwar wrapped his hand around Jeet's shoulder, "at least on one count your mother is right. That Srivastava's intentions are dubious. He would in no way give you the job. And in my opinion the time he is sparing to meet you is because of your trial report, or he wouldn't encourage even that. So, whatever we decide should have to be on these lines. What remains to be seen is why your mom is pressing upon for a representation to no less a person than the prime minister himself. For that I will speak to your mom in your absence."

After getting free from her daily chores, Kamlesh sat with her husband to discuss the issue further.

"Tell me why do you want us to write to the prime minister?" Kanwar came straight to the point.

"Two reasons."

"Shoot."

"The point, Jeet's dad, is that this person Srivastava appears to be no less than a crook. If we write to his higher bosses or even to the minister of Railways, it is possible that he might try to influence things further. There is a possibility he may have his contacts all over the Railway board."

"Yeah, right, I agree with you."

"But if we write to the PM and if, God willing, the application is even forwarded by the Prime Minister's office and marked to the Railway Minister or the chairman, they would be forced to act on it, for the reason that it has come from the PMO." Kanwar thought and thought hard. He analyzed every minute detail.

"Kamlesh," he said after a while, "It is me who works for the government and therefore is expected to know a thing or two about how our system works. But you, in your capacity as a house wife, should be the last person to have come up with such an idea. Tell me how did it come to you?"

"Are you suggesting that you agree with my argument that the representation should be sent to the PM?"

"Without doubt, but tell me how did this strike you?"

"A little bit of common sense I suppose and..."

"And?"

"Jeet's trial report, combined with the fact that he possesses a copy of the same. They won't be able to ignore it. And there is one more thing..."

"What's that?"

"Have you observed Jeet's tentativeness?"

"Yes, he is little fearful when it comes to Srivastava."

"Exactly, he believes it would be wrong to get this Srivastava's feathers ruffled up, whereas we have to teach him through our actions, that bullies like Srivastava are actually cowards and that they are likely to surrender at the first aggressive step taken against them."

"Yes, because people like Srivastava have skeletons in their cupboards and they get their tail in between their legs the moment they get the hint that someone is trying to get those skeletons out in the open."

"So, does the issue rest now?"

"Totally"

"Let me attend to my kitchen chores then." Kamlesh walked out, leaving behind a mesmerized Kanwar.

In the morning, Jeet and Kanwar got together to draft a proper representation. The trial report, certificates and paper cuttings were neatly photocopied and attached with the representation. The neat folder was then speed posted to the Prime Minister of India.

The Faculty Member

"It's taking forever Dinesh."

The friends were seated in their favourite Chinese restaurant.

"What is taking forever?"

The waiter had taken the order. Food, however, was the last thing on their minds.

"This trial thing."

Dinesh didn't respond. The waiter placed the order, but both of them were lost in thoughts. The noodles stayed untouched.

"And the deadline for the house is getting closer by the day."

Jeet looked at Dinesh in anticipation.

"You know," Dinesh spoke, "you should prepare for competitive exams as well."

"Competitive exams! You mean I should be studying now-something that I haven't done after class X."

"Precisely. And believe me you will excel at that. With your schooling, I mean with a background of a convent school, you won't find it that difficult. I mean English won't be a problem, and Maths too is class-X based. So with a little bit of brushing up, you should be ok, and in a position to clear any competitive exam you aim for. But I want to make one request to you."

"What?"

"Don't stop your practice altogether. Don't forget you have applied in various organisations for vacancies against sports quota. I mean when you are called for trials there, you wouldn't want to embarrass yourself by finding yourself out of practice. Also, do not totally give up on the Railways issue. You never know."

"Yes, you have a point. Don't worry I wouldn't stop going to the nets." After some deliberation, he asked, "But which exams in particular do you think I can prepare for?"

"There are so many exams Jeet. You may prepare for bank probationary officer or you can opt for central police organisations exam. In fact, there are a number of them, and the good thing is that they have common syllabus."

"Oh! That should be a breather, Dinesh. You mean if I prepare for one exam, I will be preparing for a number of exams at the same time?"

"Exactly."

"And how should I prepare? Do you think I should join some institute? I mean if at all there are any such institutes in the first place?"

"Of course there are. One of them is Sachdeva College which has a branch in Civil Lines not far away from your house. You go and check with them. I am sure once you talk to them, you would be able to judge their standards."

"How much would the fees be?"

"I don't exactly know the fee structure, but I suggest you carry ten thousand rupees with you when you go for admission. I believe that should be sufficient."

"Is it the fee for the entire course? I will have to ask mom for the money," he lamented.

"Yes I am talking about the entire course fee; you shouldn't be too bothered about the money part, rather consider it as an investment. If you shy away from it, there wouldn't be any returns."

Dinesh wasn't wrong. Action was needed to remain afloat. It wasn't, however, easy to demand money from his mother, but Jeet managed it.

"Here it is." Kamlesh handed over a wad of hundred rupee notes.

"Thanks mom," he put the wad in his pocket and rushed out without looking at her. Delight would have been his, had there been a way to know he would be returning the wad to her in a couple of hours, just as he used to return his pocket money. Not aware of the events that awaited him, Jeet climbed the stairs to enter Sachdeva College, the institute Dinesh had referred.

The reception area had two officials – Chiranjeev Sharma, the director of the institute, and Hansraj, the office assistant. The director had a separate cabin too but he too was seated at the reception. Both of them were busy attending to the students. It was Hansraj, the assistant, who smiled towards Jeet and asked him to be seated.

"I will talk to you in a moment," Hansraj was all politeness. An office boy offered a glass of water to Jeet..

"Please take your time," Jeet responded as he sipped water.

As his eyeballs scanned the institute, he caught sight of some papers lying in a paper tray in front of him. Inadvertently he picked one of the papers. It was an English Grammar assignment for bank P.O. examinations. For twenty-five objective questions, each carrying one mark, the time allotted was seventeen minutes. He took out his pen and started solving the objective type questions. Surprisingly, he found them pretty easy. After marking all the answers, he looked at the watch. It had taken him twelve minutes.

Not bad, he thought. *But let me ensure how many are actually correct.*

"Excuse me, Mr Hansraj," he asked the assistant who was still busy with the admission seekers. Jeet had read the official's name tag.

"Yes please," Hansraj looked at him.

"Can I have the answers of this assignment?"

"Have you solved it?" he asked with a hint of surprise.

"Just tried a little bit," Jeet smiled.

"They are at the back of the assignment."

"Right, thanks."

Jeet was surprised as well as delighted to see the result. He had got twenty-three correct answers. Just as he was pondering upon his thoughts, the director called him.

"You may please come here," the director pointed towards the chair opposite to his seat. The people he had been attending to had now left.

As Jeet got up to move, he caught sight of the message on the notice board.

"Faculty required for English."

The distance between the two chairs was not more than a few feet and it took Jeet not more than a couple of seconds to cover those couple of feet. But in those couple of seconds, he had taken a vital decision. He had decided to play a gamble, though he wasn't sure whether he would be able to pull it off.

"Yes please. I am Chiranjeev Sharma. Tell me how can I help you?" the director was polite

"Hi, I am Jeet," he said, taking the chair he was offered.

"Will you have water?"

"I have already had, thank you."

"Yes tell me, which course would you like to join?"

"Actually, I have come to apply for a faculty member's post." Jeet pointed towards the notice board

"Oh, ok," the director was caught off guard. "And what are your qualifications?"

"Well, I am...a...graduate."

"A mere graduate?"

"Yes... I mean I will be in a couple of months." Jeet fumbled

"And how old are you?"

"I am twenty."

"Well, well." The director smiled

The director thought hard for some time and Jeet watched him intently. Hansraj too watched with total attention. The students that he had been attending to, had also left.

"See Mr Jeet," the director spoke after apparently giving the issue a real hard scrutiny. "It's a pre-requisite to hold a B.Ed. degree to be able to apply for a member of faculty. If not that, then the teacher should at least be holding a master's in the relevant subject."

"I can understand that, but surely your students would judge a teacher by the way he teaches and not by the certificates he carries," Jeet tried to negotiate.

"In that case, can I know your experience in teaching Mr Jeet?"

"It's none actually," Jeet said with a straight face, "but there should be no harm in giving it a try. Give me a chance. If you feel less than satisfied, you can always say no."

"May I ask how you got to know about the vacancy, Mr Jeet?"

"I...read it in the newspaper," Jeet bluffed.

"Hmm," the director paused for a while

"Mr Jeet," the director continued, "I am sorry but..."

"Sir," Hansraj intervened before the director could complete his statement, "can I talk to you for a moment?"

"Sure."

"Sir," Hansraj continued as both the director and he moved to an empty classroom. "I believe we should try him."

"But Hansraj, he is just twenty, younger than most of the students whom he desires to teach. And more than that, he is not even a graduate as yet. How can I go against the institution's policies?"

"Sir, we do lack a good local English teacher, and because of that we have to bear with the tantrums of Mr Vashishtha who comes from Delhi and charges the moon. I believe we should give a chance to this boy. If he turns out to be a replacement, it would be a massive relief for us"

"But do you seriously believe he would be able to fit in, Hansraj?"

"Sir, look at the way he is speaking. Even Mr Vashishtha doesn't speak so fluently. I think the boy has spark. And as for his age, the students might feel a little odd in the beginning, but I believe after some time things should fall into place."

"Ok, only if you say so Hansraj. You do one thing. Bring out the toughest assignment and let's see how he performs. If he does well, we will ask him to take a class today itself."

"Sure."

It took Jeet fifteen minutes to complete the twenty-five questions.

"It was a bit tough than the one I had attempted earlier," he smiled at Hansraj as he handed over the assignment back to him after marking the answers.

Hansraj took the sheet and started tallying the answers.

"How many marks will be required for me to qualify, Mr Sharma?" He asked with a smile.

"Well," Sharma answered with a smile, "Since it's a test for the position of a faculty, ideally I believe you should be getting full marks. But let's see."

Hansraj gave Sharma an inquisitive look.

"Tallied, Hansraj?"

"Yes, sir."

"Tell us then."

"Sir, three are incorrect."

"Let me see," Sharma had a look of surprise as Hansraj handed the sheet over to him.

"I believe I should be leaving," Jeet had a sullen face.

"Please wait, Mr Jeet." The director kept the sheet aside, "Considering the fact that you had a look at the assignment for the first time, it's not bad at all."

"And what does it mean?" Jeet's heartbeats had increased.

"It means your class starts in ten minutes. Let's see how you perform there!"

The next ten minutes were spent in an intense discussion where Sharma guided him about how he should go ahead with the class.

"See, the class will be of forty-five minutes. You distribute the assignment. Give the students seventeen minutes to answer it. For the next twenty eight minutes or so you discuss the assignment, which I believe won't be too difficult for you. Also, I will be there with you for the first class."

"That would be a great support, Mr Sharma." Jeet felt obliged.

"Anytime Jeet," the director smiled. A bond of friendship had developed. "Just pay attention to one thing."

"And what's that?" Jeet was totally focussed.

"Never take any questions from the students which are outside of the assignment, and never deviate yourself from the topic. In other words, you will stick to the topic and questions covered through the assignment; nothing more, nothing less."

"Sure."

"And if you stick to that, not only will you be completing the syllabus in time, you will also nullify the chances of the students catching you off-guard with a topic that you might not be so conversant with."

"Of course."

"Let's move then, the students are waiting"

"Sure."

"And one more thing," Sharma said as they continued. "Whatever I say inside the classroom, please do not interrupt me. Even if you think I am misrepresenting a fact or two."

Jeet nodded in agreement, though he couldn't completely figure out the reference of Sharma's comment. The next moment, Sharma had an answer to his query.

"I have to nip the issue of your age in the bud, because if the students accept you as their teacher on the first day itself, it should be a cake walk for you from then on."

Jeet smiled and gestured for Mr Sharma to lead the way into the classroom.

"Good morning students," Sharma addressed the class of thirty as he entered with Jeet right behind him.

"Good morning sir," all the students stood up.

"Please allow me to introduce your new English teacher to you. Meet the young and dynamic Jeet, who at twenty-seven is our youngest and one of the most promising teachers." The class clapped.

"But sir, please excuse me, he doesn't look like he is twenty-seven," said Jyoti who was seated in one of the front benches.

"In fact, he looks younger than some of us here," added Sunita, who was seated with Jyoti.

"Well, in that case, the credit should go to his athletic build. I would take the liberty to also tell you that he is an outstanding sportsman. He plays..."

"Cricket," completed Jeet, having a hearty laugh within himself at the irony that in the guise of a lie, Sharma had actually spoken the truth.

After the class, Jeet looked as happy as a child- when he gets his favourite candy. Sharma too had a look of satisfaction on his face.

"So how was it?" Jeet asked as both of them got settled in the reception room. Hansraj was all ears.

"Not bad, Jeet."

"And?"

"And you can join as faculty today itself. I mean you can come for the evening classes. Hansraj will tell you about our salary package, etc."

"I am thankful to you, Mr Sharma." Jeet was thrilled to the hilt. His gamble had paid off.

"My pleasure. So, then your class starts at 6.00 p.m. in the evening. Please take assignments from Hansraj and go through them before you come," Sharma said to Jeet.

"Sure. By the way, Mr Sharma, can I have a look at the mathematics and reasoning assignments too?"

"You are a member of faculty now, Mr Jeet, every assignment is within your access."

"Thank you so much."

He looked at the Maths and reasoning assignments given to him by Hansraj. After some time, he looked at the director again.

"Can I ask something, Mr Sharma?"

"Sure."

"Can I apply for the position of faculty in maths and reasoning too?"

"Well..." The director smiled. "As of now there aren't any vacancies. But who knows- in the near future there might be one. Can I ask you where did you do your schooling from, Mr Jeet?"

"From nursery to class X, I was in OLF and completed XI and XII from MNSS Rai."

"Oh Rai! So I am not that much of a liar after all."

"Not at all, Mr Sharma. In fact, you had hit the nail right on the head." After talking to Hansraj for some time, Jeet left after thanking Mr Sharma and Hansraj one more time.

"Sir," Hansraj spoke after the sound of Jeet's footsteps had ceased. "It's sure a great relief from the tantrums of Mr Vashishtha."

Sharma smiled. "But sir, one thing isn't clear to me." Hansraj looked curious

"That we hadn't advertised the post in the newspaper...so how did Jeet come to know about it?" Sharma asked with a smile.

"Exactly sir."

"Actually he had come to join as a student, Hansraj."

"I don't believe this, sir."

"You have to believe it. He had a look at the assignment and then he saw the vacancy board. And taking into account both the things, he changed his mind. He thought on his feet, Hansraj. We lack youngsters like him today. Now with doing what he did, not only would he be preparing for the competitions in a much better way, he would be earning money too."

"And did he do well inside the classroom?"

"He did better than most of the established teachers. But it's not what he did that surprised me, but the fact that he knew he would be able to carry it off. It was his confidence-that he would do it-that surprised me."

"Where did he get that confidence from sir?"

"He has been educated in good schools, but more than that, I believe it's in his upbringing. If I am not wrong, he got this taking the bull by the horns attitude from his parents. And Hansraj, you mark my words, he won't be here for long. He is made for something better."

While Sharma and Hansraj were busy chatting, Jeet was returning the wad of hundred rupee notes back to his mother.

The Prime Minister's Office 2

It was precisely at 8 a.m. on a bright Sunday morning. Several months had passed since the letter was dispatched to the prime minister's office. The reply was still awaited. The visitor rang the doorbell of Jeet's house.

The uncertainty and the agonizing wait of several months had done no good to Jeet's already weakened mindset. Teaching at the college without doubt had given a new boost to him and showed him the path to a new destination, but to let go of cricket, something that had been with him for almost forever, was hardly easy. The recruitment in Railways would certainly benefit his situation. It would surely go a long way in not only keeping the sport that he loved so much alive in him, but would help him considerably in his battle against Ram Sharan as well.

But there was no opening in sight. Whereas, both he and Kanwar were now almost convinced that the misadventure of sending the representation to the prime minister was a lost cause, yet fearing the hurt it would cause to Kamlesh, none of them considered bringing the issue for discussions at the dining table. Kamlesh, on the other hand, was assured. Her belief in herself and in the situation was as rock solid as ever before. For her, it was a matter of *when* rather than *if*.

"Who is it?" Jeet called as he walked to the door. It being a Sunday, he was getting ready for his cricket match. Kamlesh was busy preparing his breakfast while Kanwar was absorbed in the morning newspaper.

"Yes please?" Jeet had never seen the middle-aged man before. The man was dressed casually in a striped T-shirt and blue trousers. He was clean shaven, with his hair beginning to turn grey at the temples. For Jeet, he was nothing more than an unwanted visitor. Jeet assumed that this man must have come to meet either his mother or father. He himself was eager to get to the cricket field, and therefore wanted to get rid of him as quickly as he could.

"If I am not wrong, you are Jeet Singh."

"Sure I am. Is there anything that I can do for you?"

"I am Charanjeet Diwan and I work for the Railway board. In fact, I am a part of their cricket team. I live in Shivaji Colony in Gurgaon itself."

Jeet welcomed him inside. The word 'Railway' was enough for him to summon his mom and dad to the drawing room where the gentleman, who held everybody's curiosity, was seated. After wishing Jeet's parents, he started to unfold in detail the purpose of his surprise visit.

"Uncle, as I had told Jeet," despite not much disparity in their age, Charanjeet addressed Kanwar as uncle, "I am a cricketer too and I am employed with the Railway board. This year our team had made a request to the authorities to get a new and talented cricketer appointed through sports quota so that our team gets strengthened. So, they have considered our request and there are several names doing the rounds that can be considered for appointment."

"That's fine, but how does it concern me?" asked Jeet.

"It concerns you because one of the names doing the rounds is yours. To cut the long story short, thanks to your recent domestic performances, your name isn't now unknown to anyone. When we came to know your name is in the reckoning, we made a request to the selection committee that it would serve the interest of our team in case you were given the seat."

Jeet was ecstatic but he didn't allow his feelings to go overboard and kept an impassive face. His parents too hadn't shown any out of the world reactions.

"Does it mean he is going to be recruited?" asked Kanwar.

"I cannot, as of now, assure that uncle, but the chances are bright. Our whole team is behind him and the team does have a say in the matters of selections."

"But as per the trial report, he has already been selected."

"But the trails haven't happened as yet. In fact, there aren't any trials. There is just an interview. And his interview letter is getting drafted. It is likely to get dispatched tomorrow."

Charanjeet was shown the trial report and was told about the related developments.

"Actually uncle, this trial report has nothing to do with the Railway board. Railways and Railway board are separate entities when it comes to sports. Both have their different administrative offices. So in a way, I would make it clear that this trial report or the interview that happened at the Railways has nothing to do with the Railway board. You should consider the Railway board issue as a fresh initiative."

"How many vacancies are there?" asked Jeet.

"That is under the wraps till now. But we would know it in a day or two."

"But tell me one thing, Charanjeet ji," Kamlesh spoke for the first time, "Jeet hadn't applied in the Railway board, so how is it that they are sending him this interview letter? Shall we then understand that it's your team who influenced them in sending the interview call?"

"No aunty. We only came to know through the authorities that Jeet's name too is getting considered. After that we made a request to them to appoint him, as he is not only talented but suits the needs of our team. "

Jeet had started thinking. "Mom's query is spot on. It is out of the ordinary that a candidate, who hasn't applied in the first case, was being sent a call for the interview. Clearly, something was amiss."

"But the name must have erupted from somewhere," Kanwar said, "After all- it cannot be simply out of the blue."

"I have no clue, but you please trust us. We are going to get him appointed. There is a possibility that he might have been considered because his name has been popping up in the newspapers now and then. After all, our sports department keeps a track of all these things. I mean it's a routine thing. Please do not give it another thought."

Thought Jeet was far from convinced, he did not speak. The gentleman had left positive vibes.

"Hopefully tomorrow itself we would come to know about the number of vacancies and the number of candidates appearing against those vacancies. Come to our office tomorrow and collect your letter by hand," he had told Jeet before leaving.

After having seen Charanjeet off, Jeet pondered over the issue for a considerable time. After having thought for long, he went to his dad.

"Dad, do you think these recent developments have anything to do with the representations we had made to the prime minister?"

"That is not possible, Jeet. Assuming the PM office decided to act on our representation, they would have taken us in the loop for sure. I mean they would have informed us that this is the action that they have taken. This is how the system works."

"That's fine dad, but how could they invite me for an interview when I haven't applied in the first case?"

"But Charan himself said that the sports department keeps a tab on the players' performances and that it's nothing more than a routine thing."

Far from convinced, Jeet simply nodded his head.

The next day, Kanwar left for office from where he was to return not before the weekend. Jeet headed to Charanjeet's office. Jeet was mesmerized at the sight of Rail Bhavan. Situated adjacent to the lawns of India Gate, its sight was nothing short of grandeur. It had hundreds of offices inside, mostly occupied by the officials of the Railway board. Not only did it house all the members and chairman of the board but also the Minister of Railways.

After getting his visitor pass made, he headed straight to Charanjeet's office on the 8th floor.

After exchanging formal greetings, Charanjeet came directly to the point, "I am in the know of everything now. Since morning I have been in touch with the concerned officers and there are exactly 116 interview letters to be issued."

"Ok, but for how many vacancies in all?" Jeet was on the edge of his seat.

"That's the tricky part actually," Charanjeet seemed defensive and uncertain.

"Tricky means?"

"Actually there is just one vacancy."

"Just one?" Jeet almost jumped out of his seat.

"Yes."

"Then?" Jeet took a deep breath. "I mean where do we stand in this scenario?"

"We are trying our level best."

"And is it confirmed that they are going to appoint a cricketer or are they interviewing people from other disciplines also?"

"Actually, interview calls are being sent to sportsmen from all disciplines. I mean cricket, football, hockey, etc."

"Fine," Jeet took a deep breath. He politely turned down Charanjeet's invitation for lunch and headed straight home.

It was almost 6 p.m. when he reached. As always Kamlesh immediately figured out all was not well. She knew something had gone wrong at Rail Bhavan. The circumstances had surely changed. The hope that appeared to have danced with Jeet all morning now appeared to have lost its sheen in proportion to the setting sun.

After indulging himself in a prolonged bath, Jeet slipped into a fresh pair of kurta pyjama. Kamlesh placed his favourite dish of rajma-rice on the table and sat beside him. Jeet knew Kamlesh had a thousand questions in her mind, but would not want her son to go through the ordeal of the day one more time without at least having finished his meal.

"Shoot mom," smiled Jeet as he pushed aside the empty utensils.

"Tell me all," she smiled back.

"There is just one vacancy."

"And the number of candidates?"

"One hundred and sixteen."

"Does it look bad to you then?"

"I don't know. There is something else also, Mom."

"What?"

"They can recruit from other discipline too."

"Hmm."

"Now you tell me how bad does it sound?"

"As bad as you allow it to sound, son," she said calmly.

"What do you mean?"

"Your job shouldn't be to count your competitors, but doing well in the interview. Do your best there and leave the rest to God."

Dressed in dark blue trousers and an impeccable white shirt, Jeet reached Rail Bhavan precisely at 9.30 a.m., a good thirty minutes before the interview was to start. Charanjeet and his teammates were pro-active in receiving him and made him feel at home.

As the list of candidates was big, several offices were vacated temporarily to make seating available to them.

Jeet's number was 56 in the list. At precisely 10 a.m., the first in the serial number was called in. The process of the candidates going in and coming out continued. On an average, a candidate was given two minutes.

The waiting candidates started talking among themselves to avoid monotony. Jeet, however, kept mostly to himself.

"This interview process is an eyewash." The candidate sitting beside Jeet suddenly addressed him.

"What makes you say that?"

"There is a rumour that they have already selected a candidate, a cricketer actually."

"A cricketer? But who?"

"Some Jeetu."

"Jeetu?"

"Yes he is an opening batsman."

"But how do you know?"

"My uncle tried to pull some strings to get me the job, but he was told by someone at a very high level that nothing can be done as the vacancy has already been filled."

Before Jeet could talk further, the candidate was called in. Next was Jeet's turn.

Had he mistaken Jeet for Jeetu? Jeet asked himself, but then he let the thought pass as he concentrated at being calm and to focus at the job at hand.

But even then his heart went out for Charanjeet. If at all it is his name that's doing the rounds, then all credit would go to Charanjeet.

He appeared to be an angel who had come to anchor his boat at the right time.

Jeet saw Charanjeet approaching him. The smile on his face seemed godly at that moment. Had it not been for the sensitivity of the occasion, Jeet would have bent down to touch his feet.

"Bhaiya, they are all saying that I've already been selected." His tone, though low, was animated.

"Who all are saying?" Even he seemed surprised as he rolled his half sleeves.

"The candidates."

"Ok." There was silence for a considerable time, after which he continued, "Jeet, you don't have to pay attention to what others are saying. Simply concentrate on the interview."

"Don't worry about that, Bhaiya. I am not bad at communicating. I'm convent educated."

"Listen," Charanjeet bent towards his ear, "When did you complete your graduation?"

"This year, Bhaiya."

"And have you joined any course after that? I mean post graduation or anything?"

"Not really."

"They are putting this question to everyone. So in case they put the question to you, just say that you have joined a correspondence course for post-graduation or for a degree in law or whatever."

"But why, Bhaiya?"

"So that it might not appear that you haven't been doing anything for several months."

"But Bhaiya, it would be a lie."

"Maybe, but it's for a good cause, so just tell them what I am telling you. In fact, they were informally asking me, so rather than saying I don't know, I said you are doing law through correspondence.

So, at least for my sake, please tell them the same thing in case they ask."

"But what if they ask for any document to certify this?"

"Tell them you haven't brought any such document as you didn't think it was required as this is a sports quota seat."

"Bhaiya, I don't know, but it isn't sounding good." At that very moment, the candidate before Jeet walked out. It was his turn to go.

"You leave the sounding part to me and tell them what you are supposed to. All the best."

As Jeet opened the door, he saw four people constituting the interview board.

Jeet greeted them.

"Good morning Mr. Singh, please have a seat."

The person seated second from the left spoke with a certain degree of charm befitting a senior government official.

This could be the chairman, Jeet thought as he got seated attentively on the designated chair.

"So you completed your B.Sc. this year?"

"Yes sir." Jeet feared the question that Charan had cautioned him about could come up, but he hadn't expected it to be the very first question itself.

"And what are you doing now? I mean besides playing cricket, of course."

"Sir I am pursuing law."

A blunt lie. Jeet thanked his stars Y.P. wasn't one of the interviewers. But did he have a choice after whatever Charan had unfolded?

"That's good." The chairman seemed to be impressed and Jeet took a deep breath.

"But you have not mentioned it in your resume?"

"Since it's my sports resume, I didn't find it necessary to mention it, sir." He spoke a second lie to cover the first.

Jeet felt the sweat in his palms, fearing that the panellists could ask him something to do with law. He tried hard and kept a calm countenance with considerable success.

To his relief, all other questions were focused on cricket.

The interview lasted for about five minutes. He was headed home after meeting Charan.

Kamlesh was happy to see the positive changes in Jeet. The gloom of the other day was now gone. His sparkling eyes exuded hope. Jeet told her about the rumour and the lie that he had spoken. He also told her about the concerns that Charan and his team had showed towards him.

"Mom do you think it was right for me to say what I did?"

"Under the circumstances I don't think you were left with too many options, especially after Charan had told you about what he had said to them. So, you did whatever you thought was right under the circumstances."

"But I am sure Y.P. sir wouldn't have endorsed this lie, despite the circumstances."

"But it's the heart of a mother that I possess, son, not that of a school principal."

Jeet hugged his mom tight, very tight.

≈

It was the fourth day from the date of the interview that Charan knocked on Jeet's doors early in the day. The box of sweets in Charan's hands told them the entire story.

"Jeet will have to join within fifteen days of the receipt of the appointment letter." He told the delighted mom-son duo as he sat in the drawing room with a cup of tea in his hand.

"Can't I receive it by hand, I mean the way I had received the interview letter?" Jeet asked.

"No, no." Charan smiled. "An appointment letter has to come by post."

Jeet smiled and felt happy at the turn of events.

"But there is nothing to worry about," reassured Charan. "It is likely to be dispatched tomorrow and would be in your hands a couple of days after that. And don't forget, there are medical and other formalities that are to be completed. Read the appointment letter carefully and act accordingly."

Jeet- ecstatic and satisfied to a considerable extent- knew his entire family would be benefitted by this elevation.

"Charanjeet has got me the job, Mom," Jeet said as both of them came inside after seeing off Charan.

"Yes, son."

≈

The medical turned out to be the most troublesome of all formalities. The stipulated medications that Jeet had to go through made him feverish to the extent that he was unable to get out of the bed. Some documents also needed attestation from local authorities, which- despite his frail health- kept Jeet on his toes.

It was only on the last day of the deadline as per the appointment letter that Jeet entered the chamber of Mr Jately, the officer concerned, to join office.

"Good morning, sir. My name is Jeet Singh." Jeet entered his office after taking due permission from the officer who seemed to be neck deep in the sea of files.

Jately looked in the direction of Jeet, but didn't speak.

"Sir, I have come here to join," Jeet opened his file and placed the appointment letter right in front of him.

"And it's *today* you have come to join! If this is your enthusiasm at the time of joining, what can be expected of you in future?" The officer appeared to be rude.

"Yes sir, it's mentioned today is the last day to join...meaning I can join today also..." Jeet chose his words carefully, *"What if he says I can no longer join."* He had got a little scared.

Jately didn't answer, but his reactions conveyed that he was not all that happy.

"Sir, actually the medical process consumed a lot of time," Jeet almost pleaded.

"But you could have joined and submitted the medical later."

"I am sorry sir, it didn't cross my mind. To be honest, I didn't know- that was an option too."

He put the file that he had held in his hands aside and put his hand forward towards Jeet's file. "Anyway, show me your documents." His frowns lessened a little. The word 'sorry' had brought about the change. As Jeet fiddled around with the documents in the file, the man with the frowns dialled a number.

"Let me talk to sahab," he said on the telephone.

He waited for a little while before speaking again.

"Good morning, sir."

Clearly Jeet was oblivious to what it was all about, as Jately listened attentively to whatever was being said at the other end.

"Yes sir, the boy has joined."

The moment he uttered the words, Jeet was all ears. The last sentence shifted his attention from the papers to the conversation. His efforts at eavesdropping on what was being said at the other end were futile.

Who is at the other end? Suddenly it was becoming a mystery for Jeet. *Is it Charanjeet he is reporting to?*

Of course it has to be Charanjeet. Who else could it be? he thought.

"Sir, was it Charanjeet Bhaiya?" he asked.

"Who Charanjeet Bhaiya?" the man shot back.

"The cricket captain."

"You mean Charanjeet, the assistant?"

"I don't know his designation, but I asked because you seemed to be talking about me."

"Of course I was talking about you, but not to any Charanjeet." *Have I said something childish,* thought Jeet.

"I am taking your papers along and would come back in a few minutes. Till then you can wait here. Would you like some tea or coffee?"

"Thank you, sir. I am perfectly fine."

The officer left, leaving Jeet behind with the unsolved mysteries. He constantly stared at the red telephone that the officer had just talked through. The answer to the mystery of who was responsible for Jeet's appointment lay in the number that had just been dialled. The person at the other end might also have the answer to how and why the interview letter was sent to Jeet despite the fact that he hadn't even applied in the Railway board.

It being his first day at office, he wasn't sure if he should take the risk. He peeped out of the office door. Seeing no one outside, he decided to take the plunge. After all he was his mother's son. He picked up the receiver and punched the redial button. It was on the third ring that the phone was picked.

"Prime minister's office. What can I do for you, please?"

Jeet's head spun and went into a flutter. The picture that got formed in his mind was of none other than that of his mom. It was not Charanjeet, but his mother who had gotten him the job.

The F-24

After a prolonged period of struggle, the roll of dice had started to favour Jeet. It was merely three months after having been appointed by Railways that he had received another call for interview from the department of Central Excise and Customs. The situation enticed him, but at the same time discomforted him too. The interview and trials were going to take place in Hyderabad. Jeet thought hard as he sat in his office with the interview letter in his hand.

It's unlikely, he thought, that a candidate from North would be given preference for the post, given the clout that the locals enjoy upon the authorities in matters of such kind. Moreover, the schedule not only demanded travelling to Hyderabad and back, but also a stay of at least five days.

It's going to cost a considerable amount of money, and since the chances of getting selected are dim, it would be nothing more than a wild goose chase and an unnecessary waste of money. But it could be that I am not assessing the situation correctly. Would I lose a good opportunity by not going? Am I making a mistake by not telling mom about this? Jeet was confused.

Ignoring the voice in his mind, Jeet made an exception by not discussing the matter of such grave importance with Kamlesh; for he knew there was no way Kamlesh would allow him to forgo the trials.

"What is it you are fiddling with?" Seeing him lost, Mrs Devyani- the section officer asked him. More often than not, the section officer and Jeet were the first ones to reach office. It wasn't any different that day. It was 9.30 a.m. and there was no one in the office other than the two of them.

"It's nothing, ma'am," he continued to grapple with ambiguity, "Actually I got a trial and interview letter from Customs and Central Excise, Hyderabad."

"That's great. Lady luck seems to be smiling on you. It's merely two months back that you joined here and now another call for an interview. What position is it for?" she beamed.

"Preventive Officer."

"Wow! It's more than a springboard to promotion, I would say. I mean, if you get selected, you would assume a position which otherwise would take you ten long years through the promotion route."

"Yes, you are right ma'am."

"When is the interview?"

"It's next week, ma'am. Just four days to go."

"It must be in Hyderabad."

"Yes, ma'am."

"But lazy bones, you haven't even applied for leave as yet!" There was affection in her mocked anger.

"Actually ma'am, I have decided not to go."

"But why?" The section officer was surprised.

"I am already working with you now ma'am, so why go elsewhere!" he said in a clear effort at putting the debate to rest.

"But it's for a senior position."

"Sure it is, ma'am. But it's in Hyderabad. So chances are that they would consider local players rather than someone from outside. So why spend money unnecessarily?"

"See, I don't know about the local thing, but what money are you talking about?"

"The money that is to be spent in the to and fro journey, ma'am, and being a recent recruit, I also don't have any leave. In case I take leave and go, money will get deducted from my salary too. I will end up losing money from two ends that way."

"And supposing there was zero money to be spent on journey and no deductions from salary?" the motherly officer curiously smiled.

"But how is that possible?"

"It seems you haven't- as yet- realized that you are working for Railway board, son?" She smiled.

"How ma'am?"

"I have the discretion to sanction leave for seven days to you, and being a Railway board employee yourself, you have the liberty to occasionally travel by train to any chosen destination in India without paying a single penny. Not only this, you are also entitled to avail travelling and daily allowances for your miscellaneous expenses. Further, your seat will be booked from here itself, from Railway board quota that is. So, would you still not want to go?"

Within two hours, Jeet had got his return pass and a confirmed berth in the Andhra Pradesh Express. Also, he got his travelling and daily allowances in advance. He was happy. The quandary, however, hadn't altogether left him. It had merely changed form.

Mom would be really angry to know I had almost let go off an opportunity, he thought. He was- however- eager to tell her everything as soon as he reached home, so that he could bask in her affection once the anger was gone.

"What did you think you were doing?" As expected, Kamlesh wasn't amused. "This kind of stupidity isn't expected from you and that too for the sake of saving some money. And look at what you were ready to put at stake! A possible jump in promotion which through the normal route would take no less than ten years! Thank God for the kind hearted section officer."

"But Mom, they are likely to prefer south Indian candidates," he said meekly.

"Do you think you know everything? Are you Almighty God?"

"No Mom."

"Are you your destiny, Jeet?"

"What Mom?"

"I asked- are you your own destiny?"

Jeet shook his head. He had no clue what his angry mother was asking him.

"Remember beta," Kamlesh had calmed down a little bit, "Your destiny has its own identity. It is a varied and detached being in its own way. At times it puts you through various tests but at other times, because of your perseverance and efforts, it gets under obligation to introduce you to your dreams. But the place and time of the intended meeting between you and your dreams is known only to your destiny and not known to you. So, it becomes imperative for you to throw your hat in at every possible opportunity, else, you risk not reaching the scheduled rendezvous. And let me tell you one secret."

"Tell me, Mom," said a spellbound Jeet.

"Destiny is very clever. More often than not, it gets the meeting scheduled when you tend to believe the odds are totally against you."

When she finished speaking, there was silence. Jeet stood lost; he pondered over what his mother had just told him.

"Did I tell you the story of Achilles?" His mother broke the silence.

"No mom, who was he?"

"He was a Greek war hero and one of the greatest warriors of all times."

"Tell me about him. You know how eagerly I look forward to your stories."

"Achilles was born to Thetis, a woman who had the powers of clairvoyance; she could look into the future. It was predicted that Achilles would die young. To prevent his death, his mother took him to river Styx, which, it was believed, offered invulnerability, and dipped his body into the water. But as Thetis held him by the heel, his heel was not washed over by the water of the magic river. So his heel remained vulnerable. You must have read a phrase 'Achilles' heel' in some of your English books. That means 'a weak spot despite overall strength'. That phrase was born out of this incident."

Jeet nodded and said he had heard his English teacher use it several times.

Kamlesh continued, "Once Achilles was summoned by the Greek kings to fight against the invincible Trojans. He initially refused by saying that it was not his battle and he would be better off not fighting it. But somewhere he thought he should fight it and so he was in a quandary."

"Then what happened, Mom?"

"As always, he went to his mother to seek advice."

"Just like I do, Mom," Jeet raised both his hands in joy and Kamlesh couldn't resist the smile on her face. "Then what happened, Mom?"

"His clairvoyant mother told her son that there was no way he could miss the war as greatness awaited him there."

"But how Mom? I mean what was so special about the war?"

"Firstly, the Trojans were invincible, so whoever defeated them had to possess signs of greatness. Secondly, the war is remembered for Achilles' battle with Hector, the prince from Troy. Hector was the greatest warrior that Troy could boast of. Achilles killed Hector outside the gates of Troy and embraced greatness."

"And what if he hadn't gone to the war?" he asked, although he thought he knew the answer.

"You tell me, now that you know the story."

"By whatever you have told me, rather than smiling on him, destiny would have laughed on his decision and he would be an ordinary fighter lost somewhere in a forgotten history text."

Kamlesh was satisfied. The lesson had been imparted.

That Ahlawat's son Pankaj had also applied for the post at Hyderabad and that he too had received an interview call was known to Jeet during his practice sessions. Further, he also learnt that Pankaj too had got his ticket booked in the same train as Jeet. *Jeet, now that you are in Railway board, we will get our berths adjusted next to each other*, Pankaj had said. The thought of Ahlawat had brought back the bitter feelings that Jeet had experienced during the under-15 matches. Along with the feelings of hatred, he could also feel the germs of revenge taking birth inside him. That the train journey was to provide him with ample opportunities for revenge, he did not know.

But despite Ahlawat's ugly actions, Jeet didn't seem to mind the situation as it had turned out to be. He had never allowed his hatred towards Ahlawat to get seeped on to his son Pankaj. There weren't any reasons for Jeet to suspect Pankaj in having a hand in his father's conspiracies. Hence, for Jeet, Pankaj was as much a fellow cricketer as anyone else. In fact, he liked Pankaj's company rather than despise it, for the fun element that it carried.

Jeet had used the sources at Railway board to get Pankaj's ticket cancelled and to be booked again to have his berth next to Jeet's own. Their berth numbers were 23 and 24 in compartment S-7. The train's scheduled departure was at 6:45 p.m. and it was to reach Hyderabad at 7.00 p.m. the next day.

The AP Express screeched to a halt at platform number 2 of the New Delhi railway station. Within a couple of minutes of the train getting stationed, the hitherto over-crowded platform bore a deserted look. The rivers of people had flown into the sea of compartments in virtually no time.

In between the hustle bustle of the passengers, Jeet and Pankaj, after having struggled a bit, finally got settled. Their one upon the other berths ran parallel to the isle. The revered cricket kit bags were placed on the upper berth while the remainder of the luggage was pushed under the lower.

"I will just be back," Pankaj rushed towards the platform.

"Where are you going? You don't want to miss the train, do you?" Jeet shouted as Pankaj meandered against the incoming crowd.

"Would just be back," Pankaj responded, more with the exaggerated movement of his lips rather than with the sound. Jeet took out *Sports Star*, a weekly sports magazine he had purchased from the vendor at the railway station. By the time Pankaj returned, he had slipped into his slippers.

"Had gone to see the chart," Pankaj barked in Jeet's ears.

"The chart?" Jeet was astounded. "You must be the only fool who gets settled down in his berth first and then traces it on the chart."

"I was not looking for *our* seats."

"Then?"

"Look at this," Jeet took out a sheet from his pocket.

"Oh God! You have torn away the chart! Don't you have some sense, some sympathy for other passengers?"

"Shun your dramatics baba, and look here!" Pankaj pointed out at the list of passengers he had marked with his pen.

"What are you doing?"

"I am highlighting the passengers that would be occupying the remaining berths of our section."

Jeet's stared at the chart spread at the centre of the berth as both of them sat facing each other.

Name	Gender	Age	Berth
Neena	F	24	17
Sushma	F	52	18
Gurjeet Singh	M	55	19
Jeet Singh	M	21	23
Pankaj Ahlawat	M	21	24

"So?" Jeet still had no clue what Pankaj was up to.

"I am sure there can't be a greater fool. Can't you see the young girl travelling with us in our section of the compartment? The one I have marked in red." Pankaj smiled.

"So?"

He smacked his forehead with his palm. "Achha, what do you have in your hand?"

"A magazine- why?"

"Why have you brought it?"

"For the journey, of course."

"This girl in that case, is for my journey." Pankaj pointed towards the name, Neena F24.

~

The passengers having finally settled down, the train moved ahead with a sudden jolt, ferrying along with it hundreds of companions who now shared a common journey for the next twenty-four hours. Jeet looked at his watch: 18:45.

As the name plate on his chest suggested, Ramavtar the TTE visited the compartment for routine ticket checks with a beeline of passengers whose tickets hadn't been confirmed constantly at his back. His countenance however wasn't affected by their exaggerated pleadings. Taking the ticket of every passenger, he would reconcile the name and other status with his own list and then move to the next.

"Sir, are you from the Railway board?" he was clearly impressed as Jeet showed him his journey pass.

"Yes," Jeet affirmed.

The TTE called the pantry man who was passing by and instructed him to take good care of Jeet and Pankaj during the entire journey.

"What would you prefer for dinner, sir?"

"Well, we have got it packed from home. You know how mothers are!"

"Of course sir, we can be no match for mothers' food but please let me know in case you need anything."

"Sure," Jeet smiled.

While Jeet continued to remain lost in his magazine, for Pankaj there was nothing that interested him more than Neena did.

Neena was petite and slender. She was fair in complexion and carried all the nuances and subtleties that came naturally to the girl of her age. But what stood out was her height. Her 5'9" frame was complemented by her dark tresses that ran down to her waist. All in all, she carried enough flair to hold the attention of any young man worth his salt.

"Jeet," Pankaj suddenly called.

"Yeah?" Jeet looked out of the magazine.

"Can you guess what is so special about Neena?"

"Hmm....wait, let me think. But why do you ask me? You are the one acting like an expert, after all."

"It is her height that has stolen my heart buddy."

"Does uncle know about this hobby of yours? I mean about your profound interests other than cricket."

"Don't talk about the old man. You know, he would beat me black and blue if he even gets a whiff of it. And you know what?"

"What?"

"He is travelling too."

"Travelling, where?"

"With us, in this very train."

"Don't tell me!"

"Yes, he is seated two compartments away from us. Don't know why, but he said I shouldn't let you know that he is travelling with us."

The presence of Ahlawat made Jeet uncomfortable. One could never gauge where exactly his conspiracies lay. Jeet felt his heart getting gripped by something.

"Why are you telling me of his presence then, in case he had asked you not to do so?" he countered Pankaj.

"Jeet, you know what, the old man had said it wouldn't matter after we have boarded the train; that I could tell you about him once you and I stepped inside the train."

"Your dad...wow...," Jeet smiled and shook his head in disbelief, "...is *some dad* I must say...."

"He is *my* dad, after all."

Both of them laughed spontaneously on Pankaj's *comment*. Jeet knew the old man was up to his tricks. But what exactly was it, Jeet had no way of knowing.

"Oh, think of the devil and the devil is here," Pankaj pointed to his father walking towards them in the aisle. Jeet smiled.

"I would just be back, Jeet." Pankaj went towards the washroom.

"So, how's it going with the Railways?" asked Ahlawat as he got seated beside Jeet.

"Railways- as in?" Jeet was desperate to get rid of him.

"I am referring to your job. How are you doing there?" Ahlawat continued with his questions.

"It's Railway board actually."

"Oh, it's one and the same thing."

Ahlawat's tone was less than friendly. Jeet knew that deep inside, Ahlawat was not able to reconcile his mind to the fact that Jeet had secured a job whereas his own son still loitered around in search of one. The sight of TTE approaching their berth sparked something in Jeet's mind. He wanted to rub further salt to Ahlawat's injury.

"Hi, Ramavtar ji," Jeet called.

"Sir, can I get anything for you?" the TTE came to him.

"Can I get an orange juice?"

"Sure sir, anything else, sir?"

"No Ramavtar ji, and sorry for the trouble."

"No trouble sir. In fact, it's a pleasure."

"Do you know this TTE personally?" Ahlawat asked as the TTE had gone out of the hearing distance.

"No, not quite."

"Then why did he address you with such courtesy. I mean, there are other passengers too but he did not even look at them."

"Yes, but the other passengers aren't from the Railway board."

"Ohh! So this is what you want to boast of!"

"I haven't boasted about anything," Jeet said plainly

"Oh yes, you have. You are behaving as if you are some IAS officer. It's just some mid-level designation you hold at Railway or this board or whatever."

Jeet was prepared for the let down comment.

"But you couldn't get even that for your son, a mid-level designation that is, despite your conspiring ways," Jeet smiled as Ahlawat continued to burn in the heat of his own anger.

"Wait for two days," Ahlawat said snapping his fingers. "He would get a far better designation."

"Ohh! Of course you mean the trials at Hyderabad uncle, but you are forgetting one thing," Jeet was calm and totally in control.

"And what would that be?"

"Topal isn't the selector there." In one sentence, Jeet had said it all. The colour escaped from Ahlawat's face as his injured ego lay scattered in the filth of the compartment's floor. He hadn't expected such a counter attack.

Words almost took forever to come out of his mouth. Ahlawat stood up and went- carrying along with him the injury caused by Jeet's words.

Pankaj had returned the moment his father had left.

"Jeet," Pankaj called.

"What's it now?" he looked out of his magazine again.

"Look at that Sardarji." Pankaj referred to the Sikh gentleman seated on the seat next to Neena's.

"What about him?"

"It seems he has never laughed in his entire life," the comment from Pankaj was witty enough to cause spontaneous laughter. Sardarji looked at them with a stern face.

"Look at his face," Pankaj continued, careful that his voice didn't travel far enough to reach the other end of the isle. "It looks like he is getting ready to go on a war against Pakistan." Their laughter continued, "But Jeet, what weapon would he take along?" asked Pankaj.

"He wouldn't need any." Jeet wasn't far behind, "The Pakistan army would surrender the moment they looked at him."

To Sardarji, it was now more than clear that the non-stop fun was at his expense. But he could do little more than curse them in his mind. At regular intervals he looked at Jeet and Pankaj, only to get embarrassed further.

"See Jeet," Pankaj shifted his sitting posture. "I think this Sardarji is the most juiceless person in the universe"

"Juiceless?"

"Yes, you know a human body consists of seventy-percent water. I believe this man is totally dehydrated. I believe it's something to do with his inherent texture. I am sure he had carried the same dried up looks even when he was born."

"You mean he had looked a dad even when he was born?" chirped Jeet.

"Exactly," both of them burst into another bout of laughter as a hapless Sardarji looked on.

After dinner, the passengers prepared for the night ahead, taking out blankets, quilts, bed-sheets, pillows, etc., to make the wintry night as cosy as possible. Pankaj had his bed ready at the upper berth while Jeet spread his bed-sheet on the lower one with his neatly folded blanket placed towards where his feet would be.

One of the centre berths was occupied by Sardarji and the other by Neena. Neena's mother slept on the top berth. Neena had her head towards the far end. Her position suited Pankaj and his voyeurism.

It was around 10 p.m. Almost all the occupants of the section were fast asleep as the train pierced through the darkness on a moonless night.

"Look Jeet," he hopped from his upper berth to sit in front of Jeet again, "I am not able to sleep."

"Oh! You mean your sleep has been plucked away by somebody!"

"Yes."

"And who is the lucky one, the F-24?"

"Of course."

Suddenly a piece of cloth fell from Neena's berth. It was Neena's handkerchief. In a split second decision, Pankaj rushed to grab it and then handed it over to Neena. She accepted it with a straight face without portraying emotions of any kind.

"What are you up to, Pankaj? You don't even know the girl," Jeet whispered as Pankaj came back to take his seat. "I mean there's no harm in talking about someone, but literally making advances is a different ball game altogether, and most of all- you aren't her servant for God's sake. Had she asked you to do it? No. The way you are behaving Pankaj, it seems you would bend your back twice to tie her laces if need be."

"You know nothing about these things," Pankaj rebutted.

Jeet returned to his magazine again. Pankaj looked out of the window, lost in his own thoughts.

"But yes, you are right about the servant bit," Pankaj forced Jeet to look out of his magazine again.

"Better late than never."

"The book wouldn't approve of it either."

"Which book?"

"Let me share this secret with you. As luck would have it, I lay hands on one of my dad's books."

"Which book?" suddenly Jeet was alert.

"*How to win girls.*"

"How to win....what?"

"Girls."

"Is this the title of the book?"

"Yes."

"And it's your dad who bought it?"

"Of course- who else? After all, it's just me, mom and dad in the family.. I had not bought the book and certainly my mom can't be buying it, so that leaves the old man. Isn't he a colourful character then- my old man?"

"Well, how can I comment on that, he is *your* dad after all."

"In fact, he is the indirect reason I could learn such techniques from the book."

"Techniques-as in- to win a girl?"

"Of course."

"And you are going to use those techniques here and now?"

"Any harm if I do that?" he smiled, ear to ear.

"How would I know? But what kind of techniques are those, can I know pleeeease?"

"It's not that complicated. To be-friend a girl, you should get in contact with her. I mean, you can obviously not pick a girl without communicating with her, can you?"

"You mean talking is important?"

"I said communicating."

"What's the difference?"

"See, talking is just one aspect of communicating. There are more ways to communicate. Sometimes it's not possible to talk, but still you can communicate."

"How?"

"I have seen Neena smiling at me. In a way, that is an example of communication."

"But I haven't seen her smiling."

"I swear."

"Means you are up to something."

"You bet I am."

"Then you keep me out of this. I would rather prefer a sound sleep."

"Your wish."

"But tell me," Jeet asked. "Do you think it won't carry risk? I mean acting fresh with a girl on a train when you are seeing her for the first time?"

"Not when the girl is smiling at you."

"Why don't you sleep now?" Jeet whispered

"She isn't letting me sleep, Jeet." Pankaj sighed.

"Then stop communicating with her."

"No way."

"So what are going to do the whole night? Keep smiling at her? "

"Can't you see I am in love with her?"

"Oh, come on! Give me a break, for God's sake. You hardly know each other."

The next moment, Jeet was stunned to see Pankaj fly a kiss in Neena's direction. Neena didn't respond. After waiting for a little while, Pankaj flew another kiss, and to Jeet's utter astonishment, this time Neena responded by flying one back by kissing her finger tips and blowing the assumed kiss in Pankaj's direction.

"This is not right Pankaj."

"Jeet, you mind your own business. If you must, please go to the upper berth and sleep."

Jeet was taken aback. Pankaj's rare show of rudeness had made him lose whatever regard and fondness he had for him. Grabbing his bed-sheet, pillow and seeds of anger, Jeet hopped on to the upper berth.

"Go to hell, Pankaj." Jeet was talking to himself. "Why should I try to help you? Are you not the one whose father had stabbed me in the back? You are no different than your dad. Sooner rather than later, your genes are bound to show their effect. Stupid person, I was trying to show you the right way. Not any more, though. In fact, I would sit back and wait eagerly to enjoy the moment when you fall from grace, if ever there is any grace left in you that is."

Jeet grappled with his thoughts. The fun in the journey was all squeezed out by now. He thought of something dangerous, something that his mom and dad would never approve of despite the circumstances. The thoughts in his mind had inflicted inner venom to the extent that the seed of revenge got rooted deeper. He promised himself that rather than rushing it, he would instead wait patiently for the right opportunity to strike.

Sleep would have come more easily had he known that the wait wasn't going to be long. Instead, the opportunities were to present themselves as early as the next morning itself.

Spreading his bed-sheet neatly on the berth, Jeet slid himself in the dual layers of blankets and stretched his legs. He felt tired. The body that didn't give a hoot to the umpteen hours of rigours on the cricket field, craved for rest. Probably different sets of muscles were used to meander through the crowd at the railway station. Within a minute of laying his head on the pillow, Jeet was lost in a sound slumber, forgetting outright that he was travelling in a train compartment.

The incessant sounds seemed to be coming from a far off distance. Jeet tried to push them away, pleading them to knock on someone else's ear drums. Finally Jeet woke up. The sounds' consistency won against Jeet's efforts at stonewalling them. It took him a considerable amount of time to realise that he was in a train compartment, and then he was as alert as ever. But despite being wide awake, he couldn't find himself equal to the chaos that confronted him as he got down from his berth. He was astonished to see Pankaj being grabbed by a policeman and everybody including the TTE, Ahlawat and the others around him.

"Beta, help me please. This lady is hell bent on finishing us totally." Seeing Jeet awake, Ahlawat rushed to him. For a moment Jeet thought everything to be a mere dream, no more than the reflections of the thoughts he had slept with.

"But what has happened uncle, what's the issue all about?"

"She has filed a written complaint with the TTE that Pankaj had tried to make advances towards her daughter."

In no time, the whole matter became clear to him.

"Only you can save him beta." To Jeet, he appeared to be a different Ahlawat. "Please talk to the TTE; I am sure he will not turn down your request."

"Uncle, let me talk to Pankaj first."

"But the TTE is not allowing anybody to talk to him. He says a police case is getting registered."

The TTE accepted Jeet's request and allowed him to have a word with Pankaj in private.

"Tell me everything that happened, and don't be foolish to hide or make things up."

"I am so sorry Jeet. I was a fool not to have listened to you last night. Please forgive me."

"Tell me the whole story."

"It's all done by this Sardar."

"Sardar! What has he got to do with all this?" "

"Actually Neena asked me to come to her berth."

"What!"

"Yes."

"Don't tell me you went there."

"Yes, I made that mistake Jeet. I apologise, my friend."

"Tell me whether she called you or did you go on your own, damn it?"

"I swear on God Jeet, she called me and we were simply sitting and talking."

"Then?"

"This Sardar woke up and saw us sitting there. Then he woke up Neena's mom and told all sorts of things to her."

"All sorts of things, meaning what?"

"That I forcefully went on Neena's berth and tried to make advances at her."

"But Neena should tell the true story. What is she saying? I mean what is her side of the story?"

"Her mom has slapped her several times and now she too is toeing their line that I forcefully made advances at her."

"Oh my God!"

"I will kill this Sardar." Pankaj almost cried as Jeet looked in the direction of the Sardar who had a triumphant smile on his face. Seeing Jeet looking at him, he twirled his moustache in a naked show of brazenness- as if-almost saying, "You laughed at me yesterday but it's me who is having the last laugh."

The policeman dragged Pankaj back.

Having no clue how to deal with the circumstances, Jeet stood and merely observed the developments. Ahlawat and Pankaj begged for mercy, but the lady did not relent and continued to get her statement recorded by the policeman. After the recording of statements, Pankaj was formally arrested. Several times Jeet thought of intervening, but then pulled himself back. Whether the TTE would accede to his request in a shameful accusation such as the one in question, he had no way of knowing. While Jeet stood in a dilemma as to what he could do to save his friend, Pankaj was taken to the security room. Jeet saw Ahlawat rushing towards the security room after a few minutes.

Jeet's decision was made. He stood up to go but then stopped. The quandary had stuck once more. But this time, it was quandary of a different kind.

"What is it that you are doing?" he said to himself as the sight when he was forced to strip his pads came to haunt him. "This is the ideal time for revenge. This is payback time for all the dreary moments of pain that Ahlawat has had a huge hand in getting inflicted upon you." The next moment Principal Y.P.'s voice reverberated in his ears, making the goodness supersede, "Forgiveness is manlier than punishment, but forgiveness should proceed from the position of strength." His mind was working overtime. Was he in the position of strength? Of course he was, for probably it was only in his discretion whether Pankaj is sent to jail for an alleged shameful act or whether he attends the trials tomorrow. The goodness in his mind and heart had prevailed over the evil. Jeet decided to do away with the idea of revenge.

"Can something be done Ramavtar ji? He is my close friend." He asked the TTE without beating about the bush.

"It's very tough Jeet ji." The TTE showed his reluctance.

"There has to be some way, please help me," Jeet wasn't the one to let go. "And moreover, Neena had called him to his berth. He did not go on his own."

"I can understand Jeet ji, but in such matters whatever the girl says is taken as the Gospel truth. But still, please give me some time," the TTE paused a little and the next second his eyes shone. "See Jeet ji, the good part is that though it's a serious enough case as it involves a girl, but certainly it's not as heinous as, let's say, rape or anything of that sort."

"So, what is it that you suggest?"

"If I am not wrong, the lady and her daughter will get down at Nagpur."

"Are you sure about that?"

"Yes, after all, I am the one who checked their tickets."

"How does it help the case?"

"It's the legal requirement that they should be provided with the copy of the complaint. In fact, I was just going to give it to them but now I won't, unless of course they ask specifically for it. In that case, I would have no option but to give it to them."

"What about the Sardarji? Is he going to Nagpur too?...He is the one who instigated them to file a complaint."

"Oh! Just give me a minute." The TTE referred to his chart. "Is he Gurjeet, M 55?"

"Yes."

"Yes, he too is scheduled to get down at Nagpur."

"Thank God." Jeet heaved a sigh of relief.

"Now it all depends whether the lady asks for the copy or not!"

"Yes, of course."

To their relief, when the train proceeded after its scheduled halt at Nagpur, neither Gurjeet nor Neena's mother had asked for the copies of the complaint or the FIR before getting down the train.

"This incident never happened, Jeet ji." The TTE tore the complaint and threw it outside the window.

"I would never forget this act of kindness." Both of them warmly shook hands.

"Beta, I have no words to thank you." Ahlawat hugged Jeet.

"Uncle, one more thing," Jeet had thought of embarrassing him. He was assured this was the least that Ahlawat deserved.

"Go ahead son."

"Please read some good and meaningful books, rather than the ones you actually do."

"I did not get you, son. What books are you talking about?"

"They cast a bad effect on Pankaj."

"Don't worry about him, son. He doesn't even get close to his text books even, what to talk of the other books!"

"That's the point uncle. Your books are far too interesting to allow Pankaj go for his text books. In fact it was one of your very own books he had read that got him in trouble."

"Which one?"

"How to win girls."

Ahlawat's face was drained. If pricked with a needle, Jeet was sure, embarrassment rather than blood would have oozed out of his veins.

"And one more thing uncle."

"Yes beta."

"I pity you."

"Pity me? But for what?"

"A few years back you chose to stab in the back of a defenceless and unarmed fifteen-year-old who at that tender age wasn't master enough of himself to realise what had hit him. Today, a few years later, despite his potency to hurt you, the same boy turned out to be your saviour."

Ahlawat's head hung further.

"And there is more. You ought to be pitied further as the one who chose to expose your real character is none other than your own son."

Ahlawat wished he would just vanish from the face of the earth.

The Miracle of Sai Baba

After being successful at the trials and the interview, Jeet resigned from the Railway board to join the department of Customs & Central Excise in the shortest possible time. It didn't take very long for Jeet to get settled in a sort of alien land. The stretch along Hussein Sagar lake that both separated and joined the twin cities of Hyderabad and Secunderabad fascinated Jeet the most. The sports officer of the department got him accommodated in the guest house on the top floor of the building that housed the department's headquarters till a rented accommodation was arranged at YMCA Secunderabad. His next target was now to get transferred to Delhi and approach the bank manager for the loan and get the house back.

"As per our rules, you cannot apply for a transfer unless you have completed one year at the parent commissionerate, i.e at Hyderabad," he was told by the administrative officer.

If I am transferred after one year that will leave six months for the house deadline, he was concerned. *Six months is a long time, and the bank manager has promised*, he thought. He shrugged off the concern taking it to be a non-issue.

With his efforts, he located an institute of competitive exams called NBS and applied for being a faculty member there. It was similar to Sachdeva College in more ways than one, but NBS prepared the candidates for bank exams only. The syllabus wasn't very different and Jeet didn't face much hardship in getting appointed as a member of faculty. His hands now appeared full.

1. 4 a.m. to 6 a.m., morning drills in the parade grounds located adjacent to the YMCA.
2. 7 a.m. to 9 a.m.: Classes at NBS.
3. 10 a.m. to 2 p.m.: Office.
4. 3 p.m. to 6 p.m.: practice at Lal Bahadur stadium located at a stone's throw away from his office.

His boarding and lodging expenses got covered by the money that he got from NBS. In this manner, he was able to save every single rupee from his office salary. The people at NBS acceded to his request of paying him in cash. He, however, did not disclose the real reason for such a request: that he was a government servant and could not legally work at any other place.

But mine are exceptional circumstances. I have to meet my daily expenses and save money too. Every penny I save will help in getting the house back, he justified to himself. He, however, had no means to know that his job in customs and central excise was in no way going to help in getting his third and final dream of bringing the house back.

A cricketer friend of his had given the address of his sister Sudha who lived with her husband in Hyderabad. He occasionally used to visit Sudha after his practice sessions. In Sudha, he found a person perfectly easy in her manners and as much ready to listen as to talk. Her husband wasn't much different either. Although Sudha was his friend's sister, she behaved in every way how a real sister should. Occasionally she would invite Jeet to her house for dinner. Sudha's husband had an instant liking for Jeet. Jeet had started sharing with both of them his most personal details. In both of them he had found a family in a far and distant land.

"You know Paddy has had a wonderful junior season," he was proud to tell Sudha regarding his younger brother one evening.

"That is great," she replied.

"Yeah, it is. But it is scary too."

"Scary! How?"

"Because he now faces trials for Ranji Trophy this coming Sunday when the story is going to get repeated once again."

"You mean the selectors aren't going to select him?"

"Do I have any reasons to think otherwise?"

"That is where you falter Jeet, in your thinking that is."

"How?"

"Paddy has his own destiny."

"Sure he does, but there are selectors too. The same bunch of cruel, heartless people who have no integrity towards their own pious profession." He went quiet, thinking for a while. "But yes, there is hope in one person."

"In whom?"

"Raghubeer Singh, the president. But there is no way to reach him."

"I think there is a way."

"What?"

"You write a letter to Raghubeer Singh, describing everything that you have in your heart. Bring that letter to me tomorrow evening."

Before Jeet could ask anything further, she waved and said bye. Jeet sat down for the task as soon as he reached YMCA. *I will have dinner only after I have completed the letter*, he promised himself.

"Have you written the letter?"

Sudha asked as he stepped into her boutique the next evening. Jeet gestured towards his office bag. The letter rested there.

"Have you been to Sai Baba temple?" She asked after giving necessary instructions to her staff.

"I will be back in around one hour," she had told them before scurrying out with Jeet.

"Tell me, have you been to the temple before?" Jeet shook his head.

"I have been a Sai Baba devotee since my childhood," she said. "He has immense powers."

"Are we headed towards Sai Baba temple?" asked Jeet as Sudha finished talking to the auto rickshaw driver in Telugu.

"Yes," Sudha replied. "You know what Jeet, a few months back I made a picture of Sai Baba, a portrait. Everybody at home was really amazed at how real and amazing the picture looked. I was surprised myself at the result because as it is I am no great artist. It appeared Baba had touched my brushes that day."

A few minutes later, Jeet and Sudha stood in the queue outside the temple awaiting their turn for the darshan.

"Keep the letter in hand and take Baba's blessings as your turn comes."

The priest took prasad from Sudha's hand and touched it at Baba's feet and handed a part of it back to her. Jeet took out the letter and brought it at Baba's feet before looking at the almighty's statue. Jeet felt like he had never felt before. God seemed to smile at him. "Give all your worries to me," Jeet heard Him say. Jeet came back to his senses when Sudha gestured him to move ahead. After coming out, Jeet could feel something unknown was keeping him happy.

"How did you feel?" Sudha finally asked him.

Both had come out of the temple.

"Incredible," replied Jeet. In one word he had said it all.

"Speed Post this letter immediately."

"That is the first thing that I will do after dropping you."

≈

It was 10 p.m. Sunday, the day of Paddy's trial.

He would be home by now, Jeet thought as he waited for his turn outside the STD booth.

"Jeet beta, Paddy has been selected for the Ranji Trophy team," Kamlesh blurted out immediately after hearing Jeet's voice at the other end. Jeet couldn't believe his ears.

"I will talk to you later, Mom," said Jeet and hurriedly put the receiver down. He was headed to the temple which he knew got closed at 9 p.m. The thanks of gratitude, he was sure, would reach Him from outside of the premises the temple too.

Serendipity

"What's the occasion?" asked Sudha. She was seated in a restaurant by the name of Garden, famous for its mouth-watering biryani. "All of us a sudden you almost dragged me out of my boutique and got me seated in this soothing ambience. I mean this is unprecedented."

"The occasion is unprecedented as well," Jeet smiled and placed a piece of document before her.

"Wow, transferred to Delhi. But it's mixed feelings for me. I am happy that you are headed home now, but at the same time a little sad because my husband and I will be missing you."

"I do understand that and thanks so much for being a home away from home to me."

Jeet held her hand.

Biryani and cold drinks were served. Both of them continued to eat and talk in tandem.

"There is something more Sudha," Jeet shot.

"More...as in?"

Rather than replying, Jeet took out a folded piece of paper and handed it over to Sudha. Her fingers felt the edges and she instantly knew it wasn't a fresh piece of paper. But it wasn't very old too. The folds were now gone and the document lay in front of her, bare and unfolded.

"It's a letter."

"Of course it is."

"Shall I read it?"

Jeet nodded his head.

Dearest Jeet,

Each day, every moment, my heart speaks to you. At times about the brilliant times that have gone by and at times about the faint hopes of future, upon which my life now delicately hangs. I had chosen to ignore its whispers and sincerely tried as hard as I could to involve myself in worldly affairs. But now, the proportions of anxiety have reached a degree where I am forced to pick up a pen and make an outlet for emotions lest they should endanger my existence with their sheer weight. Ironically, these gasps of pain, one would wonder, are also the causes of extreme ecstasy. This secret, that tears could bring such relief and indefinable joy, only an emotion as strong as love could have unfolded to me.

Last night this recurring dream visited me once again. I saw you as clearly as on your first day at school in class eleven, when you had walked to the stage or rather were pushed and coerced by the fellow students towards it. The nervousness in you had disappeared the moment you sang the first line. Sitting in the audience I watched mesmerised, as the song that you chose to sing was the very song that was closest to my heart. Out of millions and zillions of them, inadvertently you had chosen the lines that resonated in my mind all the time. This was the first of the many signs from the blue above that endorsed that you are made for none other but me. Further, I see the glimpses of you and me sitting together during the prep and whispering sweet nothings to each other. All of a sudden I notice it's not only my eyes that are focussed on you. "Have you known him before he joined our school?" my envious friends ask, I answer them with aplomb, "Forever, that's the time since I have known him."

You know what, my semester medical exams start next week which I have chosen to bunk. Your love has taught me the functions of heart which no medical science could ever have taught me. I feel saturated, as if there is nothing more to learn.

Jeet, you know you are my sweet guardian angel, but last time you had come with a fairly infirm set of wings and couldn't carry me along as you flew away in search of I don't know what. I cannot live with this loneliness any more Jeet. I am half a doctor already, and therefore I know these whirlpools of crests and troughs, if allowed to continue, would engulf my life. I wait for you Jeet. Come again, albeit with wings strong enough to carry the weight of my physical being. This time we would fly together Jeet, to wherever you wish to.

Roshni

"What is this?" asked Sudha.

"Couldn't you figure out?"

"Of course I could."

"Then tell me, what is it that you figured out?"

"Jeet, do I look so crude to you? Any person with an ability to read would know this girl Roshni is deeply, madly in love with this guy called Jeet. Moreover, being a girl myself, I can very well connect with her and listen to her sobs and can know where her grievances lie. So..., that leaves you with a lot of story-telling to do."

Jeet started from the very beginning. Till the time he ended, Sudha had laughed and cried a number of times.

"You know Sudha, my faults, if seen through the love-prism, would render me to be unworthy of her, but this letter is a testimony that she has forgiven me for our own sake."

"The date isn't mentioned in the letter. When exactly did you receive it?" asked an anxious Sudha, "I am worried about her well being."

"Around two months back. I would say this letter is timely and productive. It has been successful in its purpose of re-establishing peace, kindness and most importantly, love."

"And what have you planned to do about it?"

"As it is, I have been relieved from Hyderabad to go and resume my job at Delhi."

"When do you leave?"

"Tomorrow."

"And then?"

"The coming Sunday happens to be the Old Raist day. So all ex-students would be coming that day. I will go there to meet Roshni and sort everything out."

"It should be then be called an ex-Raist day. But why do you call it Old Raist?"

"This is in line with the school's tradition. We call it Old Raist day."

Jeet smiled. Sudha smiled too.

"I will also come."

"Where?"

"To your old raist day."

"Sure you are welcome. I feel glad you will be meeting Roshni."

"I feel more than glad."

As always, the Old Raist day was scheduled on a Sunday. As planned, on the penultimate day, i.e. Saturday, Jeet hired a taxi and picked up Sudha from the airport and headed towards MNSS. As expected, after a one-and-a-half-hour drive, they were inside the school premises. The school was bathed in the preparations for the next day. Only a few alumni who were from far-off places had made it on Saturday. Devinder, Jeet's roommate during the school, too had come on Saturday itself. The way Jeet and Devinder greeted and hugged each other pleasantly surprised Sudha.

"This bonding cannot happen in a day school," she said. "This is *some* school Jeet."

"For sure it is Sudha." He proudly smiled.

Roshni would probably come on Sunday, Jeet thought, even though his eyes searched for her. During the day, he had made courtesy visits to Y.P., Bhardwaj ma'am and other teachers. He got arrangements made in the girls' hostel for Sudha's stay.

"Why don't we visit the library?" Sudha cheerfully asked after lunch.

"You mean we should try and locate the note?"

"Yes."

"Don't you remember what Roshni had said about the note?"

"What?"

"That the lead for the note had lain hidden in that day's evening movie which I failed to watch."

"But can't we look for it randomly?"

"There are thousands of books Sudha. Not possible."

"Might be, we could get some heavenly sign. After all, Roshni believes so much in them, and not without reasons."

"Sure, but I haven't seen or observed any such signal or sign as yet. Have you?"

"Do you agree that she wrote the note in some book?" Sudha grimaced, at the same time she sounded determined.

"Yes."

"Do you then agree that book is in the library?"

"Yes, unless somebody got the book issued and never returned."

"Let us not talk anything negative."

"Alright." Jeet smiled.

"Meaning, that the book is resting somewhere in the library itself and has been teasing you all this while."

"Yes, in most likelihood, it's still in the library neatly ensconced on a shelf and yes, has been teasing me all these years."

"Then, one thing is for sure."

"What's that?"

"That you won't get it walking around in the school's neat roads and impeccably manicured lawns."

"To be honest, I don't know, Sudha."

"See Jeet, even if I agree you have missed the clue, the chances of laying your hands on it increase by being in the library and searching it there."

"You know Sudha," as if Jeet hadn't heard Sudha's last sentence. "There has to be some equation, some calculation, in the way she might have chosen the book in which she had written the note."

"What makes you think so?"

"Because I know her so well, she is too bright to have chosen the book at random."

"You mean the clue is all the more imperative?"

"Yes Sudha, but now when I am here for Roshni anyway, the note doesn't really matter, does it?"

"Maybe it doesn't matter to you, Jeet. But being a girl myself I can very well know Roshni's mind. While on the one hand I know the note or anything else is now inconsequential, on the other I can visualise a spark adorning her eyes by seeing the note or the book in your hands. That would re-affirm her faith in whatever she considers divine."

"Ok, let us go to the library." Jeet gave up. "It being a second Saturday, I am afraid library would be closed today. Anyways, let's go and check it."

As anticipated, the library was closed.

"Listen Sudha, let's do one thing"

"What?"

"There must be some English movie scheduled for evening."

"Yes, it's *Serendipity*."

"Serendipity what?"

"That is the name of the movie scheduled for the evening."

"Wow, a step ahead of me. It seems to me that you are the alumnus, not me."

"Yeah," she smiled, "the girls at the hostel told me."

"Great. I am sure the excursions during the day would have left you tired, so let me drop you to the hostel. The movie starts in another two hours, so you still have some time to rest before we meet at the school auditorium."

"Does it mean you would watch the movie too?"

"No, you would watch the movie."

"And what would you do?"

"Just sit through the movie."

"Sit through the movie, or sleep through the movie?"

Both laughed in tandem.

"And yeah, before I forget, what is the movie all about, this *Serendipity*?"

"I don't know, but seems like a love story by the sound of it."

≈

The movie started at the scheduled time. Jeet dozed off within the first five minutes of the movie. The sound seemed to be coming from a distance. It seemed irritable to start with and then grew intolerable. It was Sudha, almost shouting in his ears while nudging him.

"What's it? Is the movie over?" He looked at the screen and rubbed his eyes.

"Sit up and watch the movie. It's got something to do with Roshni's note," Sudha said in a toned down pitch, the anxiousness however clearly overflowed.

"What!" Jeet's drowsiness had vanished.

"It's as if your story is being played on the screen. At least for the 'something hidden in a book thing' is concerned."

"How?"

"Look at the couple on screen. They have written their phone numbers on a five dollar bill and hidden it in an old book and the girl has replaced the book at the used book seller stall."

"And?"

"They believe if destiny wants them to meet, then one of them should be able to trace the book, and the five dollar bill. That way, one would see the other person's phone number on the bill and make the call."

"Wh--at?" Jeet was astounded

"Ye—s."

Jeet felt numb. It's only after some time that he got back to his senses. He got up to move out of the auditorium. Sudha followed him.

"Could you figure anything out Sudha?"

"Meaning what?'

"I am dead sure it was the same movie that played that Saturday too and this is the clue that she talked about. And look at the turn of events, the same movie gets played when I sit in the auditorium years later. Now the note doesn't matter anymore. The circumstances as they got unfolded can convince even the disbeliever of the highest kind that Roshni and I are soul mates."

"But the note has to be found out. Don't forget she said it was a litmus test."

"Sure, I will find it."

"But could you catch the clue?"

"Of course, the note must be hidden in a book by the name of the movie. *Serendipity.*"

♒

The library was scheduled to be closed for Sunday too. But Jeet had reached the library sharp at ten with the librarian in tow. The latter appeared not the happiest, though. Only a few things can match the pleasures of a lazy Sunday on a cold North Indian morning. Jeet had intruded into his peace and calm of the early morning with an unusual request. Saying no to an old-Raist wasn't an option, that too on an old-Raist day.

"You said love stories, sir," he said as he punched the keys of the computer.

"Yes, most likely it should be in the love story section. How do you compartmentalise it?"

"Sir, broadly we segregate them such as fiction, non-fiction, etc., and then within fiction, we have created further sections such as thrillers, love-stories, etc."

"That's good."

Just then, Sudha entered the library.

"You are late," Jeet pointed at his wrist watch as the librarian continued to tap the keyboard.

"You had said ten," she smiled.

"It's ten minutes past ten."

"*Serendipity*? Is that what you said, sir?"

"Yes," Jeet answered.

"Sorry sir, there is no book by that name."

"How can that be? Please check properly."

"I have checked all entries, sir."

"Can you tell me when exactly the entries were transferred from the manual registers to the computer? It was all manual when I was here."

"The process is still on, sir."

"And where are the manual registers?"

"They haven't been done away with as yet; they are in the store room."

"Can you please check it there too? Just in case."

"Sure sir." If the librarian was getting irritated, he wasn't showing it.

He went to the store room and got the register for love stories.

"Got it sir." He looked out of the register

"Where?"

"There is an entry here sir that says it had been issued to Mr Kain but never returned."

"When was it issued?"

"Almost one year back."

"Is Mr Kain here at Rai still?"

"Very much sir."

"Does he possess the same house?"

"Yes sir."

"Are you sure the book is still with him?"

"Can't say sir, one year is a long time. One thing that I am very sure of is that the book hasn't been returned to the library."

"Do one thing Jeet, you rush to Mr Kain's house and I will head towards the hostel. Maybe Roshni has reached by now," said Sudha who till now has been silently listening.

"Yeah, fine."

Meeting with Kain was nostalgic. He was the same effervescent self. Kain wasn't any less delighted to see him. He talked everything under the sun and Jeet was more than desperate to come to business.

"How is Roshni?" suddenly Kain asked

"I don't know sir." Jeet was surprised by the question. "Haven't met her after leaving school."

"That's surprising, I thought you people...but leave it. Arrey..." as if he remembered something. "Wished to tell you, there is a very beautiful poem Roshni wrote for you. Don't know why but she has written it in a book that co-incidentally I got issued from the library. I forget the name of the book."

"*Serendipity*," he jumped up from the sofa. "I have come to you for the same book."

"Sure" saying this he went inside his reading room and was back in a minute.

"My bat and my books, these are two things I can never misplace. Here is your book." Kain tossed the book into Jeet's hands.

Jeet quickly flipped open the last page and saw the poem in the beautiful hand. He read it quickly and then with the book in hand, he rushed heading straight towards the girls' hostel.

"Jeet!" Kain shouted.

"Yes, sir." Jeet halted.

"Listen son," Kain had scurried close to Jeet. "Girls like Roshni don't come every day. That's all I have to say."

"I know sir, but thanks..sir." Jeet held Kain's hands. "I love you, sir."

"I love you too son, now rush to wherever you were headed too." Kain smiled

He had travelled halfway towards the girls hostel when not just his feet but even his heart almost stopped. As he turned the corner near the infirmary, he bumped into Sudha and Roshni coming from the other direction. He halted, Roshni halted too. He looked at Roshni, mesmerized. She looked pale and thin. Her features were so sad; they didn't seem to be hers. The colour seemed to have drained out of her cheeks, yet she looked beautiful.

"Where were you?" she shouted as she sat on the road, just as an athlete would after completing a long marathon. The ruggedness of the long wait had had an effect and her knees gave way as soon as she crossed the finishing line. Two rivers flowed from her two eyes, like incessant drops of rain. Jeet rushed to hold her as Sudha gestured him to halt.

"Let her cry," she whispered.

A small crowd of old-Raists and students had gathered as all of them watched with curiosity. Roshni however couldn't care about the world. After having cried to her heart's fill, she got up and rushed towards Jeet.

"Where were you?" She hit Jeet on the chest with her fists in mocked anger.

"I had gone to retrieve the message that you had put in some tin can and thrown into the vast sea. I had trouble in locating it, but locate I did, didn't I, and I am back to you." He smiled.

Roshni didn't answer, and hugged him instead, almost piercing his back with her fingers. She was less pallid now as the colour started rising into her cheeks. Her diffuseness and warmth spilled all over the person for whom it had been reserved for so long.

"Are you checking for the wings?" Jeet felt his back getting pierced by her fingers.

Roshni nodded, smiling.

"But the wings aren't on my back?" Jeet teased

"Then where have you hidden them?"

"They are here," he held her hand and brought it to his heart. The love birds hugged again as the crowd cheered and clapped.

Just then, Jeet saw the librarian amongst the crowd, waving and cheering like others. The librarian had seen the book in Roshni's hands and had understood all.

He came up to Jeet. "Sir, congrats for locating the book."

"Yeah, thanks. I got it from Mr Kain"

"No sir, I am talking about the real book," he smiled with mischief and hinted at Roshni.

Jeet laughed and shook his hand again.

"Jeet, this is such a beautiful poem," Sudha flicked open the last page.

Dearest Jeet,

The lost star
A star born to the sun and sky,
Got dropped in the sea along with its plight,
Unkind waves engulfed it, pushed it at distance far and wide,
The sun wept and the sky cried,
The broken star was never in sight;

A fisherman then so wrapped in love,
Dared the sea and fought the storms,
He pierced through the webs of deceit, the waves had along with evil spun,
The star was brought home in all radiance,
It hugged the sky and embraced the sun,
The fisherman united the family,
Bringing thus glory back to the universe.

Roshni

"Yes, I have already read it." Jeet smiled.

"But could you solve the riddle?" asked Roshni.

"There is no riddle actually. What you have tried to say is quite simple."

"Tell me then."

"Sudha could you figure out what her poem was all about?"

"How would Sudha know?" Roshni whispered.

"I have told her our story. Let us see if Sudha can figure out."

"I would say to Roshni that she excels so much in poetry that it was almost cruel to have denied others the happiness of reading it. This, in fact, is an incredible poem, where Roshni has articulated her feelings appropriately. In the poem she is the lost star, the fisherman is Jeet, who helped the star, and the sun and the sky are Roshni's parents. All in all, the poem means that Jeet is the catalyst between Roshni and her parents."

Roshni hugged Sudha while Jeet's joyous eyes watched. After some time, Sudha left. She had an evening train to Hyderabad.

"Thanks for all your support and care," Jeet was emotional.

"I will never forget this day, Jeet, and I will be your friend and counsellor till my last breath."

By evening, both Jeet and Roshni had left for Gurgaon and Sonipat, respectively. *I will share something with you after you get the papers of the house back*, Roshni had said before boarding the bus.

Taking the House Back

The eagerness in Jeet had forced him towards Dinesh's house the first thing early in the morning the next day after returning from Rai. Having parked his motorcycle outside, he entered the drawing room. Dinesh, in a striped T shirt and a white pyjama, was sipping his morning tea along with his father. After the salutations, Jeet sat silently answering Dinesh's father questions in monosyllables. Taking the hint, Dinesh's father left the room, leaving the two friends with their privacy and freedom.

"It is funny," Jeet laughed.

"What?"

"Your dressing sense! T shirt with pyjamas."

"I am free from the stress of being a pass out from Rai. Your public school mannerisms aren't for commoners like us."

"I didn't mean that. I am sorry if my comment has hurt you." Jeet was suddenly taken aback with Dinesh's reaction.

"I am just kidding!" It was Dinesh's turn to laugh. "Don't give it another thought." Dinesh patted on Jeet's lap. "Tell me what brings you here so early in the morning? And yeah, tell me about the developments related to the house. If I am not wrong, there are just a few days for the deadline?"

"It is for this very issue that I am here. Let's go to the manager for the loan. I want to throw the money at Ram Sharan and get the papers of the house back."

"Did you bring all the documents related to your job, etc?" asked Dinesh.

"Yes I have brought all that I have." Jeet handed over the folder to Dinesh.

"I-card, appointment letter, 2-passport sized photos, bank account details are all there," Dinesh flipped through the folder. "But what about the ration-card and driving licence?"

"I didn't know I had to bring those as well. But don't worry, I will go and get them in no time." Jeet started to leave.

"No, wait, don't rush! Keep your cool."

"Ok, as you say."

"Tell me," Dinesh looked at him. "Did you ever meet the manager after getting appointed?"

"No, I didn't. Are you suggesting I should have?"

"Yes, of course. It is such an important matter and you are acting at the eleventh hour."

"Do you mean things can go wrong?"

"I am not suggesting anything. But what if, you know, he asks for some documents that only your Hyderabad office can provide? I mean I am not saying he will, but what if he does? Would you, in such a scenario, rush to Hyderabad to get the documents?"

"I got your point," Jeet said, "and your concerns aren't without reasons. But all my job related documents are in Delhi now. So, such a situation shouldn't arise."

"Have you joined your Delhi office?"

"Not yet. We get ten days as joining time. I want to get over this loan issue before joining."

"Ok, let us head straight to the bank. Give me five minutes. Let me change and I will take my motorbike as well."

"Why take two bikes?"

"After the meeting, I have something to attend to."

"But we can go together."

"Where?"

"Wherever you want to go after the meeting."

"I don't want you to waste your time. As it is you are already running short of it."

"Hmm."

⩰

It was a weekday and there was considerable rush in the bank. The manager was in a meeting.

"Jeet, I forgot to tell you..." Dinesh said as they got seated in the waiting room.

"What?"

"The state government has started releasing the amount for the land they had acquired years back. Have you checked your status regarding that?"

"Have they!" asked an excited Jeet.

"Although there is no official confirmation, but yes, there is a rumour about this in the village. Do you know how much of your land was acquired?"

"They had acquired all of it. I know the amount that is due to us."

"How much is that?"

"Twenty-five lakhs."

"If that gets released, there would no need for this loan."

"True, but one doesn't know when it would be done. We know how slowly things move in government departments. Given the shortage of time, it would be foolhardy to bank on something as volatile as this."

"That is why we are seated in the bank."

Both of them smiled and waited to get the process going. The manager's meeting getting over, they were escorted to his office. The manager was courteous as expected. He was reminded of their last meeting and was also apprised of the developments having taken place with regards to Jeet's job. Cold drinks were served as he signalled towards the folder in Jeet's hands. The manager scrutinized each document in detail before allowing the first word to escape from his mouth on the subject.

"I am sorry Dinesh, but as on date, Jeet doesn't qualify for the loan."

The bomb exploded.

"But why?" Dinesh asked.

"As per the office records, Jeet is still under probation. He is yet to complete his two years in service. In that case, the bank cannot consider his case."

"But this condition wasn't laid before us when we had come earlier. What we were told was that a government employee can get a loan." Jeet tried hard to suppress his anxiety as well as anger.

"But it was then a general discussion without having touched the specifics regarding the number of years in service." The manager shot back without any emotions.

"Uncle, can I talk to you in private?"

"Sure."

Dinesh gestured Jeet to wait as he followed the manager to a vacant cabin.

"Uncle, please don't be harsh. Jeet is the only friend I have. You know and I know that you have the discretion to allow him a loan despite him being on probation."

"Yes, it is in my discretion. But if I allow him as a special case, the audit team will ask me why I had allowed the loan in one file and disallowed in others. Try to understand Dinesh, if I do this, my job would be at risk."

Dinesh looked out of the glass cabin. He could see Jeet and his desperate eyes staring at him.

"Let me be his guarantor then, uncle."

"But you can't?"

"Why not?"

"Well, because the same conditions apply for the guarantor as well. Neither you have any immovable property in your name, nor are you employed with the government."

No matter how hard Dinesh tried, he couldn't change the mindset of the stereotypical manager. "How will I face Jeet?" he murmured.

"Did you say something?" the manager asked as he halted at the door of the cabin.

"No, nothing uncle."

Jeet asked no questions. Dinesh's sullen face had said it all.

"I am sorry," Dinesh managed to say.

"It is fine. Let us go home."

The calmness in Jeet's voice disturbed Dinesh.

"I will drop you home," Dinesh said as they came out of the bank.

"I am not going home."

Jeet's reply was terse.

"Not going home! Then where?"

"I don't know. But I can't go home now. I have failed in all walks of life. Three dreams, all unrealised."

"Don't talk nonsense. Grow up."

"But you said you had something urgent to attend to?"

"That can come later."

"But I have my bike."

"I will follow you on mine."

Jeet looked at his watch as he kick started his motor bike; it was 3 p.m.

≈

Nine hours later, the stillness of midnight found Jeet wide awake. The wrinkled bed-sheet was a reflection of the grapple with the onslaught within: *Three dreams. All unrealised. I am a failure.* He looked around in the dark, in search of peace, called for doppelganger. But doppelganger was nowhere near. In fact, he was several light years away, engrossed in a serious conversation with the Supreme Power.

"What brings you here?" asked the Supreme Power.

"It is about Jeet," replied the doppelganger.

"Of course it has to be about Jeet. You are his doppelganger. Why would you be here for someone else? But what is it about Jeet that brings you here?"

"I have come for a request. Jeet feels very low at the moment. It is my humble request that his second wind be advanced and expedited."

"But it is not due yet. It is scheduled to be released after Kamlesh's illness."

"Kamlesh's illness? Is his mom going to fall sick?"

"Yes."

"Tell me it is nothing serious," Doppelganger pleaded.

The Supreme power smiled, but didn't reply.

"I humbly request you to release the second wing right now," the Doppelganger continued with his request.

"But that is against the rules," the Supreme Power smiled. "If a bank manager cannot bend his rules, how do you expect the Supreme Power to do that?"

"That is exactly my point, Supreme Power. The Supreme Power isn't some bank manager. It is the guardian of the universe it created."

"You are very witty," the Supreme Power smiled. "Alright, although the second wind will get released when it has to, but on your insistence some temporary relief for Jeet is ordered right here, right now."

"The doppelganger stands obliged, Supreme Power."

The doppelganger bowed.

The morning had arrived, though Jeet was yet oblivious to it. The insomnia had blurred his vision to the extent that even the extra brightness of the sunrays had failed to dazzle him with hope and triumph.

"Bhaiya, someone is there to meet you," Paddy entered Jeet's room.

"Tell him to please come some other time."

Paddy didn't respond.

"Or ask him to wait. I am coming."

The gentleman was well dressed. Jeet shook hands. Paddy too had followed Jeet to the drawing room.

"Are you Mr Jeet?"

"Yes, sure I am. Please tell me how I can help you."

"Actually there is cheque for you. In fact, it is in your father's name. But as he is not here, I have to hand it over to you." He opened his briefcase, and pulled something out. "Here you are!"

Reacting in a knee jerk fashion, Jeet took the cheque in his hands. It was drawn in favour of Kanwar Singh, and the amount was twenty-five lakhs.

"I am not getting you." Jeet forgot to blink.

"Sir, I am from the state land department. This is your payment for the land that was acquired by us. Whereas no one else from your village has received any compensation as yet, the director had instructed strictly that I hand it over to you without wasting any second."

"Do you mean this is the first cheque that you are handing over?"

"This is the first and the only one, sir. I doubt if others will receive it before six months' time."

"In that case," Jeet's heartbeat got faster than normal, "any reason why we have got it early?"

"I am only following orders, sir. Only the director can tell you that."

The officer shook hands with Jeet and before Jeet could know, left as briskly as he had come.

"Bhaiya!"

"Hmm?" Jeet woke up from his thoughts.

"We didn't even offer him tea."

"Call him...call him back, Paddy."

Paddy rushed outside.

"He is nowhere to be seen, Bhaiya." He came back after a few minutes. Both brothers stood staring at each other. The next moment, they hugged each other with overflowing joy and more importantly, relief.

There were no further hiccups. The manager agreed to issue the draft against the cheque despite Kanwar not being present for necessary signatures. It was agreed upon that Kanwar's signatures would be attained as and when he returns the advocates from both sides took care of the legal formalities and documents of the house changed hands. Without wasting another moment, Jeet headed home to gift the documents to Kamlesh.

The Climax

"What happened?"

Jeet was taken aback by Paddy's sullen face.

"Bhaiya...Mom had gone to the doctor yesterday." Paddy's voice had a hint of concern.

"The doctor? For what?"

"Actually she had some bleeding?"

"Bleeding?"

"Yes, from her stomach."

"Did she eat something stale? Wh..what did the doctor say? I mean is..is the issue of some concern? Answer something!"

"Don't know yet. I mean, I..I went to the doctor...with her..."

"Wait..."

Jeet went to the kitchen and brought a glass of water. Paddy drank in one big gulp.

"Stay calm, and tell me."

"Mom went to the doctor."

"Ok she went to the doctor, and then what..?"

"She said the bleeding is from the uterus."

"Ok, and what did the doctor diagnose?"

"She said she has to wait and see."

"Wait and see! What kind of doctor is she? You should have taken her to some other doctor."

"No Bhaiya. There is nothing wrong with the doctor. Actually she sent mom's sample for testing."

"What did the doctor actually *say*?" Jeet's voice was raised.

"She said it can be something serious also."

The shock loosened Jeet's grip over the papers. He sunk in the nearby sofa.

"Have you informed dad?"

He appeared calmer. It being a weekday, Kanwar was out of town.

"No, I thought I will let you know first."

"Hmm, yeah you did the right thing."

With weak steps, Jeet headed towards his room.

"Bhaiya, mom is in her room."

"Yeah I know."

"Wouldn't you meet her?"

"No, I am going to my room." As if he hadn't heard Paddy, Jeet walked on. Paddy wanted to stop Jeet. He wanted to talk to him. He wanted to be with his brother till at least they got the report. Paddy felt lonely, and scared too.

Jeet collapsed on the bed. The cricket player who could dive either side to lap on to the toughest of catches was drained of all energy. He looked at the conveyance deed of the house and then he looked at the roof of the room. Various incidents replayed in his mind's eye. He was reminded of various lessons related to life that his mom had taught him. Then he thought of Munna and the manner in which he had died. Just when Jeet was to repay his debt. Just as he held the key to the car. Like he held the papers of the house in that moment.

Will I lose again? The thought scared him to the bone. It appeared the opposite walls of the room could meet with each other any time, crushing him in the process. He felt suffocated. Not able to bear the unseen grip on his throat, he rushed out of his room initially and then out of the house altogether.

He kicked his motorcycle and headed towards nowhere in particular. Before he could know, he was out of his village, heading towards Delhi. It was then that he thought of Roshni.

Sharing things with her might bring peace.

Although it was 2 a.m., he turned towards the highway. He had a destination in mind now.

It was 5 a.m. when he reached her house. Jeet rang the doorbell just as the sun knocked at the doors of the horizon. Despite the sunrise, the haze in Jeet's mind hadn't cleared.

It hadn't taken much of an effort to locate Roshni's house, given the odd hour.

"It's the yellow house in front of D-park," she had told him. Jeet was aware of D-park and to locate the house therefore didn't take more than a couple of minutes.

"Yes please?"

Jeet stared at a pair of unfamiliar eyes of a middle aged man.

"I want to meet Roshni," Jeet was surprised to see the stranger.

"Who are you?" The stranger shouted. His tone had turned from unfamiliar to hostile.

"My name is Jeet, I am...."

"Son, please do come in." The tone had all of a sudden displayed familiarity. The stranger stepped aside leaving enough space for Jeet to enter. The stranger went inside after seating Jeet in the drawing room.

"What a surprise!"

Almost immediately, Roshni entered the drawing room with her mother.

After having greeted Roshni, Jeet touched her mother's feet.

"Actually I had come close by for some work...."

The presence of the stranger was making him uncomfortable.

"Please feel comfortable, son," Roshni's mom looked at Jeet with all the admiration she could accomplish. "Roshni I'll get the tea ready for both of you."

She walked outside with the stranger in tow.

"Who is he?" Jeet shot at Roshni the moment he was assured of privacy.

"Papa." Roshni dropped the thunderbolt. "Don't worry, I will tell you all. But what is it that brings you here at such an odd hour? I mean it is some surprise, the suspense of which is killing me. I hope all is well at home?"

Jeet started from the start and finished only after he had said all. Roshni had listened in rapt attention.

"You know Jeet, it seems happiness cannot embrace me for long." Dejection peeped through her eyes. "Have you brought mom's medical slip?"

"No, the doctor said the bleeding was from the uterus."

"And then she sent the sample for biopsy?"

"Yes."

"And when does she expect the report to come in?"

"She has sent it to Delhi. She says she will receive it by late evening today and that we can get it collected tomorrow morning. What is it that you make out of it, tell me?"

"You know Jeet, everything is in dark without the report, but since the infection is in uterus so things do not appear bad as such, but as I said only the report can categorically rule out something."

"What do you mean?"

"Actually uterus at aunty's age isn't a vital organ, unless of course, mom decides to have another kid." She smiled, despite the situation. Jeet too managed to lessen the frowns a little bit.

"I mean," Roshni continued, "Ok, let's see it like this. There can be two things: one that the report shows it was a small infection and a dose or two of medicines is all that it needs. I mean excellent, no problem. Second, let's assume it's a bit complicated and serious. In that case, we will get the uterus removed. No big deal. But there is something that I fear here."

"What is the something, Roshni? You are making me oscillate between life and death."

"We have to be practical and at the same time patient, Jeet. Do not worry, God cannot be so unkind."

The child in Roshni that had manifested despair was overtaken by the professional doctor who manifested hope.

"You think so..?"

"Yes Jeet."

Roshni's mom called out to her and she went inside the house and brought cups of tea.

"Tell me the dad story. Suddenly we seem to have our hands full, with developments good and bad, from all corners."

"Yeah, you are right." She smiled. "Dad is back Jeet. And you know who brought him back?"

"How would I know?"

"Mom brought him back."

"Mom? And he got back?"

"Not the Sonipat mom, Jeet."

"You mean not your mom?"

"Of course my mom, but not the one from Sonipat. Don't forget I have two moms now Jeet. The one from Gurgaon brought him back."

"You mean...my mother?"

"Yes *our* mother."

"But how?"

"Wait, I will call dad to tell you the whole story. It will help break the ice between the two of you."

Roshni went inside and came back with her mom and dad.

≈

"I don't know where to start beta. All I can say is your mother is an angel. She saved me, and along with me she saved the whole family. Last Monday she came to my house, I mean the place where I stayed before coming back..."

"Yes please?" Roshni's dad answered the bell. He had never seen the lady before.

"If I am not wrong, you are Mr Dalbeer Singh,"

"Yes, but I have not recognised you."

"I am Kamlesh, Jeet's mother."

"Please come," Dalbeer Singh escorted her to the drawing room. Roshni had told him about Jeet. "Tell me what brings you here Kamlesh ji?"

"I have come for a personal issue, Dalbeer ji. An issue which is personal to you of course, but as things stand, we tend to get affected the same way too. But in case you do not like to discuss about it, I would leave immediately."

"Please carry on. I am listening."

"You and I know Jeet and Roshni have decided to marry each other."

"Yeah, Roshni doesn't hide anything from me."

"Since our children are getting married, our major issues become common."

"To be honest, I am not able to get what you intend to say."

"I will get straight to the point. I am aware of the fact that you and Roshni's mother have been living separately for some time." Kamlesh paused to see Dalbeer's reaction. There was none.

"I wouldn't go into the reasons that forced the two of you into this. What I am interested in is, if there is an outside chance of any kind that can encourage togetherness between the two of you?"

"Impossible."

"Impossible! Dalbeer ji, please excuse my straight forwardness but I believe I have seen enough in life to be able to figure at least one thing if not more, that there is no such thing as impossible."

Kamlesh smiled. She had come prepared, knowing full well that a superfluous conversation wasn't going to help. She knew she had to collide with the bone of contention head on.

"Kamlesh ji, this is my family matter. How can you know more than I do?"

"Dalbeer ji, can we, for a moment, get back to the time when you got married?"

"I don't exactly understand..."

"Just bear with me for a couple of minutes, please."

"Sure."

"Did the notion that you would ever get separated come to your mind when you got married?"

"No."

"So, in a way, we may take it that at the time of marriage, getting separated occurred impossible to you."

"Hmm...ye--eah."

"And getting together seems impossible to you now?"

"Yeah."

"If impossible could happen then, what stops it from happening now, especially when the well being of two families is at stake?"

Roshni's dad was quiet and something in his calm demeanour prompted Kamlesh to continue. "I know one thing for sure Dalbeer ji, the reasons for your separation, however valid or reasonable they then might have been, cannot outweigh the combined desire of two families to bring you together again."

"I appreciate the sincerity in your efforts, Kamlesh ji, but it was Roshni's mom who asked me to get out of the house."

"And you quietly walked out?"

"That is what she wanted."

"Who said?"

"She herself said."

"Can you recollect her exact words?"

"Yes, she had said, 'Please go.'"

"Maybe she wanted you to go to another room, so that she could be with herself and fight with the frustrations of life, and moreover did she ever stop you from returning? If I am right Dalbeer ji, she begged you to come back, but maybe your male ego stopped you from the divine pleasures of being in a happy family."

"You don't know Kamlesh ji..."

"Then tell me what I don't know Dalbeer ji. I am not an outsider. Roshni is going to be my daughter soon."

"She always wanted to get rid of me. Maybe she wanted to marry someone else."

"Who told you? Did Roshni's mother say that?"

"No, but I know."

"That is what I m asking...how?"

He had no answer.

Kamlesh took the lead and asked, "Alright, tell me how long have you been separated?"

"Fifteen years and four months."

"So...is that period not long enough to marry someone?"

"Y...Yeah, it is...I mean...yes."

"Did she marry?"

"No...but there is one more thing..."

"What?"

"Bimla always leaned more towards her own family."

"You mean towards her parents?"

"Yes...her parents."

"Leaned as in..? Were the two families at war or something?"

"No..I mean she would raise her voice whenever I talked about them."

"Talk as in...generally? About them...or speaking using unkind words for them?"

"If Bimla doesn't care for me, is there any reason why I should be kind and thoughtful about her parents?"

"You mean she raised her voice whenever you chose to speak harsh words about them? You are a man, Dalbeer ji, so chances are you might not know a woman's heart and mind. A woman has immense patience. She can tolerate atrocities at her husband's house, she can work hard all day long without batting an eyelid. I have seen ladies tolerating compulsive wife-beaters. But when it comes to her parents, she cannot tolerate a word against them. She takes it that in her new family, she is the lone defender of her parents and then she can go to any extent in safeguarding them. So, by speaking ill of her parents, Dalbeer ji, I would say you have faltered immensely."

Kamlesh waited, but Dalbeer didn't respond.

"Please act Dalbeer ji, your family is waiting for you. You have wasted fifteen golden years; your daughter's and your wife's fifteen years have gone down the drain too. Don't let a second get wasted now."

"You seem to be right Kamlesh ji...for Roshni's sake at least ...I will...try...to... go back."

"In which case, it would be far better if you didn't go back at all."

"What!"

"Yes, if you think of compromising for Roshni's sake only, then it is better to let things remain the way they are. For, the foundation will still be weak. If you want to repair whatever wrong has been done, then go back for your own self first, go back for your wife for you miss her and her love, for that is the truth, and then go back for Roshni and try and compensate for what all she has till now missed. Go back and claim your home Dalbir ji. It's your home and you are the head of the family."

"And then I came back, beta, or it would be more appropriate if I say your mother, the gem of a human being, got me back."

Dalbeer looked at Jeet, as did Roshni and Bimla. Jeet smiled in pride. His thoughts were back to his mother.

"I will leave now; Paddy and mom would be concerned. I didn't even inform them before coming."

"Beta we will come too," said Dalbeer. Jeet couldn't say no.

They could reach Gurgaon only till evening. Kamlesh greeted them warmly.

"Just came to meet you, Kamlesh ji."

"I am honoured Dalbeer ji."

Dinner happened in silence, with just an occasional formal shake of the head. Roshni and Bimla were given Jeet's room for the night. Dalbeer slept in Paddy's room while Jeet and Paddy got their beds arranged in the drawing room. Then the night came carrying along the concerns of what the next morning held in store.

Jeet unfolded the bed cover, lay down on the bed and was astounded by someone's intrusion. The doppelganger sat smiling on his bed. He looked towards Paddy who was deep in sleep.

"You?" Jeet looked at doppelganger.

"Yes, are you surprised?" Doppelganger smiled.

"No, no. I am, in fact, happy. It feels nice to see you and there couldn't have been a more appropriate time."

"What's troubling you?"

"Don't you know what's troubling me?"

"Stop asking me what I know or do not know. Your sleep can get broken anytime. Do not waste your time."

"You mean I am still sleeping?"

"I said do not waste your time. Tell me your want."

"I want my mother well. Even if it means I have to sacrifice all my dreams for that. I am willing to trade them for my mother."

"You should be careful of what you speak."

"Means?"

"Sometimes, the human voice gets accepted in the exact form."

"I didn't get you."

"Are your dreams impure?"

"Not at all. They are as pure and true as my own soul."

"If your dreams are the exact reflections of your soul, then go all out to achieve the whole universe, if not for your own sake then at least for the sake of the universe. Do not settle for anything less."

The doppelganger gone, Jeet was wide awake. He looked at his watch: 3 a.m. He rushed towards Roshni's room.

He knocked and Roshni opened the door, hesitant and surprised.

"You know Roshni, mom is well. She is perfectly fine." He looked at Roshni in all desperation.

"Has the report come?"

She too was now wide awake.

"Not yet."

"But how would you know? If you haven't seen the report?"

"That is why I have come here. Let's go to the hospital."

"But the doctor said we would get the report in the morning."

"The doctor said the report would be made available to the hospital late in the evening and that we can see it in the morning."

"So, what do you have in mind?"

"We will go now. The report was to be delivered to the hospital last evening."

"To the hospital?"

"Yes."

"Hmm...ok. Let's go."

"I cannot disturb the doctor at this hour," the reply from the receptionist at the hospital was terse. "She had had a long day yesterday and slept very late."

But Jeet was adamant. If the doctor was flustered by the odd hour intrusion, she didn't show it.

"Yes the report came yesterday," she had a smile on her face. "But I didn't get a chance to go through it. Please sit down."

The two were seated in her cabin with bated breath as the doctor rummaged through her desk drawer.

"Yeah here it is," but before she could fully open it Roshni almost snatched it from her.

Jeet's eyes counted every emotion that her face manifested as Roshni was engrossed in the report. The tumultuous tsunami inside Jeet lay masqueraded in the outward calm. Initially Roshni had a straight face sans any emotion which was then followed by the expression of being engrossed to the emotion of satisfaction and then there was ecstasy.

"Jeet, Mom is fine. There is nothing wrong with her."

Jeet hugged her, looked at up at the heavens, the abode of God. The couple's silent shrieks of relief ricocheted from the walls of the hospital. Jeet bent down and bowed to the earth where he stood and then looked towards the heavens again as gratitude overflew through his eyes.

The responsibility of organising the evening party fell on Paddy. During the day, Jeet called Kanwar and told him all. Kanwar was stunned initially, then angry at having not been called earlier, but the final emotion was of relief.

"I am leaving right now," he had said before disconnecting.

The setting was a happy one. Kamlesh had cut the cake and Kanwar presented the documents of the house to Kamlesh. Roshni and her parents were there too. They had stayed back for the evening.

"And what about your dream, Jeet?" Kamlesh asked Jeet.

"My dream, Mom?"

Jeet bit into the cake his mother had offered.

"Yes son, your dream."

"Don't you think it's too late for that..now..Mom?"

"Too late?"

"Yes mom, in sports every year, every month counts. As it is I am behind the current circuit by a couple of years."

"How old are you, son?"

"What kind of question is this?" He smiled. "Don't you know my age, Mom?"

"I think I know, just want to do a re-check on my memory, wanted to ensure the semblance of illness hasn't affected it. So, tell me son, how old are you?"

"Twenty one...plus."

"Oh thank God! I was worried you would say something like fifty-one. I am relieved my worst fears aren't true. So, I have not woken up from some strange illness after some thirty years, have I, Jeet?"

She laughed. Everyone else laughed too. Jeet was embarrassed.

"Mom, I have a request." It was Roshni, coming out of the kitchen. She and Paddy had been engaged in chores.

"For sure beta, anything for you."

"Talk with me and about me mom, for Jeet has a twenty-one-year head start when it comes to interacting with you. I have to make up for that mom."

"Sure, you are my daughter. As it is I am not very happy with Jeet. He asks me, 'Don't you think it is a little too late mom?'"

Kamlesh looked at Jeet for a moment. He looked down.

"So you tell me beta," *Kamlesh* hugged Roshni, "what is it that you want?"

"Later mom," Roshni tried to smile, but could manage only a slight quiver of lips.

"No beta, tell me."

"Actually Mom, Jeet has been so fortunate. You have brought him up so well, telling him among other things so many motivational stories from the *Geeta*, *Ramayana* and *Mahabharata*. I want you to tell me one story, exclusively for me."

"Sure beta, just for you, exclusively. Not for anyone else."

Kamlesh looked at Jeet. The eyes met this time. But the next moment Jeet shifted his gaze.

"I hope you know Dronacharya was the guru of Kauravas and Pandvas both?"

"Yes Mom," replied Roshni.

"The story starts when Drona hadn't taken up the task of teaching the princes..."

Poor as they were, Drone's wife Kripi asks him to do something as poverty had stretched its cruel arms long enough to inflict hunger on their son Ashwatthama.

"To save him from embarrassment, I smear his lips with rice water to masquerade it as milk when he goes out to play

with his friends, so that the paucity of milk doesn't become the talk of the town." His wife Kripi tells him. A saddened Dronacharya asks her to wait till the next day as he would bring a cow by the evening. Dronacharya goes to his childhood friend Drupad who was now a king and who in growing up years had promised Drona to give him half his kingdom when they grow up.

"Those things were said in jest Drona, when I was a mere kid," Drupad mocks him. "You are too low in stature to be my friend. Why don't you beg me and I will give you one hundred cows in place of one."

His pride dented, Dronacharya gets too ashamed to return home and rather started teaching the Kauravas and Pandavas while Kripi, along with her son, waited for him to return with her eyes fixed on the door.

"It's time for guru dakshina, reverend guru," say his disciples as their education gets completed.

"Attack Drupad and win his kingdom for me," was the guru's diktat.

Duryodhana and Arjun volunteered but Duryodhana was stubborn and pleaded the guru to let him, and not Arjun, get benefitted by the opportunity of serving him.

"Ok Duryodhana," the guru acceded. "Go and fulfil your guru's wish."

Duryodhana, however, returned empty handed as to crush the mighty army of Drupad didn't turn out to be a cake walk. Then Arjun along with his four brothers attacked and imprisoned Drupad and brought him to their guru.

"You didn't value and respect friendship Drupad but I will," said Drona. "It isn't my wish to snatch something that belongs to my friend, so I return your kingdom and everything that

comes along with it to you. I will, however, take the one cow that I had come to take."

With the cow in tow, Drona walks back home. Kiripi, Drona's wife, is ecstatic to see her husband back after decades. Their son Ashwathama, who is now a grown up young man, too sheds tears of joy.

"I know I have sinned by being late. I know your nights have been dark and days long," Drona begged.

"When the wait ends, dear reverend husband," said an overwhelmed Kripi, "the pain of the lonely dark nights and the long days disappears by the anticipations of the good times that the future promises."

"In that case," Drona hugs her, "Go and attend to the cow and let your son drink its milk. For now you no longer need to smear his lips with rice water."

Drona then breathed in an air of satisfaction. The fatigue of so long a journey, that started in his youth and ended only in his middle age, became no trifling evil.

"So Roshni," Kamlesh looked at her. "How many years did Dronacharya take to fulfil his dream of a cow?"

"It took him decades, Mom." Roshni replied.

"So would it then be all that bad if it takes Jeet a couple of years to realise his dream?" asked Kamlesh. There was silence for a considerable time.

"So, did you like the story?" asked Kamlesh.

"Very much Mom, but for one thing." said Roshni.

"And what would that one thing be?"

"That the story was again for Jeet, not for me."

The manner in which Roshni had said it made everyone, including Kamlesh, laugh. The one who didn't smile was Jeet.

With the glass of cold drink in hand, he moved towards the stairs. Roshni tried to follow him but he gestured against it. The gusts of fresh air on the terrace triggered a soothing effect.

"Why did you leave the party?"

Surprised by the intruding voice, Jeet looked in the direction of the one who had intruded his thoughts.

"Oh!" He was glad to see the doppelganger. "So at last you could find time for me! Thank God! I thought I will have to fight alone with my onslaught of thoughts."

"I was always around," the doppelganger smiled. "Maybe you didn't notice because I spoke in different voices," each word of his soaked in mystery.

"Different voices? As in?"

"For example, umm, sometimes you heard me through Dinesh."

"You mean the guidance that I received from him came through you?"

"And once I spoke to you through your section officer."

"Does it mean it was you, rather than her, who created opportunities for me to attend the trials at Hyderabad?"

"I am just saying I spoke in different voices. I am not saying anything more or anything less than that."

"Hmmm, you know I was feeling for Munna. I feel very guilty. Maybe I should have acted early."

"Acted early, as in?"

"I mean in making efforts in reaching out to him. I could have bought the taxi earlier."

"Ha ha, who are you?"

"Hmm what?"

"You are no one but a small cog in this big wheel called universe. You do not control the world, do you?"

"No, I...don't."

"Then stop cribbing about the happenings, the threads of control of which aren't in your hands. What happened to Munna was his destiny. It had to happen the way it did. Ok tell me, where is the car you bought for Munna?"

"It's still with me."

"With you, but where?"

"I had got it parked in uncle's backyard."

"And it is still there."

"Yes, of course."

"Getting rusty and all, trying to meet its end before time," the doppelganger said sarcastically.

"Yes...I mean...I don't know what to do with it."

"There is no dearth of Munnas. Go find another Munna, the one with almost the same sets of qualities and also who is ageing and therefore possesses depleting energies. Give the car to him."

"Hmm."

"But be cautious of one thing."

"What?"

"You should help the person who really deserves to be helped."

"You mean someone poor?"

"I never said one who needs your help. I said help someone who really deserves your help."

"I don't get you. I don't know what parameters you are suggesting to be applied in choosing the person. I am getting confused."

"The one you choose has to be the one with feelings of gratitude. One who should be able to thank you for your efforts in helping him; also he should be thankful to the universe and the powers that are possessed by it for having blessed him with a gift as precious as life. If you try to help someone who lacks the feelings of gratitude and is of the cribbing sort, the Supreme Power will not allow it. In some form or the other, the gift or gifts will be taken back from him."

"Taken back from him?"

"Yes."

There was silence.

"Shall I go now?" the doppelganger broke the discomforting silence.

"You have never asked for my permission before." Jeet smiled. "It's a first."

The doppelganger smiled too.

"Did you hear mom's story?" Jeet asked.

"I hear everything."

"Is she right in talking about the pursuing my dream part?"

"Has she ever been wrong?"

"Yes, I know, she is right, but..."

"But what?"

"Why this feeling of reluctance in me to chase it? Is it the fear of failure?"

"No."

"Then what is it, if not fear?"

"Fear it is, but not of failure..."

"Then?"

"It is the fear of success."

"Fear of success, how?"

"Let us take the example of your dream. What will be considered failure here?"

"Not being able to make it to the Indian team...that would be failure."

"And by not trying, by not chasing your dream, are you not ensuring failure?"

"Umm...yes, I believe you have a point."

"By trying or making efforts, you move towards improving your chances of achieving success. So if you aren't making that move, can it be not said that you are comfortable with failure and therefore do not want to move towards success? Are you then in a way not being fearful of success?"

"Yes, my God. You are right, it is in fact the fear of success. And look at the irony of it, majority of people do not even realise it. And like fools they never try to chase their dreams thinking, 'What if I fail?' and continue to embrace failure. But...!"

"But what?"

"Since you know this secret, why don't you tell them?"

"Tell whom?"

"All the people. After all, why should so many people fail? In other words, why aren't there as many successes in this world as there are hard working men to deserve them?"

"That's because people do not chase their dreams. They do not realise that the trouble and expense incurred in pursuing a dream is nothing as compared to the fruits of a dream coming true. And even if in some cases they do, they commit the mistake of quitting it prematurely without waiting for the second wind."

"Second wind? What is that?"

"You remember you ran a cross country at Rai?"

"Yes it was a twenty kilometer cross country race."

"And what happened after fifteen kilometers of that race?"

"I was extremely exhausted and wanted to get out of the race. It felt as if I cannot go any further. It appeared as if I was drained of all my energy."

"And then...?"

"But I did not give up. I continued, despite the exhaustion."

"And then...?"

"And then as if some magic happened. It appeared as if my energy has been replenished. As if my lungs have been filled with some fresh air. It appeared as if I was never tired, as if I have not ran those fifteen kilometers and it was as good as starting afresh."

"That is an example of second wind for you. You got the gift of Second Wind because you did not quit, rather you chose to continue. Similarly, in the cross country of life, the Supreme Power gifts with the Second Wind but only to the ones who choose to continue, not to the ones who quit. It is sad that some people quit inches or moments before they are to get their Second Wind, and as a result, they fail to achieve what is or was destined for them had they not quit."

"What if the people were allowed to have a sneak-peek into their own destiny? They would then realise how close they were to the finishing line at the point when they decided to give it all up and quit."

"Yes, and that way they would realise that they have no one but themselves to blame."

"Yes, but don't you think they should know where the finishing line is? Does destiny not do injustice by not informing them where the finishing line lies? I mean, even in a small race of, let's say, hundred metres, the athletes know where the finishing line is."

"You have a point, but if people were to know all, would the thrill factor not be missing? Would it not make life monotonous and boring? But as it is, I am a mere doppelganger and not the Supreme Power. I am in no position to comment on such issues that fall beyond my capacities and powers."

"Yes, in a way I believe that would take the thrill quotient out of life but still I am of the view that people should know. At least you should tell them."

"But I am your soul, not theirs," the doppelganger smiled. "I am your doppelganger, not anyone else's. As I said, it is beyond my powers to communicate with them."

"But all of them must be having their own souls, their own doppelgangers!"

"Maybe!"

"Maybe? Don't you know for sure?"

"Yes, all others have their own souls, their own doppelgangers but most of them are dead and therefore can't talk to them anymore."

"But how...I mean a soul can't be killed. Am I right?"

"Yes, the soul is forever. But it is forced to die a premature and temporary death or let's say it lies dormant because of people's manipulating ways and pretensions, by their in-authenticicities and by the masks that they put on."

"Does it mean such people stand no chance to reach their dreams and is it that their life if is as good as over?"

"No, surely there is hope. But they have to cleanse their souls and the respective doppelgangers will speak to them and will be their compasses amidst the most dreadful of storms."

"What is needed to cleanse one's soul?"

"Absolutely nothing. Can you tell me the most impossible dream one can have?"

"Umm...to play for India?"

"Ha ha...playing for India, at best, is a tough dream. It is not even close to being impossible."

"Then...to find God is...maybe...the toughest of them all."

"Bingo, yes absolutely. Now tell me why Meera, and none other, could find and achieve the impossible feat of finding the Lord. In other words, why did God choose to come to her alone and not to others?"

"Because her soul was pure?"

The Doppelganger smiled in affirmation.

"But you haven't specified how one can get his soul cleansed."

"You know, a soul isn't like a dormant lake, it is in fact as fresh and vibrant as a flowing river. Once you stop adding your filth of manipulations into it, in due course of time it gets cleansed and hence gets alive on its own."

Silence ensued.

"Tell me about life a little bit, the journey that it is."

"The journey of life can be compared with the journey of a mountaineer: enterprising yet tough. There are three stages that a mountaineer goes through: 1. The trigger: It is the stage when one gets a whiff of the purpose of his life. 2. The journey: After the trigger comes the stage where the mountaineer gets his rucksack strapped to his back and moves towards his dream. While doing this he negotiates with deep gorges and valleys. It is when the climb gets steep that the ligaments and muscles in his legs cry that they cannot carry the weight of the mountaineer anymore, it is at this point that the ordinary call quits while the prodigious ride on the wings of the second wind to get to the third and the most difficult stage and to the real purpose of life: The Summit," replied the Doppleganger as a mesmerized Jeet devoured each word.

"So get ready," said the smiling Doppelganger.

"To chase my dream?"

"Yes, and to tell the people..."

"Tell people what?"

"To not give up on their dreams as yet, for..."

"For...the second wind might just be round the corner."

Jeet said almost to himself. He looked around. Doppelganger was nowhere to be seen. Once again, it had vanished into thin air. Jeet felt light. He felt something new, something like a small transformation inside him. He could smell the fragrance of green pastures. The little bird in him crouched to fly high. His dream appeared well within sight. He felt his lungs getting replenished by the fresh supply of oxygen. Was it the advent of the second wind? He felt eager and willing to take the leap. His dream wasn't impossible anymore.